SILENCED

A Vasily Korsokovach Mystery

Vasily Korsokovach Investigates

Book Nine

Christopher H. Jansmann

Ephram Cotte
& Company
PUBLISHING

ISBN: 978-1-960914-31-6 (Kindle Edition)
ISBN: 978-1-960914-32-3 (Hardcover)
ISBN: 978-1-960914-33-0 (Paperback)

Library of Congress Control Number: 2026901703

Printed in the United States of America

For Paula:

The one who encouraged me to find my own voice.

Books by this Author

Chronological Order

Blindsided

Pariah

Outsider

Peril

Ditched

Bygones

Downhill

Duality

Focus

Bewitched

Requiem

Vengeance

Mirage

Solitude

Masks

Belie

Silenced

Sean Colbeth Investigates

Blindsided

Outsider

Downhill

Duality

Bewitched

Vengeance

Solitude

Belie

VASILY KORSOKOVACH INVESTIGATES

Pariah

Peril

Ditched

Bygones

Focus

Requiem

Mirage

Masks

Silenced

OLIVER & VASQUEZ

Reflection in the Shadows

SHORTS

Snow Drifts

Baubles

CONTENTS

ONE
DISNEYLAND INTERRUPTUS

Our extremely delayed redeye from Boston finally landed at LAX just a hair past ten A.M. California time, ending what had turned into a grueling marathon that had started with an unexpected long weekend in Maine helping my best friend, Sean Colbeth, through the worst of what was shaping up to be a rather brutal breakup from his longtime girlfriend. I'd gotten a frantic message from his cousin on Thanksgiving day which in itself was unusual; Charlie was the epitome of calm, cool and collected, so when she was screaming into my ear that *the world was ending for my best friend and what the fuck was I going to do about it,* there hadn't been much choice other than sourcing the next available flight and spending what was left of the holiday trying to pick up the pieces. Frankly, it was a role I wasn't all that comfortable or familiar with; Sean was usually bailing *me* out, so when the shoe was finally on the other foot, I had serious doubts about my being up to the task. Alejandro's quiet support and calm assurances that simply being there to lend a thoughtful ear meant far more to Sean than any bromide I could have provided had kept me from descending into a full-on panic, especially when it was clear by the end of the weekend I'd barely made a dent in the wall of emotions surrounding my friend.

Adding insult to injury, a massive storm system had snarled air traffic up and down the East Coast and made our late-night departure from Boston on Sunday far, far later; compounding our malaise, the incessant and, at times, violent turbulence had made it impossible to get any sleep. About the only thing working in our favor was the time difference, though that did little to discount the fact we'd been quite literally up for almost twenty hours by the time we were stumbling through the terminal parking garage, looking for my Camaro only to belatedly realize we'd taken Alex's New Beetle.

Having known that our return to California was going to be well into the work day, both of us had emailed our respective bosses while we'd been cooling our heels in Boston and preemptively taken a sick day; I'd not expected much pushback from Chief Gilbert, but Alejandro had discovered a blisteringly worded response from his supervisor waiting for him in his inbox once we landed, one that all but threatened dismissal for violating multiple personnel policies. As tired as my fiancé was, by the time he slipped behind the wheel of his car, I could see he was nonetheless quietly furious and decided that it might just be best to let him channel that annoyance into navigating the Hell that was Los Angeles traffic. Still, it was hard to hide how white my knuckles were as I gripped the handle of the passenger door, for his weaving between lanes on the freeway had a certain level of mania that might have given Cruella de Vil a run for her money. Traffic thinned noticeably once we turned onto the Santa Ana Freeway and started the final leg toward our condo in Anaheim; only then did I feel comfortable breaking the silence.

"Late breakfast at the Carnation Café?" I ventured. "No one is in the park on a Monday, *especially* on the Monday after a long holiday weekend. We won't have any trouble scoring a table."

A sculpted eyebrow went up and was momentarily hidden beneath his mountain of curls. "Did you miss the part of my email where I was directed to appear as soon as I landed in California?"

"Nope," I smiled. "I hear the 5G at LAX is for crap; who's to say you actually read the message?"

"*Mi amor*," he sighed. "That's the sort of excuse my students give me. It'll never wash—"

"I can almost smell those pancakes you like," I interrupted. "The ones that come out with the granola sprinkled on top? And those massive sausage links?" I smiled again. "And the coffee. Oh man, I would sell part of my soul for a mugful of that coffee right now."

"So long as you let me keep the other part," Alex chuckled softly. "I could use a nap more than playtime at Disneyland, Vas, not to mention needing to deal with my seriously pissed off boss."

"He's just being an ass because you took that job at the B-school," I said. "And will be his peer now, not a serf."

"Maybe," Alex nodded.

The hint of a smile on my fiancé's face made me happy; somewhat unusually, he'd been an insane bundle of nerves during the interview process for the Director position at the Career Center that was part of the Business College at Cal State Irvine. I'd had no doubt that the gig was his from the get-go, a view that had been reaffirmed when the offer had been made less than two hours after his final panel interview. There were still a few details to iron out — notably, the exact date he'd be starting; that appeared to have created no small amount of friction with his *current* boss, a micromanager who seemed intent on wringing every last ounce of productivity out of Alex before he departed. Threatening to fire Alex was more for show than anything else, considering the work rules staff at CSUI worked under; still, it was a shit move intended to remind Alex who the alpha was in their work relationship. Smiling myself, I realized I'd been with Alex long enough to know he was only submissive when he chose to be — and judging from the twinkle that had appeared in his eyes, this didn't appear to be one of those times.

"Will he be any *less* upset when you turn up tomorrow?" I asked, seeing if I was reading my fiancé correctly.

"Probably not." Alex glanced at me. "Where is this truancy streak coming from?"

I wrapped my arms around my torso. "I've spent the weekend trying to patch the hole in my best friend's heart that my other friend created," I answered. "A few hours inside the berm feels like a well-earned diversion."

There was a long pause before I saw the slightest of slight smiles appear. "Yeah, it does. Fuck it."

Thankfully, the commuter exit the Five offered for Disneyland was still open despite it being close to noon at that point; coasting to the light at the other end of the bridge, Alex slipped into just the right lane in order to access the massive parking garage huddled on the northwest side of the park. I coughed up the insane amount of money for the privilege of stashing our car there, then fussed with the official app in order to purchase two single day passes for Disneyland while Alex found a spot to park. In short order, we were huddled together in the last row of the last car of the tram, channeling our inner teenagers as though we were on our first, albeit furtive, date together. I turned out to have been partially correct: while we had no trouble getting a table at the Carnation Café, the small restaurant on Main Street U.S.A. had already shifted to its lunch menu, so sadly, pancakes were no longer an option. The two of us were in the process of deciding what to have instead when my iPhone went off; pulling it from the pocket of my sweatpants, I frowned when I saw the caller ID.

"Oh, *fuck*," I breathed quietly, mindful that there were families at the tables around us.

Alex's sculpted eyebrows dipped down into the V-shape that matched his frown. "You're not *seriously* going to take that phone call after encouraging me — no, *goading* me — into ditching work, are you?"

I felt the slight touch of embarrassment flaming on my cheeks as I stood. "I'll... I'll just take this outside," I said.

Flipping the menu down on the table, Alex folded his arms against his tight chest. "I'll wait right here," he said, his eyes flashing dangerously.

Acutely aware of my hypocrisy, I scurried out of the restaurant as I answered the phone. "Hey, Chief," I said as I ducked into the small alley that led to the restrooms. "I'm still not coming in today."

"Knowing the kind of evening you had, I'm truly sorry to call," Chief Gilbert said. To his credit, his voice did sound sincere — at least, until he chuckled softly. "Though from the background music, I'm guessing you're not taking a nap on the couch."

Startled, I looked up and saw that I was standing directly beneath one of the many camouflaged speakers from which the insanely recognizable Main Street, U.S.A. loop was playing. "We're grabbing breakfast," I explained lamely. "At, uh, Disneyland."

"Expensive breakfast."

"Yeah," I replied.

"Well, I *am* sorry to interrupt your personal day," Gilbert continued, "but I need you. We've got a dead body on the construction site for that new affordable housing complex on the other side of the reservoir."

"Unless the budget situation went south while I was away this weekend, we still have detectives in the department," I said. "Honestly, Mike, I'm running on fumes; I'm no good to you until I've had a chance to recharge. Ask Miles to take the call."

"I need you on this one, Vas," Gilbert repeated softly. "We think it's Vivian Grandchester."

I felt my mind shift immediately into investigator mode. "The investigative reporter? From the *Orange County Register*?"

"Yes," Gilbert said. "We've not completely certain — it's based on evidence the responding patrol officer found at the scene; we'll know for sure once the body is recovered and a proper postmortem is done."

"Recovered?" I asked. "I'm confused. I thought you said a body had been found?"

Gilbert hesitated. "You'll understand when you see the crime scene.

How soon can you get there? Gina and her team are already on the way."

"I've got a full day pass to Disneyland, Mike," I replied testily. "And a fiancé who will probably end our relationship if I tell him I'm forsaking him for work."

"Don't be so dramatic, Vas," Gilbert laughed, which actually made me angrier. "And I'll eat the cost of your pass. Just bring in the receipt."

My anger dissipated slightly. "Not what I expected," I admitted.

"Nice to know I can still surprise even you," he replied. "Do you need me to send a car? I can get Officer Blythe to swing by with your SUV."

"That might be best," I sighed as I rubbed at the bridge of my nose. "It'll give me time to try and explain this mess to Alejandro."

"Then I'll let you get to it," Gilbert said. "Touch base with me after you've been to the scene?"

"Will do," I replied.

I waited for the triple beeps that signaled the end of the call before starting back toward the restaurant; Alex was, as promised, right where I left him, arms still folded against his chest. His eyes met mine as I pulled out my chair and sat back down across from him; not one who had ever been able to mask his emotions, Alex's anger was a nearly palpable presence as it hung in the space between us. Despite how I had clearly pissed him off, he'd thoughtfully ordered coffee for us while I'd been on the phone; I wasn't certain if I should read into the fact that mine was gently steaming into the air from a takeaway paper cup. Reaching for the brew, I took a quick sip and (somewhat appropriately) burned my tongue in the process; if I hadn't already known it was Monday, I would have assumed the gods running my life were hinting about how the rest of the day was going to play out. Based on the thin, disapproving line of Alex's lips, I began to suspect that my chances of making love to him that evening — hell, at any point in next few days — were waning fast.

Holding the paper cup between my hands, I tried to keep eye

contact as I spoke, but my guilty conscience had me immediately glance toward the outdoor seating area. "I've caught a case—"

"No shit," Alex interrupted. "I imagine you're wanted back in Rancho Linda, then?"

My eyes widened slightly. "Yes. Chief Gilbert is sending a car to pick me up." I put down the paper cup. "I tried to get Gilbert to assign Miles to the case. He has a very good reason for wanting me on it, though."

Alex's expression softened slightly; he'd been with me long enough to understand the nuances of police work. "High profile?" he asked softly.

"Possibly. Won't know until after the postmortem," I nearly whispered.

He nodded slowly, correctly intuiting what I was telling him. "Damn. Hard for me to stay pissed at you over something like that," he said after a long pause. "I'm... sorry."

"Don't be," I smiled slightly. "You have every right to be cross with me. I only hope you'll let me make it up to you tonight."

A slightly devilish smiled appeared. "I might be open to that," he said.

My eyebrows went up. "Might?"

Alex leaned across the table and lowered his voice. "Might," he replied, "though your odds would improve significantly if you managed to appear in our condo with a pint of those amazing strawberries from Bristol Farms and the chocolate fondue I love."

The sudden flash of memory from what had happened between us the last time I'd done just that created an immediate pressure in my groin and a sudden realization that the sweatpants I had on might not be the best attire for hiding certain sins. Still, I couldn't resist upping the ante. "I'll see your pint," I said as I leaned even closer and ran a finger along the strong line of Alex's jaw. "And raise you a bottle of Fairy Tale Cuvée."

"I cannot be bribed that easily," Alex whispered as his lips brushed mine.

"Maybe not," I smiled. "I'll leave you with this, then: my blue Speedos and those mouse ears you bought me over the summer." I waited a heartbeat, then lowered my voice even further. "And you can drive."

Alejandro's eyes widened. "You play dirty."

I gave him a quick kiss and pulled back. "Enjoy Disneyland," I said.

"It won't be the same solo," Alex sighed. "Then again, maybe I can finally catch the parade you never want to wait for." He smiled widely. "I might also have to drown my sorrows by eating my way across the park. I think I saw a new holiday churro out there as we came in."

"There you go," I smiled as I stood up. "Things are looking up."

"Don't be too late," Alex said. "As tired as I feel right now, I'm quite likely to turn into a pumpkin when the clock strikes eight."

"I've never made love to a pumpkin," I said innocently. "I suppose there's a first time for everything."

"Happy to be able to further your education," Alex sighed. "See you tonight, *mi amor*."

Two

A (De)pressing Situation

Post-lunchtime traffic in Anaheim was slightly worse than I'd expected. Weekdays tended to be fairly quiet around the Resort District compared to the relative deluge of humanity that appeared after five on Friday, but I had failed to account for the fact that since the calendar was now post-Thanksgiving, we were firmly within the grasp that was the madness of the Christmas Season. As frequent a visitor as I was to the parks, I'd barely taken notice of the massive Christmas tree that had appeared at the end of Main Street, nor had I even given a second thought to the garlands and other assorted decorations draped over nearly everything. I had vaguely recognized holiday music playing in the background, about the only sign that *some* part of my brain was willing to accept the reality of the season — and that I was running out of time to find the perfect gift for Alejandro. As I waited for a break in traffic on Harbor, I thought about a conversation I'd had with his mother when we'd been back in Tucson for a case and felt the first vestiges of a possibility beginning to form; any further consideration was shelved when the black and white cruiser from Rancho Linda I was trailing leapt out onto Harbor. Taking my cue, I did the same, smoothly accelerating my unmarked SUV so I could keep up with Officer Viella. I'd not been surprised that Officer Blythe's partner was waiting with her when I rounded the corner to the small drop-off parking lot wedged below the eastern pedestrian entrance to the park; the duo had been inseparable since starting together shortly after my initial hiring. I was also well aware of the whispers surrounding them; knowing a thing or two about how rumors could spread within our small department, I had quietly taken them out to lunch in late August and given them some tips to keep their personal lives, well, *personal.*

The black and white turned onto Katella, and I followed them as far as the entrance to the Five; Blythe had told me when she'd given me the keys to the SUV that they were headed to a different call, so I gently honked my thanks for the wheels as I sped past them. To my surprise, the lights on Katella worked in my favor, and in short order I was cruising along the 57 wondering what, exactly was awaiting me in Rancho Linda. If the victim was truly Vivian Grandchester, I completely understood why Chief Gilbert had wanted me; as the most notable investigative journalist in Orange County, her beat had often included covering many of the cases I had been a part of since joining the Rancho Linda Police Department. My introduction to her had been a bit rocky, though; while I had my theories about who had leaked the story of my relationship with a coworker and subsequent demotion as a result, I'd never forgiven Grandchester for making me front page material — something she'd later taken to a whole new level after my near death experience at the hands of that same former coworker. Having been an Olympic swimmer — and one of the first openly gay ones at the time — I was no stranger to having my life become an open book, but the depth of her dive into me had been borderline invasive. My departure and subsequent return to Rancho Linda had provided enough grist for a few more columns about the department; somewhat thankfully, her specific interest in me seemed to have faded over time.

Still, if I were being completely honest with myself, I wasn't having a hard time thinking someone out there might have wanted to kill her.

While not a stereotypical journalist, Grandchester was quite capable of rubbing people the wrong way when she was after a story; I couldn't remember the exact number but knew she'd won a fair share of awards for her reporting. Our interactions had become fairly frosty after her initial story broke about my assault and had never truly thawed despite her many appearances at crime scenes or briefings at the department. Forging an alliance with the media was something all law enforcement officers strived to do; with Vivian, for me it had become more an effort to *not* be the headline. Coasting to a stop at the main Rancho Linda exit from the 57, I wondered for a brief moment about who would cover her death; I had no idea how deep the bench was at the *Register*. It wasn't a stretch to presume, like most newspapers struggling to make it in the digital age, there probably wasn't much of a bench at all.

Turning left at the intersection, I set aside my ruminating over Grandchester as I navigated toward the address Gilbert had texted me. The affordable housing complex where the body had been found was on the far side of the reservoir in the heart of downtown; it was one of several multimillion-dollar projects green lit by the city to try and make a local dent in the housing crisis that had gripped Southern California for almost a decade. This particular one had been held up several times due to environmental concerns and the surprising discovery of an indigenous burial ground; I couldn't recall the exact details but knew some sort of trade had been brokered between Rancho Linda and the tribe to whom the remains belonged. My fairly regular runs around the reservoir had given me a vague sense of progress on the construction; only last week, I'd watched a truckload of lumber being offloaded from a semi, the surest sign yet that something was finally going to sprout from the acres of dirt that had been carefully leveled. Slowing, I shifted into what appeared to be an ad hoc left turn lane for an intersection that had yet to be given an official traffic signal. It took a moment for a break in traffic to appear that was large enough for me to shoot the SUV through, but when it did, I stomped on the accelerator and tried not to smile as I was pressed into the fabric of my seat.

The access road was more like a wide strip of dirt that had been carved from the landscape by a massive bulldozer; uprooted trees, bushes and other green debris dotted the edge of the throughway, carelessly discarded SoCal flora that could have been transplanted. Slowing, the SUV climbed upward until I reached the universal sign I'd found the actual construction site: a chain-link fence about seven feet in height had been erected across the dirt road and stretched as far as I could see to the right and left, disappearing into the distance. A double door of a gate spanned the width of the road, and both sections had been folded open, allowing unfettered access to the site beyond. I slowly drove through the opening, waving as I did so to one of my officers from Rancho Linda who was temporarily guarding the entrance while we worked the possible crime scene. In the space of a few yards, the road suddenly opened wide enough to become a de facto parking lot. Construction vehicles were randomly on one side, while a veritable fleet of city and county law enforcement were lined up on the other; finding an open slot, I pulled in and killed the engine for the SUV, then grabbed my backpack from the rear seat before exiting into the early afternoon sunshine. It was fairly warm for a late November Monday, though a light breeze carried the hint of how cool it would be overnight. My sweats were fine for the moment, but if we were there into the evening, I was going to need to borrow someone's parka. Adjusting the ball cap I had on backwards, I took a moment to determine how people were flowing and then set off toward what appeared to be the largest hub of activity.

From the angle of the parking lot, I was surprised to see just how far along the project actually was; my view from the running trail had been from below and obstructed by both the undergrowth and the strange geography on that side of the reservoir. Foundations for three of the four buildings had been poured, and at least one had a partial two-by-four skeleton erected for the base floor, with a hint of a second reaching to the sky. The reason for the slight hill I'd climbed in the SUV was quickly explained by the subterranean entrance to the parking garage below each of the structures; I couldn't tell how deep they went but also wasn't sure how tall each building was slated to be. Rancho Linda had some pretty strict ordinances in that regard, mostly to ensure the wealthier residents in the hills surrounding the city didn't have their million-dollar views disturbed. More sections of temporary fencing surrounded what appeared to be an open-air warehouse; carefully arranged stacks of lumber were everywhere, in a dizzying variety of shapes and sizes. As a layperson, it was hard to know what I was walking past, or which part of the site they were destined for. My particular path took me through a second gate and into the storage yard; heavy equipment that looked to me like overgrown Tonka toys were parked beside the pallets of lumber, a rogue's gallery that included several forklifts, a scissor lift and a backhoe. All of them were just as carefully lined up as the lumber, save for one forklift that had been parked at an unusual angle in the far corner. I wasn't surprised that's where I found the recognizable form of our recently promoted Chief Crime Scene Investigator Gina Carruthers; she caught my approach and finished what she was saying to a tech before I reached her side.

"Chief Carruthers," I smiled. "I love how that sounds."

"I'm still not used to it myself," she laughed. "I hear you had a hand in it, actually."

"Me?" I replied as I pressed a hand to my chest, the picture of innocence. "I'm just a lowly Deputy Chief with zero connections."

"Like hell," she chuckled before eyeing my extremely casual attire. "Apparently the rumors that you just stepped off a plan at LAX are true. I didn't know you were traveling over Thanksgiving."

"That makes two of us," I laughed as I pulled my ball cap off for a moment to run a hand through what was left of my hair.

After years of wearing it no shorter than shoulder length, I hadn't been able to accept how short it currently was; a few weeks earlier, the concussion I'd been trying to ignore had finally caught up with me, and I'd passed out in the morgue during a postmortem. My head had clipped the side of the Chief Medical Examiner's table on the way down, leaving me with a nasty gash requiring multiple stitches and, perhaps more importantly for my narcissistic streak, an incredibly ugly shaved head. Alex had done a rather adroit job of eliminating most of my anxiety over my new look by reminding me in the most intimate manner possible he preferred hairless men; while we differed on the specifics of that take, it was nice to know he might still find me sexy when the day came I was *truly* bald.

"Was it an emergency?" Gina asked, concern in her voice. "Is everyone all right?"

"The jury is still out on that," I replied. "You remember my best friend, Sean?"

"The cop from Maine?" she nodded. Her smile took on a strange fondness. "I do."

"He's going through a rough patch with his girlfriend," I said, eyeing her closely. "I think I got him over the worst of his broken heart, but you can only do so much in seventy-two hours."

"I'm sorry to hear that."

I looked at her. "You had a crush on him, didn't you?"

Her cheeks flamed slightly. "Me? Oh, no, not at all," she stammered uncharacteristically. "I mean, I could see why others *might*—"

"I'll cut you off there before you dig the hole any deeper," I laughed.

"Probably best," she smiled. "Any way you slice it, that's a long flight for a short weekend."

"And I'm feeling it," I smiled again, hoping to deflect any further questions about my getaway. "What have we got?"

"Something straight out of *The Wizard of Oz*," Gina said before motioning to me. "Step over here and I'll show you."

I followed Gina around the edge of the forklift and stopped dead in my tracks when I saw what was on the other side. "Are those... feet?"

"Yes," was her simple answer.

"Holy shit," I breathed as I took in the scene.

Gina's analogy had been spot on, for the scene before me uncannily echoed those early moments in Oz where Dorothy's house inadvertently lands atop the Wicked Witch of the East; in our modern rendition, only the lower portion of the legs were visible, protruding out from beneath a giant pallet of plywood that seemed to be a foot or more taller than me. The calves were bare, but the feet were still covered in a pair of Nike sneakers I recognized from my last foray to the local running store; unlike the aforementioned movie, the feet had settled into a rough V-formation, with the heels slightly touching. I wasn't sure if I was seeing the effects of rigor mortis or the results of what had to have been a sudden and severe compression of a human body. Stepping a bit closer, I waited for the crime scene photographer to finish before I knelt down and took a closer look at what was visible of the legs; while not strictly gender-specific, the skin had been shorn of any hair. Similarly, the light pink running socks peeking over the edge of the sneakers didn't entirely confirm there was a woman beneath several thousand pounds of lumber, either.

I looked up at Gina. "Chief Gilbert said we had a tentative I.D. on the body."

She nodded and pointed with her omnipresent iPad toward the framed building I'd seen. "I'll show you what we found; we kept it *in situ* to preserve the context."

"Okay," I said as I stood up. "I presume you're getting ready to remove the pallet, too?"

"Just waiting for your approval; that, and the coroner's van only arrived a few minutes ahead of you."

"Good."

I followed Gina once again as we retraced our steps and then set across the wide dirt of the parking area to the partially constructed building. Yellow crime scene tape was fluttering slightly in the light breeze as we approached; several construction workers clad in brilliant green shirts and hardhats were milling about nearby, carefully watching us. One of my younger patrol officers helpfully lifted up the tape as the two of us ducked beneath it; I let Gina continue to guide me along a concrete walkway that appeared to have been fairly recently poured, then up a short set of steps into what was sure to become some sort of lobby for the structure. Standing among the framing timbers, it was hard to get a true sense of how the building had been designed other than recognizing where the elevator shafts and fireproof stairwells were going. Reinforced steel was also far more visible from the inside, a reminder of California's strict building codes with respect to earthquakes. Multiple plastic evidence tents were scattered across the concrete floor in a strange pattern; I couldn't tell if they were lined up to show directionality or were truly as haphazard as they appeared. Gina stopped at the nearest marker just in front of the elevator wells, squatted down and then began to describe what I was seeing.

"Android phone," she started, pointing to the thin rectangular device with a gloved finger. "Looks like the latest Samsung non-folding model, or one generation prior; I'll know more once we get it back to the lab. We've not tried to unlock it yet, but the wallpaper is rather unique."

I knelt beside her after dropping my backpack to the ground; unzipping a side pocket, I pulled out a pair of gloves and snapped them on, then leaned as close as I dared to the phone before gently tapping it with my index finger. The cracked screen immediately glowed to life, showing the current date and time over a cropped photo of Vivian Grandchester accepting some sort of award. I looked over to Gina.

"Not entirely definitive; at least, not until we trace the owner of this phone properly," I said before seeing the slight twinkle in Gina's eyes. "You expected me to say that."

"Yep," she said before leaning to the side and pointing at another evidence marker. "This might be a bit more conclusive."

Standing with her, we moved over to the spot she'd indicated; splayed out on the concrete was a lanyard bearing the logo for the *Orange County Register* that had clearly been severed in some way. Several feet next to it, a third evidence marker was holding station beside a fairly standard plastic identification card; this one featured a non-smiling headshot of Vivian Grandchester and appeared to be her press credentials for the *Register*. Turning, I looked back at where the phone had landed, then to the forklift beyond. Again, while not conclusive, I was finding myself beginning to accept who might be beneath all of that lumber.

"She was running," I murmured. "Running away from someone."

Gina nodded. "That's my read on it."

"Footprint evidence to support that is going to be for shit," I sighed as I glanced out to the crowd of idle construction workers.

"Yeah. We'll take as many castings as we can and document the Hell out of the rest, but I don't expect anything conclusive."

"Who found the body?" I asked as we stood.

Gina nodded to the crime scene tech that had been hovering just out of earshot. The young woman swiftly moved in and retrieved the evidence as the two of us headed back to the forklift. "Site supervisor. She arrived just after first light to begin unlocking everything; given the millions of dollars of materials on the site, they have some sort of just-in-time security process where only that particular day's items are made available to the crew. The forklift was out of position and caught her attention immediately; when she went to investigate, she found the body and called 9-1-1."

I paused at the edge of the framed entrance. "Someone had access after-hours?"

"Seems that way."

"Great," I sighed. "Is the supervisor open to us reviewing the personnel rolls?"

"No," Gina replied. "At least, not without approval from someone at the corporate offices."

"Lovely," I sighed again. "I didn't catch the name of the firm when I drove in. Are they local?"

"No idea," she replied. "That's more your purview than mine."

"True," I smiled.

Arriving back at the body, we found a pair of techs from the Coroner's office waiting for us, along with an older woman with the air of one who might have been a weightlifter in a prior life; judging from how angry she looked, it wasn't much of a stretch to assume she was the site supervisor. Arms folded crossly against her rather sizable torso, the woman wasted no time accosting Gina the moment we were within earshot. "How much longer is this gonna take? We're already six hours behind."

"My apologies at the delay," I said as I donned my best retail smile and held out my hand. "Ms...?"

"Who the fuck are you?" she asked, turning her attention to me.

"Deputy Chief Vasily Korsokovach, Rancho Linda Police," I replied, dropping my hand back to my side when it became apparent she was in no mood for standard social niceties. "I'm running this investigation. You discovered the victim?"

"Yes."

"Good. I'll be speaking with you later, then," I said before nodding toward what appeared to be the portable office I assumed she worked out of. "If you wouldn't mind waiting in your office, I'll be with you shortly."

"I'm not going anywhere until I get—"

"Please wait in your office," I said, my smile getting a bit strained. "I won't ask a second time."

"Or you'll do *what*?"

"I'll have you escorted to the station, and you'll wait for me there," I said. "Which, I assure you, will be far less comfortable. Your choice."

She looked at me and for a long moment, I thought she might try and challenge me to a round on the mat; instead, better sense won out and she curtly nodded. I waited until she'd moved far enough away to call up to the constructor worker who'd been patiently waiting behind the controls of the forklift. "Nice and easy, please."

The guy gave me a thumbs up and then started the forklift; there was a momentary plume of black smoke from the exhaust pipes, and then the engine began to hum as he carefully slid the forks into the appropriate slots on the pallet. Revving the engine slightly, it began to sound strained under the load of the pneumatics slowly raising the pallet off the ground. It didn't take long to expose the rest of what turned out to be an extremely flattened human form; as the forklift slowly backed away with the wood so it could be fully examined by the crime scene techs, I stepped forward and felt myself slowly shaking my head. I'd read about earthquake victims getting crushed beneath tons of debris but had yet to work such a scene; seeing what was left of Vivian Grandchester made any imaginings I might have had seem far less violent than the reality actually was.

Despite the carnage, it was clear it was Vivian; her attire — or what was left of it — made it seem that she'd been out for a run, with three-quarter length leggings in a dark color that hid most of the blood and what might have once been a white tank-top that didn't. Shards of bones were poking out everywhere, but that, oddly, wasn't quite as nauseating as the puddle of brain matter beside the head; the angle made it almost seem as though the skull had been popped like a giant grape, which I supposed it probably had. What struck me the most, though, was a slightly rectangular pile of glittering translucent plastic about where the forehead once was; based on the darker plastic around it and a fabric band that might have been attached, I felt like I was seeing something familiar.

"Is that a head lamp?" I asked Gina as I knelt beside the body and, after swallowing hard against the rising bile in my throat, pointed a gloved finger at the glittering plastic.

"Maybe," she said after a long moment. "Certainly looks like the right sort of electronics."

"Did we locate her car?"

"No," Gina replied. "The supervisor says she was the only one here when she arrived; we've accounted for all the vehicles here currently."

I looked beyond the buildings and at the reservoir shimmering in the late afternoon sunshine behind them. "She must have gotten here from the running trail," I murmured. "We'll have to pull her DMV record and then search the public lots on either side of the recreation area."

"She could live close enough to the trail that she didn't drive," Gina said.

"Maybe," I replied, "but something tells me she wasn't a resident of Rancho Linda." I glanced back down at the body. "I don't think I'm going to stick around for the next part."

"Probably wise," Gina said as she waved the photographer over. "Peg will likely be in touch for the PM."

"Definitely not looking forward to that, either," I sighed.

THREE
SUPERVISOR TALK

The portable office for the site supervisor appeared to have seen better days. Weatherbeaten and dinged in more than a few places, it appeared to have lived a rough life on the move. Two wooden steps led to the only door, beside which was a copper nameplate emblazoned with both the name of the construction firm (The Cardinal Group) and, in far smaller font, the current supervisor (Izzy Lift). A second, far smaller plaque had the requisite *days accident-free* counter, which stood at sixty-seven. I wondered as I knocked on the door if they would consider the death of a non-employee in such statistics, as though death of a human could be simply reduced to a number.

Izzy Lift pushed the door open with enough force that it brushed me back and nearly off the small staircase; judging from the barely hidden smile, that appeared to have been the intent of her action. "About time."

They also serve who only stand and wait, was the reply that sprung to mind; I decided the literary reference might be lost on Lift, so I shifted to something more accessible. "Often our most important conversations are done at the end," I said with a slight smile. When her harsh expression softened a bit, I pressed my advantage. "Any chance you have coffee in there? I've been on the go since six yesterday morning."

Lift's eyes widened. "I thought even cops got holidays off."

"Crime never sleeps," I said with a tired smile, opting to let her continue to draw the wrong conclusion. "And our department is pretty fucking understaffed at the moment."

Those same eyes narrowed slightly. "Management never gets it, do they?"

"Never," I agreed (despite being part of said management).

"You okay with instant?"

"Yes."

"Then c'mon in."

She held the door open for me and I stepped inside; to my surprise, and contrary to the personality I thought I had seen, the interior was actually quite comfortable. The walls had a light wood paneling that complemented a dark carpet; under the small window at the narrow head of the trailer sat a couch and end table that were clearly from the same collection. A small buffet was against the far wall and held a microwave, hotplate and dorm-sized fridge; the shelves below stored precisely arranged office supplies, each carefully labeled with what I suspected was a catalog reorder number. A U-shaped desk was pressed against the other wall and held an impressively large widescreen monitor attached to an unseen computer; there was a small door in the rear wall that presumably led to a bathroom. The standard overhead fluorescent fixtures had been replaced by something in a softer white, bathing the entire area in a warm, almost homey glow. Lift went to the hotplate and put a kettle on top of it, then reached into a small basket beside it to retrieve a packet of warehouse-brand instant coffee. After snapping on the appliance, she waved me to the couch and leaned against the table. We considered each other for a few moments with the sound of the kettle heating up filling the silence. Only when she started to fold her arms against her chest did a small light bulb go off in the back of my head.

"Shot put? In college?" I asked.

Startled briefly, Lift's face settled into a slightly warmer expression. "UC San Diego, class of 1991," she said with a trace of pride. "I finished in the top ten at the NCAAs three of my four years."

"That's no easy feat," I observed. "Well done."

Lift shrugged. "It was a means to an end," she continued. "No way I was going to be able to pay for college on my own, even back then."

"I completely get that."

The kettle began to boil, which appeared to be Lift's cue to search the cabinet for a mug. "How did you guess that?" she asked. "Most people just assume I'm fat for no reason at all."

"I swam in college," I replied, "so I hung out with athletes, like, all the time. You kind of figure out the various body types for each sport pretty quickly."

"Never thought about that," Lift chuckled before turning back to me. Her eyes narrowed slightly again, almost as though she were looking into the brilliant sun. "Fuck. You're that gay Olympic swimmer, aren't you?"

"Yes," I nodded.

"I knew your name sounded familiar. My nephew is a huge fan; he swims for Cal State Santa Barbara."

"I'm flattered that he even knows who I am," I laughed. "I've been out of the spotlight for quite some time."

"Legends never fade away," Lift said with such earnestness it almost took my breath away. "How do you take your coffee?"

"Black, please."

She tore open the packet of coffee and dumped it into the mug, then poured the boiling water over it; after a few circuits with a plastic spoon, she handed me the steaming concoction. "I'm too lazy to get a real coffeemaker," Lift said apologetically.

"This will be perfect," I said as I tried not to crinkle my nose at the acrid smell of the coffee. Taking a sip, I quickly confirmed it was as bad as I suspected it would be. "How long have you been with the Cardinal Group?"

"Twenty-two years this past July," she replied as she moved behind the desk and took her seat.

"That's quite the tenure," I observed.

"I like what I do, and the company pays me well for it."

"Have you always been a field supervisor?"

"Yes," she nodded. "I've never wanted to be cooped up in a cubicle farm."

"I get that," I smiled. "I had one, briefly, and hated every minute I was stuck in it."

"Exactly," Lift nodded. A hint of a genuine smile appeared. "Deputy Chief, you said?"

"Yes," I nodded, "but please call me Vasily."

"Your departmental dress code seems kind of casual."

I waved at my sweats. "I literally stepped off a plane from the East coast a few hours ago and have yet to actually get home," I explained. "This is not my normal work attire, I assure you."

"Maybe it should be," Lift said after a moment of consideration. "It suits you."

"Thanks."

"Isn't it unusual for a Deputy Chief to be running an investigation?"

"Not in Rancho Linda," I replied. "Like I said, we're pretty thin right now." I paused. "But I also get dragged out when the case looks like it could be high profile."

Lift nodded out toward the yard behind us. "The body?"

"The body," I confirmed. I took another sip of the coffee and felt it burn all the way down to my stomach; even the worst gas station coffee was better than whatever it was Lift bought. "Do you mind if I record this conversation? I hate taking notes and, honestly, haven't been able to read my handwriting in years."

I hadn't missed Lift blanching slightly at the word *record,* but she recovered quickly. "Sure."

Setting the coffee down on the end table, I pulled my iPhone out of my pocket and started the voice recording software. After announcing the date, time and who was in the room, I looked back at Lift. "The site is locked down after hours?"

"Yes," she said. "With the insane amount of building materials we have to have on hand, we've had to make sure everything is secure to cut down on theft."

"Do you have overnight security?"

Lift nodded. "Rent-a-cops from a firm out of Los Angeles, but they only swing through at random intervals between nine P.M. and four A.M."

"Why not station someone on site?" I asked. "That seems like very little coverage for something so valuable."

Lift shrugged. "Above my pay grade," she said. "And that wasn't always our policy. As late as five years ago, we *did* have someone staying onsite overnight."

I decided to file that away for later review, for it felt like a strange non sequitur to me. The need for caffeine overrode my distaste for the poor coffee substitute Lift had brewed for me, so I reluctantly retrieved the mug from the end table; as I did so, I spied that day's edition of the *Orange County Register* sitting beside it, folded in half to expose the crossword puzzle. Several answers had already been completed, with exquisitely precise letters carefully inked into each box; I'd seen such a handwriting style somewhere before but couldn't immediately place it. The uncapped pen resting at the top of the page made me smile, for it was the hallmark of a no-nonsense puzzle solver — though it did give me pause. When had Lift had time to work the morning crossword?

Raising the mug to my lips, I tried not to grimace as I took another sip, then continued my questioning. "Can you walk me through how you discovered the victim?"

Lift frowned. "I've already gone through this with the other cops."

"I realize that," I said, noting that she'd folded her arms against her chest again. It seemed to be a defensive posture, so I adjusted accordingly. Smiling gently, I adjusted my tone to sound more like Alex when he was trying to talk me down from my current angst. "I've done this for a long time, and what I've found is that when a witness is exposed to a traumatic situation, they often only focus on a few key aspects of what they endured. That can unintentionally blind them to important evidence they don't even realize they saw." I took a sip from the mug, idly noting it said *Childless Cat Lady* on the side; I wondered briefly if there was a male version and whether Alex would like one. "So, we tend to ask our witnesses to go over their experience more than once, for each time we do, they often wind up recalling something they didn't remember the first time we took their statement."

"Oh," Lift said, her expression relaxing again. "Oh... yeah, I could see that. Sorry."

"No need to apologize," I replied. "This is not a normal situation; humans aren't wired for this sort of experience."

"No kidding," she said. It seemed like a hopeful sign that what passed for her smile had appeared again.

"Now, if you would, take a moment to think back to when you arrived on the site this morning. When you're ready, guide me through your actions."

Lift nodded. "Well, I got here about five," she started. "Cardinal used to pay for spotlights, but this build doesn't have 'em; that means the workers can't start until first light, so there's no real reason for me to be here too much ahead of that."

"When is that?"

"About six-thirty," she answered. "There are a few times during the build when I'm here at three to accept delivery of materials; it's a bit tricky without spots, but most of the trucks have mounted lights that make it doable."

"Is this a five-day or six-day worksite?"

Lift smiled. "Cardinal would have you believe five, but it's actually six — especially when we get closer to crunch time. OT kicks in for Saturday; site is locked down for Sunday."

"So you, what, unlock everything when you get here?"

"That's about the size of it," she nodded. "More for my own sanity than any security reason, I walk the site, too, and kind of eyeball where everything is; I do inventory twice a week just to make sure a pallet of drywall hasn't disappeared or so that we don't inadvertently run out of nails."

I felt an eyebrow arch. "How does a pallet of drywall walk away?"

"You'd be surprised," Lift chuckled. "I was the site supervisor on that high end apartment building on the far side of Rancho Linda — the one up in the hills?"

"I know it," I nodded. It seemed best not to admit I'd also recently investigated a murder there, too.

"Eight refrigerators disappeared one weekend, the inventory for an entire floor we were about to complete."

"Ouch," I said, keeping my face impassive. Such larceny would -- *should* — have been reported to the Rancho Linda Police, but I was hard pressed to recall having seen one. "Did you get them back?"

"No," she shook her head. "We had to scramble to replace them — and I've maniacally walked every site, every day during construction, since."

This time, I did frown. "*Every* day?"

"Yes."

"I thought no one was here on Sunday."

Lift looked startled. "None of the *workers* are," she amended. "I still swing by, just in case."

"Ah," I nodded. "Trying to make up for the lack of regular security?"

"Yeah."

"Unpaid, I take it."

"Unfortunately," Lift sighed. "But I'll be damned if I have another theft on my watch."

"Totally get that," I smiled.

"Anyway, that's how I knew something was off this morning," she continued. "We always park the forklifts together, in a spot next to our lumber yard; when I saw number four out of position, it was clear someone had been here and moved it."

"When were you here on Sunday?"

She smiled slightly. "I sleep in a bit that day, so seven."

"And you were here at five this morning?"

"Yes."

"So, you went to the forklift...?"

"Yes," she nodded. "I climbed up into the cab so I could move it back to the yard, but when I reached down to start it, I was high enough to see the, uh, sneakers."

"Was that when you called 9-1-1?"

"No," she replied. "I got back out of the cab and then went to confirm what I'd seen; once I was sure there was... someone... under the pallet, that's when I called for help."

"When was that?"

Lift looked thoughtful. "I think 6? Maybe a little before? I wasn't really paying attention at that point."

"I can understand that." I swirled the coffee in my mug and realized there was a stray ground floating on the surface. *How is that even possible?* I thought. *Instant coffee is supposed to be... instant.* "How long did you have to wait for the patrol officer to arrive?"

"Not long," she replied, then looked a bit uncomfortable. "I was glad for the company, if I'm being honest. I was a bit freaked out by the body, enough that I wouldn't let the operator go until I saw the police car pull up."

"And that's when you showed the officer the scene?"

"Yes. Once I'd retraced my steps with them, they asked me to wait in my office," she added, her eyes momentarily going to the crossword. "That was a terrible suggestion. I lasted about an hour and then went back out to see what they were doing to my job site."

I tried not to smile. "Not the first time I've heard that sentiment. Tell me, how much lumber was on that pallet?"

"I'd have to pull the shipping manifest, but we typically order everything in units that are assigned to specific parts of the construction timeline. That pallet was for the second floor, northeast wing; specifically, the two bedrooms for the corner unit; it won't be needed until sometime mid-December, so there would be no reason to move it yet."

My eyebrows went up. "I'm impressed."

Lift shrugged. "You do this job long enough, you become a sort of savant," she said before smiling slightly. "But in this case, I happened to have caught the lading tag stuck to the side of the pallet when I found the body."

"Ah," I smiled. "You mentioned doing daily inventory — is that how you keep track of everything?"

"Partly," she nodded. "Each label has a special QR code that gets scanned at every step of the way — right up until we begin to unwrap the lumber. Then we scan each piece of lumber as it goes into the building."

"That's a lot of effort."

"When you're talking a project this big, with margins as thin as they are, every board foot counts."

I put the mug back on the table, definitely done with the brew. "Do you think it was an accident?" I asked.

Lift looked at me like I had grown a second head. "Hardly. I can't see any way that woman would have willingly laid down beneath the pallet and waited for death to be lowered on her."

I'd already come to the same conclusion, but it was interesting to hear Lift's take. "You said you'd done your normal security rounds when you got here; besides the forklift being out of place, did you find anything else unusual?"

"No," Lift said, then looked away.

Hmm, I thought. *That's the classic tell that I'm not getting the whole truth.* "In that case, any idea how two people might have gotten inside the fence?"

"Two?" Lift repeated, frowning as she did so.

I nodded. "I presume the forklift isn't of the self-driving variety; someone had to move it and then lower the pallet on top of our victim."

"Oh, right," Lift said. "Yeah, that makes sense."

"Any thoughts on how they gained access to the site?" I pressed.

"Maybe they climbed over the fence?" she replied tentatively, glancing away again. "I honestly have no idea. Isn't that more your department?"

"I'm sure our crime scene techs are already looking into that," I said. "Who else has keys to the locks?"

"I'm the only one with a master," Lift immediately answered. "The rent-a-cops have one for the gate in the outer fence, and most of the foremen have sub keys for lumber yard and things in their specific zone."

"Zone?"

"Yeah," Lift explained. "We break each portion of the site down into a zone, and each zone is managed by a specific foreman; I have direct oversight over the entire project, but it falls to them to actually build whatever is within their area."

"Interesting strategy. What do their keys unlock in each zone, exactly?"

Lift shrugged. "Toolkits, mostly; and the portable outhouses. Everything else requires a master."

"Where are the keys for the equipment stored?" I asked, my eyes scanning the small office as I spoke. "I presume those are handled by you as well."

"Yeah," Lift replied uncomfortably. "They're in a safe under my desk."

My eyebrows went up. "And you are the only one with a key to your office?"

"I have a master, yes," she replied, "but there's a duplicate at the home office just in case."

"Who has access to that duplicate?"

"I wouldn't know," Lift replied. "You'd have to ask someone at corporate."

I nodded. "Your office was locked when you arrived?"

"Yes," she replied. "I also leave it locked when I'm out on my rounds or otherwise not here."

Shifting apps on my iPhone, I shot a quick text to Gina as I continued. "Was the key to the forklift in question missing this morning?"

"No," Lift said after an excruciatingly long moment.

"When did you check?"

"Right after the cops sent me here to wait for them."

"Did you mention this to them when you went back out there?"

"I... didn't," she admitted.

I pushed myself off the couch and came around to stand beside Lift's chair; the key safe was neatly tucked away under the return and only fully visible if you knelt down. Squatting slightly, I could see the small numeric keypad where the combination would be keyed in; the cabinet itself was less than four inches deep, clearly intended solely for small items such as keys. Looking up at Lift, I caught the shadow of fear on her face.

"You opened this earlier?" I asked as I stood.

"Yes."

Lift rolled her chair backwards defensively; it was a non-subtle reminder than my six-five frame could sometimes be construed as threatening, depending on my attitude. Considering I was beginning to get pissed at having been lied to — even if it was a lie of omission — it was definitely shifting into something aggressive. Folding my arms against my chest, I narrowed my eyes at her in my best *this is gonna get messy* expression and was rewarded by seeing her swallow. Hard.

"Who else knows the combination to this safe?"

"I'm the only person on site," she replied, swallowing a second time.

A tiny bead of perspiration had formed along her hairline. "Loss Prevention sets the codes and provides them to us; I would assume someone there might know."

"Loss Prevention? Is that a department within Cardinal?"

"Yes."

"You'll need to provide me with a contact to speak to them, then," I said. "Presumably the person who gave you the codes in the first place."

"I can do that."

I waited a beat. "How do you know Vivian Grandchester?"

"The journalist?" Lift answered quickly. "Only from reading her in the paper."

"You've never met her before? In person?"

That tell — looking away from me before responding — happened again. "Nope."

"Izzy," I sighed as I pinched the bridge of my nose. "I've been awake since six Sunday morning, have a headache and am missing out on playing at Disneyland with my fiancé so I can chat with you." I looked at her, hard. "When did you first meet Vivian?"

"I've never met her before," Lift replied. The beads of perspiration had banded together to become a small trickle down her temple.

Every instinct I had as an investigator told me that was a prevarication, but seeing as though I had zero leverage at the moment to convince Lift of the error of her ways, I settled instead for a grim frown and the determination to find out *why* she was lying as I moved around her desk. "Okay," I said as I tapped the voice recorder app on my phone and ended the session. "I'll have your statement transcribed by someone back at the station; you'll need to stop by and sign it sometime in the next twenty-four hours." I paused. "If you don't sign it, I'll be forced to insist you come to the station and have this little chat in one of our interview rooms instead."

"I can stop in tomorrow afternoon," Lift said.

I nodded. There was a knock at the door, and I quickly opened it before Lift could object. "Gina," I smiled. "I figured you'd delegate this to someone."

Gina stepped up and into the office. "They're all doing other things," she replied. "And I had a spare moment."

"I won't say no," I said. "The safe is under the desk; there's a chance that someone other than Ms. Lift accessed this office and borrowed the keys to the forklift — and then returned them."

Sensing what I was intimating, Gina looked at Lift. "I'm going to need to dust everything, then. Did someone take your prints already, ma'am?"

"No," Lift said, her eyes wide.

Gina put down her bag and rummaged through it to retrieve the digital scanner we now used. Part of me missed forcing suspects to get ink on their hands. "Well, taking them will be the easiest part of this task," she sighed, then looked at me. "I guess I will borrow someone to help; as good as I am, it will take too long if I fly solo."

"Grab anyone you need," I said as I moved to the door. "And call me when you have anything."

"Don't I always?" she laughed. "Now, Ms. Lift, if you'd place your index finger on this spot here..."

FOUR
HOME, FINALLY

Since the Camaro was already in my designated parking space, I was forced to pull the unmarked SUV into the last open visitor spot of our condo's underground parking garage. I didn't tend to bring the SUV back to Anaheim as a rule, but when I realized just how late it was after getting through briefing Chief Gilbert on the investigation's progress, texting Alex to retrieve me felt like a colossally bad idea. Knowing an apology would be in order, I made two emergency side trips on my way home, the combination of which put a bit of dent in my checking account. Grabbing my bags from the back seat of the SUV, I locked up the truck and then hurried across to the elevator lobby; waving my fob at the lock flipped the light from red to green, allowing me access to the small space. As I waited for the elevator to land on my level, I considered what I was going to say to Alex; it wasn't the first time I'd been late or had missed a planned outing due to my obligations as a Deputy Chief, of course, but I'd grown increasingly worried that his patience with the demands Chief Gilbert placed on me was wearing rather thin. By the time I was putting my key into the lock of our condo's door, I'd still not found what I thought were the proper words. Quietly thumping my head against the closed door, I closed my eyes and prayed to... something... that I wouldn't mess up the best thing that had ever happened to me in the next ten minutes.

The first thing I noticed when I pushed the door open was the fragrant smell of onions, peppers and garlic being roasted together; taking a deep breath, I thought I could also detect something vaguely like warm bread in the air as well. Curious, I carefully wandered down the short hallway and found my beloved humming to himself in our small kitchen; multiple pots and pans were on the stove, all burbling along with something, and it appeared the oven was on just below, though the interior was shrouded in darkness. My favorite Disney salad bowl was on the breakfast bar, filled to overflowing with greenery; the bright red spots of cherry tomatoes, when combined with the square brown chunks of croutons, made it look somewhat festive, even though the calendar had not yet turned to December. Two place settings had been laid out on the other side of the bar, complete with currently empty wineglasses standing like sentries over the silverware.

"Wow," I breathed as I set my own bags down on the sliver of open space atop the breakfast bar. "Someone's been busy."

Turning, Alex smiled. "Seeing as though you ran out of the Carnation Café this morning with just your coffee, and knowing you as well as I do, I assumed you'd be hungry when you finally arrived."

I felt my face heat slightly. "I ate," I said defensively.

Alex placed the wooden spoon he was holding on a small Mickey-shaped trivet and came over to me, then put his hands on my arms. "*Mi amor*, we've been over this. Protein bars a meal do not make."

"I suppose they don't," I replied sheepishly. "Caught."

"Indeed," he laughed as he leaned in for a kiss that immediately made my toes curl. Leaning back, his eyes danced with merriment. "Welcome home."

"Thanks," I replied. "What are we having?"

"Carne asada," he replied, "with cilantro rice, a salad and some fresh sourdough from the bakery at Disney's California Adventure. If you were a *really* good boy, I might also let you have some of my refried beans, too."

"What is your definition of good?" I asked.

Alejandro's eyes drifted to the bags I'd put on the counter. "It depends on what you picked up."

Smiling wider, I opened the first bag and retrieved the bottle of Fairy Tale Cuvée I'd ordered from the bar at the Grand Californian. "As promised."

"Well done," Alex said appreciatively as he picked up the bottle. "I almost hate to open it."

"That's why I got two," I laughed as I pulled the second one from the bag.

"Vas! That had to cost a *fortune!*"

I shrugged. "Does true love really have a price tag?"

"We may need to set some upper bounds," he replied as he eyed the second bag. The logo for *Marceline's Confectionary* was clearly visible, causing one of his sculpted eyebrows to rise ever so slightly.

"Oh no," I said as I pulled it away from him and then carefully stowed it on the bottom shelf of the fridge. "That's for later."

"Now I'm *seriously* worried about your spending proclivities."

"I'm allowed to spoil my fiancé," I smiled. "It's in the small print of our marriage contract."

"I hesitate to point this out," he said as he pulled me into a hug, "but we've not quite crossed that threshold yet."

"Soon enough," I breathed as I gently kissed him. "And, perhaps, not soon enough."

"Right there with you," he laughed. "Food's just about ready; the tortillas only need another minute or two in the oven to be heated enough. You've got time to change into something more comfortable if you want," he added, a slight twinkle to his eyes.

"Okay," I smiled. "Be right back."

Alex pulled me into another kiss before I could escape, though this time, it held barely restrained passion. "Don't keep me waiting."

"Wouldn't dream of it," I said as I reluctantly pulled away.

I picked up my work backpack and hurried to the master bedroom; as I closed the door behind me, I was somewhat amazed at Alejandro's rather accommodating attitude, and began to seriously wonder if I'd dropped into one of those bad science fiction movies where people get replaced by alien body doubles — or worse, robots programmed to look and act like a loved one. Concerned that he might be trying to cover his actual displeasure by burying himself in his cooking, I closed my eyes for the second time that evening and wondered if I were finally paying the price for being a lapsed Catholic. Opening them again, I started across the carpet to my side of the bed and stopped halfway there when I caught sight of my favorite electric blue Speedos; they had been carefully placed against my pillow, just below the classic pair of Mickey Mouse ears Alex had finally talked me into purchasing. Dropping my backpack next to the nightstand, I sank down onto the mattress as I picked up the ears; turning them in my hands, I smiled fondly when I saw my name embroidered on the back. Glancing to the dresser, my eyes fell upon the matching set of ears that had pride of place beside the small collection of colognes Alex rotated through; in an instant, my heart melted for the man I had fallen in love with — and then ached for all I had put him through over the past couple of months.

Standing, I went over and looked at the little vignette formed by the mouse ears and the eclectic collection of fragrance bottles; nothing screamed *Alejandro* more than that tiny corner of the dresser, especially when compared with the side I claimed as my own. I ran a finger along the edge of the photo I'd bought the first time we'd ridden Splash Mountain together and smiled at how well the camera had caught his look of pure childish delight; he'd lost his first set of mouse ears as we'd careened toward oblivion, giving me the best of many excuses to shower him with more. Beside that was a second, larger photo of the two of us in costume at Rosie's recent Halloween party; I'd had it framed by a little shop around the corner from tuxedo rental place we'd discovered earlier that year, and marveled yet again at just how damn hot Alex was.

Glancing back at the ears and swimsuit on the bed, I decided to take the hint and quickly swapped my boxer briefs for the Speedos, then took a few more moments to try and align the mouse ears on what was left of my hair at *just* the right angle; once I was satisfied with my image in the bathroom mirror, I deviously tied a knot in the cord for my sweats and then wandered back out into the kitchen. Alex was just finishing pouring a rather healthy amount of the wine into each of our glasses. His eyes immediately went to the mouse ears perched on my head, then dropped to my waistline before coming back up to my face.

Smiling slyly, I hooked a thumb in the waistband of my sweats. "I figured you'd be distracted by my Adonis-like form were I to completely fulfill my obligations at this time," I said mischievously. "However, I am quite happy to comply, but I cannot guarantee how far we'll make it through this excellent dinner you've prepared should I — as they say — drop my drawers."

Alejandro's eyes twinkled with delight. "You really know how to push my buttons, Vas."

I moved to him and pulled him into a warm embrace — tight enough that there was no way he could miss how certain parts of me were anticipating the dessert yet to come. "Yes," I said, "though sometimes I push the *wrong* ones. I am truly sorry about today. I know I keep doing that kind of thing to you, and I'm... seriously worried I'm screwing things up between us." I brushed back a lock of his luscious curly black hair so I could see his dark brown, expressive eyes. "I love you, Alejandro Ortega-Cortez, and I will do anything to make sure I don't lose you."

Alex put a hand to my cheek. "I know you do, and, frankly, I love you more," he smiled. "And like it or not, my heart has been completely captured by a cop — and a damn good one at that. Do I like the hours you keep? I'll be honest," he sighed, "I don't. There *are* times when I wish you were some sort of business wonk at a Fortune 500 whose sole worry is the price of soybean futures. But I also know that I would likely have never fallen in love with whatever *that* version of Vasily would have been."

"Soybeans?" I laughed. "Not my style."

"Exactly," he smiled. "You've gotten better at this work-life-balance thing since we've been together; there's still work to do, but dammit you're the best thing that's ever happened to me. I'm not about to let my fears over what your job might do to you overwhelm the happiness we have together."

I felt tears welling up. "That's... that's absolutely beautiful," I whispered. "How did I get so lucky?"

Alex smiled. "You tried to drown yourself in the right hot tub," he breathed before he pressed his lips to mine. When we came up for air, he smiled wider. "You're right," he nodded. "Better keep your clothes on; I'm famished, and I'm sure you are too. Besides," he smiled wolfishly, "I need you to have enough energy to get through the rest of the night."

"Your wish is my command," I intoned.

As we settled onto the matching barstools, I reached for my napkin and was just placing it across my lap when that cold shiver of fear over having forgotten something important shot down my spine. Glancing behind us at the empty cat tree in the corner of the living room, I groaned. "Shit. We forgot to pick up Chat from Rosie."

Alejandro chuckled. "I've already spoken to our favorite author, and she happily agreed to keep our fur baby for another night," he said as he turned my head toward his. "I think she likes the company, and I felt like we needed a night to ourselves."

I had a mental image of our black feline scampering about the massive mansion Rosie owned on the far side of Rancho Linda and frowned. "So long as Chat doesn't forsake us," I replied. "With that much space to explore, he'll never want to come back to our tiny condo."

"He loves us," Alex said as he pressed another kiss to my lips. "Don't worry, he'll be back. Even if his grandmother spoils him rotten."

"Grandmother?" I asked, my eyebrows going up. "When did *that* happen?"

"The moment we asked Rosie to take care of Chat the first time," he laughed. "Now, eat."

I did as instructed; unsurprisingly, the food was amazing, and as hungry as I turned out to be, it didn't take long for me to plow through multiple helpings. After helping Alex clean up the dishes, we turned off the lights and took what was left of the first bottle of wine back to our bedroom; I'd barely put the bottle down on the nightstand before a pair of warm hands had encircled my waist and made short work of the knots I'd tied. There was a gentle tug and then the sweats were pooled at my ankles; those same hands then carefully turned me around so I was facing my beloved. In the half-light coming through the window, I could still see his dark eyes twinkling with delight as he looked me over; lifting my arms slightly, I saw the flash of his smile as he got the hint and reached for the edge of my t-shirt. Somehow, Alex managed to guide the shirt around the mouse ears as he pulled it off; stepping back, he took another appreciative look before pressing me back onto the mattress. While it was a clear message that he intended to drive that evening, I smiled wickedly and decided to put up a bit of a fight. Prior to meeting Alex, I'd rarely ceded control in matters of the bedroom; one of the many joys of our relationship had been the discovery that it was just as erotic to be on the other side of the equation. Still, try as I might, letting go of my need to be the alpha was never easy.

As Alex began to pull off his shirt, I reached over and drew him toward me; the maneuver elicited a surprised gasp from my fiancé and managed to keep him temporarily trapped in the fabric that hadn't quite made it over his mountain of curls. I seized on the opportunity and began to slowly kiss each of the many impressive ridges that framed his lower abdomen, then smiled slightly when I drew another gasp after quickly darting the tip of my tongue into his belly button. My hands crept upwards along his sides, slowly probing every muscle as they inexorably made their way toward his very sensitive nipples; sensing my plan, he squirmed above me to try and free himself from the shirt. The world around me shrunk to a singular focus on every square inch of his exposed skin; each tattoo I passed on my unrelenting journey upward got special attention, enough that I could feel Alex's body begin to arch into every kiss. As our breathing became ragged, I could hear the pounding of my pulse in my ears — a clear warning I was closer to the edge than I realized. Slowing down at that point was a tall order, especially when I was so near the prize; still, I took a moment to lean back and take in the landscape that was my lover, just long enough to knock the edge off of my libido.

My pause allowed Alex to finally shuck out of his shirt, which was casually tossed to the ground beside the bed; as he leaned inward for a quick kiss, I ghosted the palm of my hand across his left pectoral just light enough that Alex involuntarily shuddered. His guttural moan when I slowly — oh so very slowly — traced a circle around his right nipple with my tongue told me I had his complete and undivided attention; I pulled his gorgeous lips down to mine and began to kiss him with a passion that was becoming increasingly hard to hold in check. Eyes closed for a moment, I felt him gently push me down so my back was on the bedspread; sensing where we were going — and that I was happily losing the fight to take the lead that evening — I scooted back further, and then allowed him to adjust me so my head was on our pile of pillows.

I watched as he straddled me and then leaned down for another kiss, his signature whale-tale pendant dangling in the small space between us. I reached up with both hands and pulled him toward me for a full-on exploration of his magnificent lips that left both of us breathing even heavier. Expecting that might mean we were getting closer to the main event, I was surprised when he instead flattened himself against my body and embarked on another series of incredibly hot kisses. It wasn't lost on me that his position had pinned my cock between us, nor could I ignore how even his slightest movement against me managed to rub the thin fabric of the Speedo across my throbbing need in the most horribly erotic manner possible. The tension was excruciating, and in moments I found that I was completely at his mercy, unable to resist any of his efforts — which I supposed had been his intention from the beginning.

Pure instinct began to take over, and I heard myself moaning as I tried to get just *enough* friction for the release that seemed just beyond my reach. Alex appeared to have planned for that as well, for each time I thought I'd found a position that would do the trick, he deftly adjusted his attack, distracting me slightly with a trail of little nibbles along my neck or by lightly tracing the outline of a pectoral muscle with a finger. That he had managed to figure out how to keep me on the edge spoke to how long we'd been together; time lost all meaning as I teetered above the abyss. Waves of desire began to overtake me, pulling me upward from the bed as though I were on puppet strings; I was only half-aware that Alex's curls had begun to stick to his forehead, his body as slick with sweat as my own. Coming up for air from an especially fierce set of deep kisses, Alex's beautiful face was flushed and his mouth half open as he tried to steady his breathing. Running his hand along the side of my face, he looked at me questioningly.

"May I?" he asked, his voice husky.

"Fuck yes," I said, my voice equally as taut.

Almost as though we had carefully choreographed it, Alex rolled off me and onto his side of the bed, allowing me to untie the Speedos and kick them to the floor; he reappeared what seemed like a fraction of a second later and quickly pushed my legs apart so he could kneel just in front of me. Leaning back on the pillows once more, I watched as he tore open the small aluminum packet for his favorite flavor of condoms; it took every ounce of what was left of my willpower to keep from going over the edge as he slowly rolled it over me, kissing every newly exposed inch of latex as he went. I nearly lost it again when he quickly drew me into his mouth, then shuddered slightly when I felt him tentatively probing my ass with the edge of his cock. My rape some years earlier had left me with a level of PTSD that I'd never been able to fully shake; Alex understood that, and (aside from our rather disastrous first time together) always went to great lengths to ensure I was both willing and ready when the moment came. I closed my eyes and fought back the sudden panic that seemed to wash over me each time I allowed him inside of me; putting my hands to the small of his back, I pulled him forward, my not-so-subtle message he could keep going.

My last conscious moments before the blinding white light of release overtook me centered on an observation I'd made not long after the two of us had met: as a diver, Alejandro had exceptional flexibility, something we often used to our mutual benefit during lovemaking. That night, it meant he was able to somehow keep his mouth focused on my now extremely sensitive cock while simultaneously — albeit deliciously slowly — thrusting in and out of me. I fisted the sheets under the pillow in a futile attempt to hold back just a little longer, then let out a nearly feral grunt as I scissored up and into Alejandro, shuddering fiercely with each wave as it rippled through my body. My fiancé timed it as perfectly as any dive in his repertoire and gave himself over a fraction of a second later, his back arching up and away from me as he let out a low moan with each involuntary spasm. Then, with every ounce spent, Alex collapsed on top of me, his head nestled just below my pecs. Those gorgeous eyes of his sparkled in the dim light, his face flushed with the pleasure of our exertion.

I ran a hand through his luxurious curls and relished in the simple pleasure of hearing the two of us breathing; once my pulse returned to something close to normal, the muted sounds of the street traffic dashing by our building became a subtle, comforting soundtrack, underscoring the domestic bliss I'd found with Alex. Pushing the damp curls back from his forehead, I smiled again at the thought of how lucky I was to have him in my life — and, surprisingly, felt a subtle twinge in my groin that hinted I might not necessarily be done for the evening.

Alex must have felt it too, for the white of his teeth became apparent in the near darkness. "Someone is in a mood tonight."

"Can you blame me?" I asked fondly. "I've got the love of my life right where I want him."

"Do you now?" he replied. I couldn't help but notice he was still inside of me, and that a hand had appeared at the base of my cock. "I think you might have that backwards," he observed as that hand slowly began to encourage, shall we say, another reaction — one that my body appeared very ready to accommodate.

"Maybe," I replied. "Or perhaps I just want to see how—"

With the insane timing that came with being a police officer, the vague sounds of my iPhone going off somewhere in the condo floated through the air, quickly quelling the resurgence the two of us were feeling. Cursing under his breath, Alex carefully pulled out of me and moved to his side of the bed; as I rolled off the mattress and began searching for my phone, I realized any apology at the interruption — or any promise that it would be brief — would be ill received at best. Padding across the carpet, I felt a slight amount of anger rising that my personal time was being ignored yet again; that dissipated slightly when I finally located my phone on the breakfast bar and saw who was calling. Tapping the answer button, I took a deep breath to steady myself before speaking.

"Gina — it can't be good that you're calling at this hour."

"And good evening to you, Chief," she said cheerfully. "I hope I'm not interrupting anything."

I tried to ignore the condom I was still wearing. "Just dessert," I said with a slight smile. "With the events of the day, I had a... late dinner with Alex."

There was a long moment of silence. "Ah," Gina finally replied after a slight cough. "Well, I hope it will keep."

"That makes two of us," I said with a wistful glance toward the master bedroom. "What did you need?"

"I wanted to let you know that we located the victim's car," she answered. "It was parked in one of the outer lots at the Rancho Linda Mall; I'm on my way over there now and thought you'd want to be there, too."

I closed my eyes and groaned inwardly. "Absolutely," I said. "I'll grab my things and leave after I hang up."

There was another pause. "No need to hurry," she said carefully, confirming without a shadow of a doubt why she was the best crime scene tech in Southern California. "You should be able to finish what you're doing."

I glanced at the bedroom again. "I suspect I've had all I'm gonna get for tonight," I replied ruefully. "See you in twenty."

Five

The Curious Case of
the Missing Technology

While I'd intuitively known it was close to the witching hour when Gina called, actually seeing the cold, hard evidence the week had suddenly flipped to Tuesday was a bit off-putting. In some ways, it felt like the clock on my Camaro's dashboard was mocking me; at the very least, it served as an uncomfortable reminder I'd been up for the better part of a day and a half at that point. Bleary eyed and fighting back the crash from my extracurriculars with Alex, I turned into the first twenty-four hour Starbucks I passed on my way to the 57 and ordered the largest black coffee they had on offer; the price of such a luxury was nearly enough to shock me into full consciousness by itself, though not enough to wipe away the strange cobwebs that seemed to be hanging at the edge of my thoughts. I managed to get a third of the insanely hot cup into me before I turned onto the 57, and by the time I'd brought the Camaro up to highway speeds, I felt like my brain had finally reached them, too.

That there was even traffic on the freeway at one in the morning always surprised me; never as rough as its daytime counterpart, it still served as a reminder that Southern California tended to be a round-the-clock operation. Small trucks bearing the logos of local produce ware-

46

houses vied for space alongside longer semis hauling freight from the various ports we had to destinations unknown; a healthy smattering of passenger cars were also sprinkled across the lanes, clearly driving with the intent to get to wherever they needed to go as quickly as possible. A county SUV suddenly appeared in my rearview mirror, lights all ablaze; as it weaved in and out of the traffic and then whooshed past me in pursuit of something I couldn't see, I wondered if the officer behind the wheel had drawn the short straw, or was a natural night owl and had asked for the assignment. I'd spent my fair share of time on overnight duty during my early years in law enforcement, though back in Windeport that had pretty much consisted of keeping my phone on and by my bed; more than once, I'd been roused at two in the morning to help herd a wayward dairy cow back to the barn for their first milking of the day.

Life had seemed far simpler then.

The main exit for Rancho Linda appeared in the distance, and I dutifully switched lanes myself so I could reach the ramp; coasting to a stop at the bottom, I rolled through the red light and hummed down the main drag, the engine of the Camaro a comforting purr as I drove. I slowed a second time at the light for the mall and then slowed further as I took my bearings; based on what Gina had told me, I stuck to the outer access road and looped around to the far side of the massive structure. Soon enough the strobing from multiple police vehicles became visible, along with the harsh glare of temporary spots that had been brought in to illuminate the entire scene. I found an open spot beside a van from the Orange County Office of the Medical Examiner and killed the Camaro's engine; pulling my beanie down a bit, I grabbed my sweatshirt from the passenger seat and slipped out from behind the wheel.

As late Novembers went, it had been a relatively mild start to our winter, though as I shrugged into the warmth of my hoodie, I sensed that might be about to change. While I couldn't entirely see my breath, the crispness in the air made me wish I taken more time to dress than to have simply tossed on the first set of workout gear I could find in our as-yet unpacked luggage from the trip to Maine. I thought longingly of my thermal running tights and chuckled inwardly as I recalled days in Windeport when I'd thought temperatures in the low fifties meant wearing shorts and a muscle compression shirt. It certainly hadn't taken long for my blood to thin once I'd returned to California.

One of my newer recruits was standing just in front of the requisite loop of crime scene tape that appeared to have been run in a large square around a late model Honda Civic. He smiled at me as I approached, and for a moment, the old Vasily wondered what it might take to get him into my bed; shaken slightly that my sleep-deprived mind had so easily drifted in that direction, I returned the smile and vowed to find another super-sized cup of coffee at my earliest convenience. Holding the tape up for me, I ducked under and then made my way over to the action; Gina was standing behind the open trunk for the Civic, staring at it almost accusingly. Multiple sarcastic witticisms flashed through my head as I came up beside her, all of which immediately evaporated when I got a look at the trunk's contents myself.

"What the fuck...?" I breathed.

I caught Gina's smile out of the corner of my eye. "And good evening to you, too," she chuckled softly.

"I was wondering why you were scowling," I continued. "Someone was searching for something. Or they were looking for a clean outfit."

She nodded and used the edge of her omnipresent iPad to point at a gym bag that had been completely torn apart; workout gear in a shocking variety of vibrant colors was strewn throughout interior, almost if the bag had exploded. "I think the former," she said. "The bag was sliced open with something sharp. Same goes for that computer satchel."

My eyes drifted to a high-end leather briefcase in the opposite corner of the trunk; an uneven gash across the side had created a sizable opening, allowing easy access to the contents. I leaned down to get a better look and saw the usual cornucopia of the tech-savvy worker: power cords, adapter dongles and data cables were all tangled together and had spilled slightly out onto the carpet of the trunk. There might have also been a random manilla folder or two pressed to the back of the satchel, but without shining a flashlight on the mess, I couldn't really tell. Turning back to Gina, I asked the obvious question.

"Laptop?"

"Nowhere to be found," she replied. "At least, not in the car," she added before waving at the spotlights. "I called in help to do a grid search of the lot but I'm not hopeful."

I nodded, for that was my first thought as well. Setting my backpack down on the ground for a moment, I pulled a pair of gloves out of a side pocket and snapped them on. "Can I poke around in here?" I asked as I leaned in.

"Not quite yet," Gina replied. "Still waiting for a photographer."

"Oh shit," I breathed, looking at her. "Jocelyn's out of town for that funeral, isn't she?"

"And Francis is still on Family Leave," she sighed. "Honestly, I'm not loving having to lean on the Sheriff's Office like this. It feels like a hint of how things will be in the future."

"Not if I can help it," I replied darkly.

Prior to leaving for Maine, I'd had a rather heated discussion with my boss over the proposal to merge more of our department with Orange County's; frankly, I probably shouldn't have gone after the messenger like that, for Chief Gilbert was just as much a pawn in the city's efforts to cut costs by eliminating any services they felt the County were already offering. I knew he was as pissed off at the whole mess as I was, but he'd caught me just after I'd read the memo we were to vacate our current building by November 30 and decamp to the modern Glass Monstrosity at the fringes of Rancho Linda. My foul mood wasn't truly an excuse for such bad behavior on my part, so I'd quickly apologized to him with a six-pack of his favorite microbrew and a private promise we'd work together to try and stem the tide of stupidity.

Returning to my backpack, I rooted around until I found a pen and then used it to carefully lift the ersatz flap on the satchel just a little bit more; Gina was on the same wavelength and helpfully triggered the flashlight function on her iPad, then held it closer to illuminate the interior. The light revealed the cables were a far more tangled mess than had first appeared, almost as if they'd been hurriedly gathered up to clear the way to the true prize. Gingerly lifting the flap even more, I got the sense the laptop that *should* have been in the padded slot was just that. My eyes drifted to what I could now clearly see were several manilla folders, thick with material; their tabs were angled away from me, so short of unzipping the bag, I couldn't immediately see how they were labeled. It wasn't much of a stretch to presume they contained research for one or more articles the journalist might have been working on, though I did wonder why it wasn't stored digitally on some cloud server.

I withdrew my pen and stood back up to face Gina. "Someone *really* wanted that laptop," I said. "But why cut it out of the satchel? I didn't see a lock on the zipper; it would have been fairly easy to retrieve."

"There isn't one," Gina confirmed. "Nor on the gym bag."

Looking back at the yard sale in the trunk, I slowly nodded as my investigator brain began pulling the threads together. "This is all for show."

"It is?"

"Yeah," I continued. "Leave behind clear evidence of a search and the common assumption on our part would be they were looking for something valuable; I think we're meant to assume the laptop was the target."

"Huh," Gina said thoughtfully. "If not the laptop...?"

"Something smaller," I said, leaning down to inspect the gym clothes. "Something that could be hidden more easily — a thumb drive, maybe. Or a SIM card; maybe even one of those two-factor authentication token devices. Hard to know until we can dig into this pile of stuff ourselves." I looked at Gina and smiled slightly. "This reminds me of a case I worked with Sean last Christmas; we found a journalist's voice recorder hidden in her underwear drawer."

"I thought that was where you put your emergency cash?" Gina asked with a smile.

"I keep mine next to the condoms," I replied innocently. "But to each their own."

"TMI Vas," Gina sighed. "Want the rest of the tour?"

"Yes, please."

She nodded and drew me around to the driver's side. "You're looking at a three-year-old Honda Civic hybrid with remarkably high milage," she began. "We had to pop the lock but found the keys in the glovebox — alongside the vehicle registration and insurance card. I cross-checked the VIN with the Department of Motor Vehicles and was able to confirm it belongs to our missing and presumed dead journalist, Vivian Grandchester."

"I think you've probably added to our certainty over who we found," I said before gesturing at the empty parking lot surrounding us. "Why is it parked here? There are multiple public parking lots around the reservoir that are far more convenient to the running path." I looked in the general direction of the soon-to-be-former police station. "I like a long workout just as much as the next runner, but starting from here would have made it close to a half-marathon distance."

"Maybe she was in training for something," Gina offered. "You'd know better than I would, but the gear she was wearing — and what's in the bag back there in the trunk — looks fairly high end. I don't think she was a casual runner."

I frowned as I thought back to the crime scene I'd been at nearly twelve hours earlier. "I don't remember seeing a watch on what was left of our victim's wrist," I said.

Gina tapped on the screen of her iPad. "I've got the photos, hang on... yeah, here we go," she said as she turned the device toward me. I tried to repress a shudder at seeing the flattened remains again, and instead focused on the arms. "I don't see anything, unlike the debris you think were for a headlamp."

I nodded. "Any runner worth their salt would have recorded their workout," I mused. "Especially if they were in training."

"Maybe she was using her phone?" Gina offered. "You're trying to confirm her movements, aren't you?"

"Yes."

"The phone might help either way," she continued. "I'll have the geeks check it for workout data and also cross check its location data with the towers surrounding the reservoir." Gina paused. "You don't think she parked here, though, do you?"

"No," I replied. "If I recall correctly, the mall has surveillance cameras?"

"Already got one of your officers visiting with the overnight rent-a-cop stationed in the security office," Gina said. "So far they're volunteering to help, but you might want to have a warrant ready to go just in case."

"Noted," I nodded. "Who doesn't love doing bureaucratic paperwork at two in the morning, anyway?"

"I don't," Gina chuckled. "If the video turns up anything, I'll let you know; leaning into your assumption about our victim not driving here herself, this happens to be a corner of the lot where there are fewer cameras."

"Someone knew what they were doing," I mused. "You know anyone in Transportation? Maybe one of those new fancy cameras they installed to catch red light runners might finally be useful."

"So cynical," Gina laughed. "Especially when they didn't cost the city anything to implement."

"Clearly you've not seen what it's costing us to store the video in the cloud," I sighed. "The grant didn't cover that."

"There's always something," she said. "I'll reach out to them; we might get lucky, since the main entrance to the mall has one of those gizmos."

"That's my hope. Is this car new enough to have an onboard black box?"

Gina smiled. "It is indeed. We'll be able to pull the last fifty hours of telemetry; I've not done more than a cursory review of the navigation system, but it looks to be of the type that connects to a smartphone. I'm not going to be able to get much from it without having the device it's pared with present."

"Well," I smiled slightly, "it helps the victim's phone is still in relatively good shape."

"I'll connect everything up once we get it back to the barn," she continued. "We still need to dust for prints and obviously take photos; aside from some dirt in the well of the passenger seat, the car appears to be relatively clean and well taken care of. Dashboard says it's got a half-tank of gas and just under 260k on the odometer."

"Shit," I breathed. "I guess reporters really do have to get around."

"Apparently. I did notice the low tire pressure indicator is illuminated; it's hard to say without a tire gauge, but I think the left rear is actually looking a bit soft."

"Seriously?" I asked, my eyebrows going up. "All this equipment and no tire gauge?"

"What can I say?" Gina replied. "It's never come up before."

"This might be your lucky day, then. Give me a second."

"Ok."

I left Gina standing by the Honda and made a quick round-trip to my Camaro; having driven cross-country in the car multiple times, I had a small road repair kit in the trunk that included all sorts of goodies, including a nifty little battery-operated digital tire pressure gauge. Ducking back under the tape (and heroically ignoring the cute officer who was *definitely* giving me the eye), I handed the device to Gina. "Will this do?"

"Nicely, yes," she replied as she deftly triggered it. "While I measure the tire, see if you can track down what the manufacturer recommends for pressure."

We split at that point; I pulled open the door to the driver's side and then leaned in so I could read the small sticker that was just inside the frame. "Looks like 38," I called out before standing again and moving around to the side of the car she was on. "What are you reading?"

"Twenty pounds," she replied from where she was kneeling beside the wheel. "This must be one of those run-flat tires, for it doesn't look *that* soft to me."

"Modern tech," I said as I crouched beside her. Playing a hunch, I reached into the alcove and gently ran my gloved fingers over the treads; it took but a moment to find a solid, cold mass beneath them. Leaning closer, my eyes caught the glint of metal beneath the spots. "A nail, I think," I said as I leaned back on my haunches. "And if I'm *really* lucky, it will match the type used at the construction site."

Gina looked at me. "What a tangled set of clues," she said. "The victim is dressed for a nighttime workout; you think she drove to the site before or after her run?"

"I'm not sure yet," I said thoughtfully. "But I do wonder now if the headlamp was more for scouting the construction site, not for her run. Whatever data you can pull from the victim's phone might help shed some light on that."

"Pun intended?"

I laughed. "Oh yes, totally." Looking back at the car, I continued to muse. "If we assume she was at the site, the next logical assumption is the killer had a specific reason why Grandchester's car couldn't be found there."

Gina frowned. "Moving it wouldn't have delayed identifying her," she said.

"No," I said as a I stood. "But it did give someone more time to search the car. This might narrow down our window a bit," I continued. "Lift told me she gets to the site pretty early in the morning; she didn't mention having seen the Honda, so it had to have been gone by six."

"Unless Lift is lying," Gina reminded me.

"There's always that," I laughed. "But I think I managed to tease most of the truth out of her."

"Not all of it?"

"No," I replied. "My gut tells me she knows something else that she wasn't willing to say — at least, not yet." I smiled again. "I'll just have to turn my charming personality up to ten so I can get it out of her."

Gina's mouth quirked. "I thought that only worked on guys?"

"Hey, I can be equal opportunity when needed," I laughed before glancing at the officer who was *still* paying close attention to me. "Though, admittedly, I don't seem to have as much success with women."

"Good thing you're gay, then," she chuckled. "Though I could see you as bi."

"Been there," I said as I grabbed my backpack, "done that and got the scars to prove it. Let me know when you've got the video from Transportation?"

"Will do," she answered. "Just a head's up, though: I have to oversee the move of some of our more sensitive equipment to the new lab space later this morning, so don't expect anything too quickly."

A bolt of realization shot through me. "Shit, is that today?"

"Sadly, yes." She paused. "I take it from your expression you forgot."

"I've been out of town," I said, though even to my ears the explanation felt weak. "Or, more honestly, I've been trying to forget it's even happening in the first place."

"Aren't we all. I'm going to miss our old building."

"Me, too," I sighed. "Well, maybe I'll see you over at the new space later, then."

"I'd better," she laughed. "Since you're the one signing off on our move."

"Am I?" I asked innocently as I turned and headed for the Camaro. "Go figure."

Six
Practice Makes Perfect

Seeing as though I was already wide awake and less than a mile from the station, I killed the time before I could get into the pool for swim practice by treating myself to a modest carafe of freshly brewed coffee at the diner across the street while filing a stream of electronic warrants for the case, including the surveillance footage from the mall's parking lot. By the time the clock on my laptop's screen showed it was quarter to four, I'd put in what felt like the equivalent of ten hours of work; filing bureaucratic paperwork — electronic or otherwise — always felt a bit like a soul killer, even if it was necessary to ensure the legality of my investigation. One thing Sean had drilled into me in our decade working together was the importance of dotting every "I" and crossing every "T" for you never knew when you were going to run up against a high-priced lawyer capable of scrutinizing every last detail in the hunt for a mistake that would clear their client. My successful close ratio reflected how seriously I'd taken that lesson to heart; as I shut down the laptop and shoved it into my backpack, I wondered a bit at how my friend was doing and toyed with the idea of giving him a quick call. Doing the mental calculation of the time difference told me he was probably still in the pool, wrapping up his own start-of-the-day calisthenics, so I tapped out a quick text message with an offer to speak later, grabbed my gear and headed for the Camaro.

The gate to the pool was open when I pulled into the parking lot at Rancho Linda High School, the clarion signal that any and all were welcome to partake in what awaited just beyond the chain link fence. Save for our coach adjusting one of the lap clocks, the deck was clear and the lanes empty, not an unusual situation given *official* practice started at five; Coach tended to get her workout in before we arrived, and had a standing initiation to join her should they want to get some extra yardage in. Most days it was just the two of us in that bonus hour; on the few occasions when I'd not been alone, it had generally been a visiting college swimmer there for the holidays trying to maintain their edge (and avoid the wrath of their team coach upon their return for having slacked off). Ducking into the locker room, I grabbed my spare Speedo from the locker along with my backup goggles and cap; typically, I never left the condo without a fully stocked swim backpack, but I'd barely had time to unpack from our trip to Maine, let alone prep for the coming week. Eying what little shower gel I had in my supplies reminded me I'd also planned on restocking the locker, too; adding it to my mental to-do list, I found myself wondering if I'd even have time to buy groceries, let alone grooming supplies in the coming days.

Exiting the relative warmth of the locker room was a stark reminder that winter was about to descend on Southern California; the sudden chill against my exposed skin raised goosebumps in places I never thought I'd feel them. Somewhat wisely, I'd opted to ignore County regulations and had skipped the shower in favor of stepping directly up to the block and then doing a smooth racing dive into the lane I favored; kicking to the surface, I made short work of the first lap and flipped to return to my starting point at the other end. By the time I was bobbing there beneath the starting block, Coach had conveniently leaned her small whiteboard against it, her devious workout for me spelled out in blocky red letters.

Someone had a bad night, I groaned inwardly as I looked it over.

The breakdown of strokes, distances and time requirements were quite harsh, even for former Olympians like me. Still, I was always up for a challenge — but not before pulling myself out of the water to hunt down one of those energy gel packets she kept in a special drawer for emergencies. Grimacing slightly at the horrific taste of the stuff, I tossed the packet into the trash and then stepped to the block again; throwing myself into the air, I parted the surface once more and smoothly executed a nearly perfect parabola before popping up and beginning the first of six sets of butterfly. It was my best stroke — and the one that also took the most out of me; by the start of the final 800 yards, I was truly feeling it in the small of my back, a leading indicator an extended session in the hot tub might not be enough to keep from being stiff later in the day. My mind went completely blank save for a singular focus in completing — no, *surviving* — the set; when I finally hit the tile of the wall for last time, my lungs were on fire and my arms felt like they'd been made from rubber. Gasping for air as I bobbed at the edge of the pool, I cursed for the millionth time the insanity of maintaining an Olympic-caliber workout routine; on the other hand, I knew my body craved the rush of endorphins that were always unlocked with the madness, the prize for having sold a portion of my soul to the God of Chlorine. It also didn't hurt that it kept those very muscles Alejandro had been paying especially close attention to a few hours earlier in tip-top shape; I smiled to myself at the irony that both of us had body image issues we rarely spoke about, issues that drove us to our respective pools upwards of six days a week. Despite everything I had accomplished in my life, I still saw in the mirror the thirteen-year-old version of myself that had struggled to bulk up, the kid who'd felt neither attractive nor desirable. Alejandro had repeatedly assured me he'd love me even if I grew fat and bald; my inner teenager had steadfastly refused to believe it.

Or, more accurately, adult me has never allowed himself to accept it as truth, I thought as I felt my breathing begin to normalize. *So here I am, putting in grueling exercise nearly every day of the week. Is this a gay thing? Maybe this is a gay thing. I feel like I read somewhere gay men tend to worry about growing old... perhaps I'm just right there in the middle of the bell curve...*

As I moved to the next item on my workout agenda, I sensed the pool had shifted around me; turning slightly, I saw the regular crew had arrived and the main workout session was in full swing. Looking up at the clock mounted by the locker room, I was dismayed to realize my first set had taken nearly an hour — an eternity by my standards; it was little solace it had been close to five thousand yards of fly. Sighing, I ducked underwater for a moment and then kicked away from the wall, intent on trying to get in as much of the remaining instructions on the whiteboard before dragging myself out of the water at six. I managed to make a good dent in what was left, and ultimately only skipped the short cooldown set so I could keep to my self-imposed schedule; as I truly hated the showers in the pool's locker room, I tossed my sweats back on over my still damp Speedo with the intention of using the far better showers at the station. I also had a spare set of business casual clothes in my locker there as well, something that would be a bit more professional to wear to the postmortem I had to get to later that morning. My plan immediately hit a snag, though, for when I exited the men's lockers, I ran right into Rosie Frankenhoffer; clad in the super-thick, super-comfy workout gear that seemed to be from a different era, she appeared to be searching for something in her swim backpack and looked up at me as I approached.

"Hey," she smiled before dropping the bag and pulling me into a big hug. "How are you doing? Did you pull Sean back from the brink?"

"Jury's still out," I replied.

Rosie's eyes narrowed. "That sounds like a story you can tell me over breakfast."

"I'd love to," I said, "but I've got—"

"I think the Deputy Chief can be spared for thirty minutes," she interrupted with a smile. "Meet you over at the diner."

I'd known my millionaire friend long enough to realize there was no getting out of the invitation — even if I'd wanted to. Ever since Rosie appeared in my life, I'd found it pretty damn hard to refuse her anything; Alejandro seemed to have a similar predilection, if his recent agreement to be the main attraction for her at an upcoming Christmas Eve fundraiser were any indication. She felt like the grandmother I'd never had, and it often seemed she thought of Alex and I as family. As loquacious as she often was, Rosie hardly ever spoke of her own relations; despite being an investigator, I'd never felt the need to press her, for it often felt like an area of deep sadness better avoided than discussed.

"Fine," I sighed, "but I'll have to eat and dash. I still need to shower and then get down to the Coroner's office."

Rosie glanced meaningfully at my sweats. "I seem to recall you conducting more than a few investigations in far more casual attire," she said.

I rolled my eyes. "Not intentionally."

"Uh huh," she laughed. "See you at the diner."

Feeling as through I had lost yet another round in whatever friendly game we were playing, I shifted my backpack on my shoulder and sighed audibly as I walked across the pool deck and out the gate for the parking lot. True to form, Rosie's nearly pristine Oldsmobile Cutlass Calais was parked in her usual spot next to my Camaro; shaking my head at how easily I had folded, I tossed my backpack into the backseat then slid behind the wheel. The engine started up with a quiet roar that seemed to underscore my mood; leaning into that, I may or may not have backed out my space at Warp 6, then kicked up what little dirt was in the parking lot by stomping on the accelerator to leap forward even faster. Needless to say, I returned to the diner in record time — not that it mattered, since it was, literally, just down the street from the pool. Despite my antics, as I got out of my car, I discovered Rosie's Oldsmobile had turned in right behind me and decided to wait for her on the concrete walkway just below the iconic Googie arches of the diner. Before long, the two of us were cozily ensconced in my favorite semicircular booth, gazing at the plastic-coated menus despite knowing pretty much what we'd be ordering already.

Turning to the waiter — the latest in a long line of Emo surfer guys who never seemed to quite measure up to the first one I had met the day I'd arrived in Rancho Linda — I handed him the menu with a smile. "The usual, Rigoberto."

"I figured," he replied. "Same for you, Miss Rosie?"

"Pancakes today, Bert," she said, which caused me to raise my eyebrows. "Chocolate chip."

"*Sí*," he replied, as astonished as I was. "Coffee?"

"God yes," she replied.

"Back in ten," he said before moving to the next booth.

As I watched him smile and begin to scribble down their order onto his notepad, I realized I'd not thought about Drew in some time; for a while, I thought something had developed between us, but in the end, the allure of moving forward in his chosen vocation had been impossible to compete with. His kindness in the aftermath of my rape was something I'd never forget, but I'd always been struck by how he'd more or less completely disappeared from my life once he'd moved away from Rancho Linda. On the other hand, the part of my ego that was still smarting over how easily I'd been cast aside had long tempered my desire to look him up. The amazing hunk that currently shared my bed might have also had something to do with it, too.

Rosie as always seemed to be tuned into my thoughts and cocked her head slightly as I turned back toward her. "You dated Drew when you first moved here, didn't you?" she asked.

I smiled. "I'm not sure 'dated' does justice to what we had," I replied. "But yes, we were together for a while — right up until... well, until I went back to Windeport that summer."

"Ah," she said, tactfully opting not to bring up *why* I'd so abruptly skipped town. "Have you heard from him since he moved up the coast?"

"Not a peep," I said, with just enough of a tone to indicate I'd prefer a new topic.

Rosie's eyes narrowed slightly, but she got the hint. Unfortunately, that meant zeroing in on why she'd invited me to breakfast in the first place; taking her coffee cup into her hands and raising it to her lips, she paused long enough to look over its rim in the most Lauren Bacall way I'd yet seen. "How's Sean doing?"

With anyone else, I would have simply smiled and provided a witty joke about how relationships come and go, but Rosie had long ago moved into that small, select group of people I felt were like family. The look of genuine concern on her face wasn't an act; without my having said a word, it was clear she'd already divined my trip hadn't been a complete success. I played with my spoon for a moment as I pondered how much to tell her, and then just as quickly decided to screw it all and unburden my soul to a friendly ear.

"Not great," I replied with a long sigh.

"What the fuck happened?" Rosie asked. "I know I only met his girlfriend once, but she seemed to have her shit together."

I smiled wryly. "Like so many of us, she managed to hide what was truly going on behind a façade of normalcy," I answered. "I don't know if I told you that they had a bit of a meltdown in their relationship this summer."

"You didn't."

I nodded. "Yeah. Sean made the mistake of suggesting they move into his bungalow and that, apparently, uncorked a whole shitload of PTSD for Suzanne. Her ex-husband was a controlling personality, to put it mildly, so the thought of being beholden to another man was too much."

"That's not Sean," Rosie said. "I got to know him pretty well when he was recovering at the mansion from that gunshot wound. There isn't a nasty bone in his entire body."

I smiled slightly at that, for it seemed wise not to tell her about the unsanctioned side investigation my best friend had run into Suzanne's ex-husband after she'd finally explained to him why she'd dropped out of his life for a week. It was one of several extremely questionable actions my otherwise stalwart by-the-book mentor had taken in the aftermath of her disclosure, actions that had landed him in hot water with his new bosses at the Maine State Police. While I'd had a sense from our regular texting and phone calls that *something* had gone awry between Sean and Suzanne, I'd not been prepared for the shell of a man I'd found when I landed on his doorstep in Windeport after Thanksgiving. I'd had my share of bad relationship exits, to be sure, but Sean's heart had been wounded so deeply I feared for its recovery. As much as I loved Rosie — and trusted her — none of what I now knew had happened felt like information I could share with her, not without violating the unwritten understanding I had with my best friend. So, I decided to shade the story ever so slightly to both satisfy her and, hopefully, forestall any further probing on her part. The downside, of course, was that as an author, Rosie tended to have quite the inquisitive mind; I felt badly I'd be leaning into my skills as an investigator to slightly mislead her, but it seemed justified.

"Sean lived in a bubble during his formative years," I reminded Rosie. "When he wasn't swimming, he was *thinking* about swimming while pulling down straight As in school. I love my friend to pieces, but the dude is barely out of his teenage years when it comes to dating; while he can read a suspect like no one else, Sean is still learning how to do the same when it comes to his significant other." I shrugged. "He sees now that Suzanne had been leaving him little hints — he never stayed more than a night at her place, and she seldom spent more than two at his. They always split the costs when they traveled, even if it was just a long weekend in Portland to volunteer at the Children's Ward. The pattern only became apparent when she pointed it out to him," I added, then smiled wanly. "The irony wasn't lost on him that it's the second time he misread the situation."

Rigoberto chose that moment to reappear with our breakfast; Rosie waited until he'd refilled our coffee mugs before speaking. "You're talking about his ex-fiancé?"

"Deidre," I nodded as I stirred my oatmeal. "Though I'm also inclined to think that the death of his mother was more of a contributor to that one going down the tubes. It took Sean a long time to process what happened; his father couldn't deal with it and sort of pulled up stakes, leaving him to wander through the barren wasteland of grief on his own."

"I didn't know that."

"Sean doesn't tend to talk about it," I said. "Not even with me. I did what I could at the time, but it was impossible to break through the protective shell he'd weaved around himself."

Slicing off a piece of her pancake, Rosie carefully speared it with her fork, then added a piece of bacon to it before looking at me again. "'Not great' sounds like a Vasily euphemism for 'shitty.'"

So much for keeping her out of it, I thought. "Yeah," I agreed. "It pretty much is. Suzanne's ex passed away two weeks ago, and through a strange series of legal shenanigans, she wound up with his entire estate. Don't ask," I hastily added when I saw her eyebrows arch. "All I know is that means she's now the proud owner of a few acres in New Hampshire hosting what is apparently her dream home. Sean says she's been spending every weekend there — the weekends that she's not on rotation at Maine Medical."

"Meaning she's keeping her distance," Rosie correctly intuited.

I nodded. "They pass like two ships in the night if they happen to cross paths at the local grocery store."

"That's... that's *awful*."

"Yeah," I said again as I tore off a piece of my sourdough toast and stared at it for a moment. "The two of them are supposed to be in our wedding; I'm not entirely sure how we're going to handle that." I looked up. "Sean's decided to take a leave of absence from his new job and drive to Florida so he can spend the holidays with his father; he'll join us at Disney World for the wedding, then head back to Maine after."

Rosie looked thoughtful. "He doesn't seem like the type to run from a problem," she observed.

"No," I agreed. "But he *does* need a change of scene, and he declined my offer to host him for a bit out here. He could do worse than reconnecting with his father; they used to be pretty close, and only recently patched things up."

Rosie continued to eye me. "Keep Suzanne on the guest list," she said.

I felt an eyebrow arch. "I haven't decided to boot her yet."

"Haven't you?" Rosie asked. "Let her come. It will give me a chance to talk some sense into that woman. There may yet be time to save Sean's happily ever after."

This time, both of my eyebrows went up. "How did you know—"

"That he was going to propose?" she smiled. "You forget how much time the two of us spent together while you were out trying to solve that case." Rosie smiled wider. "And I am quite capable of ferreting out information from someone when the need arises. Sean told me about the ring he was planning on buying, and the various scenarios he'd come up with for proposing."

"Scenarios?" I asked, incredulous. "*Plural?*"

"That man can plan," she laughed. "He deserves a chance, and it sounds to me like Suzanne hasn't yet been willing to give him one."

"What makes you think you can change her mind?"

This time, the smile was sad. "Let's just say I know from experience that passing on a guy like Sean could be a mistake that she'll regret for the rest of her life."

I thought about that for a moment and slowly nodded. "You had a beau, didn't you?"

"A lifetime ago, yes," she replied.

"What happened?"

"I fucked up," she said quietly. "And therefore learned a lesson that I think I could share with Suzanne."

Curious, but sensing there was a boundary that could not — yet — be crossed, I let the tantalizing chance to peek into Rosie's past go. "I doubt it will be that easy."

"I'm sure it won't," Rosie agreed. "But we'll be together for a week. Magic has happened in less time."

"I love your optimism."

"Anything is possible if you believe in it," Rosie replied as she flagged down Rigoberto. "I've got to go — and so do you, if you intend to make that postmortem. We can plan further when you come to dinner tonight."

"Dinner? *Tonight?*"

"Yes," she smiled. "Chef has prepared a feast in honor of Chat's parents coming to retrieve him. There will be plenty of wine, so plan on spending the night."

"I'm not sure that's such a good idea. I'm in the middle of a case—"

"You can tell me all about it," Rosie grinned, "over dinner."

"It's really not the best time," I tried again, though I could see in her eyes it was a losing argument. "I've got research to do, reports to write—"

"I suspect you have people who can do that for you, *Deputy Chief.*"

I sighed. "I don't suppose I'm getting out of this, am I?"

"Nope."

"Then we'll see you tonight," I sighed again.

SEVEN
PM in the AM

My plan to swing past the station for a shower and a change of clothes ran aground as soon as I slid behind the wheel of my Camaro; as I reached for the ignition, I felt my iPhone buzz in the pocket of my sweats and preemptively groaned and what I suspected was an unwelcome omen. The push notification I found on the lock screen after I fished the pesky device from the pocket of my sweatpants confirmed the rest of the morning was off to a rocky start, for a semi had flipped on the 405, spilling what Dispatch was euphemistically referring to as an "environmental hazard" across what had been six lanes of busy rush-hour traffic. Having breakfast with Rosie had eaten into the already slim margin I'd left myself that morning for getting to my appointment with the Chief Medical Examiner on time; even leaning on my extensive knowledge of the surface streets in Orange County to get around the mess, I knew — at best — I was going to be a good thirty minutes late, and that was before I stopped to pick up the sugary coffee treats I never failed to appear with each time I met with Dr. Pembrooke. Sighing — and slowly banging my head against the steering wheel in mute protest of how the universe was currently unfolding — I decided the shower would have to wait. I figured there were far smellier things in the morgue, anyway; if I were lucky, no one would even notice one swimmer trailing *eau de chlorine* in his wake.

After shooting Peg's admin assistant a quick text that traffic might delay me, I started up the Camaro and pulled out of my spot, then turned onto the main drag for Rancho Linda. Despite how far upstream the city was from the accident, drivers trying to get between the 5 and the 57 had made it bumper-to-bumper. Somewhat predictably, the lights couldn't keep up with the unusual volume and made the whole mess worse by constantly changing; what should have been a quick three-minute drive to the 57 took me nearly ten, melting much of the Zen I'd gained from my workout in the process. Weaving around cars trying to get up the onramp for the 57, I found some relief as I drove across the rest of the city; traffic began to thin as I crested the ridge and coasted into Irvine. The sprawling Cal State campus appeared and then rolled past me; smiling, I triggered the Bluetooth on my car and speed-dialed Alex. As always, he picked up on the first ring.

"Hey," he said curtly, a faint note of frustration in his voice.

"Uh oh," I replied. "Someone's grumpy."

"Maybe a little," he admitted with a slight chuckle. "I'm stuck on the 5 at the moment. Any chance you can dispatch one of those police helicopters to rescue me?"

"If Rancho Linda had one, I'd send it," I answered. "Sadly, we don't. I thought the accident was on the 405?"

"I didn't know about that one," he said. "Though it explains why the 5 was so busy. Apple Maps says there's a wreck a few miles ahead of me; I'm stuck between exits with no place to go until it clears."

"Shit."

"You could say that again," he sighed. "I suppose I shouldn't complain. I'm missing a meeting I hate attending anyway."

My mouth quirked. "Are you *sure* you didn't know about the pileup on the 5?"

The momentary silence was telling. "Can I plead the fifth?"

"Only if you get arrested," I laughed. "Why did you want to avoid this meeting?"

"Various reasons," he said. "Not the least of which is our new CFO is a dick, and I can't stand to be in the same room with him."

Dodging a car that decided to pull out into the street without looking in my direction, I smoothly accelerated around it and slipped back into the proper lane for my turn. "I didn't realize they'd finally hired someone," I said, frowning slightly at the omission from my fiancé. "I take it this wasn't the candidate your hiring committee recommended?"

"Hardly," he replied. "Our top selection wanted more money, though, and wound up taking another offer."

"What's wrong with this guy, then?" I asked. Alex had regaled me for weeks regarding the Byzantine interview process his university now required for executive-level candidates; he'd been tapped to lead the search committee when the last head of the financial arm for Cal State Irvine had unexpectedly retired at the beginning of the Fall semester. It was another in a long line of high-profile appointments my fiancé had received since joining the college, a sign (at least in my book) that his star was in ascension. When I'd made that observation while cuddled into him one evening, he'd snorted and reminded me that he was a simple diver just trying to make his way forward in the world. I was pretty certain now that the world had other ideas.

"He's a stepper," Alejandro replied.

"Don't you mean climber?"

"No, I mean *stepper*," he answered emphatically. "As in he's incredibly willing to step on anyone's toes on his way to the top. CSUI is just a waypoint toward a better position elsewhere."

"So much for being in it for the kids."

"Exactly," Alex said darkly. "He was detailing his new plan to focus on centralizing business services across campus to stave off future financial troubles, though from the numbers I'm seeing, I have my doubts it would do anything but seed chaos at the unit level and trash what little efficiencies we already enjoy."

That quirk turned into a full smile. "I presume you made your position known?"

"As did the head of the Faculty Senate," Alex replied. "Along with the rest of the committee. It won't make a bit of difference at this point as the fucking idiot is clearly the darling of the president at the moment. We're all just silly numbers a spreadsheet the second-rate MBAs in his office generated anyway. Who are we to actually try and make sense of his plans?"

I smiled at the thought of seeing Alex fired up in a meeting about something he was passionate over. "There are days when I think your management could be interchangeable with mine."

"Aren't you a manager?"

"So they tell me," I laughed. "I avoid it when possible."

"Probably wise. Will you be home on time tonight? I might need to be soothed."

"Funny thing about that," I said as I turned again and found myself fairly close to the Starbucks I needed.

"Oh?"

"Yeah. Rosie has invited us to dinner and a sleepover tonight, in honor of our retrieving Chat."

There was a long pause. "I don't want to sound disagreeable, but her spare bed makes far too much noise for what I'd hoped to be doing to you this evening. Can't we just spirit our fur baby away and leave a raincheck in his place?"

"She *was* rather insistent," I said.

"That translates to you being unable to say *no* to her."

"Pretty much," I chuckled. "Can you blame me?"

"Hardly," he laughed. "Good thing we still have some clean stuff in our bags from Maine. I'll throw in a few other items and meet you at the condo after work."

"Sounds like a date."

"No, *mi amor*," Alex replied. "A 'date' would be you taking me to that boutique hotel on Catalina Island, hanging the 'do not disturb sign' on the door and then slowly having your way with me."

"I kind of like that idea," I said.

"I thought you might," he laughed. "See you tonight."

I was still smiling when I pulled into an empty spot at Starbucks and then dashed in to retrieve whatever the latest concoction was from the chain. Considering we had crested Thanksgiving, all of the festive holiday options had appeared on the menu, including a rather egregious eggnog-flavored one that felt uncomfortably close to a nutmeg drink Peg had resoundingly rejected last year. Betting on a past favorite, I stuck with something that appeared to have plenty of chocolate in it and then hurried back to my Camaro with a loaded drink carrier. Locating an open spot in the parking lot, I glanced at the clock on the dashboard and realized the law enforcement gods were smiling down on me that day; somehow, I'd managed to only be about twenty minutes late despite all of the hurdles thrown in my way. Locking up the car, I dashed across the lot to the Law Enforcement entrance for the morgue and went directly to the reception window at the end of the lobby, fingers crossed that Dr. Pembroke would still be able to perform the postmortem despite my tardiness. The handsome young man behind the glass looked up at my approach and smiled as he slid the window open.

"Hey Chuck," I smiled back. "Please tell me Peg is still expecting me."

"Is she ever," he replied. "She's in Exam Four, but you might want to hustle in."

I felt an eyebrow arch. "The accidents?"

"Yeah. We're already backed up as it is," he sighed. "From what I'm hearing on the loop, we're looking at a half-dozen victims from the one on the 405."

"Ouch," I frowned.

Chuck shrugged. "They hand out overtime around here like candy, so there's that. Maybe, someday, we'll have enough medical examiners that I won't have to keep juggling the schedule for Peg."

"I had no idea your budget issues were as bad as mine."

"We're the County," he smiled again. "It's probably *worse*. Everything is bigger here."

"Naturally," I laughed as I moved toward the double doors leading into the morgue.

Deviating quickly through the locker room to change into a pair of dull green scrubs, I trotted through the equally drab interior corridors of the morgue as fast as the full drink tray would allow; pushing through the swinging metal doors with my back, I found the doctor herself standing in her usual position beside the exam table, tapping away at the portable computer that had been positioned beside the head of the cadaver. Her masked face turned in my direction at the sound of the doors parting; I could see her eyes immediately drop to the cups in the carrier.

"Ah," she said with relief. "I cannot tell you how much I need one of those."

I moved over to the console and held the cardboard carrier up to her. "Long day already?"

"And it's getting longer by the minute," she nearly moaned. "What did you bring me?"

"Peppermint mocha," I replied. "It's now officially Christmas."

The way Peg's eyebrows crunched down told me the mask was hiding a deep frown. "I'm *so* not ready to hear that," she groused as she carefully plucked one of the drink containers from the carrier.

"I presume that means I'd better not tell you how many shopping days are left, then?" I asked as I tactfully put the carrier on the back counter with the spare drink I always brought. Two years into paying my penance for trying to lie my way to the top of her line, Peg still didn't seem to notice I avoided partaking in the sugary treats I never failed to bring as part of my ongoing apology. I'd begun to wonder if it was deliberate blindness on her part, or whether she'd fallen in love with what had become, essentially, a fun ritual each time I appeared in her exam room.

"You do and you'll find yourself on one of my tables," she replied darkly before pulling down her mask just enough to take a huge gulp from the container. How she was able to eat while standing so close to a dead body was something I tried not to contemplate.

"Message received," I laughed. "This is clearly a holiday-free zone."

"Clearly," she chuckled. Putting down her drink, she pulled her mask back up and then waved at the body on the stainless-steel table. "As always, you seem to have brought me yet another edge case."

"That sounds ominous."

"Depends on your perspective," she sighed. "I've done my share of autopsies on earthquake victims who perished under tons of building material; it's never pretty, and as you might expect, most of the time death is due to what we often refer to as 'compression injuries.'"

I chanced a glance at the cadaver; it was still extremely difficult to see what was left of Vivian Grandchester, though it was apparent Peg (or one of her minions) had cleaned away the worst of the stomach-churning evidence the poor woman had been essentially squeezed like a lemon. Without turning, I also knew that the more-than-normal collection of plastic biohazard containers on the rear counter held what had been removed from the body; I wasn't looking forward to reviewing the carefully catalogued items that were sure to be in the case file later that day. It had been years since a postmortem had me running to the nearest trash bucket so my guts could turn themselves inside out; as I carefully tried to swallow back the bile rising in my throat, I thought perhaps I might be closer to that moment than usual. Looking at Peg, I could see she was carefully watching me, her eyes filled with concern.

"Are you okay?" she asked quietly. "Do you need to step out for a moment?"

"Not yet," I replied honestly. "This is... this is a bit harder than normal," I added.

"Yeah," she agreed. "If you need a break—"

"You'll be the first to know," I interrupted.

Peg waited a moment, then slowly nodded. "As you can imagine, positive identification of your victim will only be possible through DNA at this point; however, I am reasonably certain based on a few key characteristics that this is likely Vivian Grandchester. Hair and eye color match what is listed on her current driver's license, and body measurements roughly align to the height and weight on file."

"That's reasonable," I said, then frowned. "That won't be enough probable cause to send Gina's team to Grandchester's home to collect a comparison sample."

"Sorry," Peg apologized.

"I might get lucky with next-of-kin; I've not done her background yet but presume there's someone out there that can get us there, DNA-wise."

"That's kind of what I figured we might wind up doing in this case," Peg said as she moved to the far side of the exam table. "Like I said earlier, COD is going to be pretty hard to figure out given the state of the body. Just about every bone was fractured, resulting in plenty of internal injuries; any one of them could have been fatal. However," she added as she leaned down and pointed to what was left of the head, "there is this very unusual indentation behind the left ear that's not consistent with your victim being crushed by a pallet full of building supplies."

Against my better judgement, I walked around to join Peg and looked at where her gloved finger was pointing. "Trauma?" I asked, looking at her. "Something hard, from behind?"

"And possibly fatal," she nodded. "There's no way to know for sure, but my professional instincts tell me she was dead long before the forklift lowered the boom on her — so to speak."

"It does kind of answer how she wound up beneath the pallet," I murmured. "I didn't think she laid down willingly, but it also didn't look like she'd been bound, either."

"I didn't find any ligature marks," Peg confirmed. "At least, none that were evident beyond the bruising from having been crushed. I have a few tricks up my sleeve that might confirm or deny that, if you want us to pursue it, though."

I nodded. "Yeah. Just in case."

"All right." Peg moved to the midsection of the body, forcing me to shift toward the feet. "I can't tell you much about the overall health of our victim, at least not from my observations. We're running the usual tests on everything, of course, so we might uncover some biochemical markers that will fill in some blanks." She looked over to the counter at the rear of the room. "We had to slice and dice what was left of the clothing, but it was still fairly easy to tell it was high-end fitness material; the mass spec will tell me more. I might be able to get you a manufacturer."

"I'm not sure it would help in any way," I said. "But you never know."

She pointed a gloved finger at a bag on the rear bench holding a pair of sneakers. "Footwear is a different story; those we were able to determine are from Brooks."

"Do you have a model?"

"Yes," she nodded as she went back to her computer. Tapping at the keyboard, she read something from the screen. "Cross trainers specifically for pronating runners, fairly recent release that has only been out since April. They replaced an earlier version that had been on the market for about a year."

"Fitness companies are notorious for that sort of planned obsolescence," I sighed. "Just when I think I've found something I like, they go and discontinue it."

"Tell me about it." Peg looked up at me. "About the only good news I have to offer is that it was not sold widely; based on our admittedly quick research, it appears to have only been available in select retailers. I presume it was intended as a marketing tool for independent running shops to attract customers."

I nodded slowly. "I shop at one myself; there are only a handful of those in Rancho Linda, and maybe a half dozen total in Orange County. I'll have Gina's team get me a list of who might have stocked that particular sneaker."

"Would that be important?" Peg asked. "I did match the tread to castings taken from the scene, but it's not outside the realm of possibility that someone *other* than the victim wandered the construction site wearing a pair of these sneakers."

"True," I answered as I felt myself frown. "The construction site *is* too damn close to the running trail to rule that out. I guess if nothing else, it'll give me background on Grandchester."

"We'll try to get something forensically off the victim's footwear to nail it down more," Peg said. "I'll be honest, it probably wouldn't be anything that would stand up in court given the state of the victim."

"I'll take whatever I can get," I said before smiling slightly beneath my mask. "Is it too much to hope for that you find a strange little worm stuck inside the tread of her sneaker that's only found in our fair city's reservoir?"

Peg chuckled as she wandered back toward the computer stand and her waiting coffee drink. "No, but I wouldn't hold my breath, either."

I chanced another glance at the body. "I imagine *any* sort of trace evidence will be hard to find."

"On the contrary, we found a *ton* of trace," Peg sighed. "The real question is whether we found anything of significance, and the answer to that is still pending."

"I feel like we're going to be pushing your lab geeks to the limit on this one, Peg," I said as I returned my attention to the medical examiner. "Anything they find could be useful."

"It's always an adventure with you," Peg laughed. "Honestly, it might be the only thing keeping some of those techs on my team."

"If that's the case, I fear the world has gone upside down."

"Too late, I think," she laughed again. "Everything will be in the file shortly. I'll ping you when the lab results come in, too. When do you think you'll have a DNA sample for me?"

"No idea," I sighed. "If I am truly lucky, our victim has a relative living here in Southern California and will consent to a cheek swab; otherwise, it all depends on how well I can sweet talk a judge into a search warrant for her home and office – not, I think, an easy proposition considering she was a journalist. Since I also have a missing laptop to recover, though, I think I've got a pretty strong justification."

"As strong as any," Peg said. "In this day and age of cloud storage, I can't imagine you'd find anything on it that wouldn't also be stored elsewhere. Especially since she was a journalist."

I folded my arms against the thin fabric of the scrubs. "Which is why the fact that it wasn't in her car is troubling me. We found her briefcase, so clearly, she *should* have had it with her." I shrugged. "Then again, I've been wondering if its absence is intended to throw us from something more salient."

"Like what?"

"Memory cards, maybe," I mused. "I told Gina at the scene that I thought the victim's car had been staged for our benefit; with time and distance, I'm leaning further into that view."

Peg looked thoughtful. "You know, if she were working on a story that was sensitive, she might not have wanted to keep that in the cloud. Or on the laptop."

I nodded slowly. "That fits with the literal files we also found in the car; I think she had hard copies of whatever research she'd been doing. I've yet to go through it."

"I've read her stuff in the *Register*," Peg said after looking down at the cadaver. "She doesn't strike me as the sort to use paper files."

"Having been on the receiving end of her research, I would agree."

"I'd forgotten about that. This must be a weird one to investigate for you."

"Yes and no," I replied. "On the one hand, I feel like it might be her revenge for not giving her an off-the-record quote for any of my cases."

"Maybe," Peg agreed. "And the other?"

I started for the door. "I can't shake this feeling her ghost is watching my every move," I said with a smile. "And breathlessly reporting all of it to the Almighty."

"It's not like you to be superstitious," Peg said.

I paused with one hand on the cool steel of the door. "I may be a lapsed Catholic," I replied, "but that doesn't mean I've forgotten all of the old tales about saints passing judgment on our lives." I paused. "So, yeah, I can fully buy into a spirit following me around until I solve her murder."

Peg's eyebrows went up. "You are a very complicated man, Vasily."

"So Alex keeps tells me," I laughed as I pushed through the door.

EIGHT
OUTFOXED

After a quick shower to wash away the worst of the morgue from my body — and, perhaps, one of the many layers of chlorine from the pool that had accreted on my skin over the years — I emerged from the Office of the Medical Examiner feeling more like a detective and less like a gym rat who'd been called in on his day off. I tossed my swim backpack into the rear of the Camaro and then paused after closing the door to consider my reflection; no amount of wishful thinking had caused my hair to grow out any faster than it was capable of doing, leading to the frown I could clearly see. Short wasn't really my style, and as I ran my hand through what *had* finally appeared, I also realized why I had bleached it for as long as I could remember. Whatever my natural color was supposed to be, it didn't fit the mental image I had for myself; even the salt-and-pepper style I'd donned for the Halloween gala had seemed more like me, despite it also feeling as though it had added a decade to my age. Sliding my sunglasses down from their perch on my head to cover my eyes, I sighed as I slid behind the wheel and wondered for the millionth time if I were the only gay man in the entire universe as hung up on appearances as he was.

Setting aside my near-constant body image issues for the moment, I started up the Camaro and then pulled out of my spot; I paused at the exit to the lot just long enough to punch in the last known address for Vivian Grandchester, then bravely darted into the last vestiges of rush hour traffic. As I headed back to Rancho Linda, I felt like I had the law behind me in terms of searching the journalist's home. At the very least I'd be able to argue to a court that a wellness check had been necessitated based on the evidence from both the scene and what Peg had provided during the PM; any clues I might stumble over while performing said wellness check would likely be admissible. Smiling slightly, I thought back to one of my first cases after my final return to California; I'd been digging into the death of a gymnastics coach from Cal State Irvine and had pretty much used the same logic to enter his home. Still, I thought it prudent to cover my bases and before stepping into the lukewarm stream of hot water that passed for the morgue's shower had called Miles back at the station; he'd promised me the request for a proper search warrant would be in the hands of my favorite judge by the time I reached Grandchester's residence.

Aftereffects from the earlier pileup made traffic on the 5 intense, and it didn't get any better once I shifted to the 57. An accident close to the Katella exit had me questioning my life choices once again; by the time I'd finally crawled past what appeared to have been a collision between a motorcycle and a semi, my patience had frayed enough that a throbbing headache had appeared between my eyes. Leaning into my training as a law enforcement officer, I threw the Camaro around slower vehicles and then accelerated well above the posted limit to try and regain some time; when the primary exit for Rancho Linda appeared on the horizon, I deftly shifted lanes and coasted down the ramp far faster than I should have. The light was in my favor, though, allowing me to smoothly slide out onto the surface street that sliced right through downtown. Siri guided me past the mall and our current office, then beyond the library and our modest town hall; the first left turn she had me make put me into one of the older neighborhoods, one full of what I liked to think of as the traditional California Arts and Crafts bungalow.

Most dated back to the midcentury era and had lush green lawns shaded by mature trees full of wide leaves. Sidewalks bordered both sides of the street and appeared wide enough for four people to walk shoulder-to-shoulder, another callback to an era that no longer existed. Somehow, while each bungalow looked as though it had been based on the same general floorplan, no two had been decorated the same. Some had flower boxes, others had tiered fountains bubbling over with brilliantly blue water; one even had a modest flagpole reaching for the sky with a Pride flag proudly waving in the light breeze. It was an eclectic neighborhood, and one that I knew was so far out of my price range that I wondered just what sort of a salary Vivian Grandchester had pulled down.

A partial answer to that question appeared when I slowed to a stop in front of the address I'd been given. Pulling to the curb, I killed the engine to the Camaro and then took a second look at the late model Toyota minivan sitting in driveway; it had clearly seen better days, as evidenced by the ancient brown-and-gold California license plate that seemed nearly as old as the house. The disability placard hanging from the windshield looked a bit newer and seemed to underscore the reason why a ramp had been built just beside the normal three-step staircase to the front door of the bungalow. Getting out of the Camaro, I pulled my backpack from the rear seat and started up the concrete walkway to the front door; flowerbeds had been planted along the edge of the front porch for the bungalow, but the plants had been pruned for the winter. That hadn't stopped someone from beginning to carefully string Christmas lights through the bushes; while the job appeared to be incomplete, I could see more lights had begun to snake upwards along the posts supporting the roof of the porch. Pausing at the base of the steps, I realized I'd only known the professional side of Vivian; I'd honestly never given a moment's thought to what her life might have been outside of her job as an investigative journalist.

Moving up the steps of the porch, I caught the movement of a sheer curtain covering what had to be one of the windows to the living room; glancing in that direction, I saw an orange tabby cat with expressive eyes carefully watching me as I approached the front door. "Hey there," I said as I knelt to the window. "How are you?"

The cat pressed itself into the glass in a friendly manner before dropping from the windowsill. A moment later, I heard the lock being opened; thinking for a moment that the cat was some sort of circus-trained performer, I was immediately disabused of that notion when the door was pulled inward to reveal an elderly woman standing somewhat unsteadily behind one of those commercial walkers. Idly, I noted that the small basket in the front of the gizmo held an assortment of gardening tools, including an impressive trowel.

"Good morning," the woman said, her voice clear and strong. Her eyes were soft hazel and didn't appear to miss anything. "It can't be good when the Deputy Chief of Police lands on your doorstep."

Taken aback slightly, I donned my best retail smile. "I didn't know I had such a reputation," I replied.

"Not you, personally," the woman replied. "In fairness, when Viv didn't come home last night, I suspected I might get a visit from you, or one of your deputies." She watched me closely for a moment. "Something *has* happened to her this time, hasn't it?"

"Might I come in, Mrs. Grandchester?" I asked, making an intuitive guess.

"Please," she said as she deftly backed up and allowed me through the door.

I paused just inside the threshold and found myself in a small foyer; as I suspected, a living room was off to the left, stuffed to overflowing with comfortable looking chairs all facing a large flatscreen television that looked to have been professionally mounted on the wall. Directly opposite and through a decorative arch was the formal dining room; it looked like a puzzle was in progress on the cherry wood of the table. A small hallway provided access to the kitchen in the rear, flanked by a right-angle staircase that led to the second floor. Stepping slightly sideways, I let her close the front door behind me, then followed her as she moved into the living room; contrary to the walker, she seemed quite steady on her feet, deftly weaving around the furniture before pausing by the couch. Waving at the easy chair opposite, she quickly took a seat, then pushed the walker out of the way. The orange tabby cat took that moment to hop onto the rounded arm of the couch, then settled in facing me, paws tucked beneath it; I tried to ignore how it felt like it was somehow passing judgement on me.

Settling into the easy chair she'd offered, I watched for a moment as she picked up what appeared to be an in-progress sweater being knitted from a skein of yarn full of brilliant colors bordering on psychedelic. Seeing my expression, Mrs. Grandchester smiled slightly as she resumed working on the item. "I hope you don't mind," she said apologetically. "I'm part of a group at church that crafts Christmas gifts for kids and I'm three sweaters behind."

I smiled slightly. "Not at all," I replied before arching an eyebrow. "Forgive me, but you don't appear to be following a pattern."

She smiled. "I've made so many of these over the years it's nearly second nature now."

"That I can believe," I said before my eyes went back to the shocking colors in the skein. "Timothy Leary might like that particular sweater."

"Maybe," she laughed, though there was still a bit of tension in her eyes. "This one is for a kid who is a fan of the late Bill Walton."

I nodded slightly. "He used to love those tie-dyed shirts, didn't he?" I asked before looking at the sweater anew. My eyebrows went up again as I finally took in the pattern. "How did you figure out a way to replicate the pattern? That's incredible."

"Lots of trial and error," she replied, then paused. "Why are you here, Chief Korsokovach?"

"Call me Vasily, please," I said.

"Only if you call me Hope."

"Deal." She eyed me for a moment. "You're not quite what I expected, Vasily."

I smiled slightly. "You can't believe everything you read."

Hope nodded. "Viv went after you pretty hard when you were driven out of the Department."

"I'm used to the spotlight," I shrugged. "You take the good with the bad."

There was a long pause. "Were you... actually...?"

"Raped?" I finished for her. "Yes."

Hope looked at me again then slowly shook her head. "Then I am very sorry for how she covered it," she said. "In my day, we would have shielded the victim more."

My eyebrows went up. "You're a journalist too?"

"Long retired," she nodded. "My beat with the *Times* was similar, though. I covered the LAPD in particular and had a front row seat to the riots in 1992."

"Not a good time for Los Angeles in general," I observed.

Hope did another row on her sweater; I felt like it had grown a foot just in the short time we'd been speaking. "Why are you here, Vasily?"

I thought about the best way to respond and decided to cut to the chase. "We found the body of a woman matching the description for Vivian at the construction site for the new affordable housing complex," I began. "Due to the circumstances of *how* we found the victim, we don't have a definitive identification, though. I'm here because I was hoping to find a personal item that might have some of her DNA on it; barring that, a relative who might be willing to provide a comparison sample."

Hope nodded. "I see."

"I didn't know Vivian well," I continued, "so I must confess that I didn't expect to find you at her last known address. Was she living with you?" I asked, correctly intuiting who owned the bungalow.

"Since the death of my late husband," Hope nodded again. The knitting needles in her hand made a rather soothing clicking noise as she worked. "About six years now. She stayed some nights prior — toward the end, we were taking shifts keeping Hal company."

"Cancer?"

"Among other things," she said softly. "Spinal issues put him into a wheelchair twenty years ago; we converted the den to the master so he wouldn't have to climb the stairs. Viv uses that as her office now."

I filed that away. "I'm sorry for your loss," I said, then nodded toward the walker. "Hip replacement?"

Hope's eyes widened. "Yes," she replied. "How--?"

"A friend of mine has spent a ton of time in the hospital over the past few years," I said, thinking of Rosie fondly. "You pick up a thing or two while you're there. For what it's worth, you look like you won't need that much longer."

"Another week or so." Hope smiled slightly. "Which is just as well, for the physical therapy really sucks."

"I know a thing or two about that as well," I laughed.

She looked at me. "Swimmer, right?"

"Yes. Still, actually. My fiancé and I can't seem to shake the habit of being athletes."

"Somehow I can believe that." Hope paused. "What happened to Vivian?"

"I can't really say at this stage," I answered. "Other than to confirm we're treating it as suspicious." I paused. "I'm sharing that with you with the caution that the investigation isn't public yet."

"Off the record, then," she smiled. "All right. What else can you tell me?"

"That depends," I said. "When did you last see her?"

"She had dinner with me Sunday night," she replied. "Then abruptly told me she was going for a run using the path around the reservoir."

"Did she do that often?"

"Run around the reservoir? Yes, but usually in the morning. I was a bit worried about her going so late, but she assured me there was plenty of lighting and would be safe."

"I've used that same path myself at night, and she's right," I confirmed.

"Well," Hope smiled slightly, "that didn't prevent me from insisting that she still take a headlamp; she wasn't happy with me but grabbed the one her father had in the closet for emergencies and then took off."

I nodded. "What time was this?"

"About eight."

"When did you expect her home?"

"She was on deadline," Hope answered. "Whatever she was working on had to be in by one in order to make the Monday edition. I know she'd written most of it but intended to polish it before submitting it to her editor."

"Do you know their name?"

"Howard something," she replied. "Never met him."

"Did she like him?"

"No," Hope said instantly. "Viv said the guy was a bastard, always looking at the bottom line and not wanting to make waves politically. Fortunately, she had enough awards hanging on her wall that he couldn't kill many of her stories."

That caught my attention. "But he had? Killed a story?"

"Several."

"About what?"

"Viv never told me specifics."

Something in the way she'd said that made me think otherwise. "Did she tell you anything about the current story she was writing?"

"No," Hope said a bit too quickly.

The sense she was hiding something became more pronounced. I decided to tack slightly to try and shake out more details. "You mentioned Vivian was using the den as her office."

"Yes," she nodded. "And before you ask, you cannot review anything in there."

My eyebrows went up. "I can, actually."

"Not without a warrant."

The sudden left turn also felt significant. "Which I will have within the hour," I said.

Her smile gave me more pause. "I think not. Most judges frown on law enforcement pawing through source material from a journalist."

I started to slowly nod. "You reached out to a lawyer already."

"When I saw your car pull up," she replied.

"I see." I thought for a moment. "You realize that something in her research might lead to us understanding what happened, right?"

"We have the Constitution for a reason," she replied.

It took a Herculean effort not to roll my eyes; most people who quoted the foundational document for our democracy to me tended not to have any clue what was actually in it. Then again, it was quickly becoming apparent that Hope Grandchester was not like most people.

Time to play hardball, I thought.

"As you wish," I said with a partial smile. Pulling out my iPhone, I glanced through the text messages and idly noted the push notification from Bristol Farms that apples were now five pounds for a dollar. "We'll just wait for the crime scene techs to arrive, and then we can go through your house with them. They should be here within the hour; I hope you didn't have plans for lunch."

Hope stopped knitting. "Did you not hear me? You aren't going to get your warrant."

"Oh, I think I will," I replied easily. "I probably should have mentioned that Vivian's absence from work triggered a missing persons investigation; that gives me a rather large amount of latitude in terms of evidence gathering."

She blinked. "You just said you found my daughter—"

"I said I found a woman matching the *description* of your daughter," I corrected. "There's a difference."

"That's pure semantics!"

"Legally, it isn't," I replied, then leaned forward. "Look, the team is going to turn this place inside out to get the DNA sample I need; whatever we find along the way will become part of the investigation and therefore excruciatingly public." I held her eyes for a long moment. "As you might imagine, I have some experience in this area; I suspect such public disclosure might not be in the best interests of either you or your daughter. Or," I continued, dropping my voice into the deadly serious range, "you can tell me what the fuck Vivian was working on and save both of us a shitload of time. Your choice."

Hope looked at me for a long moment. "I never got the sense from Viv's reporting you were so vindictive."

"I'm not," I replied as I sat back up and folded my arms against my chest. "And never have been. If what you are truly asking is whether what Vivian wrote about me over the years will affect how I investigate her death, the answer is an unequivocal *no*; I simply don't have time to play any games. I believe there is a strong possibility your daughter was murdered, and her killer has one hell of a head start on me. Whatever you know — whatever *she* knew — might be critically important to my finding out who did this."

"You'll have to find another way," Hope said as she put her knitting down and reached for her walker. "It's been nice meeting you, Deputy Chief. Now, get the hell out of my house."

"My team—"

"Won't be coming," she said as she pushed the walker ahead of her and began to move toward the front door. "Good day, Deputy Chief. Don't come back until you have a *legal* reason to be here."

I waited for a moment before standing; it had been a long time since someone had outfoxed me so deftly. Following her to the door, I paused in the threshold and turned back toward her, smiling ruefully. "Until we meet again, then."

A flicker of a smile wafted across her face. "Ever the optimist, I see. *That* was in Viv's reporting."

The opening was too good not to take. "You can't believe everything you read," I replied before turning on my heel and walking back to the Camaro.

NINE
FIRST AND FOURTH

Despite the chilly temperature of the late November day, I rolled down all the windows in the Camaro and let the breeze try to cool off my temper. The text from Miles confirming that my favorite judge had declined to sign the warrant had come in mere moments after I'd slid behind the wheel; whatever lawyer Hope had reached out to had made enough of a persuasive argument that what little evidence we'd gathered at the scene was circumstantial at best in terms of identifying our victim. While it felt a bit circular to me to demand positive proof of who we had lying in the morgue *before* being able to gather DNA to validate our assumption, the law (for the moment) was working in Hope's favor. What options I had left weren't great, but the good news was that I still had some — including visiting Vivian's former employer later that afternoon.

Maybe I'll get lucky and find she had a toothbrush in a drawer of her desk, I thought bleakly as I came to a stop at the entrance to the residential neighborhood. Per usual, making a left turn looked like it might require an act of Congress. *Or an overnight bag with dirty laundry she didn't unpack—*

Despite the appearance of a perfect opening in traffic, my mind froze.

Shit.

Spinning the wheel, I darted right and bullied my way into the flow of vehicles; accelerating, I kept one eye on the road while trying to pull up the location for the *Orange County Register*'s headquarters. I was reasonably certain their tall building wasn't far from my condo but had never had an occasion to actually visit it. Grandchester's usual modus operandi had been to ambush me at the station or over the phone; sitting down for a proper interview back at her office had never been in the cards. Scanning through the addresses, I tapped the proper one and then deftly switched lanes again so I could get to the onramp for the 57 south; speeding up more, I made short work of the distance and coasted at speed down the exit for Orangewood, barely making the light. As I worked my way along the surface streets toward my destination, I tried to temper my anxiety at possibly being outplayed a second time in less than an hour; there was a chance — albeit a slim one — that Hope's actions were driven by something personal and therefore hadn't included reaching out to Vivian's employer. Still, as I braked hard to avoid running a red light a few blocks from my destination, I knew I'd been foolish to take her statement about not knowing Vivian's editor at face value; frowning, I realized Hope had probably guessed my next move and had given them a heads-up moments after I'd left her house. I had to assume she'd beaten me to the punch; cooling my heels for a few moments while I waited for the cross traffic to clear knocked the edge off my anger, paving the way for me to think a bit more strategically about what I needed to do. While the prudent move would have been to get Judge Spenser on the phone so I could charm him into reversing himself on the wide-ranging warrant I needed, I had a sense that probably was the wrong move; journalists tended to run to the courts when anything even vaguely related to a First Amendment violation landed on their doorstep. My own personal history with the *Register* would add even more fuel to the fire, garnering large font headlines on their front-page hinting at some sort of retribution for perceived slights in their past reporting on me.

No, I needed a different angle; forcing the issue with a warrant would cause more harm than good.

The last flames of anger had flickered out by the time I turned into the parking lot that hugged the modestly tall building that the *Register* called home. Pulling into an empty spot under a tree that looked as though it had seen better days, I killed the engine and stared at the tower for a few moments.

I need a way in, I thought. *And I might know who can do it.*

Reaching for my iPhone, I tapped the speed dial for Alejandro; my heart did that funny two-step as soon as his beautiful voice filled my ear. "Hey," he said warmly. "Your timing is perfect. I was just fantasizing about this hunk of a swimmer whispering sweet nothings into my ear."

Despite everything, I felt myself smile. "Oh?" I asked. "That sounds like one hell of a fantasy. Was this hunk having his way with you, too?"

"Most definitely," Alex replied. "How's your day going?"

"Not as good as yours, clearly," I laughed.

"You forget I was stuck in traffic, *mi amor*," he said. "And had that shitty meeting to go to. But enough about me," he continued, a slight note of concern entering his voice. "What happened?"

"I got caught with my pants down," I answered baldly.

"In some contexts, that's a good thing," Alex said. "Like, say, later tonight at Rosie's."

My smile grew a bit wider. "I'll keep that in mind."

"I hope you do. Especially if you happen to have that swimsuit I love on underneath said pants."

"I guess I'll be doing a late workout in Rosie's pool, then," I laughed, suddenly feeling much better. "God, I love you."

"I know," he chuckled. "And ditto."

"Listen, do you have any kids interning or working at the *Orange County Register*?"

"I'm sure we do," Alex answered. "I don't tend to deal with Journalism majors, though, so I'd have to check with a colleague to confirm. Why?"

"Your fiancé is trying to figure out a way to get around both the First and Fourth Amendments," I sighed.

"And you want to use one of our students to do that?" It wasn't hard to miss Alejandro's note of incredulity.

I looked out of the driver's side window of the Camaro and considered the set of pigeons sitting rather contentedly along the roofline of a squat warehouse that was the next building over. Honestly, they looked as though they were having a far better day than I was, and for a moment I felt a stab of envy. "I didn't say it was a *great* idea," I admitted.

"I'd agree with that wholeheartedly," Alex replied. "And I'm the last person you should be going to for advice in law enforcement matters."

I smiled to myself. "I suspect having been with me as long as you have means you've picked up a thing or two about the business."

"Perhaps," he chuckled softly. "I guess I do know enough to point out that whatever evidence you managed to obtain using this harebrained scheme would quickly be tossed out by any lawyer that can breathe." He paused. "Well, maybe not the sort of lawyer who advertises on bus shelters."

"Actually, those are *just* the sort who'd make my life miserable," I sighed. Glancing back to the tall building for the *Register*, I sighed again. "What *am* I doing here?"

"Following the evidence," Alex replied. "Just like you always do." He paused again. "It's not like you to question yourself. What the fuck actually happened this morning?"

"Such language," I laughed. "Especially from someone with an advanced degree."

"I've heard worse in the Ph.D. carrels," he said. "But the point remains: trust your instincts, just like you always do."

I thought about that. "Then I'd better let you go," I said.

"Call me when you get done there?" he asked. "So I know whether I need to find one of those bus shelter lawyers for you?"

I smiled again. "I shan't need one, my love, but I will call you nonetheless."

"Good," he said before chuckling. "'Shan't?' Seriously?"

I shrugged. "That's what you get for dating a well-read guy."

"Oh, I know," he laughed wickedly. "Some of the things you say when—"

"Gotta run," I added hastily as I felt my face heat up. "Love you."

"Love you *more*," he replied before I killed the connection.

I grabbed my backpack from the rear seat and exited into the midday sunshine. Despite it having started off chilly, the weather had shifted into standard SoCal brilliance of the sort that had initially attracted the first settlers from the East Coast. As I walked toward the front doors of the office building, a significant part of me wanted to ditch the whole police officer thing and spend some time communing with the waves; my foot might have even hesitated on the first step leading up to the entrance, especially when my inner truant reminded me I was driving the Camaro (which was conveniently stocked with both my favorite knee board and one of my wetsuits). Sadly, my professionalism won out, and I continued up the steps and through the automatic sliders – but it was a near thing.

For whatever reason, I'd assumed the lobby for the *Register* would be similar to that of the original location for the *Los Angeles Times*; I'd once visited the historic newspaper as part of a high school field trip and fondly remembered the Art Deco space with its slowly rotating globe. Pausing just inside the threshold, I was dismayed to find the *Register* had gone in a completely different direction; the modest space felt like it was one uniform shade of blasé, from the uninspiring white walls to the generic industrial linoleum in alternating shades of gray. Rounding out the dullness were recessed overhead LED lights of the sort any home improvement warehouse stocked; the only thing missing were fake potted ferns casually spread through the space. It didn't take long for me to get my bearings, for the only activity was centered on a small security desk that guarded the bank of elevators directly behind it. Having not really thought through my plan of attack — hell, if I were being honest, there wasn't really a plan at all at the moment — I tacked toward the desk and braced myself for a chilly reception. I'd often found that rent-a-cops seemed to hold a dim view of *actual* law enforcement officers and was fully prepared to be turned away short of my goal.

My prospects improved slightly when I caught the eye of the hunk of a security guard sitting behind the desk. He appeared to be in his early twenties, with an extremely toned upper body that was threatening to split the button-down uniform shirt he was wearing. Long, black hair had been pulled into a businesslike ponytail that looked far more professional than anything I'd ever done; a slight haze of dark stubble grazed the chiseled cheeks, perfectly on point for those of us working in California. Heading toward the desk, I smiled my megawatt model smile just as the acting coach had taught me and hoped to God I'd never have to admit to Alex how frequently I leaned into my sex appeal to get information out people. Propping an elbow on the counter so I could subtly flex, I noted how the kid's eyes had gone to my bicep before quickly returning to my face.

"Hey," I said casually. "Busy day?"

"No," he said before smiling. "I was getting bored, actually."

"Good thing I turned up, then."

"Yes," he nodded. That close, I could smell his aftershave — and could easily see he was far younger than I'd thought. "How may I help you?" he asked.

There were so many levels of innuendo baked into that question I immediately knew the kid was new to the game. That, and he looked vaguely familiar; it took me a moment to finally place him. "*Bobbie*? Bobbie McCallen?"

The kid looked at me for a long moment. "Do I know you?"

"We met a few years ago," I said. "I was the lead detective—"

"On Chase's case," he finished for me. "You and that guy from Maine. I remember now."

I reached across the counter and shook his hand. "It's actually nice to see you again. You've been missed at *The Alternative Way.*"

Bobbie smiled slightly. "I don't have a ton of free time these days," he replied. "I work two jobs just to try and stay ahead."

I frowned slightly. "Shouldn't you be in college?" I asked. "I thought you were on scholarship somewhere for track and field?"

"I wasn't as much of an athlete as Chase," he answered. "I was good but not good enough for a full ride anywhere. I had to change my plans slightly as a result — I'm just finishing up two years at Orange County Community College on the California Promise Program and will be at CSUI this fall." Bobbie frowned slightly. "How long I *stay* at CSUI depends on working here and at Vons."

"That... sucks," I said, reading between the lines. "I presume that means your parents are out of the picture."

"Right after they discovered *why* Chase had been murdered," Bobbie replied quietly.

I nodded slowly, for it wasn't hard to recall the specifics of the case Sean and I had been investigating. Chase Cromwell had been the full package: a high school star athlete with deep volunteering roots in the community for all sorts of important causes, most notably one that helped teens trying to find their way through the turbulent waters of gender identity. Bobbie had been one of those teens, and Chase had been brutally murdered for those efforts. With a shock, I realized I might have accidentally misgendered my young acquaintance and moved to quickly correct my mistake.

"Do you still go by Bobbie?" I asked. "And what pronouns should I use for you?"

Bobbie smiled slightly. "I'm intentionally presenting as male today," he said, correctly reading my expression, "so please don't feel bad about getting me wrong. I've found it's just easier to appear as people want me to appear when I'm working."

I frowned again. "You shouldn't hide who you are," I said. "I don't."

He eyed me. "Easier said than done."

I leaned closer. "I didn't say it was easy," I said softly. "I certainly pissed off my fair share of people over the years who couldn't stand to be breathing the same air as a gay man."

"I can't believe anyone has ever given you grief about that."

"Oh, dude," I laughed. "Come get a cup of coffee with me sometime and I'll tell you tales that will curl your toes."

"Those I would like to hear," he smiled. "So, what can I do for you?" he asked, before adding a slightly embarrassed smile. "And... sorry about earlier."

"My ego appreciated it," I smiled, "though my fiancé might not. I'm actually looking into a possible homicide," I continued, watching him carefully. "Can you tell me if Vivian Grandchester is in today?"

"Vivian?" Bobbie asked, his eyes widening. "I highly doubt it. Not since she fell out with the Editor-in-Chief, Howard Burbank."

"When did that happen?"

"Oh, maybe a month ago?" he replied. "I don't have all the details, but from what I heard, she's still employed by the *Register*, but works remotely." Bobbie smiled slightly. "I know the guy who does the mail run upstairs, and he told me the fight they had was epic, including a few chairs being thrown around."

"Indeed," I said, my eyebrows going up. "Over what?"

"No idea," he replied.

"But if you had to guess?" I asked, prodding him for the answer I knew he had.

Bobbie scanned the lobby again. "Scuttlebutt is that she had a hot story, but the publisher wanted it killed for some reason. Mr. Burbank was the one to deliver the message."

"Did her story make it into the paper?"

He shrugged and smiled sheepishly. "I just work the desk, man. I don't actually read our paper."

"It's not a job requirement?" I asked, arching an eyebrow.

"Fortunately, not."

"Wild," I smiled. "Any chance Burbank is in today?"

"He's *always* in," Bobbie smiled. "I think he's got a cot in his office."

"I *do* read the *Register*," I said with a frown, "and there isn't enough breaking news in it to warrant that sort of work ethic."

Bobbie shrugged. "You want to go up? I can give you a visitor pass."

"I do," I nodded, then looked at him askance. "Are you going to get in trouble for admitting a police officer?"

"There are days I don't think they realize I'm even down here," he said with a smile as he slid the pass over to me. "Burbank's office is on the top floor. Can't miss it when you exit the elevator."

"Thanks."

I clipped the badge to my belt and walked over to the elevators; one arrived nearly instantly after I pressed the *up* button, and mere moments later deposited me in a wood-paneled lobby that was the antithesis of the one I'd just left. Windows looking toward the hills in the distance made the room seem even larger; a small desk in dark wood guarded a half-open office door, though the person who should have been a sentry was nowhere to be found. Taking this as a positive omen, I stepped around the desk and gently knocked on the half-open door.

"What?" was the brusque reply. "Did I not *just* tell you how I wanted my burger cooked?"

Raising my eyebrows, I poked my head into the office. "Actually, no," I said with a smile.

The guy sitting behind a desk twice as massive as the one that Sean Colbeth had back in Maine glanced in my direction; his eyes narrowed at me. "Who the fuck are you?"

Taking that as an invitation, I moved inside and paused a few steps from the desk. There were two uncomfortable looking guest chairs facing the desk; behind Burbank was a bookcase jammed to overflowing with hardcovers that didn't appear to be ordered in any sensible way. Actual mockups for the paper were lying flat on the desk in front of

Burbank, presumably for the next edition of the *Register*; I was a bit floored they still did it manually, especially given the size of the monitor on the workstation off to one corner of the gargantuan desk. Three different mugs of coffee sat close to a multiline phone; a small ashtray was nestled between them and held an ancient looking pipe that appeared to be lit. That explained the odd odor in the room — a mix of tobacco and, if I weren't mistaken, a touch of rum. Burbank himself was wearing a pressed white button-down with suspenders and a modest tie in blue; his hair, though white, was professionally cut and styled, and he was clean shaven. His suit jacket had been carefully hung on a coatrack in the corner and had the requisite pocket square. Everything screamed that the guy was an old-school journalist, backed up perhaps by his salty language; still, I found I was having a hard time not laughing, for all the guy needed was a bushy mustache to complete the whole J. Jonah Jameson look.

"Deputy Chief Vasily Korsokovach," I said, holding out my hand. Burbank took it without rising. "I was wondering if I could ask you a few questions about Vivian Grandchester."

"Korsokovach," he said as he picked up his pipe and sat back in his chair. After taking a puff, he narrowed his eyes. "You're that fucking gay cop who was raped by a coworker, aren't you?"

"I prefer 'former Olympic Swimmer turned decorated investigator' but to each their own," I replied, slightly irritated.

"Didn't Rancho Linda fire your ass?"

"I was on leave for a few weeks," I answered mostly truthfully, "but returned to active duty once I'd recovered from my physical injuries."

That seemed to give him pause. "Injuries?"

"Injuries," I nodded. "I believe Vivian's articles about my situation were rather explicit as to what those were, if you're truly curious."

"I suppose they were," he replied after a long moment. "Hope already called, Deputy Chief. I've got nothing to share with you unless you have a warrant to compel me to talk."

I held my hands out. "No warrant," I smiled, "nor would I need one to confirm that Vivian Grandchester was working on a story at the time she died."

Burbank blinked. "Hope didn't say Vivian was dead—"

"Interesting," I interrupted him, playing a hunch. "I wonder why? For I was rather explicit with her."

"Hope and I go way back," Burbank said with a slight air of reproach. I nodded slightly at confirmation of what I'd suspected. "We've butted heads for decades."

"Seems like an odd thing for her to neglect to share with you. Especially," I added as I watched him carefully, "since her daughter was your star journalist."

Burbank literally scoffed at me before taking another deep lungful of pipe smoke. The way he blew it back out from his nose was something I could never unsee. "Star. More like a pain in my ass. Had been for years."

"Why did you keep her on, then?"

He tapped at the mockups on his desk. "She managed to sell more of these than I thought would ever be possible," he said. "Her stories are the only thing keeping us afloat."

"Was she working on a new story?" I tried again.

Burbank looked at me for a long moment. "Get the hell out of my office."

Arching an eyebrow, I stood my ground. "That's not exactly a *no*, Mr. Burbank."

"Nor is it a *yes*," he snapped.

"Isn't it?" I smiled slightly as I turned for the door. "I'll be in touch."

"Not without a warrant you won't."

I paused at the threshold to the office. "As you wish," I replied sweetly. "Until we meet again."

"Like hell."

As I took the elevator back down to the lobby, I sorted through what Burbank had said — and what he *hadn't* — and realized Bobbie had actually been far more helpful. Still, my gut was telling me I was on to something; finding out exactly what Grandchester had been working on slipped into the top spot on my priority list. Striding across the entrance lobby a few minutes later, I found the young man still seated behind his counter.

"How did it go?" he asked.

I rolled my eyes. "Burbank is quite the character."

"That good, eh?" he laughed. "Sorry."

"Not your fault," I replied before pausing. "It's classic jazz night Friday at the *Alternative Way*; the house band from the bar down the street will have the stage."

"I remember them," Bobbie said. "They're pretty good."

"That they are. You must get a dinner break or something from Vons — why don't you stop in for a set and get a cup of coffee to go?"

"That wouldn't leave you much time to tell me your tall tales," he smiled.

"I can get to the point when needed," I replied. "I hope you can be there; it would be fun to catch up."

"I'm not sure I can," Bobbie said. "But I'll try."

"Good," I smiled as I turned for the door.

Ten

The Glass Monstrosity

Given how the day had gone so far, visiting the glass monstrosity that was our new headquarters building was the perfect way to end it. Located on the furthest edge of the city, it wasn't nearly as easy to get to as our current spot in the center of downtown; in some ways, I felt like the City Council was telegraphing just how they felt about us — that, in fact, they'd be willing to shift the border between us and the next municipality over just to be rid of the headache we seemed to represent. Years of cost cutting and shifting services to the County had reduced our ranks to the bare minimum needed to do the basic work of keeping our taxpayers safe, but even that seemed to be in their budget crosshairs. I'd yet to receive formal approval to hire the traditional set of graduates from the Justice Academy in the spring, a telling, glaring clarion that the fight over the fiscal year budget was still far from over. My mood continued to darken as I drove up the wide but rather steep four-lane highway that climbed slightly into the hills surrounding Rancho Linda; about the only positive to the whole move was the fact that most of our offices had million dollar views back down into the heart of the valley, an unexpected perk that didn't quite wipe away the sting of being a good fifteen minutes away from anything.

The irony that our new space was four times the size of the old building had apparently been lost on the City Council; then again, I fully expected the rest of the municipal infrastructure would ultimately join us, paving the way for the core of downtown to be transformed into some sort of boutique shopping district. I'd seen that movie before, though, and had my doubts it would bring in even a fraction of the tax revenue the politicians were hoping for.

Pausing at the light guarding the entrance to our new building, I turned left into the short driveway and waved my badge at the brand-spanking-new card reader that had been installed just the prior Wednesday; the arm for the gate snapped open with an efficiency that was hard not to appreciate, given how derelict the system for our current parking lot had become. Driving along the gently curving access road to what had been designated the non-public parking lot, it wasn't hard to see how the entire campus had once been a tech startup angling to be the next Microsoft or Apple. Carefully manicured trees that were too mature not to have been transplanted from elsewhere cast long pools of shade over much of the lot, giving the whole area a quiet, bucolic feel thoroughly at odds with the kind of work we were expected to do from there. I found an open spot beneath one of the tall trees and parked the Camaro, grabbed my bag from the rear seat and then started down a winding stone pathway leading to what was to be the Law Enforcement entrance to the building. Since things were still very much in flux, the door had been propped open with a big bucket of drywall mud; a burly woman I recognized from our Facilities crew had her boot up on it as she took a deep drag from her cigarette. My eyes flicked to the small *This is a Non-Smoking Campus* sign that had been carefully tacked above the card reader, then back to her; she rolled her eyes and took another hit of nicotine as I made my way past her.

We all rebel in our own way, I thought as I wandered down the hallway.

The pungent odor of fresh paint assaulted my nose as I came into the new booking area, so I took care not to accidentally lean on anything lest I ruin yet another polo. Benches had been installed since my last visit, arrayed just beyond the plexiglass windows for the on-duty booking officer; peering through the plastic still clinging to the glass, I could see the actual furniture had yet to be installed. I decided not to check out the new holding cells and instead turned left at the corridor intersection; my badge got me through to *another* hallway, though in truth it was more like a lobby for the four elevators dedicated to our staff. I hit the button to call a carriage only to rather annoyingly remember I had to tap my badge to the pad first; updated security had been a top priority, though I was finding it more of a hindrance than an upgrade. Doors to the elevator behind me immediately snapped open, and I stepped inside; here I found an upgrade I *did* like, that being a digital control panel that knew who had just entered the elevator (since I'd tapped my badge) and defaulted to the common floors I might head to. In my case, it was offering to take me to the seventh floor, home of my Major Crimes unit; just below that, the button for the Crime Lab on the second floor had appeared, and beneath that, the lighted indicator for the tenth floor — the unlucky location for all things Administrative, including my boss, Chief Michael Gilbert. As I tapped the button for Gina's domain, I wondered how long it would take for me to get used to *not* having Mike in the office beside me; it was part of the secret sauce in terms of how we ran the Department, and I worried quite a bit about whether separating us had been another intentional decision by the powers-that-be.

Thoughts of doom and gloom dispersed slightly when the doors snapped open again to reveal a more industrial looking elevator lobby; turning, I followed the corridor to a set of automatic glass doors that appeared stuck halfway open. Three overall-clad techs were frowning in unison at a small control box in the corner and mumbling technical terms that didn't mean anything to me, so I risked slipping through the slight opening between the two halves of the portal and then continued my quest to find Gina.

I found the Chief Crime Scene Investigator herself sitting at a horseshoe of a desk just in front of a wall of glass that looked into the lab proper; from the activity I could see behind her, equipment was being unwrapped, plugged in or otherwise checked out after having been moved from downtown. Gina looked up at the sound of my footsteps on the ugly industrial tile and smiled tiredly at me.

"Hey, stranger."

"Something wrong with your door?" I asked, pointing my thumb back the way I'd come.

"Circuit fried the first time one of my techs tapped their card at the reader," she sighed as she leaned back in her chair.

"That can't be good."

"Seems to be par for the course," she sighed again as she rubbed her eyes. "This place wasn't built to house a state-of-the-art crime lab, let alone all of the tech needed for modern law enforcement activities."

"I seem to recall having told the City Council just that," I frowned. "Repeatedly."

"And yet, here we are," she laughed. "I'm not sure you should sign off on stuff, Vas," she added more soberly. "This is a bit of a shit show at the moment."

"Is *anything* working around here?" I asked, frowning.

"Not much; the list is far shorter than what's in the queue to be fixed." She nodded at the lab behind her. "About the only good news is that County IT knows how to deal with our smart equipment; I've had very little trouble bringing those items online. Filing timesheets is an entirely different story."

I groaned. "Don't tell me the corporate network went down again."

"Get used to paper for the next few weeks," she chuckled. "If you can find a printer that stays online long enough to generate the forms for you. And don't get me started about the copiers."

"There's no way we're going to make that move-in date."

Gina smiled. "You must have just missed the moving truck that was here earlier. My understanding is they pulled the last of us out this morning."

My eyes widened. "I hadn't finished packing!"

"Then you'll have fun searching through the boxes in your new office," she giggled. "Sorry. I know it's not funny, but if I don't laugh, I'm gonna start to cry."

I thought about that for a moment. "Yeah. Yeah, that about sums it up," I sighed. "Shit. Do you have any *good* news for me? Or should I drive over to that bar I saw on the way in and drown my sorrows over whatever's on tap?"

"Well, even with one arm tied behind my back — such as it is — we were able to get some stuff analyzed," she said as she stood. "Come on out back and I'll show you what I've got. It's not much, but it might fill in a few more details."

"I'll take anything at this point," I said as I followed her through a second set of automatic sliding doors; these, while operational, seemed to stutter uncomfortably as they parted, almost as if they were reluctant to continue. I hurried through just in case they opted to snap shut on me. "My morning has been anything *but* productive."

"I heard that the warrant was quashed for Grandchester's house," Gina said as she led me through the lab. It was a bit of an obstacle course, littered with half-unpacked moving boxes and the personnel trying to sort through them.

"News travels fast around here," I sighed.

"Gossip is faster-than-light in law enforcement circles."

"No kidding. I nearly went two-for-two at the *Register* but found out she'd not physically worked there in a bit. My discussion with the editor wasn't very fruitful other than to confirm she was focusing on an investigative piece he was intending to spike."

"Intriguing. What was it on?"

"*That* is the question of the hour," I sighed again. "Reading between the lines? I think it was something big, especially given how her mother was so adamant about protecting her home office from me."

Gina smirked. "So much for that vaunted charm of yours, Vas.

Usually, you smile your megawatt smile and people pour out their souls to you."

"I must not have been at the top of my game today."

"Indeed."

We came to a stop at a lab bench in the far corner of the lab; several translucent tubs were arranged on the surface holding what appeared to be the evidence that had been collected at the construction site. Sliding a lid off one of the tubs, Gina reached in and pulled out the phone we'd recovered, placed it on the counter and smiled slightly as she turned toward me. "This might salvage your day then," she said as she pulled a pair of latex gloves from a box mounted to the wall and snapped them on. "My tech nerds were able to dump the contents of Grandchester's phone and uncovered a few items of interest."

"Oh?" I said as I reached for a pair of gloves myself. "Tell me more."

Carefully sliding the phone from the small bag it was inside, Gina tapped at the cracked screen. "Just off the top, it takes a hell of a lot of force to crack one of these foldable screens," she started. "I don't want to read into it without more evidence, but my informal take is that it was either thrown down or ripped away from your victim."

I thought back to the scene where we'd found the phone and the ID for our reporter. "I still think she might have been running at that point," I mused. "This lends more credence to her being attacked and subsequently subdued in some way before being moved to the forklift."

"Exactly. I'm going to head back out to the construction site later and take some measurements; we'll run some simulations on the computer that has yet to be unpacked and see if we can come up with the right amount of force, the proper angle and maybe the speed it would have taken to create this sort of damage."

My eyebrows went up. "Our supercomputer is *also* offline?"

"Yes," Gina replied with a frown as she gestured to the darkened screen of the computer sitting on the bench. "Apparently, the slot they'd carved out in the County's data center isn't big enough for our hardware."

"Clearly no one down there watched *This Old House*," I sighed. "'Measure twice, cut once.'" *

"Exactly. There's some emergency rejiggering going on as we speak, but it might be a day or two before we're able to bring it online properly. And before you ask," she smiled slightly, "yes, I've already reached out to LAPD to see if we can borrow some computer cycles if it goes much longer."

"Our friends in Orange County aren't going to like that."

"They'll get over it," she laughed. "Now, I don't want to oversell what we've got, so let me preface this by saying while we were able to access the phone, we don't have some of the key passwords for services on the device."

I nodded, for I'd had plenty of experience cloning phones during investigations; occasionally we got lucky when a suspect or a victim chose not to use a strong passkey or PIN, but that was the exception and not the rule. "Getting those will be problematic."

"Yes, but all hope is not lost," Gina continued. Holding the phone up slightly, she tilted it so something on the cracked screen caught the light. "See those smudge marks?"

I leaned toward the device. "They're more like streaks," I said with a smile. "Is that how you figured out the PIN?"

"Exactly," she nodded. "Turns out it was only four digits, and we were pretty certain of at least two of the numbers based on the routes of these smudges. We got it on the fiftieth try."

"*Fiftieth?*" I asked. "I'm a bit rusty in my math but that seems fairly fast."

Gina shrugged. "We knew what numbers we had to work with, so that shortened the process. Most PINs are four digits and can re-use a number, so ordinarily there would be around six thousand possible

---

* Author's Note: *This Old House* was a show on PBS for many years that featured Master Carpenter Norm Abram. This phrase was one that he used often, especially when working out a tricky solution.

combinations. Knowing two of the numbers cut that down to about eleven-hundred options; a little bit of intuition got us the rest of the way."

"Intuition?" I asked. "Did she use a street address or something?"

"You're in the ballpark," she laughed. "Literally. She used the last year the Angels won the World Series."

I frowned. "When did that happen?"

"2002," Gina answered. "As any long-suffering fan such as your victim probably lament."

"Still," I frowned deeper, "I would never have pegged Vivian Grandchester as a baseball aficionado."

"I'm not sure it was her," Gina replied as she reached back into the tub to retrieve a small wallet. "She must have been an old soul to carry around something like this," she continued as she snapped the leather billfold open. "No one has physical photos of anything these days, but I suspect this particular one is significant."

I leaned down to look at the small photo that appeared to have been carefully inserted into the sort of plastic holder that had long since gone out of style; slightly faded with age, it was still clear enough to make out the fact that it had been taken in the stands at Angels Stadium. A far younger version of Vivian Grandchester was smiling into the camera, standing next to a man in his twenties wearing a ball cap bearing the Angels logo and a jersey with their traditional white-and-red color scheme. Behind them and slightly out of focus was the baseball diamond, with the unique waterfall out in center field just barely visible. The seats had to have been right behind the plate, given the angle to the pitching mound; the last time I'd been there for a Red Sox - Angels matchup, I'd barely been able to afford the cheap seats on the upper deck, so I was pretty sure someone had spent a tidy sum on their day at the ballgame. Peering closer at the photo, I had the strangest sense I'd seen the guy before; his chiseled body spoke to hours at the gym, but his brilliant white smile made me think of one of those defense attorneys who advertised on late night television. More importantly, though, was how his arm was draped around the shoulders of Grandchester, speaking volumes as to their relationship.

"We'll run the photo through some of our stranger tests once those stations are up and running," Gina was saying as I examined the photo. "I'll be able to get you an approximate date it was printed, but we'll also cross-reference anything we can make out in the shot to get the time we think it was shot."

I squinted at the photo. "The scoreboard is partially visible," I said. "Maybe you can piece together something from that?"

"Maybe."

I tapped at the photo with a gloved finger. "They must have records of who bought those seats, too," I mused. "Get me a date range to work with and I can cut a warrant request for the system that sells those tickets."

"I can do that," Gina replied, "but you already know who those people are."

I blinked. "I do?"

Gina looked at me. "You've been away too long, Vas. That's Anton Cardinal."

I blinked again. "As in *Konstantyn* Cardinal's son?" I asked, mind slowly spinning.

"A bit younger, but yes," Gina replied as she picked up her tablet and tapped at the screen. It lit up under her touch to display a website featuring a more current photo of the same guy. "I cheated and used one of those online AI tools to scan the photo and it hit almost immediately. I'll run it through our normal system if it gets online sometime this century."

"I thought he'd left the country," I said, still churning the revelation around in my head. "I know I'd departed by then, but I remember some sort of national story about the son of a major SoCal developer embarking on a voyage of self-discovery and leaving his father's business in his wake."

"Apparently that voyage ended right back here in Orange County,"

Gina chuckled. "Or daddy's money ran out. Either way, according to Forbes he's now the one running The Cardinal Group — and has been for the last half-dozen years."

"Interesting," I said as my eyes went back to the snapshot in Grandchester's wallet. "These two look like they were close."

"Check out the ring finger on your victim."

I squinted. "Hell. Is that a *diamond*?"

Gina nodded. "Large enough that even such a lousy photo could pick it up."

"We didn't recover a ring from the body, did we?"

"No," Gina answered. "I checked twice."

"Interesting. Given how she hounded me, I had no idea Vivian even *had* a personal life," I continued. "Or that she was once engaged. I'll have to hit the archives and see if there was an engagement announcement."

"Do people still do that?"

"Oh yes," I nodded. "It cost a pretty penny for me to put ours in the *Register*, I assure you. But I'm a bit of a traditionalist; Alex didn't care one way or the other."

"Good for you," she smiled. "It can't be a coincidence that your victim was killed in a development project owned by her former fiancé."

"You know me and coincidences," I replied. "I wonder what ended their engagement?"

"Well," Gina said, her eyes twinkling as she picked up the phone again, "who says it did?"

My eye narrowed. "You have text messages?"

She nodded. "And voicemail," she said. "Some of which are not suitable for work, I might add. Seems the flame never truly went out for either of them."

"I'm not looking forward to reviewing them now," I sighed. "Feels a bit too voyeuristic. When was the last time they spoke?"

"A few hours before the coroner thinks she died," Gina answered.

I looked at the smiling corporate version of Anton Cardinal. "Then it seems I have someone else I need to chat with."

"Don't poke at that bear too much," Gina chuckled. "They're the ones renovating this building for us. And tearing down the old one."

My eyebrows went up. "Really? I thought we did competitive bidding — how did they wind up with *both* jobs?"

"Real Estate Development is a bit of a closed system," she replied. "The large firms tend to be able to outbid the smaller ones, which leads to a consolidation. That, and I'm sure The Cardinal Group has donated to more than a few of our City Council members."

"No doubt. Anything else?"

"Quite a bit," she replied before nodding to the remaining tubs on the counter. "Before I get to *those*, unlocking the phone also gave us access to its GPS data. The team is still processing it, but I should be able to provide the victim's recent movements to you without having to hit up the wireless carrier for cell tower stats."

"That would be welcome."

"Also, we pulled the nail from the tire mid-morning and were able to determine it's of a variety in use at the construction site. Not exactly a smoking gun, so to speak, but it *does* hint the victim was in the lot recently. The math on the leak the nail would have produced tells us tire likely went flat within an hour of picking it up."

I thought about that. "Maybe parking at the mall was more of a necessity than we realized," I mused. "Without changing to the spare, they wouldn't have gotten much further. I bet they didn't even know it was soft."

"Not immediately, but that model vehicle has pressure sensors; the dashboard probably lit up as soon as they turned onto the main drag."

"Interesting," I said. "Nice work with one arm tied behind your back."

"And yet, there's more," Gina smiled as she tapped one of the tubs on the counter. "We did a complete inventory of what was in her satchel — the one we found in the back of the car? Your guess that the files were research material might be on the money. They appeared to be financial statements for several real estate developers, including The Cardinal Group; there was also a smattering of reporting from various outlets about projects Cardinal has worked on over the past twenty years, including — drumroll please — this building and the one where we found the victim."

"Financials?" I said as I eyed the tubs. "That makes me think Grandchester was doing a cross-cutting comparison. Maybe she uncovered something one of our regulators had yet to find."

"Or something hidden cleverly enough it would take years to discover," Gina added. "I've seen that before."

"Same. Sounds like I have some quality spreadsheet time coming up."

"You will — once we scan everything into the system."

"Maybe I should take the tub with me, then," I suggested. "I had to paw through manual files a few cases ago; it'll be like old times."

"I think you are a bit too young to remember those," Gina replied. "And as welcome as you are to take the files — after signing for them, of course — I suspect you have enough on your agenda at the moment that you can wait for us to get this digitized."

"Probably true." I pulled off my gloves and nodded at the darkened computer in the corner. "I'd ask when this will all be in the system, but I think I already know the answer."

"I'd heard you were a clever detective," Gina laughed.

"I have my days," I smiled as I turned to leave. "Let's hope this turns into one of them."

ELEVEN
DINNER AT ROSIE'S

In all honesty, I'd been avoiding unpacking my new office as a way to deny the fact that the move was actually happening in the first place. It was a shit teenager kind of move that only served to make me angrier about the whole situation, one that I truly had very little control over in the first place. Still, as I entered the waiting elevator, my rebellious streak won out, and I pressed the lighted indicator for the main lobby and freedom. The air of the early evening felt somehow fresher to me after being subjected to the acrid combination of fresh paint and new carpet; taking a deep breath, I realized that as high as the office was in the hills surrounding Rancho Linda, there was a weird kind of peace to the location that our current — or rather *former* — location in the center of town lacked. Birds were actually chirping in one of the trees in front of me, and when I concentrated slightly, I thought I could hear the gentle bubbling of the decorative fountain in the public court-yard. As I walked over to my Camaro, I grudgingly admitted that maybe the new building wasn't all that bad after all.

Maybe.

Sliding behind the wheel of my car, the clock on the dashboard cheerfully told me I still had time to make the evening practice; deciding it was just what the doctor ordered, I fired up the engine and pulled out of my spot, then made my way back down out of the hills and over to the Rancho Linda High School pool. Rush hour had just gotten underway, but I still managed to make excellent time; I wasn't all that surprised to find the parking lot overflowing as that tended to be the far better attended time; only the truly dedicated seemed to turn out for the five A.M. version. Grabbing my backpack from the rear seat, I locked up the car and headed to the locker room, then returned to the pool deck a few minutes later properly attired in my favorite electric blue Speedos. Coach had seen me arrive and had positioned a small whiteboard beside the lane along the far wall; as I pulled on my goggles and swim cap, I wondered what I had done to deserve the masochistic set scribbled out in black. Stepping up to the block, I leaned over, grabbed the edge and then flung myself out over the brilliant blue of the water before cleanly slicing through the surface to begin my workout. Given the sort of day I'd had, I focused like a maniac on my workout and forced the case to the back of my head; I knew myself well enough to understand that I wasn't anywhere close to the proper frame of mind for chunking through what I knew — or more importantly, what I *didn't*.

I let the stress flow away from me as the yards I swam increased; each time I hit the wall for a flip turn felt like another knot of tension had been released. The endorphin rush from pushing myself to the limit was intoxicating, so much so that it was with a great deal of reluctance that I pulled myself out of the lane so the age group team waiting in the wings could claim the pool for their workout. Knowing I was heading to Rosie's for dinner meant I simply threw on a pair of shorts and my favorite muscle t-shirt; in a nod to how it had begun to get rather chilly in the evenings, I added my UEM sweatshirt and then hurried out to the Camaro for my rendezvous with Alejandro. This time, rush hour traffic was not in my favor; whatever Zen I had gleaned from my workout had completely evaporated by the time I pulled into our underground garage at the condo. My mood immediately lifted when I spied my beloved standing at the doors to the elevator lobby; his muscle-hugging long sleeve shirt left nothing to the imagination, nor did the tights that appeared to be painted over his strong legs. His beautifully curly, thick black hair had been partially hidden behind a Nike-branded kerchief; it was slightly damp, hinting that, like me, Alex had just finished his evening workout. Two small suitcases sat beside him; I pulled over to the loading zone and popped the trunk, then waited impatiently for him to slide into the passenger seat so I could grab him for a kiss that (hopefully) reminded him just how much he meant to me. Judging from the way he narrowed his eyes after we parted, I may have also telegraphed something else entirely.

"And hello to you too," he laughed as he went in for another slightly less passionate kiss. "I take it your day didn't get any better."

"I don't know about that," I said as I turned around and then exited the garage. "A gorgeous hunk stepped into my vehicle. Things appear to be looking up."

"I see," he chuckled. "I had no idea wearing my gym gear would get such a reaction."

"The *hell* you didn't," I laughed. "Dry land today?"

His response was just a tad too slow. "Yes."

I glanced over to him as I waited for the light to change on Katella. "Alex, my love, if you have any hope of diving in Rosie's charity event, you've got to let that wrist heal."

Alejandro's chiseled cheeks flamed slightly. "I know. But I also know I need to keep my form."

It was hard not to feel for him; he'd tweaked his wrist while training back in August and had been struggling with it ever since. Like me, he was having a hard time adjusting to the notion that his body wasn't quite as resilient as it once was; an entire drawer in the master bathroom vanity was dedicated to the wraps, ointments and other supplies we needed in order to patch ourselves up between workouts. The reason he was wearing a long sleeve shirt suddenly became obvious when I finally saw the slight bulge of athletic tape around his wrist.

"I'm the last person to tell you to tone down your workout," I said as I pulled into traffic. "But I love you too much not to worry you might be doing real damage to that muscle. Did you see that sports medicine doctor I recommended?"

Alex shifted uncomfortably in the passenger seat.

Despite the heavy traffic headed toward the 57, I chanced another look at my fiancé. "What's wrong?" I asked softly after seeing his face. Reaching for his hand, I interlaced it with mine. "Tell me."

He took a deep breath. "Before I tell you, promise me you won't go into full Protect Alex Mode."

My eyebrows went up. "That's one hell of an ask."

"Promise me," he pleaded.

The look of terror I saw on his face when I glanced at him was enough to quell any protest. "Promise," I said.

Alex took another moment. "The exam was inconclusive, so she ordered an MRI. And... not just for my wrist."

"I'm not sure I like where this is going," I said as I shifted lanes to get onto the 57.

"That makes two of us," Alex chuckled ruefully. "You know how hard I hit the water when I go off the ten meter; since I've been favoring my injured wrist, that's shifted my form a bit — and now my shoulder is spasming." He looked out the window. "And so's my back."

"Fuck," I breathed. "You should have said something!"

"And risk having you pull me from the water?" he asked. "Not likely."

"I wouldn't have—"

"Oh yes," he interrupted. "You would have." Alex paused. "And I would have let you," he added quietly.

"So, by not saying anything, you had license to continue?" I demanded, my anger growing. "Shit, Alex, this is serious! I've been telling you for months now that—"

"I won't quit diving any more than you'll quit swimming," he interjected. The quiet fury in his voice was rare; when I heard it, I knew I was wading into dangerous waters. "I know my body; don't presume that you know it *half* as well as I do."

My anger was immediately punctured by an image of the two of us entangled among the sheets of our bed. "*Mi amor*, I've done nothing *but* get to know your body from the moment we first met."

"That's not what I meant," Alex huffed, but I could see a slight hint of a smile out of the corner of my eye.

"Point taken," I said as I reached for his hand again. "You can't blame me for being worried about you."

"No," he sighed as he kissed my knuckles. "It's one of your most endearing qualities. And the most frustrating, honestly."

"Seriously?"

"Seriously."

"I just want us to grow old together," I said, "presumably with everything functioning."

"As do I," he replied. "That's why I scheduled the MRI."

"I want to be there."

"I figured you might say that," he sighed again. "Which is why I didn't tell you."

"You already did the scan?" I said as we coasted off the 57 and down into Rancho Linda. "Without me?"

"Just before we left for Maine. The results haven't come back yet."

"Alex—"

"I didn't want you pacing back and forth in the waiting room, worried to death about what was happening," he continued. "As stressed out as you are about Sean and your job—"

I swerved off the ramp and onto the verge and put the Camaro into park. Turning to a very shocked Alejandro, I took both of his hands into my own and looked him directly in the eye. "Alex, you are the center of my universe — my very reason for existing. Everything else is secondary to you, my love."

"Vas—"

"*Everything*," I emphasized. "I would move heaven and earth just to ensure you are happy. Being with you as you face life's worst moments is what it means to be your husband."

He smiled slightly. "Even if it's just a silly old MRI scan?"

"*Especially* if it's a silly old MRI scan," I said. I waited a beat and then went in for the kill. "Besides, those outfits they make you wear don't *exactly* cover—"

Alex rolled his eyes. "You've seen everything I have to offer already, *mi amor*."

"Doesn't mean I don't like a good tease every now and then," I laughed as I pulled out into traffic.

Navigating the worst of the rush hour traffic forced me to focus on driving for a bit, so we lapsed into a companionable silence; ultimately, traffic faded the further into the hills we climbed, allowing me to cogitate on our conversation. As the Camaro hummed with the effort of tackling the slight incline to reach our destination, I thought a bit about what I had said and how I had reacted to Alex; as always, I felt a significant level of self-recrimination for even being the slightest bit upset that he had done what he'd done — especially because my past actions had driven him to it. By the time the twin golden lions flanking Rosie's driveway appeared in my headlights, I'd figured out how to make it up to him.

"Look," I said softly as I turned between the lions and then started up the paved stones of the driveway to the grand entrance for the mansion, "I am sorry to have put you into that position. I guess I am still figuring out where our boundaries are, as well as what level of bubble wrap I am allowed to use on you. For that, I truly apologize." I glanced at him. "I'll do better."

"I know," he smiled back. "We're both pretty new at this relationship thing, aren't we?"

"That we are," I answered as I parked the Camaro just beyond the steps to the massive double wooden doors for the entrance. "Forgive me?"

"Already done," he said softly as he leaned in for a kiss. "Come on, let's go rescue our feline."

We grabbed the bags from the trunk and then let ourselves into the mansion; Rosie had long since given us our own keys to the place considering how frequently we were guests there, though it always felt odd unlocking the front door as though we owned the place. The massive foyer had finally been returned to its normal, albeit empty, splendor; no trace of the fateful Halloween party a month earlier was left, though I was surprised to see a massive Christmas tree standing just to the side of the entrance. In all the years I had known Rosie, she had never once decorated the mansion for the holiday; my eyes went wider when I saw the fragrant garland wrapped along the curving banisters for the movie-star staircases on either wall leading to the second floor.

"Holy hell," Alex breathed next to me. "We leave for a long weekend, and she goes and decorates."

"And rather tastefully, too," I added.

"I don't remember — did she do this last year?"

"No," I shook my head as we headed upstairs to drop our bags off in what had more or less been made our permanent home-away-from home. "Nor the year prior to that."

"I wonder what put her into the spirit," Alex said as he pushed open the door to our bedroom.

"Joy," I sighed as we dumped the bags on the bed and then started to change for the pool. "Another mystery to solve. Just what I need."

Alex had pulled his shirt off, exposing his ripped physique and the smattering of tattoos he'd acquired since we'd moved to California; the white of the bandage around his wrist confirmed my suspicions, but I tactfully decided to ignore it. I always tried to avoid looking at the piercings in places that seemed as though they would be positively uncomfortable, but the rest of the canvas was so compelling it was often hard not to be distracted. Alex seemed to know he had my undivided attention, as evidenced by the way he managed to slowly flex his extremely well-defined biceps as he rolled up his t-shirt. It took every ounce of willpower I had not to jump him on the spot.

"Then don't," Alex said.

I reluctantly pulled my eyes away from his toffee-toned torso. "Don't? Solve it?"

"Exactly," he smiled as he shrugged out of his tights and then pulled on a pair of vibrant purple swim briefs. "Relish in the not knowing."

"I don't do that well," I said, arching an eyebrow.

"I know," he smiled. He tied off his briefs and then unhelpfully pulled me close enough that I could smell the faint whiff of chlorine on his skin. "Roll with it," he whispered as he leaned in and nibbled at my neck.

"Alex," I said, my voice growing husky, "I might well do that if you keep this up."

He pulled away and then glanced meaningfully at the front of my shorts; it was impossible to hide the effect he was having on me, so I wasn't surprised to see the nasty twinkle in his eyes. "Someone is all hot and bothered. Do you need a shower to cool off before we go downstairs?"

"I can think of another way to take the edge off," I said as I started to untie my shorts. "Rosie won't mind if we're a little delayed."

"Oh no," Alex smiled impishly. "We're not going to keep our host waiting. Besides, I'm hungry."

"So am I."

"Clearly," he chuckled as he pulled away from me and grabbed one of the beach towels Rosie had thoughtfully left on the massive bureau. "Here," he said as he tossed it to me. "This is big enough to hide a multitude of sins."

I narrowed my eyes at him as I kicked out of my shorts and then wrapped the towel around my waist. "I will seek retribution," I said menacingly. It might have played better had the towel not been printed with a cartoonish dinosaur.

"I look forward to it," he laughed as he took my hand in his. "Come on, *mi amor*. Let's go rescue our cat."

There was something so completely *right* in having Alejandro by my side; as we trotted down the massive staircase hand-in-hand, the sense I was living in the perfect moment was hard to shake. All of the tensions of the day were washed away when his dark eyes caught mine; my heart did that funny two step each time our shoulders brushed and I could feel the heat of his skin against my own. By the time we'd reached the door to the solarium, I was nothing more than the man who loved Alex, willing — and quite able — to do anything he asked of me.

I paused at the fogged over door and quickly pulled Alejandro in a deep, passionate kiss. When we parted, I saw his eyes dancing merrily. "That's quite an appetizer," he said. It wasn't lost on me that he was flushed and breathing a bit hard.

"Just wait for the main course," I said before drawing him back into a second, equally as deep kiss.

Parting a second time, I decided not to comment on how he quickly unfurled his own towel and hastily wrapped it around his waist. Coughing slightly, he nodded toward the door. "Shall we?"

Pushing the door open, I stepped into the moist embrace of the solarium and nearly immediately began to perspire; reaching for Alex's hand, we followed the winding path of slate stones through the towering forest of trees better suited for places along the equator than Southern California. By the time we reached the main clearing for the pool, sweat was running liberally down my face and chest; I suspected that, per usual, the towel would soon be rendered useless. The woman of the hour herself was sitting in her favorite spot on a wicker loveseat, clad in at least two layers of thick warmup gear; despite the intense tropical heat of the space, Rosie always managed to look like she was chilled to the bone. About the only thing that had actually cooled off was my libido, allowing me to unwrap the towel long enough to mop my face a bit before we took our customary positions on the wicker seats facing her; a low wicker coffee table sat between us and held enough take out from Olive Garden that I expected the rest of our swim team to arrive at any moment.

"*Dios mío*," Alex breathed as he sagged into his chair and ran a hand through his now damp curls. "It feels three hundred percent warmer than normal in here. What did you do, Rosie? Is there a heat pump hiding under the ferns now?"

"Hardly," Rosie laughed. It was a deep, resonate affair that always reminded me of Lauren Bacall. "This time of year, the angle of the sun is such that I get far more of it, and once the place warms up, it takes time to radiate it back out." She sighed contentedly. "Isn't it wonderful?"

"It's an advertisement for why we should fear Global Warming," Alex replied as he fanned himself. "And a reminder of why I hated visiting Mexico City in August."

"It couldn't have been that bad," I said with a sly smile. "You didn't use the heat as an excuse to lounge at the pool in your Speedo so you could work on your tan?"

"You forget I grew up in Tucson, *mi amor*. I looked good year-round."

"And still do," I observed.

"You're biased."

"Undoubtedly."

Alex ran the towel through his curls and then tossed it over the back of his chair. "All the same, I'm starting to feel a little overcooked."

"You can take a swim after dinner," Rosie smiled. "And what took the two of you so long? I'm not sure the lasagna is still warm!"

Alex eyed me. "Someone kept getting distracted," he replied wickedly.

"By work," I hastily added, feeling my cheeks flame slightly. "It was a rather long day," I continued as I leaned down and served myself a healthy portion of lasagna. "Emphasis on long."

"Your new case?" Rosie asked.

I rolled my eyes. "You know I'm not supposed to talk about it, right?"

"That's never stopped you in the past," she pointed out.

"Mostly because you ply me with wine and pepper me with questions until I give in."

"I would never stoop so low," Rosie replied before waiting a beat. "Wine's open, by the way."

"Rosie!"

Alex was laughing into his breadstick. "You might as well bring her into the loop, *mi amor*. She'll be insufferable if you don't."

I looked at him. "*Et tu*, Alex?"

"Just pointing out the obvious."

I glared at him, then shoved another forkful of lasagna into my mouth to buy some time. It wasn't that I didn't trust Rosie — far from it; on more than one occasion, her counsel had proven quite useful at getting to the root of a case. My concerns always stemmed from involving her, even tangentially, in crimes that often reflected the worst society had to offer; even as a trained professional, I knew the toll it took on me, though thankfully, having Alex in my life meant I always had a reminder of my own humanity. Rosie, for all her noble charitable causes and extensive network was in truth something of a recluse; Alejandro and I were the closest thing she had to family, so bringing such darkness to her doorstep felt like a betrayal of our friendship. And yet, as I considered the woman I now thought of as my adopted mother and saw her expectant expression as she waited for me to divulge my secrets, I couldn't deny how much I valued her opinion. I felt the same way about Alex and knew in that instant that the two of them had helped me solve far more cases that the entire team back at the department.

"We think we found Vivian Grandchester last night," I said as I balanced my plate on the arm of the wicker chair, then bowed to the inevitable and reached over to the table to pour myself some of Rosie's favorite Olive Garden table wine. "She appeared to be visiting the new affordable housing development being built along the reservoir after normal business hours."

"How did she die?"

"I can't tell you that," I replied carefully, "mostly because the coroner is running a few more tests for me. But we're reasonably certain she died at the scene."

"What was she doing there?"

I sipped at the wine. "I'm not sure yet," I hedged.

"But you have a thought?" Rosie pressed.

"That's partly why it was such a long day, *no?*" Alex interjected. "You have a sense of what she was doing but can't prove it."

"Yet," I nodded. "I'm reasonably certain — no, dammit, I'm *definitely* certain she was doing some sort of investigative piece on The Cardinal Group."

"Konnie's old company?" Rosie asked, her eyebrows going up.

I frowned. "You know Konstantyn Cardinal?"

"Yes," she nodded. "Or did. He passed last year."

"I'm lost," Alex said.

"Konstantyn Cardinal created The Cardinal Group around the time my father made his fortune," I explained. "I was too young to truly know who he was when he attended parties at my family's home in Newport Beach, but I have vague memories of a guy who spoke the same language as my parents."

"And he's dead?" Alex asked.

"Yes," Rosie supplied. "He'd stepped away from running the company, oh, fifteen years ago, I think. His son took over the reins and grew The Cardinal Group from a small local developer to a regional real estate investment firm that dominates most of Southern California." Rosie looked sad for a moment. "I've tried for years to get Anton to do more for the community, but he's even *more* of a tightwad than Konnie was."

"That's one way to stay rich," Alex snorted.

"True," Rosie laughed. "Not one I subscribe to, however." She looked at me. "You think Vivian uncovered something at Cardinal?"

I shrugged. "That's the working theory. I'm also fascinated by the fact that Grandchester might have been engaged to Anton."

Rosie actually looked shocked for a moment. "Holy *shit*. I'd forgotten about that. A bit of a scandal at the time now that I think about it."

Remembering the photo Gina had shown me, I eyed Rosie. "When did the engagement happen?"

"Twenty years ago, give or take," Rosie replied after a moment. "It made quite the splash — the rakish heir to the Cardinal fortune falling for a local up-and-coming journalist. Whole star-crossed lovers from different worlds vibe."

"Clearly the wedding never happened," I prompted.

"No, though I couldn't tell you why," Rosie said. "I can ask around if it would help."

"It might," I nodded. Smiling slightly, I took a longer sip from my wine. "Assuming you want to be involved."

"I wouldn't have offered if I didn't," she replied before picking up the bottle. "More wine?"

"For you, Rosie," I laughed as I held out my glass, "anything."

Twelve
Seeing Red

The headache that greeted me the following morning was a stark reminder that Olive Garden wine was best in small quantities; blinking to clear the cobwebs from my brain as I reached for my iPhone to mute the alarm, I wondered what had possessed Rosie to open two bottles for dinner — or why I had been so willing to help her polish them off before heading to bed. It wasn't like me to drink to excess, but then again, I'd long ago realized that Rosie was capable of drinking almost anyone under the table; that she also seemed to relish the challenge of turning her two favorite male hunks into foolishly grinning teens who couldn't hold their liquor was, of course, an added bonus.

Carefully propping myself up on an elbow, I wondered if I should take careful inventory to determine if I'd gained a tattoo or another piercing; the last time I'd gotten drunk, the silver hoop earrings I still wore had appeared out of thin air. Eyeing Alejandro as he softly snored into his pillow beside me, I figured he was off the hook for such malfeasance this time; frowning, I realized I had but a hazy recollection of actually getting back to the bedroom after dinner — one that didn't seem to include any of the hot sex I'd actually planned on.

Damn, Vas, I sighed as I curled into Alex. *Oh-for-two when it comes to cagey old ladies.*

Alejandro shifted at my touch and turned toward me; in the darkness, I caught the slight sparkle of his eyes as they blinked open. "Hey," he said, his voice thick with sleep. "What time is it?"

"Half past time to fuck Alex?" I asked hopefully.

The soft chuckle was accompanied by brief kiss. "*Mi amor,* as much as I would love to accommodate your request, there's some sort of mariachi band roaming in my head right now that's kind of killing the mood."

"Tell me about it," I lamented as I hugged him closer. "Raincheck, then?"

"Definitely." He yawned massively. "What time is it, actually?"

I squinted at my phone; at least I'd remembered to take out my contacts at some point along the line. "Four-ish. I've got just enough time to make the roundtrip to Anaheim and still get to practice."

"I knew I should have driven," Alex groaned. "All I want to do is pull the sheet over my head and snooze."

"Maybe we could call in sick—"

"Not twice in the same week," Alex interrupted as he sat up and then slipped out of the bed. "Let me throw some clothes on and then I'll track down Chat."

"Rosie said he'd made her writing room his base of operations."

Alex chuckled as he pulled his t-shirt on and then tied off his shorts. "With all of the rooms in this place, I think it's on point he chose the one where Rosie would be the most. Besides the solarium."

"That kitty is smart," I said as I rustled up a new pair of Speedos and then tossed some warmups on over them.

Less than ten minutes later, we were on the road headed down into Rancho Linda; at that early hour, I made excellent time — and set a new record for the roundtrip between the condo and the pool. While I missed the optional pre-workout, I still managed to slide into the water with a few minutes to spare; the throbbing in my head lessened slightly as I checked off the items on the workout, but never completely went away. Not having been one of the collegiate athletes that partied every weekend, I wasn't completely up on hangover remedies save for getting plenty of liquids into me; still, there was only so much Gatorade a human body could take before it began to rebel.

Food would have been a logical option after the grueling workout, but when even the *thought* of trying to eat my usual no-frills oatmeal created a wave of nausea, I opted for a full-strength Coke from the vending machine outside the locker room of the pool and called it good. I was halfway to the Public Safety building for the weight training portion of my workout (it *was* leg day) and a shower when I remembered there was no point to visiting the original brick structure in the center of town; frowning, I continued on past what had been my professional home for the past two years and headed toward the edge of town. Slurping at my Coke as I rose into the hills, I tried to remember if the gym was actually ready for prime time; the pounding in my head was hard to ignore, but I felt like I'd walked past it recently during one of the interminable pre-move planning meetings I'd been forced to lead. About the only thing I could recall for certain was watching two burly moving men carrying a treadmill into the space with enough ease it might well have been a slim two-by-four instead.

The light for the non-public parking lot was in my favor, and I was impressed yet again with how smoothly the automatic gate operated as I turned in. More cars were there than I would have expected at such an early hour; seeing the Orange County logo on most of them hinted that it might be our new technology overlords, attempting to get ahead of the day's problems before the rest of the staff arrived. As I parked my Camaro beneath an old oak tree I'd begun to favor, I mentally wished them all the best; aside from being an informed consumer and user, information technology as a vocation had never appealed to me. The few people I knew well in that field were, in my opinion, underappreciated professionals with the patience of saints. Nobody cared about them when everything was working, but the minute you couldn't print the agenda for your meeting with the boss, they inevitably got an earful. Sliding out from the driver's side, I grabbed my swim backpack and wondered how Brian Knotgrass was doing; with the consolidation of our former I.T. group with the main one in Orange County, he'd been whisked away to their headquarters in Santa Ana to manage the wider set of county assets. Kids who looked like they'd barely left middle school now roamed our offices instead; despite their apparent youth, they seemed to know what they were doing — or, at the very least, had yet to accidentally delete anything critical to running our organization.

Tapping my ID at the reader for the side entrance to the Glass Monstrosity, I slipped through the door and quickly made my way to the far side of the first floor; as I'd feared, my badge didn't work on the RFID reader for glass doors protecting the new gym, despite several attempts (and a few oaths) to encourage the light to flip from red to green. Pressing my hands to the glass — and what was with having glass doors everywhere, anyway? — it was hard to see anything inside the darkened room; the fact that the overhead lights were out seemed to be a leading indicator it hadn't officially opened. Trying my card one final, futile time, I briefly lamented the interruption to my dry land training plans and then turned to head for the locker rooms that were just down the hall. Those were in a slightly better state of affairs; with the rolling move in for departments, they'd needed to be ready when the first wave had landed.

Pushing through yet *another* glass door — albeit a frosted one — I decided *ready* might have overstated the situation. Lockers were indeed installed and waiting in one half of the space, but it looked like the four sinks had been roped off for repair already; peering around the corner, I could see the urinals still didn't have their privacy shields installed, but the doors to the toilets appeared to have finally arrived. Sighing, I walked to the proper aisle and located the new locker number I'd been assigned, then completely spaced on what the PIN code for the fancy digital gizmo that served as the handle was. Digging out my iPhone, I scrolled through my notes app and then chuckled softly when I realized I'd used a variation on my favorite four numbers; as I punched them in, I wasn't sure Alejandro would appreciation knowing I was using his height and Speedo waist size in such a fashion.

Unzipping my swim backpack, I carefully hung my polo and khakis on the hooks, then retrieved my body wash and towel; stripping down, I locked everything up and then risked the showers for the first time. Unlike our old digs, we'd gotten something of an upgrade in that each stall now had a small changing room just in front of it with a short bench. I dropped my towel on the bench and then stepped into the shower proper, turned the dial all the way to boiling and then prayed the water heaters were actually hooked up and working that morning. The blast of icy water that nearly pinned me to the tile wall confirmed my worst fears, though I was rather impressed with the water pressure. I went through my ablutions faster than should be humanly possible, dried off and then returned to my locker to dress. Running a hand across the slight burr of stubble on my face was a reminder that I'd not shaved since returning from Maine; other parts of me also needed attention, too, if Alejandro's not so subtle hints were any indication. That brought a slight smile to my face; despite my distaste for shaving down for any other reason than a championship swim meet, it was hard not to appreciate the effect my efforts had on him — nor ignore how he was usually willing to step into the shower to assist me with the process.

Maybe this weekend, I thought as I twisted in front of the mirror on the back of the locker door. *I think I can get away with a few more days. We haven't had good shower sex in a bit anyway.*

The thought of him running the loofa sponge over me — and my body's reactions to it — confirmed my suspicion that my libido hadn't gotten much of a workout, either; wondering if I was going to be hounded by erotic images of my fiancé all day, I tossed on my clothes, grabbed my swim backpack and left the locker room to start my day as Professional Vasily.

And immediately faltered.

I'd originally planned on reviewing what I could find on The

Cardinal Group before heading over to their world headquarters, but as I stood there in the elevator lobby of the Glass Monstrosity, I found I was less inclined to see if the network was actually functional in our new office than I had been earlier. You didn't need to be a detective to intrinsically understand that having a parking lot full of I.T. nerds prior to eight in the morning wasn't a great sign.

Screw it, I thought to myself.

Shifting the backpack on my shoulder, I headed out to the parking lot and my waiting car. Tossing my gear into the rear seat, I slid behind the wheel and then punched up the address for The Cardinal Group on my phone; I smiled at the irony *they* were in the heart of Rancho Linda, close to all of its amenities and easy access to the 57. Leave it to a real estate firm to understand it was all about location; sighing, I started up the car, backed out of my spot and then headed down the hill to the center of town. My headache had become more of a dull ache, allowing me to appreciate the spectacular sunrise over the hills surrounding the city; I had to admit, the angle from the new office afforded me vistas that our old spot could never match. It was a grudging admission that I would never reveal to anyone publicly, however.

Coasting into the center of town, I shifted lanes and waited to make a left for a sedate business park a few blocks from the Rancho Linda Mall. It appeared to be quite similar to one I had visited a few years earlier, comprised of two- and three-story buildings in the Spanish Colonial style that had been extremely popular in the city during the late sixties and early seventies. Mature trees that were clearly not native to California were everywhere, shading well-manicured patches of lawn and the various parking lots surrounding each cluster of offices. It was a bit tricky finding the exact address Siri was claiming was the one for my destination; for whatever reason, I'd assumed an organization purportedly as large as Cardinal would have had a massive lighted sign pointing the way to their world headquarters. When one didn't appear, I pulled into the lot next to the most likely candidate, locked the Camaro and then wandered over to the small plaque listing the organizations in that space to discover if I'd completed that part of my quest successfully.

"Huh," I murmured aloud when my eyes finally found the proper entry. "Suite 300," I added to no one in particular, leaving unasked the larger question of *why* they only seemed to occupy a small portion of one floor of one building.

Concrete pathways that appeared to have been freshly painted with some sort of non-skid material crisscrossed quads of green lawn much like a college campus; I chose the most likely option and headed toward the building number the map had indicated. Eschewing the elevator, I took the exterior steps two at a time to the third floor, then had to make three circuits before *finally* locating Suite 300; it was sandwiched between a custodial closet and Madame Rochelle's Palm Reading Services in Suite 310. All sorts of warning bells were going off in the back of my head as I read the name of the business etched on the window of the door — and the business hours, which were listed as Monday to Friday (with no time given). If I hadn't recently been wandering a construction site owned and managed by Cardinal, I would have immediately assumed they were some sort of shell corporation that had leased a space simply to get a California address for their incorporation paperwork. It also seemed completely at odds with the kind of organization Izzy Lift had described; peering into the space beyond the door, I could barely make out a small desk and maybe a water cooler.

What the fuck? I thought. *Maybe I got the address wrong...?*

Pulling my iPhone from a pocket, I went into Safari and did a quick internet search; landing on the official home page for The Cardinal Group allowed me to verify that their corporate headquarters were exactly where I was standing, though their website also made them look far larger (and more professional) than the reality was hinting at. Two phone numbers were listed at the bottom of the site, one for inquiries and the other for faxes; setting aside for a moment that *anyone* still faxed *anything*, I tapped at the inquiries number and immediately went to a computer voice telling me the office was currently closed; leaving a voicemail wasn't apparently an option, so I hung up and then turned to lean on the ornamental railing running around the outside walkway. Staring at the grassy quad below me, I felt a slight frisson in my gut that told me I'd stumbled onto something important. Exactly *what* that might be was unclear, but I also knew myself well enough to know that wouldn't be the case for long.

Movement at the corner of the quad caught my attention; my eyes were drawn to a tall man in a classically tailored business suit briskly walking toward the building along the same concrete path I'd used. He was carrying a leather briefcase and for all the world looked like he'd have been far more comfortable on Wall Street in New York City than Rancho Linda. As he grew closer, I could see the light-colored pocket square was a perfect match to the necktie; given how the sun was reflecting off the polish of the shoes, they had to have been recently touched up by someone who knew what they were doing. When the figure disappeared into the small alcove for the elevator, I thought I'd stick around a bit longer to see if I'd guessed right about who I'd just seen.

The chime of the elevator arriving on my level sang out merrily, though the man I'd been watching appeared to be anything but as he rounded the edge of the building. He had a phone pressed to his ear and was frowning deeply, enough that a groove had formed between his eyebrows. Whatever it was that he was discussing, though, was hard to ascertain; the moment he saw me at the door to Suite 300, he pulled the phone from his ear, hung up abruptly on whomever had been unlucky enough to call him and then focused his attention on me.

"Anton Cardinal?" I smiled as I held out a hand. "Deputy Chief Vasily Korsokovach. Do you have a moment? I'd like to talk to you about your housing project down by the reservoir."

He stared at my hand for a long moment before briefly shaking it. "I'm incredibly busy, Deputy Chief," Cardinal said, more or less confirming my suspicion.

Age had been kind to Anton Cardinal; despite his hair now being completely white, he still retained much of that college jock look I'd seen in the photo Gina had shared with me. The cut of his suit emphasized the fact that he was still solidly built, though there was a slight hint that the cocktail hours endemic to making deals in his profession had, perhaps, extended his waistline slightly. A close-cropped beard did make him seem far more distinguished, though the cynic in me immediately assumed it was just one more marketing tactic he employed with his clients.

"This won't take long," I smiled again, trying my million-dollar model move. "Though I would be happy to schedule something if that were more convenient. Either here," I added, "or down at the station."

His eyebrows went up; I noted idly that they had been professionally shaped. "Are you accusing me of something?"

"Hardly," I chuckled, though I thought it was interesting that he immediately went there. Eyeing him for a moment, I nodded slowly. "You don't know, do you?"

"Know? What?"

I cocked my head. "I assumed your site supervisor had already filled you in."

Cardinal seemed to be getting more irritated the longer we stood there together. "I don't deal with day-to-day operations," he explained as though I were a ten-year-old. "I have people for that."

"Okay," I nodded again. "Who would those be, and when do they get in?"

"Business operations are handled out of our office in Lake Buena Vista," he said.

"I thought The Cardinal Group was based in California?"

"We are," Cardinal smiled. It looked a bit like a grimace. "Though employment laws here make that rather impractical and quite unprofitable — at least for those positions I can't move to a more tax-friendly state."

"Like Florida?" I asked, a bit agog. "That's three time zones away from what you do out here."

He shrugged. "They work California hours," he replied.

"All right," I sighed. *Travel to Orlando* hadn't been on my BINGO card. "Who do I need to speak to out there?"

"About what?"

I felt my patience begin to wane. "Mr. Cardinal, a dead body was recovered from your construction site Monday morning. I'm going to need to know a bit about your operation beyond what your site supervisor has already told me."

The fact his face didn't so much as twitch told me everything I needed to know about just how hands on Anton Cardinal was. "I'm not sure what you'll get from them," he said after a long moment. "Especially without a warrant — something any court in Florida is unlikely to provide to a California detective."

"This is still a California company," I replied. "Regardless of where your employees are working and processing information, our laws apply. My warrant will be just as valid there as it would be here."

I watched him closely, trying to keep my face impassive. While it wasn't exactly a lie, it was a tiny bit of an exaggeration regarding how such things worked. Still, the fact that he backed down told me he might not be as brilliant a businessman as he looked. "Fine," he said as he looked to his phone. "Talk to Myrtle McKenna; she's my Chief Operations Officer and can get you anything you need."

Myrtle? Seriously? I thought. "Will you email her and let her know I'll be there in the morning?"

His eyes bugged out. "You can just do a Zoom meeting or something—"

"I prefer to do these things in person," I smiled. "Especially when records might be involved."

"Fine," he said before glancing to his phone again. "I've really got to go — we've got another round of financing for a new project, and I'm about to meet with some investors."

"What kind of project?"

"Student housing," he said distractedly as he tapped at his phone.

"Where?"

"Irvine," he said before reaching into his pocket to retrieve a business card that he shoved at me. "Next time, make an appointment."

"Of course," I smiled again. "One last thing, while I have you, though. I understand you were engaged to Vivian Grandchester."

Cardinal frowned. "That was a long time ago," he replied.

"When was the last time you saw her?"

He frowned deeper. "I think she covered the groundbreaking of our new housing project beside the reservoir for the *Register*. That was a few months ago; I gave her an interview and that was that."

I smiled slightly. "I take it the way things ended, grabbing a cup of coffee and reminiscing about the good times you had together was out of the question."

"Quite," he nodded. "Is there anything else?"

"No," I replied, which wasn't entirely true. Given the text messages and voicemails Gina said they'd found on Grandchester's phone, I had a *ton* of follow-up questions, but it was clear those would have to wait for a better moment. "Thank you for your time."

The Chief Executive Officer of The Cardinal Group nodded as he fished a key from his pocket and unlocked the door to their world headquarters; had the entire situation not been deadly serious, I would have openly laughed when the door stuck and required some effort to open fully. Wondering if it was a metaphor for the organization, I pulled my iPhone out and placed a call to our internal travel department.

My chances at a night of hot, steamy sex with the hunk of a guy I called my soulmate appeared to be diminishing.

THIRTEEN
THERE'S MORE HERE THAN MEETS THE EYE

"You're *what?*"

Alejandro's incredulous voice echoed in my Camaro. "Flying to Orlando," I repeated. "Looking for answers."

"And you leave tonight?"

"The flight's at six, actually. You can come with me," I suggested helpfully. "Maybe sneak in a visit to Universal while we're there? I hear they opened a new park."

There was an audible sigh across the connection. "*Mi amor,* in case you've forgotten, we just got *back* from a cross-country trip. I haven't even had time to unpack."

"Perfect!" I laughed. "Then I can pick you up and go straight to the airport."

"Vas—"

"This will be more fun," I said, a faint note of pleading leaking into my voice. "Not as much angst."

"You're going out there because of a *murder,*" he reminded me.

"Okay," I admitted. "No angst but lots of drama."

"Babe," Alex said slowly, "as much as I would love to go with you—"

"I've even got us a room at the fancy Marriott—"

"*Vas*," he said louder. "I can't go. Any other week I could."

"Oh," I said as I turned out of the business park and then headed for the construction site. I'd decided a second walk through the scene was in order after speaking with Cardinal, more to clear my head than anything else. "Your extra day off is still a point of contention?"

"And then some," he replied. "Besides, we've just gotten Chat back home. As much as he loves his grandmother, I'm not sure I want to impose upon her so soon."

"Rosie would do it in a heartbeat."

"Probably."

"Huh," I said somewhat sadly. "I didn't use to hate traveling alone."

"You just like showing me off," he laughed. "And who could blame you?"

"Exactly!" I agreed. "Are you sure you can't work remotely or something?"

"I suspect we'd be engaged in other pursuits were I to accompany you," Alex chuckled. "Besides, most of our time will be spent in the air."

"Together."

"True," he chuckled again. "And there is no one else on earth I'd want to hang out with, *mi amor*. Just not this time."

"Damn," I sighed dramatically. "I don't know how I'm going to get through it."

"You'll find a way. You flying out of LAX?"

"Yeah," I groaned. "So I've got to make sure I'm on the road by two just to beat the traffic."

"Well, at least our suitcases are still packed," he reminded me with a laugh.

"With dirty laundry. I might just go straight to the airport with my swim backpack and call it good."

"Wouldn't be the first time you've run around in workout gear," he said. "Or that you've had to wash your clothes in the sink of the hotel."

"I'm told the major hotels now have laundry service."

"Wise ass," he laughed. "Got to run. Call me when you get to the airport, okay?"

"Will do."

I let the call drop and shook my head sadly. While I'd expected Alex might not be able to come with me, my heart had hoped he'd agree; the reality that I was facing a five-hour flight and a lonely hotel room didn't take long to set in. I'd only been partially joking about not liking to travel solo; there had been a time when I'd felt footloose and fancy free, but once Alex had become a permanent fixture in my life, going anywhere without him — even the grocery store — felt like a missed opportunity. Orlando wasn't the sexiest place in the world for couples; Paris continued to have a lock on that title. And if I were being honest, Florida's recent tilt away from supporting the LGBTQ+ community was insanely troubling; we'd had a long talk about continuing with our plans to get married at Disney World in January after that state's legislature went after our favorite company for having the audacity to recognize our community was just as much a part of the American kaleidoscope as any other. In the end, we'd opted to support Disney in our own, albeit small, way; still, no small part of me worried endlessly about what might happen to us if we found ourselves on the wrong side of town. I was confident I could protect both of us, but I also didn't want to tempt fate, either.

My musings came to an abrupt halt when I recognized I'd reached the nascent intersection for the new housing development; without the light, it took a few more minutes before I was able to scoot across to the construction entrance. I wasn't surprised to see that my officers were no longer standing watch in front of the temporary gate; the de facto parking lot was quite full of vehicles of all shapes and sizes, making it nearly as difficult to find a parking spot as the local mall. Sneaking the Camaro between two pickup trucks, I killed the engine and got out, then slid my sunglasses on. Considering the area was abuzz with all sorts of activity, it was hard to peg the site as one where a dead body had been discovered less than forty-eight hours earlier. Taking my bearings, I started toward the small shack I knew Izzy Lift used as her headquarters with the intent of telling her I was going to take another look around; halfway there, I saw her burly form appear in the doorway. Unsurprisingly, her face took on a deep frown, and she moved with alarming speed in my direction.

"You again," she nearly yelled as she trotted across the hard-packed earth.

"Good to see you again, too, Izzy," I laughed. "You sure know how to greet your guests."

The frown shifted to something vaguely like a smile. "Last time you were here, I lost a full day of work."

"Not this time," I replied as she came to a stop in front of me. "I'd like to take another walk around the site if I could."

"Oh," she said. "That's it?"

"That's it."

"All right," she nodded. "Let me get you a hard hat. But I'll need to escort you."

"Deal."

I followed her across to a freestanding cabinet I'd missed before; unlocking it, she looked at me and then reached in to remove an obscenely brilliant yellow hard hat, then grabbed a second one for herself. It took a moment to get the strap on the inside sized correctly; once we were done, she looked at me expectantly.

"Where do you want to start?"

I pointed to where we'd found Grandchester's phone. "That building?"

"You got it." I could see wheels turning and wasn't disappointed when she continued. "I understand you saw the boss this morning."

"News travels fast," I nodded as we headed toward the building.

"Especially when he's annoyed," she sighed. "You must have really pressed his buttons. I normally only talk to the people in LBV."

"I think I caught him at a bad moment."

"*Every* moment is a bad one for him."

"LBV?" I asked after a moment. "You mean the office in Orlando?"

"Technically, Lake Buena Vista is its own little spot," she said, "and yes."

"You didn't mention the people you report to are in a different state when we spoke on Monday."

"It wasn't intentional. The change is fairly recent; Myrtle — that's the COO — her parents are in Winter Park, and she wanted to be closer." Little paused. "What is this, December?"

"Don't hurry Christmas," I smiled. "I'm clinging to the end of November for a bit longer so I can avoid thinking about shopping."

"I'm right there with you," she laughed. "Anyway, I think the office packed up and relocated back in March." She smiled. "Cardinal gets a twofer because payroll taxes are less out there."

"They moved *everything* just to keep Myrtle as an employee?"

"She knows where the bodies are buried," Izzy said before realizing who she was speaking to. "Not literally, of course."

"Of course," I nodded sagely. "I guess the part that confuses me the most is what you told me earlier about the key safe — that the duplicate master key to it was at the home office."

"It is," she replied.

"The one here in Rancho Linda?" I pressed. "Not Florida?"

"Yes," she answered as we reached the edge of the building. I was a bit surprised that the entire second floor had been roughed in since my last visit. "The bulk of the administrative people may have moved, but the core of Cardinal Group is still here."

"It's a pretty small office," I observed.

"Not as small as you think," she smiled. "I'm told the old man was somewhat thrifty and wouldn't pay for windows; the entire operation is essentially in the center of the building, behind other orgs that were willing to pay for better visibility."

"Interesting." A thought crossed my mind at that moment. "Did you ever work with Konstantyn?"

Lift smiled wryly. "'With' would imply something of a relationship," she replied. "I don't think the old man was into that kind of thing. But yes, I've been here long enough that I remember the days when he'd walk the construction site, taking notes about the prior day's progress — or lack thereof."

"Sounds a bit like a hardass," I said.

"The old man was old *school*," she chuckled. "A product of his generation, to be sure. I'll say this for him: he knew his shit. He could read a construction plan like he'd been the one to design it and had been known to swing a hammer every now and then just to prove his bona fides to the crews he hired." Lift smiled again. "Until this moment, I'm not sure I realized how much I've missed seeing him pop up."

"His son doesn't do the same thing?"

Lift frowned. "Anton? Hardly," she said before remembering who she was talking to. Coughing slightly, she continued. "I mean, when his father was grooming him to take over, he forced Anton to work at whatever site was under construction at the time so he could get a feel for the business; not something the typical college student wanted to do, for sure, but he turned out to be a quick study." She smiled slightly. "Although I don't think Anton ever forgot how much he hated the experience — either that, or he never forgave his father for forcing him to do it; either way, once the old man stepped down, the kid pretty much stopped any kind of site visit unless it was necessary for the investors."

"So they rely on you for that sort of oversight now?"

"Pretty much." Lift paused. "I will say this, Anton's time as an intern led to some of the inventory processes we now use; we're far more efficient in that area than we used to be."

"Are you talking about those barcodes on the lumber?"

"Among other things," she nodded. "It also helped their bottom line, since we don't employ the same number of people to manage all of that any longer."

"Savings that I'll wager have been eaten up by the cost of materials," I said as I eyed the edge of the building.

"It's a vicious cycle," she agreed. "Looks like the electricians are working this floor, be sure to watch your step."

I let Lift lead me across the concrete walkway and up into the main lobby area Gina and I had visited earlier. A small group of electricians appeared to be running a conduit through the still-open ceiling; slightly further away, a plumber was putting the finishing touches on a sizable plastic tube that disappeared into the floor above us. Sounds of air hammers filtered down from above, along with snippets of raucous conversation in both Spanish and English. I was struck once more how unaffected everyone seemed to be; death, it appeared, had done little more than cost them a full day's wages. Stopping in what I had originally pegged to be the elevator alcove, Lift turned and looked at me expectantly.

"What did you want to see?"

"Is there access to the running path from this building?"

"There will be," she replied and then led me deeper into the building. We sidestepped a partially used stack of two-by-fours as she continued. "In fact, this is the only building that will have direct access from the rear entrance. The rest of the development can reach it via a pathway that will loop around the property."

"A paved path?"

"Concrete," she replied. "Though there had been a plan to make the section along the water more of a natural surface. I think our insurer nixed the idea."

"Sounds about right. Will there be a gate to the property from the trail?"

"Right now, yes. Once construction is done, no," Lift shook her head. "That was part of the deal with Rancho Linda."

We stopped at the edge of the concrete pad; that side of the building hadn't yet seen any proper landscaping save for the hint of a graded pathway leading from where the door would be down to the running path circling the reservoir. I wasn't an expert by any means, but to my eye it looked like it was less than the length of a football field. Looking at the hard packed surface of the temporary path, I had little faith Gina's team had managed to locate any shoe impressions that would have been remotely usable, though I'd not actually looked at the file yet. I was struck by how few of the tall trees surrounding the reservoir had been removed from that corner of the development; it was likely the reason I'd not been able to see how quickly construction had been progressing during my midday runs. It also meant that anyone on the path would have been unlikely to have seen anything the night of the murder, too.

Vivian would have had to come this way if and when she used the path to get here, though the nail in the tire makes me think she actually didn't use it the night she was killed, I thought as I folded my arms against my chest. *Makes sense, though; it's the best access to get to the center of the site, and... to the construction supervisor's shack. Hmm...*

"I'm going to miss this," I murmured.

"Miss what?" Lift said.

I looked at her. "We're moving the department to a building at the edge of town," I explained. "Our old location is just across the reservoir and also has great access to this running path."

"That's right," she nodded. "The new Government complex — the one that used to house that tech startup."

"They may have been in tech, but the building barely supports it," I sighed.

"We built that one, too," Lift said. "There were... a few items that got value engineered."

I felt an eyebrow arch. "Is that a clever way of saying 'cost cutting?'"

"Quite."

Something sizzled in my gut. I looked back toward the elevator alcove. "Can I get a copy of the construction plan?"

Lift started. "They are on file with the City already."

"Yours are probably more current," I said. "With any updates that had to be made once you broke ground."

"Those get filed with the City, too."

"Do they?" I asked, continuing with my hunch. "Always?"

"Yes."

I cocked my head. "I don't think so," I said softly. "And I think that's one reason Vivian Grandchester reached out to you."

Lift's eyes went round. "I have no idea what you're talking about."

"Oh, I think you do," I said. "How often had you been meeting?"

"We weren't meeting," Lift replied firmly, but then quickly glanced away.

It also wasn't hard to hear the slight note of panic in her voice. I decided to take a slightly different approach. "I've got an out-of-town errand to run," I began carefully. "I'm leaving tonight but will be back Friday."

"That's a quick turnaround," she observed.

I shrugged. "The glamorous life of a detective. And I have to be back in time for classic jazz night at the *Alternative Way*."

Lift eyed me. "I've heard that's a good venue for music."

"It is," I nodded. "You should stop by. The quintet that's the house band at the bar down the street will be there. They're one of my favorites."

"I... think that would be a nice change of pace," she said. "I usually stream something on Netflix; it would be good to get out for once. What time do the doors open?"

"I'll be there at four," I replied. "I like to find a good seat before the crowd descends. That's also when the fresh pastries come out of the oven, so I can get first crack at them."

There was a hint of a smile on Lift's face. "You don't look like the kind of guy who goes for sweets."

"That's thanks to many hours at the pool each day," I smiled. "I hope you can make it."

Lift nodded, then looked at her watch. "Do you need anything else? I really should get back to it."

"No," I replied. "I've got to get to the airport anyway."

"Safe travels on your trip, then," she said.

"Thanks."

I followed her back out of the building and then parted ways with her in the parking lot; as I got behind the wheel of the Camaro, I felt reasonably confident Lift wouldn't make an appearance on Friday. Whatever information she had was locked up behind a fear of discovery — that much I was certain of; her non-answers about Grandchester made me more confident that I was on the right track. The question of the hour, though, was what the hell the reporter was working on; I felt like I had enough pieces to make an informed guess, but also knew I needed to be on more solid ground before crafting the kind of warrant I knew would land me in front of a judge asking hard questions about the First Amendment. Shifting gears mentally, I decided to go in a different direction and fired off a series of text messages to Miles Guernsey, a key member of Major Crimes; a warrant for the financial records of The Cardinal Group wouldn't be all that hard to get, given that the victim appeared to be interested in them as well, nor would it be a stretch to grant me access to corporate records regarding the relocation of personnel from California to Florida. If either of those held what I suspected they did, getting my broader warrant for Grandchester's home and office materials would be far easier to obtain. Just for good measure, I threw in a request for Grandchester's finances as well; I had some suspicions now about her activities in the days preceding her death, and her banking records might well confirm them.

Thinking about that for a moment, I shifted gears again and speed-dialed Miles. He picked up on the first ring. "I've barely read your text message," he said. "You can't possibly—"

"No, I don't," I laughed. "I have related questions that are too long to type as a text. Did the warrant come through for our victim's cell phone records? Specifically, the location tracking?"

"It did," Miles said. "Though as wonky as our network is at the moment, I'm not sure I can access any of the data for you. Are you looking for something specific?"

"Beyond matching it to the GPS data on the phone itself? Yes; I obviously want to know her movements on the day of the murder, but now I'm also curious if she popped up in Orlando recently. How broad was our location data ask?"

"The usual," he replied. "Though we don't typically use anything beyond California."

"But it won't be a stretch of the warrant?"

"I don't think so, but I can go back to Judge Spenser if you want clarity before proceeding,"

"Do that," I said. "Tell him I have enough probable cause that I'm heading there myself tonight."

"That will pique his curiosity."

"And, hopefully, give me the answer I need."

"I'll let you know what he says. Are you really flying to Orlando tonight?"

"Yeah," I replied. "The Cardinal Group moved all of its administrative operations there last Spring."

"You could just do a Zoom call," he said, echoing Anton Cardinal.

"And miss the chance to sneak in a visit with the Mouse?" I laughed as I started up the car.

"Figures," he chuckled. "Good hunting."

"Thanks," I said as I backed out of my spot. "Here's hoping I actually catch something..."

FOURTEEN
MCO by Morning

LAX wasn't exactly the *worst* airport on the planet — I think one overseas held that title — but it sure had to rank in the top ten. In all the years I had lived in California, the place never seemed to cease being under construction in some form or another; random changes to parking and traffic flows seemed the norm, making any sort of navigation software mostly meaningless. I wasn't a huge fan of the outer Economy lots, so after fighting my way into Los Angeles, I spent another frustrating half hour crawling around the airport so I could park in the garage closest to my terminal. Finding a spot in the extremely full garage was even more frustrating, but ultimately, I slipped into a slot between a post and a Prius that looked to have seen better days. I'd opted not to go to Anaheim and retrieve my suitcase; my swim backpack had a spare RLPD polo and boxer briefs for emergencies and, of course, enough workout gear to cover the difference. Having done substantial traveling for regional swim meets meant everything in the backpack met the requirements for going through the TSA checkpoint, eliminating the need for checking anything; I did have to spend a few minutes arranging everything so I could slide my MacBook and all of its adapters into the mix.

The terminal proper was a chaotic mess, with people in lines almost everywhere; it took a moment for me to deduce that a whole series of flights had been cancelled due to a massive snowstorm hugging the East coast; it felt a bit like *déjà vu*, considering the exact same thing had happened to Alejandro and me just that Sunday. A scan of the monitors said my flight wasn't affected, but the gate had been changed to accommodate one that had; I was in the process of thanking my lucky stars when the departure time shifted right in front of my eyes, delaying me by at least an hour. Frowning, I knew it wasn't really an issue; despite the relatively early departure from California, I had a significant layover in Atlanta. With the time change and connection, I wasn't due into Orlando until almost seven the following morning; whether I spent an hour of that in LAX or Atlanta didn't really matter, save for the fact that the pizza was far superior in California.

Security proved to be as fun as always; for the fifth time in a row, I seemed to have triggered something on the particle scanner that required a full hand pat-down of my groin. Whether it was a weird area of focus for the TSA or just the way I happened to wear my underwear was hard to know, though it was clear the agent charged with doing the actual examination was about as thrilled as I was. The sign at my gate said we'd picked up thirty minutes already, so instead of a pizza, I opted for a steak grinder loaded with onions and cheese, and further splurged on a small bag of Doritos; despite it being airport food, since I'd not had *anything* solid to eat since dining at Rosie's the prior evening, the meal felt like a divine moment of nirvana. We boarded the flight soon after; owing to my late booking, RLPD Travel had been forced to stuff me into First Class, which meant the seat was able to recline sufficiently enough to get a few hours of sleep before landing in Atlanta.

As with most round-the-clock airports, Atlanta was quietly bustling despite it being nearly two in the morning; since I had the time, I opted to walk the underground tunnels between terminals instead of taking the train, something I tried to do whenever I could. Amazing art installations were hiding down there and often changed from season to season; I never failed to be impressed by what I discovered, nor to appreciate just how *not* artistically inclined I was. Alex had more of an eye for those things, a talent that had led him to slowly redecorate our condo in Anaheim. Originally, I'd been a bit reluctant to let him have full dominion over the space, given how I felt about the condo, but the longer we were together, the more I considered it just as much his home as mine. And, in the end, his tweaks had been worth the initial angst — even if he might have gone just a bit overboard with the cat furniture.

The only café open in my departure terminal looked a little sketchy, but my opinion changed the moment my nose caught wind of the beautiful smell of a fresh pot of coffee being brewed. I talked myself into a chocolate-filled croissant to compliment the large cup I bought, then wandered to the extreme far end of the terminal for my gate. Several hardy souls had curled up on the extremely uncomfortable seats for a quick nap, but I figured that ship had already sailed for me. Snarfing down the croissant in a matter of seconds, I tried to pace myself with the extremely hot coffee, but that, too, disappeared long before the gate agent appeared and began taking upgrade requests.

Orlando was more or less an up-and-down flight from Atlanta, barely long enough for the attractive flight attendant to serve me a relatively decent breakfast of scrambled eggs, bacon and a blueberry muffin. I thought I'd seen his eyes linger on my biceps as I'd handed him back my tray; the phone number on the back of the napkin he'd handed me for my second cup of coffee was a pleasant reminder that I still had some sort of sex appeal. Glancing down at the engagement band Alex had given me, I was a bit shocked at how forward the approach was, considering I was essentially telegraphing I was already taken; then again, the kid looked barely street legal, so it was possible he was doing nothing more than looking for a one-night stand. Pre-Alex Vasily might have eagerly accepted the overture, but older and wiser Vas knew he'd get his ass smacked — or worse — if he even took a second look.

I'd better not let on that Alex is running the show, I thought to myself with a smile as we descended into Orlando International. *Then again, there's no one else in this universe I'd let run me around by the nose than him.*

Only having carryon proved to be a blessing; I was able to hustle directly to the rental car area and track down the vehicle that had been reserved for me. I'd assumed something in the Economy class would be mine and wasn't disappointed to see an ugly white Ford something sitting beneath the sign bearing my name. Sighing, I managed to cram my six-foot-two frame into the cramped front seat, though it felt a bit like my knees were in my chest as I pulled out of my spot. It took a moment for me to get the right address for the J.W. Marriott I'd booked into punched up on my phone, and then somewhat longer to wend my way around the various circles of access roads for Orlando International. The sun began to peek over the horizon, and then immediately disappeared into an unusually thick layer of clouds that looked ominous; while not a frequent traveler to Florida, I could count on one hand the number of times I'd experienced bad weather. *That* thought reminded me of the flight cancellations, which in turn triggered a guilty conscience for not having called Sean as promised. Reaching into my backpack with one hand, I pulled out my AirPods and then speed-dialed my friend; as it was nearly eight, I figured (correctly) he'd be done at the pool.

He picked up on the first ring. "Hey," he said. My eyebrows went up at how tired he sounded. "Little early for you, isn't it?"

"If I were in California," I answered. "As it happens, I'm in Orlando chasing a lead."

"No kidding," he replied. Sean seemed to have suddenly perked up. "When did you get in?"

"About an hour ago, plus or minus. Took forever to get the rental car out of the lot; I think it's one of those mazes used for research, honestly. The winner gets a free tank of gas."

"Doesn't sound like you won, then," he laughed.

"Nope." I paused. "Sorry I didn't call earlier this week; I picked up a case as soon as I returned to California."

"It happens," he said. "Must be one hell of a case if you're in Florida."

"Early days," I smiled. "But it's certainly turning into one."

"You can tell me all about it over dinner."

It took a moment for me to register what he was saying. "You're *here*? Already?"

"Nearly," he laughed. "GPS says I've got about six hours left to hit my dad's place; if you don't mind an overnight guest, I'll shift directions and meet you at your hotel."

"When did you leave?" I asked.

"Right after you did," he replied. "I've been taking my time, seeing the sights." He paused. "Swimming at different pools. Found a few I really like, actually."

"Enough to move?"

"Enough to consider it."

"We do need to talk, then," I said. "I'm going to be at the J.W. Marriott in Grande Lakes; I have no idea how long I will be, so I'll add your name to the room so they can give you a key."

"Okay," he said. "That's the one closer to Universal?"

"Yes," I said. "And the website says it has a really nice pool, so if you beat me there, you can chill out with a piña colada or something."

"Sam Adams is more my style."

"I'm sure they can accommodate you," I chuckled. "It will be good to see you, even if it's only been a few days."

"Yeah," he replied. "Yeah, it will. See you later, then?"

"Deal."

I let the call disconnect and then tried not to focus too much on why my best friend had left weeks earlier than planned to spend the Christmas holiday with his father; it now seemed there would be plenty of time to delve into that later. Instead, I tried to avoid the tourists who seemed determined to kill me by changing lanes at the absolute last minute anytime a directional sign appeared bearing the word "Disney." Fortunately for my sanity, the hotel I had reservations for was far closer to the airport than the massive theme park complex further east and south; turning off the highway, it was but a few minutes more to get to the massive tower for the hotel. Strictly speaking, I could have checked in using the mobile app, but since I now needed Sean to be able to access the room when he arrived, I had to speak with a clerk to adjust the reservation slightly. To my surprise, that led to an unexpected upgrade to a suite on the Concierge floor, one that came with access to the lounge that apparently had a reasonably good view of the fireworks from Seaworld. Wondering if that was a sign of how the day was going to go, I crammed myself back into the shoebox of a rental car I had, punched in the location for The Cardinal Group (East Coast Version) and set off in search of my quarry.

Nine o'clock in the morning turned out to be when the heaviest flow of traffic was surging toward Disney World; unfortunately, the address I had in Lake Buena Vista forced me in the same direction, and unlike California, surface streets seemed few and far between in that part of the county. It was with a massive sense of relief that Siri finally told me to exit the bumper-to-bumper traffic full of out of state plates; the city I descended into — if it could be called that — appeared to cater extensively to the traveling tourist, with block after block showcasing some low- to mid-budget hotel or chain restaurant. Aside from random retail stores hawking everything from clearly unlicensed Disney merchandise to surf boards (in central Florida?), I didn't get the sense Lake Buena Vista was a hotbed of corporate office space. At the outer fringes of the main drag, though, the nearly outlandish advertisements for hotels and eateries disappeared, replaced by a variety of squat buildings that seemed purposefully indeterminate. Siri had me turn into the parking lot for one that had four or five stories; most of the spaces were full, but I found a spot beneath palm tree that had seen better days. Locking the rental, I headed across the faded pavement toward the front door; just inside was a fairly standard elevator lobby, with a framed directory at the far end. The Cardinal Group was listed as being in the basement, which wasn't much of a surprise given what Lift had told me earlier. Eschewing the elevators, I found the stairwell and quickly descended down a floor; there were only two offices on that level, one for the management group maintaining the building, and the other for Cardinal.

Pausing outside of the wooden door that had been stenciled with the name of the firm, I checked my iPhone again and frowned at the lack of confirmation my warrant had been granted. I wasn't entirely surprised, for there were real jurisdictional issues that I had intentionally minimized while speaking with Anton Cardinal — issues that Judge Spenser would not take lightly, no matter how much favor I curried with him. Sliding my iPhone back into the pocket of my khakis, I put on my best retail smile and sent up a prayer to the law enforcement gods that I'd catch a break and get what I needed; otherwise, the whole round trip to Orlando would be for naught.

The door swung inward easily, revealing a handsomely paneled reception lobby; tasteful artwork hung on the walls over comfortable couches that were surrounded by potted greenery. Soft lighting filled the space, as did music from a light classical station. A small cubicle sat at one end, just below the logo for The Cardinal Group and guarding two closed doors that presumably led to the inner sanctum. The desk was currently occupied by a woman who looked to be far closer to retirement age than mid-career, which, given the demographics of Florida, seemed on point. Her long white hair had been pulled back from her face and held by a hair clip in the shape of a hummingbird; it matched a cloisonné version on the lapel of a smart blazer in light blue. Perls that Barbara Bush would have loved ringed her neck, complementing a wardrobe that seemed a bit beyond someone who was answering the phones. Without windows — and without the decorating — the space would have felt claustrophobic; instead, it felt comfortable, cozy and a world apart from the office I'd peered into back in Rancho Linda. It said something about both the organization and the people running it, something I filed away in the *useful in the future* box.

Shifting my approach slightly, I wandered over to the transaction counter and placed a hand on it. "I'd love to get the contact information for the firm that did your decorating," I said. "What they were able to do in such a small space is remarkable."

"I'll take that as a compliment," the woman replied with a warm laugh.

I looked at her; that close, I could see that her makeup, though light, had been expertly applied. "You did this?"

"I did," she nodded. "I used to run the design center for Cardinal when we were building single-family homes in Orange County, California."

"Wow," I replied. "How did you land out here?"

"No good deed goes unpunished," she laughed again. "I got promoted into management."

I rolled my eyes. "I completely get that," I said. "You must be Myrtle."

"I am," she frowned slightly. "And you are?"

"Deputy Chief Vasily Korsokovach, Rancho Linda Police Department," I answered as I reached over to shake her hand. "I would ask if I'm catching you at a bad time, but since you're currently sitting at your reception desk, I'm going go out on a limb and assume the day's not started off so well."

"It hasn't," she nodded. "My receptionist ruptured his ACL playing pickle ball; he's in surgery today, and his wife — who also works here — is at the hospital with him." She smiled slightly. "Therefore, the COO is running the desk for the day."

"So much for being promoted," I laughed. "You don't have anyone else to cover?"

"Fallout from Thanksgiving," she shrugged. "Just about everyone takes time off between now and Christmas, which is about the only place on the calendar when we can get away with it. Year end is an all hands-on deck kind of thing, so I'm woefully understaffed until then."

"Ah," I nodded sagely. I'd done enough digging through financials over my time as a detective to gain an appreciation of the cyclical nature of accounting. "I'm surprised you don't have more depth, considering how large The Cardinal Group is."

Myrtle smiled slightly. "We're actually quite small; Cardinal is a family-owned corporation with a board that keeps a keen eye on the bottom line. That translates to a lean payroll, among other things."

"You can't possibly cover all the bases that way," I observed with an arched eyebrow.

"We backfill with consultants as needed," she replied, then waved at the desk. "Or we wear more than one hat at a time. The team has become rather adept at multitasking."

"I suppose a short change of scene can't be all that bad," I said, though I had my doubts.

"The early returns look promising," she smiled. "I don't often get a former Olympic swimmer landing on my doorstep."

"I see my reputation precedes me," I laughed. "Or Anton Cardinal called ahead."

"A little of both," she chuckled. "He phoned right after you spoke to him; I did a quick internet search after that since your name sounded familiar. I used to live in Long Beach, so I remember the spread in the *Los Angeles Times* about you." Her smile widened slightly. "You were wearing quite a bit less in that article, if I recall correctly."

"As any good swimmer would," I smiled.

"Indeed. I have to admit, I thought Mr. Cardinal was kidding when he said you'd be here today."

"I go where the leads tell me to go," I shrugged. "Did Anton explain what I was looking for?"

"All he said was to give you whatever you asked for," she replied as she placed a small USB stick on the transaction counter. "I assumed you'd be most interested in the housing project where the victim was found, so I took the liberty of downloading all of our records for it."

My eyebrows went up. "That was proactive."

"I've done this for a long time, Deputy Chief," she replied. "It's not my first rodeo with oversight."

I reached for the drive. "Sounds like there's a story in there."

"Or four," she smiled. "I've given you all of the financial records for the project and tossed in the overall plan for construction so you can see how they tie together. That includes the status reports we get from the field, which in this case, come from the site manager, Izzy Lift."

"Nice." Looking at the drive in my hand, I thought for a moment. "Does this also include your list of contractors and suppliers?"

"For the project? Yes."

I looked at her. "You have different contractors or suppliers for each of your projects?"

"We have a master list we draw from for all of our bids," she replied carefully.

"I'd like to see the full list The Cardinal Group uses," I smiled.

Myrtle's face lost some of its mirth. "I feel like that is out of scope for your investigation."

"Could any of the organizations or people on that wider list have been used in the housing project?"

"I suppose so," she replied slowly.

"Then I'd like that full list, too."

"It will take a minute to download."

"I can wait." I smiled. "Otherwise, I might sneak off to Walt Disney World."

"Hard not to," she replied, but there was no trace of humor in her voice.

"Do you have a head of security?"

"We outsourced that years ago," she replied. "It's a line item on each project, you'll see that in the data I gave you."

"For such a large organization, isn't that a little unusual?" I asked, trying not to frown. Lift had given me the impression there was more heft in that area than it appeared to have. "I feel like you likely have millions of dollars on the line with each of these projects. Not having direct security oversight seems unusual."

"Margins are pretty slim in our business," Myrtle replied. "And it's pretty much industry standard now to eliminate anything you can pay someone else to do for less."

Capitalism rears its ugly head again, I thought. "I see. We're going through some of those changes now at the department; I have to admit, I miss having my own I.T. department."

"We've never been big enough to have one," Myrtle sighed. "I'd kill to be able to speak to someone who could fix my laptop," she said before her eyes went wide. "Metaphorically speaking, of course."

"I hear you," I laughed. "Want some advice?"

"Sure."

"Get a Mac," I said. "I've never had any trouble with mine."

"Does it run Excel?"

"Among other things," I nodded. "It can even surf the internet."

"Sold," she smiled. "Let me get that list for you. Do you want some coffee while you wait?"

"I thought you'd never ask," I smiled.

"Hang tight, and I'll be back," she said as she stood.

I watched as she disappeared behind one of the two doors, surprised that she didn't invite me to the main office proper; the fact that there was a computer monitor sitting on the reception desk also made it seem odd that she needed to go elsewhere to get my data. Waiting just long enough for the door to close behind her on its pneumatic hinge, I leaned over the transaction counter and immediately learned two things: first, the computer monitor was just that, a monitor, and didn't appear to be connected to anything. That was intriguing, but not as much as seeing an old-fashioned multiline Nortel reception telephone straight out of the late 1990s; I held my breath just long enough for one of the lines to light up, then slowly let it out. Somewhat promisingly, the small digital window on that station helpfully displayed the number being dialed (and which extension it was coming from). Embracing the historical irony completely, I grabbed my iPhone and snapped a picture of the phone just before the line went out — but not before noting it was one of the area codes I knew covered Orange County, California; it wasn't hard to guess who might have been at the other end of the line. Figuring I had but a few seconds before my host reappeared, I straightened back up and made it look as though I were checking my text messages.

Right on cue, Myrtle reappeared holding a cup of coffee and a very earnest (though likely fake) expression. "Speaking of computer issues, I don't seem able to access that database at the moment. I've put a call into the firm we use for tech support, but it might be a while. Do you want to come back this afternoon? Say, around three? I should have this resolved by then."

I took the coffee. "Sure," I smiled before glancing at the door. "That'll make for a slow day for your team."

"As I said, we're running on a skeleton crew. It's just me today."

"Really?" I smiled again. "Anton Cardinal isn't paying you enough."

"Please let him know that the next time you see him," she replied. "See you this afternoon."

FIFTEEN
UNEXPECTED GUEST

Somewhat ambivalent that I would actually get anything from Myrtle later that day, I pocketed the USB stick and drove back to my hotel. I had a ton of time to kill before reappearing at the appointed hour, but not quite enough to justify the steep cost of a side trip to any of the theme parks that were a short distance away from where I was staying. That pretty much left hanging out at the pool until Sean arrived; that familiar guilt I always got when I skipped a workout convinced me some time frolicking in chlorine would be wise, so I stashed the shoebox of a car in the self-parking lot and made my way to the room I'd been given so I could change. The suite that I found myself in went well beyond anything I'd ever stayed in before; not only did it have a full-sized living room with three couches and a massive 60-inch flatscreen on one wall, but there was also a full bar in the corner stocked with every conceivable type of spirit imaginable. Two queen beds were in their own room, in a space nearly as large as my entire condo back in Anaheim; the attached bathroom had both a jacuzzi and walk-in shower spacious enough to accommodate the wildest hijinks Alex and I could have ever dreamed up.

Dropping my swim backpack on one of the beds, I took a moment to appreciate the upgrade before digging through my gear to retrieve a swimsuit, goggles and my swim cap; quickly changing into my Speedo, I bowed to the inevitable and stuffed what I'd been wearing into one of the helpfully provided on-site laundry bags then called downstairs to request same-day service. Digging through one of the outer pockets of my bag, I came up with a half-full tube of sunscreen and began to slather it on my already tanned skin; I'd made it to my chest when I heard the door to the suite unlock. Glancing at my phone sitting on the bed, I felt an eyebrow begin to arch. It went up further when I heard the *thunk* of a backpack dropping to the ground and a familiar voice call out.

"Vas? Are you here?"

"In the bedroom," I replied with a smile. "You made good time," I added as I turned to see my best friend appear in the archway separating the two spaces. "What did you do? Turn on the lights and sirens and put the pedal to the metal?"

"I can't read a map for shit," he lied, though that crooked smile I loved nearly sold it. "I was closer to Orlando than I thought."

"Right," I narrowed my eyes. "What are you driving, anyway? Last time I checked, you didn't have a car."

"I do now," he replied. "Charlie drove me to the Ford dealer in Bangor, and I bought a Mustang GT Convertible." Sean looked a bit uncomfortable. "In, uh, Vapor Blue."

"You... bought a convertible?" I asked, slack jawed. "A brand-new *Mustang*? And drove it *here*?"

"Yes."

"Dude," I breathed. "You're having a midlife crisis, aren't you?"

"Most definitely." His keen eyes quickly appraised the situation. "Headed to the pool?"

I nodded. "My one and only appointment this morning resulted in a follow-up for later this afternoon," I replied as I continued to slather sunscreen on myself. "One that I am reasonably sure isn't actually going to happen. As much as I would love to go to Disney World, there's just not enough time. So, the pool it is."

Sean seemed to consider that and ran a hand through his head of extremely disheveled curls as he did so; it gave me a moment to take stock of my friend. The lack of hair product to tame his wild hair was telling, leading me to think that maybe he'd not truly been taking in the sights as he'd claimed. It also wasn't like him to skip shaving, even when traveling, so the significant start to a beard felt like another leading indicator my best friend was still not in the best place mentally. The UEM Men's Swim and Dive t-shirt and matching nylon wind pants were an unusual sartorial choice for Sean; while I seemed to have a predilection for roaming the known universe in what we both jokingly referred to as "workout professional" attire, Sean tended to reserve it for times when he considered himself off duty. I found it hard not to think that the absence of his unofficial uniform of polo-and-khakis stood as mute testimony as to how he'd put more than just his career on hold.

Shit, I thought as I twisted the top closed on the sunscreen tube. *I think he's gotten worse.*

Almost as though he were reading my thoughts — a common and mutual occurrence when we'd been working together — Sean smiled tiredly. "I might have exaggerated how frequently I stopped along the way," he said as he scratched at his chin. "Or the number of pools I'd swum at."

I put a hand on my hip. "You drove straight through, didn't you?"

The slight shading of embarrassment beneath the stubble underscored how bad a liar my friend was — outside of an interrogation room. "I think I should plead the Fifth on that."

"Probably wise," I laughed. "I'll bet you've not had a proper meal in a bit, either."

His cheeks flamed darker. "I don't suppose protein bars count?"

I rolled my eyes. "Not according to Alejandro." I glanced at the sunscreen in my hand. "Let me toss some clothes on and we'll see if they are still serving breakfast at the restaurant."

"I have a better idea," Sean said. "I need a quick shower to get presentable, and then I'll join you at the pool. We can order something while we lounge by the water and you can fill me in on your case."

"Are you sure?"

"Yes," he nodded. "Now go and save me a good seat."

"All right," I smiled. "Bathroom's over there. Try not to use up all of the hot water?"

"No promises," he laughed.

More for form's sake than any modesty concerns, I yanked my microfiber shorts from the backpack and pulled them on over my Speedos, grabbed my sunglasses and then headed for the pool; I wasn't all that surprised to find it was rather quiet when I pushed through the safety gate, given how it was a weekday just after a major holiday. I also suspected the initial heavy skies might have sent vacationing tourists to other activities that were under cover; whatever the reason, I had my pick of brilliantly white lounge chairs and chose two that were part of a small alcove overlooking the lazy river. Kicking out of my shoes, I slipped off the shorts and made my way over to the larger pool; like most major four- and five-star hotels, there was a small section set aside for those who wished to swim laps, though barely wide enough for two lanes at best. Both were empty at that hour, so I slipped into the waist-high water on the outer lane, pulled on my goggles and swim cap, then set about making up for having missed my normal workout. The water was far warmer than I would have liked, owing to the pool being more of the recreational variety, but I still managed to sneak in what felt like a standard four-thousand-meter set. What was more interesting to me, though, was how my mind *didn't* shift into investigator mode as the tiles went by below me; no, instead I found myself focused on my best friend, trying to unravel the context clues woven into his sudden appear-ance at the hotel. I'd assumed my trip to Maine over Thanksgiving had gotten him through the worst; as I flipped at the far end of the pool for my final lap, it dawned on me that Sean might have simply made me *feel* like I'd helped, and had instead hidden away his still-crumbling heart behind the standard unemotional Maine persona he often wore. Very few could pierce that outer armor of his; I thought I was one of them, but as I stretched my arm out to hit the edge of the pool, I realized I'd overlooked the obvious signs all was not well during my visit.

Popping up at the edge of the pool, my thoughts went on hold when I saw Sean sitting there, legs dangling in the other open lane. He had his goggles and swim cap on and was wearing the sort of face I'd only seen when he was intent on beating his last personal record. We'd swum together long enough that I was intimately aquatinted with every muscle in his tall body, a body that had once inspired fantasies of a life that could never actually have taken place. Still, I took a moment to appreciate the fine work of art that had been presented to me, then pushed my goggles up to my forehead.

"I hope you put some sunblock on," I said, nodding to his very white, very not-tanned skin. "Even as overcast as it is today, you're going to burn in minutes."

"If I stay in the water, I can avoid it," he replied with a slight smile, repeating the lie we had often told ourselves when the team had traveled to tropical locations for training. Typically, we all wound up as red as the lobsters they served at Millie's in Windeport.

"Wanna race?"

"It depends," I said. "What do I get if I win?"

"Bold to think you can still beat me," Sean replied as he slipped into the water.

The trash talk immediately made me feel like we were still on the team at UEM; my eyebrows went up when I saw that he was deadly serious. "I can beat you any day and twice on Tuesday," I smiled. "Especially if it's butterfly."

"Game on," he nodded. "Up and back. If I win, you have to take me on as a permanent consultant."

I frowned. "I'd do that in a heartbeat anyway," I replied, wondering if I was getting confirmation of his status with the Maine State Police.

"Sounds like a safe bet, then," Sean smiled.

"All right," I continued. "If *I* win, which I will, by the way—"

"Not likely."

"—you'll drive me over to Disney World in that fancy Mustang of yours and treat me to dinner at the Flying Fish."

Sean narrowed his eyes at me. "I take it that place is rather expensive."

"Shouldn't be a problem for someone who just up and bought a new car," I snarked with a smile. "Besides, you're going to beat me anyway, right?"

He put on his goggles and then pulled his swim cap over his curls. With the shading of his beard gone from his cheeks, he looked every bit like the twenty-something I'd first met at UEM nearly two decades earlier. "I am," he said with confidence. "Ready?"

I pressed my goggles back on, then gripped the edge of the pool. "On three?" I asked as he mirrored my move.

"Yes," he nodded as he dipped his body down a bit more.

"Ready..." I said as I twisted forward and put my chin on the surface of the water. "One... two... three—"

I was startled slightly by the tremendous splash of Sean diving into the race, and even more surprised that he'd essentially intentionally false started. Recovering my wits, I hurled myself up and into the water, trying to reduce the body-length lead he'd created. In all honesty, while Butterfly was my best stroke, the only person who'd ever beaten me — consistently — had been Sean; as I threw myself into the full body effort that was swimming fly, it became clear fairly quickly that Sean had kept his immaculate form. The best I could do was halve his lead by the time we hit the far wall; flipping in the opposite direction, I decided two could play at this game and dove slightly deeper than normal to allow myself some additional distance of underwater dolphin kicking. Surfacing about a third of the way down the lane, I risked a quick sideways breath and saw I'd pulled even; the discovery provided enough of a jolt of adrenaline to propel me forward just a little bit faster. With less than three body lengths to go, I risked another sideways glance and discovered Sean was doggedly matching me stroke for stroke; kicking harder, I put my head down and dug into the water above me, furiously holding my breath so I could keep to a perfect streamline. I hit the edge of the pool a moment later hard enough I created a mini tsunami over the edge that washed along the light-colored concrete; breathing hard, I turned and saw Sean was right there, gasping. Only then did I realize I had no way to verify which of us had touched first; pushing my goggles to my forehead, I scanned for and found the slack-jawed lifeguard who'd been prowling the perimeter with his rescue float.

"Hey," I called out. "Did you see which one of us touched first?"

The kid — he looked all of sixteen — did a quick scan of the empty pool before walking over to us. "That was *sick*," he breathed. "You two swim like Olympians."

"Probably because we are," Sean laughed.

"*Seriously*?" the lifeguard said. "When?"

"2004 and 2008 for me," Sean replied before pointing to me. "2008 for him. We also swam together in college."

"I would have loved to see those sessions," the kid replied. "Our high school team is kinda lame, but my age-group is cool. We practice at the local college pool and there's a national swimmer there trying to make the next Olympics." He looked at us. "Do you do clinics? I bet Coach would have you in a minute."

I glanced at Sean. "He's available for that kind of thing," I offered without asking. "I'm here on business and have to head back to California tomorrow."

He looked at Sean expectantly. "I... I guess I could," he said after shooting me a look that said *you're gonna pay for this*. "I'm going to be in Florida for a bit."

"Sweet," the lifeguard replied. "I'll text him when I go on break. Are you staying at the hotel? I can track you down if he says yes."

"Yes," Sean replied. "Until tomorrow."

"Cool," he smiled. "And it looked like a tie to me."

"Diplomatic," I laughed. "Thanks."

"My pleasure," he said before he went back to scanning the empty pool.

Sean smacked me on the shoulder almost immediately after the kid left. "Hey!" I howled as I rubbed where he'd hit me. "What's that for?"

"Volunteering me," he replied darkly. "I've never done a clinic in my life."

"Oh, that's not true," I smiled. "We used to run the age group for Coach back in the day; that's not a lot different."

"Maybe not," he allowed, "but herding a pool full of teens wasn't on my agenda."

"And what *was*?" I asked meaningfully.

Sean's face darkened slightly. "I had plans," he said defensively.

I looked at him. "I'm having a hard time buying that," I said as we stood there in the pool. "Sure, you drove to Florida, but are you *really* here to visit your dad?" I asked, before adding softly, "Or are you actually escaping what happened back in Maine?"

My best friend looked away. "Vas, for the first time in my life I don't know the answer." He turned back to me. "And it's scaring the shit out of me."

"I can believe that," I replied before moving closer to the lane line. "I think I should have stayed longer over Thanksgiving. I knew you were at loose ends when I left, but not on this order of magnitude."

Sean smiled that slight smile of his. "This isn't on you, Vas. In fact, you and Alex pulled me out of the worst of the funk I'd sunk into. All of this—" he said as he waved generically at the hotel, "—was sort of in the back of my mind. And had been for months." He looked back at me. "I'm not happy working for the State; Suzanne's little escapade just complicated things more."

"Did you really take a leave of absence?"

"I tried to quit," was Sean's surprising reply. "Jimmy — Captain Roberts, that is — talked me out of it and instead granted me unpaid leave until the end of January." He shrugged. "About the only positive to having been fired by Windeport was forcing them to pay out my accumulated vacation and sick time. I had quite a bit — you know how hard it is for people like us to take time off."

I nodded slowly. "That's how you paid for the car?"

"Yeah," he replied. "And I still have enough left over I can stay out for a few months without hurting my savings."

"Sounds a bit like what happened to me when Rancho Linda initially forced me out."

Sean smiled. "I paid attention," he said. "And had a good lawyer."

I was distracted for a moment by a rivulet of water as it snaked along Sean's well-defined pectoral but managed to pull myself back. "I don't imagine you spoke to Suzanne before you left."

He shifted his position, causing small ripples in the water. "She's pretty much been MIA in Windeport for a few weeks now. I assumed she spent the holiday at her place in New Hampshire; now that her clinic is part of a medical group, she's better able to pull in doctors to cover for her."

"You didn't call her, then?" I asked. "Like we talked about?"

"No," he answered before quietly laughing. "I bought a car instead. And then immediately left the state with just my swim bag and a laptop."

I shook my head. "You really don't have a plan, do you?"

"Nope," he admitted. "Not even a *concept* of a plan."

"Definite midlife crisis," I sighed. "At least now I know what to expect when I get there myself."

"Happy to help," he laughed ruefully.

"Where's your dad living?" I asked thoughtfully.

"Over on the West coast," Sean replied. "He's got a beachfront condo somewhere around Naples."

"How far away is that from here?" I asked, frowning. "Florida geography isn't my specialty."

"GPS said a few hours," he replied. "I think I have to head over to Tampa first, then down to Naples. Why?"

"I think I'm going to take you up on that offer to be a consultant," I replied. "I suspect I'm not going to get what I need before I have to head back to California. It would be handy to have someone on the ground here in Orlando, assuming you can hang out for a few days."

"I've not gotten a better offer," Sean replied. "And... Dad doesn't know I'm coming."

I smacked my face with the palm of my hand. "Dude..."

"I know," he sighed. "But remember: no plan. I'm pretty much flying by the seat of my pants."

"No kidding—"

My iPhone chose that moment to sing out the merry ringtone I had set for Alejandro. I nodded at Sean and then pushed myself out of the pool; after quickly drying off the worst of the water, I dug through my shorts to locate the infernal device and tapped at the answer button. "Hey—"

"Vas," Alejandro interrupted. "I think you've hit a nerve on that case you're working."

Something in his voice made my blood run cold. "What happened?"

"Two very burly manly men cornered me on campus," Alex began. "They wanted me to deliver a message to you."

"They did?" I asked, my blood pressure rising. "What was it? Are you okay? I'm catching—"

"I'm fine," Alex interrupted again, "and I have no idea what the message was. But you might be able to ask them yourself when you get back."

I blinked. "That sounds like a story and a half."

"It is," he laughed. "Do you have time to hear it?"

"Hell yes," I said.

Sixteen
Mess with a Diver, Get Your Ass Kicked

Alejandro

Vasily's career had taken him out of town on enough occasions now that Alex didn't feel his absence as keenly as he once did; those first few weeks after he'd arrived in California, it had taken some effort not to have a full-on panic attack when he'd been left to his own devices, with all of the usual fears swirling around in his head. Was Vasily really coming back, or would that trip be the one when Alex discovered just where he really stood with the man he loved? Somewhere along the line, Vas had correctly figured out why Alex grew so tense each time the small duffel bag came out of the closet; it had taken some effort — and no small amount of fevered, passionate sex — before Alex fully understood the depth of his soulmate's commitment to the former Mexican National Diver. Not that he *loved* it when Vas took off without him; to the contrary, Alex often twisted his schedule inside out to make sure he *could* dash off with the Greek God he loved whenever possible, for spending time with Vas — no matter where it was — always centered his soul and made him feel whole.

This sudden trip to Orlando was more of a trigger for all of those pent-up fears than he would have thought, though. As Alex headed down to the parking garage for their condo and his waiting New Beetle, he groaned inwardly at the long day ahead of him, for most of it would be spent with his recently discovered nemesis, namely his current supervisor; the closer Alex got to the start date for his new position at the business college, the harder it was becoming to deal with the incessant micromanaging he got from the crap-for-brains millennial. He didn't need his counseling degree to divine where the antipathy was coming from, for José had been pretty upfront with the fact that *he'd* also applied for the Director position Alex had ultimately gotten; as trite as it was, it seemed his current boss couldn't look beyond the diving portion of Alex's resume and therefore had deemed him incredibly unqualified for the gig. If the two of them hadn't also been of Hispanic descent, Alex was nearly certain José would have filed an EEOC complaint alleging discrimination.

That might still happen, Alex thought morosely as he slid behind the wheel of his brilliant yellow vehicle. *It's not a secret that I'm gay; assuming he's not hiding in the closet — which seems doubtful — he could make trouble on that front.*

But would he? That seemed to be a question that continued to linger on Alejandro's mind despite having already signed the offer for the position. The other truth was that he *had* set a start date, but had thoughtlessly (or purposefully, depending on one's perspective) failed to relay that to José. Every now and then, Alex's inner teenager rose up and allowed him a measure of rebelliousness, something he'd not had while *actually* growing up in an extremely strict, extremely conservative Catholic household. As he started up the car, Alex caught the smile in his rearview mirror as he considered — briefly — how he'd finally been able to do some of the *other* stuff he'd long fantasized about as a teenager once he'd met Vasily. His tutelage beneath the talented hands of his fiancé had checked off a number of boxes, but there were still a few left open, some that he was reasonably sure Vas would be into; he just needed to screw up the courage to ask, something he'd been so far unable to muster — despite the depth of their passion. Nonetheless, that didn't stop him from flashing an image through his mind of Vas wearing that skintight latex costume he claimed was for cosplaying as Chat Noir; Alex didn't consider himself into any particular fetish, but it was hard to deny how erotic it had been the one and only time Vasily had modeled the outfit. The screen-accurate Spider-Man costume was a close second and, fortunately, was something Vas seemed to repeatedly find excuses to wear; Alex had spent many a happy evening slowly unzipping his partner from the embrace of the Spandex, something he was certain Vasily had noticed.

Pulling out of his spot in the garage, Alex realized he was already daydreaming of his partner and shook his head to try and clear it. *Gone barely twelve hours,* he sighed, *and I'm already missing you. This is gonna be a fucking long day.*

Traffic on his route to Cal State Irvine was typical for that mid-morning hour; he generally didn't leave the condo until close to eight, allowing enough time for him to do his dry land workout at the small gym in the building. Looking down at his wrapped wrist, he frowned a bit; he'd planned on doing a full session on the ten meter after his kids had finished their portion of diving practice that evening, but the slight twinge he'd felt while shaving seemed like a warning he couldn't truly ignore. The results from his MRI scan were due any day now, though he couldn't deny his deep fear that they would only confirm his worst suspicions. Before Vasily had come along, diving had been his entire world; even now, despite knowing Vas had his back (and every other part of him, for that matter), Alex still fretted about someday not being able to step out onto the end of the ten meter to do his thing.

Thy will be done, he sighed again. *Though if you are still listing to me, Díos, please let me keep diving.*

Predictably, there was no answer from on high, so he returned his focus to the road. Only then did it finally register that a mid-sized Honda had been following him since getting onto the 57; while he didn't have the same instincts as Vasily, he'd driven in California long enough to know the odds that the *same* car would follow you for miles *just because* were fairly low to infinitesimal. Having lived with a cop for some time now meant he knew a few tricks of the trade; curious if he were right, Alex snapped on his turn signal and then immediately shifted lanes. There was a pause, but the Honda mirrored him; frowning, he accelerated around a massive semi carrying a load of cables and then snuck into a spot just ahead of it. The Honda came roaring past him in the lane to his left, then shifted lanes to drop in a few cars above Alex's current position. He wasn't all that surprised when it preceded him off the 57 at the exit for Irvine, nor the way it managed to slow down just enough to pull in *behind* him as the road up the hill to the college went from four lanes to three.

They're not hiding, Alex thought as he continued on to campus. *They want me to know they are there. That tells me something, doesn't it?*

Glancing at the clock on his dashboard, Alex debated calling Vas but thought better of it; the last thing he needed to do was rile up his fiancé while he was half a continent away. So he decided to let it play out, if for no other reason than to attempt to determine why he'd attracted someone's attention. He kept one eye on the Honda, and one on the road; at length, the turn for Cal State Irvine appeared, and he slowed to take the corner while the light was still in his favor. Slowing further, he watched as the Honda paused at the corner to allow a car in between them, then smiled to himself when he realized it was likely going to follow him all the way to the faculty/staff lot. As with most college campuses, the roads at CSUI tended toward majestic arcs that favored views of the building architecture; for his purposes, that meant it remained rather easy to ensure he could keep tabs on the Honda. Slowing again, he turned into his designated lot behind the athletics building, then paused long enough for the license plate reader to kick in and raise the arm. Alex noted that his shadow rather smartly drove on past the faculty lot and disappeared from view; it spoke to a knowledge of the campus that they didn't even attempt to access the lot. Sliding into a spot beneath an old tree, he debated again calling Vasily; doing the math in his head, he figured it was close to lunchtime out in Orlando, and yet he continued to dither.

Grabbing his backpack from the passenger seat, Alex locked up his car and then headed for the sidewalk. As a gay man — and as a negative commentary on society writ large — he tended to be more alert to his surroundings; his campus was a far more welcoming atmosphere than most places he frequented, but he kept a weather eye out for anything that seemed more unusual than the normal craziness a college with such a diverse population as CSUI had might offer up. Halfway across the grassy quad in front of the dilapidated building that housed Career Services, he caught the two men in well-tailored business suits sitting by the Art Deco fountain and conversing. It might have almost been believable save for the fact they were trying too hard to *not* look like they were watching him; arching an eyebrow, Alex adjusted his backpack and continued onward as though it were just another day despite the pit in his stomach telling him otherwise.

Feeling a bit like he was in a spy movie, Alex used the reflection in the glass of the doors to his building to confirm Business Suits had indeed left their position at the fountain and were making their way in his direction. Vasily had taught him a long time ago that there was no such thing as coincidence; with that in mind, he pulled open the door while quickly sorting through his options. Confronting the duo with witnesses felt like the safest option, but he also suspected they wouldn't allow that to happen; if he wanted to figure out *why* they were so interested in him, he was going to have to provide them with an opportunity that would make them *feel* like they were controlling the situation. As he went down the worn steps to the basement of the building, he smiled grimly at the notion he'd spent nearly his entire diving career making the judges see something that wasn't always there; fooling a pair of stalkers couldn't be all that different.

The plan began to coalesce when he saw one of his favorite student workers behind the half-moon reception desk protecting Career

Services. "Will," he smiled as he sidled up to the counter. "I need a favor."

"Sure, Alex," the young man smiled. "What do you need? More photocopying?"

"Something a bit different," he replied. "I need you to do two things for me. First, two gentlemen are about to appear, looking for me. Kindly tell them I've stepped into the restroom and will be back momentarily."

Will nodded. "All right. And the second item?"

"Call Campus Police and report an assault in progress."

The color drained out of the poor kid's face. "An assault...?"

Alex leaned over the counter and lowered his voice. "I believe strongly those men intend to do me harm," he said softly. "I'm going to lead them away from the career center so no one else sees what's going to happen. But I need you to make sure Campus Police is on the way. Do you understand me?"

Will nodded again. "You want me to call *after* they appear?"

"Yes," Alex replied. "You can't miss them. They're wearing matching business suits and look like they've stepped out of *The Godfather*." He reached over and put a hand on the student's shoulder. "You've got this."

"Okay," Will nodded. "Are you... are you—"

"Going to be okay?" Alex asked before smiling. "Have faith," he answered a fraction of second before he heard the telltale sound of expensive loafers on the stair treads.

Adjusting his backpack, he hurried down the subterranean hallway; the restrooms weren't more than a few yards from the main entrance to Career Services, and maybe a handful further from the staircase. They were also somewhat unusual in that they'd been built to accommodate the special needs of the students who might be interviewing with employers in his office; despite now being in one of the least desirable buildings on campus, whoever had laid out the facility back in the day had thoughtfully accounted for the need to provide a place for students to change into proper attire for meeting with prospective employers —

and to store said attire when classes interfered with their schedule. Pushing through the door to the men's side of the facility, Alex spent precious seconds to ensure both the locker room and showers were empty, then wasted a moment more to verify he was the only person on the bathroom side proper. Hefting his backpack, he smiled grimly as he set it beneath one of the sinks, just within reach; pulling out his iPhone, he propped it up against the mirror on the svelte ledge over the faucet, tapped the recording button for his camera and then turned on the water. He let his hands hover over the flowing water and waited; it took every ounce of the control he exerted while diving to keep his breathing and heartrate close to normal, and it paid off when the door to the restroom opened a second time to admit both of the Suits. Leaning down as though he were just finishing up, Alex steeled himself for what he expected was coming next.

"Hey, asshole," he heard from behind. "Are you the dude fucking Vasily Korsokovach?"

He tried not to let the fear show in his voice. "It depends," he replied with as much equanimity as he could muster. "Who's asking?"

"That's above your pay grade."

Shutting off the faucet, he slowly turned; mindful of where his phone was, he made sure to stay just off center in the hopes his camera was getting the full angle. Somewhere in the back of his head he thought perhaps he was violating a campus policy by recording inside such a space, but figured it was the least of his worries at the moment. This close, he could finally tell that each Suit was different; one of them was slightly taller than the other, but both were wearing identical slicked-back hairstyles Wall Street raiders had made famous back in the mid-1980s. The cut of the suits spoke to something tailored, a perception reinforced by expensive looking silk-ties and matching pocket squares. Both were clean shaven but one already had a five o'clock shadow; the other seemed to have experienced a bad run of acne at some point in their youth, and, if the red tinge to the bulbous nose were to be believed, was now a rather exuberant participant in cocktail hours. Taken together, the duo fairly screamed *mob enforcers*, though for the life of him, Alex couldn't recall Vasily mentioning any crime families in Orange County — or Southern California, for that matter. For a brief, awful moment, he thought maybe he was the victim of some sort of candid camera prank, but that reasonable explanation evaporated when he saw the slightly shorter of the two Suits pull out an honest-to-God set of brass knuckles from his suit pocket.

Oh, shit.

"That wouldn't be hard to assume," Alex smiled, aware that the Suits hadn't noticed his hands weren't even wet. "I'm but a lowly paid State Employee."

Suit One — the shorter of the two — began to put the knuckles on, an elaborate process Alex assumed was designed to intimidate the potential victim. It might have worked, too, save for how incredibly over-the-top his performance was; Alex wondered if the stress of the situation was getting to him, for instead of fighting back his fear, he was actually struggling to keep from laughing. "I'm only going to ask you one more time," Suit One said. "Are you the *fucking* dude currently *fucking* Vasily Korsokovach?"

Alex arched an eyebrow. "I'm obviously standing here with you right now," he replied reasonably. "So, the literal answer to your question would be, 'no.'"

That seemed to give both of them pause, allowing Alex to downgrade their IQs a few points. Suit One looked at Suit Two, who for his part appeared to be chewing through a math problem he couldn't quite grasp. At length, he finally sneered — actually *sneered* at Alex. "You wanna be a wise ass, then?"

Alex shifted slightly, allowing his leg to bump up against his backpack. "What do you gentlemen want, exactly?" he asked, careful to keep his voice steady. "I have a full day of appointments to get to."

"We need you to take a message to Korsokovach," Suit One said. He emphasized his point by gently smacking the brass knuckles into the palm of his other hand.

Having picked up a thing or two from dating a detective, Alex was reasonably sure where the conversation was now heading; much like when he was striding across the concrete of the ten meter platform mere moments from performing his diving finale, he felt himself shift into a different place, one where his senses were far more heightened and time seemed less linear. Alex was therefore prepared when Suit Two suddenly leapt forward, arms outstretched in an attempt to grab him, presumably so he could be held for a pummeling from Suit One; shifting sideways, Alex yanked on the strap of his backpack and hurled it at the face of Suit Two with all he had. Loaded with two weeks of resumes to review plus his rather hefty MacBook laptop, it made a satisfying *crunch* when it smashed into the nose of Suit Two; Alex had but a moment to appreciate the varied string of curses that immediately filled the air before he lowered his head and tackled Suit One into a metal door for one of the stalls. The portal was ripped from its hinges with the force of their impact and landed on the porcelain throne itself, which in turn was torn from the wall under the weight of the two grown men atop it. Water started to gush from the now-exposed plumbing, covering the industrial tile with a slick sheen.

Momentarily entangled in the limbs of Suit One, Alex wasn't fully able to duck the roundhouse that came up and at him; he felt the cold kiss of the brass knuckles as they connected just below his left eye, followed by something warm trickling down his cheek. He managed to intercept the second blow with his injured wrist, but the pain from *that* hit nearly made him moan in agony. Stumbling backwards, Alex fell directly into the waiting bear hug from Suit Two and immediately found his arms pinned to his sides. Alex attempted to twist out of his embrace only to find that despite all of hours he'd spent in the weight room over the years, he was unable to shake the surprisingly iron grip of Suit Two; that didn't mean the idiot didn't still have a few weak spots, though — one of which could be rather useful to a diver. Bracing himself for the worst, Alex leapt up and backwards, smacking the crown of his head into the lower jaw of Suit Two; clearly dazed by the hit, Suit

Two stumbled into the sink behind them, releasing Alex in the process. Ignoring the stars at the edge of his vision, he dropped swiftly to the ground and rolled away; coming out of his roll into a crouch, Alex found himself facing the mess just as the sink crumbled beneath the weight of Suit Two and unleashed a new torrent of water, adding a slightly post-apocalyptic flavor to the entire scene.

Breathing hard and blinking back a slight bout of double vision, Alex tensed up when Suit One managed to pull himself out of the stall then purposefully started toward him; he spared nary a glance at Suit Two, who appeared to be moaning about missing a few teeth, and was instead focused with a rather murderous fury on Alex. Stepping backwards slightly, Alex belatedly realized he'd landed in a corner and had nowhere to go; leaning down, he was preparing to ram Suit One again when the door to the restroom flew inward, admitting several uniformed Campus Police officers and, to Alex's surprise, Chief Paula Compton-Burnett herself.

"*Freeze, asshole!*" she cried, her Glock trained unwaveringly on Suit One. "*Hands on your head, now!*"

With a glance heavily laden with malice, Suit One dropped the brass knuckles to the tile and then did as instructed. The uniformed officers — all of whom looked nearly as young as the students Alex worked with at the Career Center — swarmed around his attackers; Chief Compton-Burnett kept her gun trained on them until both had been handcuffed. Only then did she slide the gun back into her holster and move over to Alex; eyeing him, she shook her head slightly.

"Damn," she breathed as she put an arm around his waist. "Let's get you looked at; then you can tell me what I think is going to be a really good story."

"I can do one better," Alex said as he nodded toward the sinks. "My phone should have recorded most of what happened."

Her eyebrows went up. "You know we have rules against doing that sort of thing in a bathroom," she said.

"What if I told you I was prepping for a presentation when they jumped me?" Alex asked innocently as he tactfully escaped her embrace and retrieved his phone; that it had come to no harm at all was some sort of minor miracle. Turning off the recording, he watched the Police Chief as she considered him.

"A presentation?" she asked dubiously.

Alex shrugged. "We tell our kids the best place to practice for interviews or any kind of speaking engagement is in front of a mirror."

"I see." The Chief took another long moment before finally nodding. "You can download it for me once the EMTs see to that nasty cut you've got. They're out in the lobby."

A few minutes later, Alex found himself sitting on one of the couches in the reception area for Career Services, being attended to by an extremely hunky EMT. "I don't think you're going to need stitches," the guy was saying as Alex watched a second set of first responders push the gurney Suit Two was strapped onto toward the elevator. Between the gauze stuffed up his nose and the continuing moans, Alex figured the guy might never mess with a diver again. Suit One trudged along behind the gurney, handcuffed but also looking a bit worse for wear; apparently, despite how expensive the suits had appeared to be, they didn't take kindly to getting wet. "But it is going to be tender for a day or two — and it will bruise up something awful."

"Just as long as it's healed in time for my wedding," Alex smiled as he returned his attention to the hunk. "My fiancé won't be very happy if I look like a prizefighter in all of the photos."

"When is that?"

"January."

"It should be," the EMT said as he reached into his small satchel. Retrieving a pair of small plastic bags, he twisted one until it crackled, then handed it to Alex. "Ice it down as much as you can tolerate so the swelling remains minimal," he continued as he pressed the icepack to Alex's cheek. "I've only got two of these packs, but you can pick up more at any pharmacy."

"Thanks," Alex replied. He'd tried — and failed — not to wince at the pain when the pack was applied; he needed to get to a mirror to see just how bad he looked.

"You'll have a bump on your head for a bit, too, but you don't seem to be concussed. I'd still take it easy for the next few days if you can and check in with your primary care doctor if headaches or blurred vision develop."

"Can do. Thank you."

The EMT nodded again and then withdrew; Chief Compton-Burnett had been waiting in the wings and immediately settled in on the cushion beside him. Alex only knew her by reputation, which was incredibly positive by all accounts. She wore the uniform like she'd been born to be a cop but also exuded the air of one who would defend the rights of the underrepresented without question. Her salt-and-pepper hair was cut short but in a very feminine style; he wasn't surprised that she was free of makeup, though it wouldn't have been necessary in the first place. Her natural beauty needed no accentuation.

She smiled slightly as she watched him appraise her. "Not what you expected in a Police Chief?"

Alex smiled back. "Just the opposite," he replied as he shifted the ice pack. "My fiancé taught me a long time ago no two police officers are identical, but that each fills a necessary role just the same."

"Sounds like something Vasily would say," she chuckled.

"You know him?"

She nodded. "Through Chief Gilbert, mainly. And by reputation."

"Good, I hope?"

"Yes," she nodded again. "Terrible thing they did to him in Rancho Linda. I'm glad Mike got it all straightened out."

"Yeah."

Compton-Burnett looked in the general direction the cops had gone. "I'm not inclined to believe that was a hate crime in progress I broke up," she began. "And I've not seen brass knuckles like that since I worked the Back Bay in Boston."

"I'd agree with you there," Alex said. "Despite the mafioso overacting—"

"They destroyed a bathroom, and nearly you with it!"

"—I think they were trying to send Vas a message," he continued. "Through me."

She narrowed her eyes. "Enforcers?"

"You'd know better than me," he shrugged. "But that's how I read it."

"Is he working a case?"

"Yeah. It took him to Florida; he'll be back Friday."

"It could be related," Compton-Burnett said. "What do you know about his case?"

Alex knew he looked uncomfortable. "He, uh, doesn't always tell me what he's doing," he hedged.

She rolled her eyes. "Just like I don't tell my husband anything, either," she sighed.

"Exactly," he replied, though he could feel the flame of embarrassment against his cheeks. "I, uh, don't know how jurisdiction works in a case like this, Chief, but it might be wise to hand those two over to the Rancho Linda Police."

"Indeed," she smiled. "I suspected you might make that suggestion."

"Really?"

The Chief stood. "I've already spoken to Mike; we're not really equipped to handle a case like this, anyway, so he offered to house those two down in Rancho Linda until we get the paperwork sorted." She paused. "I think that means they'll likely still be on ice when Vas gets back."

"He's going to want to talk to them," Alex said.

She looked meaningfully at his bruised face. "I would think so."

Seventeen
Thrown for a Curve

It was probably wise that Sean was by my side when I hung up from my call with Alejandro; he could see the steam billowing out from my ears and quickly pre-empted any rash actions by handing me an ice-cold Samuel Adams he'd ordered from the poolside bar. Glaring at him for his presumption — and, frankly, getting even more irritated over knowing he was actually right — I gulped down more than half of the brew before finally getting myself under control. Whether it was from the sudden infusion of alcohol or the inevitable dip in adrenaline, I found myself smiling at the insanity of the universe, as well as my inability to do shit about *any* of it.

Well, that's not entirely true, I thought as I drained the last of the bottle. *I can control what I can control.*

Eyeing my now empty bottle, Sean arched an eyebrow before taking a sip of his.

"He's fine," I answered to the unspoken question. I was relatively certain he'd heard all of my end of the conversation, which in itself was enough to have filled in the blanks on what happened to Alex back in Irvine. "And he was rather definitive in not wanting me drop everything and return to California on the first flight I could get." I smiled grimly.

"I hate to say it, but it's not the first time my work has affected my personal life — or those close to me."

"Do you think it's related?"

"To the case? I think so," I said. "At least based on how Alex described the attack."

Sean whistled. "Mob enforcers? A shady real estate company? The dead journalist investigating them? You sure can pick 'em."

I tapped a finger on his bare chest. "I learned from the best." I observed before realizing how odd it was that the two of us were just standing there, drinking beer a few feet from the edge of the pool. Aside from the friendly lifeguard, we had the place to ourselves; it was pretty clear we'd stumbled into a weird dead zone between Thanksgiving and Christmas that under other circumstances would have made for a lovely, relaxing getaway. As it was, the piped in Muzak accentuated just how empty the place was.

"I take no credit in that," Sean smiled as tipped up his beer bottle again. After taking another swig, he got that look I used to see back in Windeport when he was itching to interview a suspect. "I'm going to go out on a limb here and say you want to drop in unexpectedly at that office you visited earlier today."

"Do I ever. You want to come with?"

"Like you even have to ask," he chuckled. "I'll drive."

Sean finished the last of his beer and then we made our way back to the hotel room with the intent of changing into more appropriate attire; that proved futile for one of us, for my laundry order had yet to be returned. Sighing a bit at how the universe appeared to enjoy watching me interview suspects in workout gear, I shrugged into my favorite muscle compression t-shirt and then waited for Sean. Having seen my dilemma, he decided on solidarity and slid a pair of microfiber shorts on over his still-damp suit before retrieving another of what had to have been an endless supply of UEM Swim and Dive t-shirts he owned. As we left the room and headed for the elevator, I wondered if it was one of the many ways Sean continued to support the program that we had both been members of; despite what he'd claimed earlier, I knew from my time back in Windeport that he was often the first to volunteer for meets or any of a number of training needs that had come up over the years. I'd never asked him if he had thought about becoming a coach; most Olympians wind up trying their hand at it eventually, though it wasn't an idea I'd ever found all that appealing. While we waited for the valet to retrieve his Mustang, I thought of all the shenanigans we'd gotten up to while members of the team — teens and twenty-some-things with raging hormones can be pretty creative — and felt a new respect for anyone brave enough to take on the challenge.

All thoughts of swimming vanished, though, when I heard the rumble presaging the arrival of Sean's midlife crisis. The portico had an appropriately sweeping driveway leading up to it, which meant I was treated to a slow reveal of the sports car as it climbed the slight slope to get to us. I had to admit, the particular shade of blue he'd chosen was actually quite attractive; I'd pictured something a bit darker, though, and was pleasantly surprised it was much closer to the electric blue I favored. It was also clear that the car was itching to go far faster than the sedate two or three miles an hour the valet was piloting it at; the sleek lines screamed speed, something I was reasonably sure the engine hiding beneath the hood was quite capable of providing. The car pulled to a smooth stop in front of us, allowing the young valet to pop out of the driver's seat. He was wearing a smile that said he'd won the equivalent of the lottery, then walked over to Sean to hand him the keys; my friend slipped him a tip, and then the two of us got in.

After dropping his phone on what I noted was a built-in charging plate, he glanced at me before starting the car with a slight roar. "If you want to punch in the address, I'll try to get out of here without hitting anyone."

I felt an eyebrow arch while I tapped at the nicely sized touchscreen. "This car is smaller than the SUV you typically drive, Sean."

"A fact I am still getting used to," he laughed.

"You're getting old, my friend."

That dry expression he often wore appeared. "I hear forty is the new twenty."

"I wouldn't know," I replied as I trigged the GPS navigation. "Seeing that I'm still only twenty."

"I'd better take notes, then," he laughed again. "So you know what to expect."

"Love you too," I chuckled. "Now, let's go shake down my contact."

Sean pulled out into the major artery that ran parallel to the Marriott. "I've been giving this some thought," he began tentatively. "Are you sure you want to go in there, guns a-blazing, like those over-dressed enforcers in California?"

"I do."

"It might not net you anything," he continued. "And could, in fact, make them clam up further."

"I'm aware of that," I replied, feeling a bit of my good humor evaporating. "This second round is more of a message visit, honestly." I looked at Sean. "I didn't get the warrant I needed so all I'm truly left with is whatever legerdemain I can muster to reveal what I *know* they are hiding."

He glanced at me. "That's not all you want to do."

"No," I said after a moment. "I also want them to know they can't fuck with my fiancé."

"It sounded like Alex already sent them that particular message."

"I'm not opposed to reinforcing the notion with the full weight of my badge."

"The one from California?" Sean asked.

"Stop poking holes in my not-quite-a-plan plan," I said with a slight smile. "It's hard enough to make it up as I'm going along."

"Clearly," he smiled again. "Who, exactly, are you sending said message to? I can't imagine it's this person running the Orlando office."

"Anton Cardinal," I answered. "The CEO. I think Myrtle McKenna — she's serving as his Chief Operations Officer — has a direct line to him. When I was there this morning, she disappeared to the rear of the office to get the additional info I needed; I may or may not have obtained evidence that she made a phone call to a California number before returning to tell me it would take some time to retrieve the data."

"Interesting. And telling."

"Completely," I nodded. It wasn't lost on me that the palm trees seemed to be slipping by at warp speed, but I thought better of mentioning that to Sean; for the first time since I'd flown back to see him, he seemed more like himself. Folding my arms against the thin fabric of the compression t-shirt, I felt myself frown slightly. "I don't have all of the pieces yet, but my working hypothesis is that the victim uncovered something — probably financial in nature — that Cardinal doesn't want or can't afford to have exposed. Without her research materials, though, I'm shooting in the dark; I might find a hint of whatever it was in the data Myrtle did give me."

"That feels like a long shot."

"Yes," I smiled, "but I've built cases around far less from the footnotes of a profit-and-loss statement."

"Don't you have the victim's laptop?"

"Nope," I sighed. "I have *some* paper files that we located in the victim's car, but so far, we've not been able to gain access — legally — to anything else, either in her home or in the cloud. The home part really pissed me off, too; the victim's mother read me the riot act for trying to violate her dead daughter's Constitutional rights."

"What did you find in the files you do have?"

I smiled slightly, for Sean had quite easily read himself into the case in the short time it had taken for us drive to Lake Buena Vista. "I've not actually reviewed them yet," I replied. "I'm loathe to admit this, but with the move to our new building the technology situation has been a bit unreliable. The crime scene nerds hadn't had a chance to scan anything into the case system before I left for Orlando; I'd hoped to review it while I waited for my return flight but haven't logged in yet."

"Then we're going into this a bit blind," Sean observed as he slowed to make the now-recognizable turn into the parking lot for the building we needed. That he'd set a new land speed record getting there went without comment. "Not something I like doing."

"Me either," I agreed. "And my megawatt smile didn't get me very far earlier, so that's, like, two strikes."

Sean pulled into a spot in the surprisingly empty lot and shut off the Mustang. "Maybe I'll provide just the turn of luck you've been waiting for."

"I'll settle for her fawning over your six-pack abs and well-defined biceps if it gives me anything I can use."

Sean laughed. "Glad to know I could be of service."

I paused with my hand on the door. "I thought this was a convertible?"

"It is," Sean replied, though his face shaded slightly. "I've, uh, not had the top down yet."

I looked at him askance. "How is it possible you drove all the way here without trying it out?"

"I *have* tried it out," he replied defensively.

"The dealership doesn't count."

Sean's face flamed a dark read. "Does to," he replied lamely.

"Man," I said, shaking my head, "you're making the rest of us sports car owners look bad. C'mon, let's see if we can work a little of our magic."

Sean followed me across the lot to the entrance for the building; I skipped the directory this time and simply went directly to the stairwell and the basement. My first clue that the case was about to become far more complicated came when we exited into the hallway and discovered the door to office for The Cardinal Group (Orlando) was cracked open; I came up short when I saw the lock had been sheared off. My hand immediately went to where my Glock would normally be and grasped at air, an uncomfortable reminder I was far from my normal jurisdiction. Looking at Sean, I could see he'd made the same inference from the destruction; he pulled out his phone and tapped at it, then nodded to let me know the video had begun to record. Using an elbow, I gently pushed the door further open.

"Myrtle? It's Chief Korsokovach. Are you injured?"

I waited a full four count before trying again, though deep in my heart I was reasonably sure I wasn't going to get a response. Pushing the door open wider with a toe, I carefully moved into the tiny reception area; the smell of what had happened hit my nose before I saw the slumped over figure behind the desk at the far end of the space. While not an expert by any stretch in blood spatter patterns, even my untrained eye could see that Myrtle had been sitting right where I'd found her earlier that day when she'd been shot; edging closer, I nodded grimly when I saw someone had made quite the mess digging the bullet out from the wall behind her.

There didn't seem to be a point to checking for a pulse from what was left of McKenna, but I did it all the same more for form than for anything else. It took but a moment to confirm the obvious, but once I did, I nodded at Sean who ended his recording. "This can't be a coincidence," he said softly.

"No," I agreed before my eyes went to the door that McKenna had disappeared through during my visit.

Seized with a hunch that needed to be explored, I moved to that side of the desk and used my elbow once more to carefully open the door; pushing it open with my toe, I wasn't all that surprised to find the space completely empty, save for a small cardboard box holding another Nortel phone. Shaking my head, I turned around and found Sean right behind me; his eyes went wide as he registered what *that* meant.

"What did she give you this morning, exactly?" he asked.

"A thumb drive," I sighed. "Which I've not had a chance to check yet, either."

"It's probably blank."

"No," I shook my head. "I'm sure it has *something* on it; they were expecting me, after all. Whatever is on it, though, is likely meaningless."

"Well, fuck," Sean breathed.

"Exactly," I sighed as I pulled out my iPhone. "Here's hoping Chief Gilbert has a friend out here," I said as I pulled my boss's name up from my contacts.

"Mike's address book is legion," Sean replied.

"True." Looking at Sean, I smiled slightly. "Well, you didn't quite bring me the stroke of luck I was hoping for, but I'll take it."

Sean frowned. "How do you figure?"

"Now I *know* I'm onto something..."

Eighteen
Orange County, Redux

I wasn't entirely sure what to make of the fact that Chief Gilbert took it completely in stride that I had landed myself in the middle of what appeared to be another murder, albeit on an entirely different coast; he'd quickly given me the name of his contact in Florida, then promised to reach out personally to them in order to vouch for my credentials. After adding the contact to my phone, I made the call to 9-1-1, then retreated with Sean to the exterior steps of the office building to await the arrival of the locals. The first to appear on the scene was an *extremely* junior deputy who looked barely old enough to have hit puberty, an impression that was reinforced by the sheer look of terror on his face when we confirmed the reason we'd called it in. Since it was clear this was the kid's first homicide, Sean and I subtly coached him on the proper steps to get the scene under control. Not wanting to step on any jurisdictional toes, we were pretty careful in our suggestions for how best to cordon off the scene; once he'd strung enough crime scene tape to have mummified nearly all of the Pharaohs entombed within the Valley of the Kings, I tactfully suggested he might want to commit our statements to the record. He was just finishing with Sean when a late model Ford Crown Victoria pulled into the lot, followed closely by two vans bearing the county seal on their sides; it wasn't much of a stretch to assume the boss had arrived, especially when the Crown Vic bypassed the parking lot proper and instead pulled onto the grassy sidewalk just in front of the entrance.

The most prominent feature of the petite woman who emerged from the sedan wasn't how well she wore the tan uniform of her department; despite my tastes lying on the other side of the aisle, I could still appreciate the fine lines of a female who had curves in all of the right places. No, it was actually the mountain of Dolly Parton-esque hair in the most extraordinary purple shade that really caught my attention; as the officer approached us, it became clear that her hair color wasn't consistent but rather had been dyed with an unusual gradient that made the middle sections seem three shades lighter. I assumed my expression had been telegraphing my thoughts when I saw the quirk of a smile appear on her lips; coming to a stop on the step just below us, she pulled off her sunglasses to reveal eyes of deep green that had been accented with a touch of light blue eyeshadow. On anyone else, it would have looked awful; on her, it was nothing short of perfect.

"Bernie Carver," she said simply. "I hear you're gifting me a dead body."

"Deputy Chief Vasily Korsokovach, Rancho Linda," I said as we showed her our badges and then each shook her hand. I was a little jealous that Sean's badge looked a bit shinier. "This is Commander Sean Colbeth from the Maine State Police; he's been working on my case as a consultant. I'm sorry to have to meet you like this, and yes, we do seem to have stumbled into something here."

Carver looked at Sean. "Colbeth? As in the Olympic swimmer?"

"Yes," he nodded.

Her eyes travelled over him for a moment. "Damn," she said appreciatively. "I see a lot of formers down here, and hardly any of them look as good as you."

"Formers?" I asked, trying not to smile at Sean's obvious discomfort.

"Former Olympians," she amended. "Especially swimmers. They seem to flock to Florida for training, then retire here. Especially in Central Florida. Something in the water, I think," she chuckled.

"Ah," Sean coughed.

Carver turned back to me. "Tell me about your case and why you landed in middle of my jurisdiction investigating it without so much as a how-do-you-do."

It wasn't the first time Sean had been recognized when we worked a case outside of our respective jurisdictions; oddly, that afternoon it grated on me I *hadn't*. I thought perhaps it was a reminder of what it had been like to work in his shadow all those years, something I had willingly done at the time just for a chance to be close to him. The epiphany that I could never go back to that hit me far harder than I expected, so it took me a moment to gather my thoughts; it didn't help that Carver's frown grew deeper the longer I paused. Trying to salvage myself, I smiled my model smile and tucked away my introspection for another more appropriate time.

"That's on me," I apologized. "I usually coordinate with LEOs when this sort of thing happens, but I've literally been on the go since Monday morning."

Her eyebrows went up. "This happens a lot to you, then?"

"More often than you might think," Sean rather unhelpfully added.

"*Anyway,*" I continued after shooting Sean a *thanks for throwing me under the bus* look, "I'm investigating the death of a journalist back in Rancho Linda. From what I've pieced together so far, she was working on an article about a business based back in California and may have stumbled onto something that led to her death." I nodded back toward the building behind us. "For oddball tax reasons that I haven't fully looked into yet, a part of that *same* organization was being run out of an office here in Lake Buena Vista. I flew out to obtain records pertaining to my case that the owner had agreed to provide."

Carver smiled slightly. "Didn't trust the old 'we'll email those to you' line, I take it."

"Exactly," I replied, returning her smile. "I was also hoping to get a better sense of why the office was truly here — something that is kind of hard to do remotely."

"I see. And the victim my people are now taking a look at? She worked here?"

"Yes," I nodded. "Myrtle McKenna. She was the COO for the organization."

"Did you get what you needed?"

I pointed to the young officer that had been the first to arrive. "I have no idea. McKenna gave me a USB stick allegedly containing the files I had asked for; I've not yet had a chance to review what was on it. I turned it over to your junior assuming it was now evidence in your investigation."

Carver nodded. "We'll make a copy for our records and then release it back to you," she said. "Would that be acceptable?"

"Completely."

"All right," she said as she started up the steps. "Better walk me through the scene."

I glanced at Sean who shrugged and then fell into line behind Carver; I followed along like we were on some sort of elementary school field trip. Stepping under one strip of tape, I waited for Sean to hold up the next strip so we could get into the main lobby; techs from Carver's crime lab had begun to work over that part of the scene, dusting for prints around the elevators and the door to the stairwell. She nodded at the tall gentleman that seemed to be in charge; much like Gina Carruthers, he appeared to be holding a state-of-the-art tablet onto which he was transcribing his notes as he walked the space. Pausing at the door to the stairwell, Carver turned toward us but not before digging multiple pairs of latex gloves from a side pocket of her uniform trousers. Handing each of us a set, she nodded back at the activity in the lobby.

"I presume you came through here?"

"Yes," I replied as I snapped the gloves on. "The space was empty, much as it was earlier this morning. Aside from The Cardinal Group in the basement, I got the sense from the rather sparse building directory the rest of the offices were mostly vacant."

"Not surprising," Carver said. "Disney used to lease a lot of space in LBV during their explosive growth in the 1990s; they've pretty much downsized now to whatever they can fit in their building on property. Universal did the same thing a few years ago."

"Must have made the lease attractive to The Cardinal Group, then," Sean observed.

"That or they scored a tax credit," Carver added. "Did you take the elevator?"

"No, the stairs."

"All right."

We waited for the tech to finish dusting the doorknob and then entered the stairwell; a moment later, we exited into the basement lobby. Pausing in the middle of the space, I pointed to the now wide-open door for The Cardinal Group's office. "I was standing about here when I noticed the door to the office was ajar; it had been closed during my morning visit."

"And that struck you as unusual?"

"Yes," I replied.

Carver walked over to the door and held the tape up so we could duck under it. "Then what?"

"I pushed the door open a bit with my toe and called out for McKenna," I answered. "Without my gun, I was feeling a bit cautious."

"Left it back at the hotel?"

"It's still in California," I answered. "On such a short turnaround, I didn't have the time to file the proper paperwork to take it with me."

Carver looked at Sean. "Mine's back in Maine," he said. "I'm officially on leave, so it seemed best to keep it locked up."

"Well, that rules out having to run ballistics on the two of you," she said, "though I'll probably still need to test for GSR just to be thorough."

"Understood."

"So, you called out to McKenna?"

"Yes, though honestly, I didn't expect an answer."

"Why?"

I glanced at Sean. "I was already suspicious she was going to ghost me," I replied. "The USB stick I mentioned? In theory, it only contains a portion of the data I wanted — assuming there's actually anything of use on it; I'd requested more when I'd met with her this morning. That prompted McKenna to make a phone call, after which she informed me it would take until this afternoon to retrieve it. I fully expected to find her MIA when I returned."

Carver smiled slightly. "Classic. Who did she call?"

"I have a hunch it was her boss, Anton Cardinal," I said. "But I'd need to see the phone logs to confirm it." It seemed best not to divulge at that point I'd snapped a photo of the number in question.

"I think we can provide that."

More techs were scouring the reception area; I was beginning to think the minivan they had arrived in had some properties of a circus clown car, for it hadn't seemed large enough to have held so many people. Two techs wearing dark overalls were carefully working over the dead body of McKenna; one had a tape measure and was determining the space between the seat and the blood spatter on the wall, while the other was carefully putting something nauseatingly amorphous into a small evidence bag with a pair of forceps. The door to the rear office had been propped open, and I could hear sounds of work going on back there as well. There was no question it was a well-oiled machine that Carver had deployed, though I wondered about the inference I could draw from that — namely, it was called into action rather frequently.

"Is this how you found the body?"

Carver's voice drew me back to our conversation. "Yes," I nodded. "She was slumped over just like that."

"You didn't move the body?"

"No. I checked for a pulse, but it was pretty clear it wouldn't have mattered at that point."

"Got it. Did you touch anything else?"

"Just the door to the rear," I replied. "With my elbow."

She looked at Sean. "And you?"

"Both doors to the stairwell," he answered. "Upstairs and the one down here. That's it."

"That's *it*?" Carver's eyes widened. "Are you sure?"

"Not our first rodeo," Sean chuckled. "You're welcome to take our prints, of course, but I think you'll find they're already on file. I also filmed us entering the space, if you'd like to see it."

"Indeed," she replied. "You two are a matched set, aren't you?"

"There are days," I chuckled, "but I think I'm the cuter one in this relationship."

Carver's eyes momentarily flicked to Sean. "I'm not so sure about that," she replied.

My eyebrows went up, but I kept the snarky comment that tried to leap from my lips at bay; fortunately, she wasn't my type — literally — so my ego easily withstood the assault. Still, I'd been getting vibes ever since Carver appeared that she seemed rather intensely focused on Sean. Glancing at Sean, I realized he seemed to also have picked up on that subtle undercurrent; my eyebrows went up further when I saw that strange half-smile he used to use when he flirted with Deidre on the deck of the pool at UEM form on his face.

What the fuck?

"I'm flattered, Madam," Sean replied, "but Vas has a far better tan."

Her eyes turned back to me, then down to the ring on my finger. "That he does," she nodded. "What did you do next?"

"We poked our heads into the rear office long enough to clear it, then called it in," I answered, then smiled a bit myself. "As much as I wanted to dig around what little was here, we instead went back upstairs and waited for the calvary to arrive."

"A wise choice. Anything else?"

"Other than giving your officer our statements? No."

"All right. How much longer will you be in Florida?"

"I was hoping to head back tomorrow," I replied. "I have an insanely early flight in the morning; I've already asked Sean to work this end of the investigation for me."

"I'm on my way to visit with my Dad," Sean said, answering the unspoken question we could both see on Carver's face. "He lives a bit south of Tampa; I'm taking an extended leave so I can spend Christmas with him and then be here for Vasily's wedding in January. It was a fortunate happenstance Vas was in Orlando as I crossed the state line into Florida."

Carver looked at me, then the ring on my finger again. "Congratulations."

"Thanks. I can change my flight if you need me to stay...?"

"I don't think that will be necessary," she replied. "We'll get you both tested for GSR and then you can get back to enjoying our Florida weather."

"The sights are definitely better than Maine," Sean said.

It was such a terrible pickup line that I had to turn away to hide my smile; *why* my best friend seemed to be flirting wasn't exactly an open question, though it did seem to cement where things stood between him and Suzanne. I realized I might need to huddle with Alejandro to see if any changes were in order for our guest list in January.

"I presume you're going to want access to our case file?" Carver asked.

"Yes," I nodded. "I'm happy to be reciprocal on that and share what we've got on the California end of things. I'll also want our coroner to coordinate with yours."

"Sounds like a plan." Carver said, then got a knowing smile. "Go ahead, ask."

"Your hair," I began. "Were you cosplaying? Maybe *Star Wars*?"

"Nicely done," she nodded slowly. "And sort of. My family celebrates Thanksgiving, Rebel Style."

"Rebel Style?" Sean asked, looking at me. "I've not heard of that."

Carver smiled warmly. "You must have led a sheltered life."

"You don't know the half of it," I laughed.

Nineteen
What Is It with Redeyes, Anyway?

By the time the detectives from the Orange County Sheriff's Office had finished with the two of us — and yes, the irony that the Florida version was far easier to work with than my future California overloads hadn't been lost on me — it was late enough that I graciously allowed Sean out of paying his debt to me and instead agreed to dinner at the hotel restaurant. That he was somewhat unwilling to admit that I had, indeed, won the quasi-swim meet was a point of contention that we discussed at length over an amazing prime rib and an even better bottle of Cabernet Sauvignon; by the time the plates of Key Lime pie had been removed, we'd also settled on what his role would be moving forward. With McKenna's extremely suspicious death, I figured it would be handy to have him hang around a few more days to act as my liaison; to that end, I swung past the reception desk in the lobby and had them extend my reservation through the middle part of the week so Sean could have a base of operations.

As early as my flight was the following morning, I knew I'd have a better chance of getting some sleep on the plane than trying to grab a few hours in the suite. Sean didn't seem all that anxious to head to bed, either, so we broke into the mini bar for more wine and then settled into the extremely comfortable couches in the living room area. Our conversation was open and free-flowing — and also managed to steer completely away from the true reason Sean had appeared in Orlando in the first place. Each time I tried to poke a little bit at it, he'd smile and deflect with a story about a case he'd worked after my departure to Rancho Linda, or a shared memory of our time at the Olympics. While we never addressed anything, by the time I was hiking my bags across the lobby to pick up my car from the valet, I had the distinct impression that he was actually in a better place than when he'd arrived; whether that had more to do with being pulled into a case than spending twenty-four hours with his best friend, I wasn't sure. I still felt like I was on unsteady ground when it came to diagnosing my friend's emotional health; Alex was far better at it than I, so I filed away my impressions so I could run them past my fiancé later.

The drive back to Orlando International was uneventful; at that ungodly hour, I had to leave the keys for the rental in the small overnight return box. I was a bit surprised at the long lines snaking into the TSA checkpoint, though the reason became apparent once I finally reached the agent checking IDs: whatever scheduling software they were using seemed to have assumed no one flew out at three in the morning, and therefore had only provided for a handful of personnel to run the various pieces of the operation. It was another in a long line of indicators I'd seen over the past four or five years that efforts to automate staffing in any situation — grocery stores, retail shops or even at my police department — all suffered from the same basic problem, that being the actual needs based on historical trends tended to be overridden by the budgetary concerns of the moment. In the end, the software was no better than the white-lined paper my old boss at the Newport Beach Lifeguard unit posted weekly on the front of his office door; while it had our schedules listed, there was always a note at the top that said *subject to change*, which it often did.

My flight boarded on time, and after munching on a reasonably decent breakfast of scrambled eggs and home fries, I asked the flight attendant for a pillow and then tried to get some rest. I didn't expect to drop off to sleep as easily as I did, though, given how much was on my mind; having been literally on the run since leaving Sean's place nearly a week earlier caught up with me, however, and made short work of the flight. Before I knew it, the attendant was gently shaking me on the shoulder so she could retrieve the pillow — and then I was on the ground, striding through the muted hubbub of the terminal at LAX. I found my Camaro right where I left it, paid the obscene amount of money for parking at the terminal and then worked my way around the airport so I could get to the 105. With the time change and the magic of a direct flight, I'd landed just a hair after five local time, well ahead of the worst of rush hour. It also helped that I was headed out of the city, though there were days now when I didn't think that mattered any longer. Traffic thinned appreciably when I shifted to the 710; once I'd turned onto the 91 East, I began to wonder whether to go to the office or instead head down to Anaheim for a proper shower and a clean change of clothes. As appealing as the option of going home was, the text I'd received from Chief Gilbert upon landing had been a stark reminder the clock was running on the two thugs currently cooling their heels at the Rancho Linda Police Station, so in the end, it wasn't really a hard decision. Catching my tired face in the rearview mirror, I knew I was running on fumes; still, the hot knot of anger that flamed into being each time I thought about what had happened to Alex was enough to chase away the worst effects of my fatigue.

The need for more caffeine forced me to sidetrack into the Starbucks perched beside the offramp for the 91; I didn't normally come in from that side of town, so it wasn't one of my regular haunts — not that any of the other ten thousand locations I swung through on a regular basis counted as such, either. Pulling into the parking lot, I took a moment to consider the very bland exterior of that particular location while I shut down the Camaro; it was a visible reminder that the chain had been busily remaking itself to seem less like the comfy coffee shop it once was and more like the kind of spot you'd find in the lobby of any four-star hotel. While I missed the original vibe of the place, the coffee -- while overpriced — remained the star attraction, one that made it worth suffering through whatever other growing pains might be taking place behind the scenes.

After placing my order for the largest size available of their featured holiday drink, I stepped over to the corner and contemplated the similarly bland holiday decorations that had been nonetheless carefully applied nearly everywhere. My head still thought it was Halloween, so seeing the red-and-green Christmas theming was a stark reminder I needed to get my act in gear and finish my scheming for Alejandro. Something he'd said to me months earlier had suddenly popped into my brain while I'd been in Orlando, and out of that, an idea had begun to form for a gift that I thought might have some deep meaning for my fiancé. I was a little afraid I'd waited too long to successfully pull off what I now wanted to do for him; in many ways, I felt like I'd been avoiding writing a term paper that was now mere hours from being due. Then again, some of my best grades had come from projects I'd completed literally at the eleventh hour; grabbing my coffee from the barista as it came out, I headed back to my car but not before making a mental note to sneak in a call to Alejandro's mother at some point during the day. If nothing else, she'd be able to confirm whether my idea was sound enough to pursue.

It took a few more minutes to climb into the hills surrounding the city to reach our new headquarters. The sun was still not quite up as I pulled into a spot beneath one of the mature trees, so the parking lot was awash in the strange warm glow from the LED lamps that dotted the area. Grabbing my backpack from the rear of the car, I locked it and headed for the law enforcement entrance, then used my ID to get inside. The smell of new paint and carpet still hung heavily in the air, but the modest amount of activity I found inside the booking corridor was the best evidence yet that operations were closer to being in full swing. I nodded at the sergeant behind the bulletproof plexiglass and then turned right at the end of the corridor to head toward the holding cells.

My badge got me through to another austere corridor that didn't look all that different than the one we'd had at the original office. There was a small, raised desk at the far end where the officer on duty was stationed; behind them, the gated entrance to the dozen holding cells that had been carved out of what had once been storage rooms for the original business. Ten pairs of doors were on the opposite wall; nine were interrogation rooms, with the final one at the end being our fancy all-electronic observation center. The irony that we had more holding cells than places to interview suspects wasn't lost on me, nor the fact that, somehow, the space had managed to be far smaller than our old one. It felt like a foreshadowing of what was to come, namely that anything having to do with suspects would likely be handled at the county facility in the very near future. I wasn't sure it was a change I was looking forward to, but also knew I was powerless to stop it. Mostly.

In keeping with the theme that our new headquarters were supposed to be state-of-the-art, small lights had been installed above each door on the interview side of the hallway; they could be illumi-nated with special colors to indicate what was currently going on inside. Most were off, but two were lit yellow — a flag that suspects were present but not (as yet) speaking to anyone from law enforcement. I had a suspicion as to which *particular* suspects were cooling their heels in those rooms, one that was confirmed as soon as I made my way over to the duty station and smiled at the geriatric officer sitting there; his face was mostly hidden behind a mustache that made him look like a grand-fatherly giant walrus.

"Morning, Ted," I said with as much enthusiasm as the caffeine had granted me. "I understand the pair that tried to beat up my fiancé are in holding."

Ted smiled — or at least, I *thought* he smiled. The mustache could hide a ton of sins. "They were. Chief Gilbert called down about an hour ago and had us move them into Interview 4 and 5."

I felt my eyebrows go up. "Either he's psychic or he was tracking my flight."

"Probably a bit of both," Ted replied. "The Chief's in observation and asked that you join him for a moment before you go in."

"I'm sure he did," I said. "What's your read on them?"

Ted looked thoughtful; he'd been with Rancho Linda long enough to have developed a keen sense of the sorts of people that landed in the rooms he managed. I'd learned early on that his insights could often be quite helpful. "Aside from the expensive suits — nothing off the rack about those, for sure — they seem like rather common thugs. We rarely get those here in Rancho Linda; more likely to see that in Los Angeles, honestly."

"Not local, then? Hired, maybe?"

Ted nodded. "You can order anything over the internet these days," he replied with a shrug. "Why not thugs?"

"Good point. Thanks."

It was just a few more steps to get to the observation center; knocking once, I opened the door to find Chief Gilbert sitting in one of the chairs facing the bank of monitors mounted on the far wall. A kid who looked like he was getting ready for a marathon session of *Call Of Duty* was seated beside him, wearing a full television producer-style headset barely visible in his wildly messed up hair; he tapped away at a keyboard while his eyes flicked across the various screens of information that were reflecting in his rimless glasses, so fully engrossed that he didn't even acknowledge my presence. Gilbert turned at my arrival and stood; he was holding a small manilla folder which he handed to me.

"We've got about four hours before they get arraigned," he said without preamble.

"And good morning to you, too, Chief," I laughed. "You're in damn early."

"It happens when a member of my senior staff gets themselves involved in a murder on another coast," he sighed. "Considering I'm still going through the intra-agency request for assistance that your peer in Lake Buena Vista sent, I'm not going to ask how your trip went."

"Probably for the best."

"Especially since it emphasized you were the one who found the dead body," he continued. "Was it related to this case?"

"Yes," I replied. "The victim was the COO for The Cardinal Group; she was killed a few hours after meeting with me."

"Definitely connected," he sighed. "Damn."

"My sentiments exactly."

"Are you going to have to go back out?"

"I don't think so, no," I replied. "Sean happened to be in the Orlando area when I arrived, and he's agreed to take point there as our rep."

Gilbert cocked his head. "Why the hell is he in Florida?"

"He's taking an extended vacation to spend Christmas with his dad," I replied, shading the truth slightly. "So unless things get really thorny, I think we'll be good."

"All right. Make sure he signs the latest version of our consultant agreement; the city's general counsel gave me grief after you, uh, forgot to have him sign the last one."

"Did I do that?" I asked innocently.

"I won't dignify that with an answer." There was a long pause. "Ordinarily, I would counsel against what you are about to do," he began, addressing the elephant in the room.

"And yet, the suspects appear to already be in the interview rooms, awaiting me."

"They are, and only because I am *trusting* you to be professional," Gilbert replied. "No one would blame you for wanting to... explain to them... how badly they erred in trying to rough up your fiancé, but you know better than most how that would go down with the courts."

I smiled slightly before nodding at the screens. "So, unplugging the cameras is out, then."

"Most definitely." Gilbert paused again. "Alex is still planning on pressing charges?"

"I presume so, but I've not talked to him since I returned."

"Okay." Gilbert paused a third time; it was clear he was choosing his words more carefully than normal, which sent up all sorts of flares for me. "Do you want a protective detail assigned to Alex?"

I blinked. "I'd not thought about it," I replied honestly. "And had frankly assumed this was a one-off."

"Maybe you're not seeing the whole picture here, Vas, but from where I'm standing, this feels a hell of a lot like you've landed in the middle of some sort of weird quasi-organized crime situation. You might want to consider if there will be any fallout from questioning people who from all appearances seem like some sort of enforcement duo; we send them to the County Jail, there's a good chance you might get another visit."

I leaned against the wall. "Maybe we want that," I mused. "It might tell me something."

"More than you *already* know?" Gilbert asked. "Are you honestly telling me your predilection for getting into dangerous situations has expanded to allow putting your fiancé into harm's way, too?"

"No, I'm not," I said, irritated slightly that my boss would even think that. "And he's got me—"

"You can't protect him *and* run the investigation," Gilbert interrupted.

"Maybe it's national take-your-fiancé-to-work-week," I replied gamely.

"Right."

"Fine," I sighed. "Go ahead but try to keep them in the background if you can. The last thing I need is him not being able to do *his* job because we've got a cordon of protection around him."

"I'll do one better," Gilbert replied. "A couple of our recent recruits look like they should still be in college; they'll do a bit of undercover work on this one and blend in with the students."

"That might work. I'll call Alex and let him know... hang on," I said as I saw his knowing grin. "You've already got this in motion, haven't you?"

"Since last night," Gilbert chuckled. "I'll be damned if anything happens to a family member on my watch."

I smiled slightly. "If I weren't so pissed I'd say thank you."

"Roger that," he laughed. "Touch base when you get done with the interrogations? I'll be upstairs... enjoying the view from my new office while I consider how much it's costing me."

"Absolutely," I laughed.

I exited the observation room and randomly selected the nearer of the two interview rooms as my first target; pausing outside the door, I opened the folder and briefly scanned the items Gilbert had included. Aside from the standard ten-print cards, I appeared to also have hard-copy versions of their motor vehicle records and, more impressively, a bit of a criminal dossier. Both seemed to have previously been guests of the County for brief stints, serving out time for prior assault and battery charges. Flipping up a page, my eyebrows went sky high when I saw the photos of their last victim; right then and there I decided not to tell Alex who he had accidentally tangled with — ever.

So much needless violence, I thought, anger building again as I reached for the handle. *I feel like I've stepped back five decades.*

Pushing the door open, I strode into the small room and immediately came up short. Having expected to see some version of the MVD photo sitting across the table from me, I wasn't prepared for the deep black eyes and severely broken nose that had appeared to have been hastily splinted by an EMT; the suit jacket was slung over the spare guest chair, exposing an expensive looking white button down stained with blood and torn in one spot. More amazingly, perhaps, was that the tie was still properly tied in a full Windsor knot, offset slightly by the dried blood it sported as well. Jet black hair that had originally been slicked back had shrugged off the holding power of whatever product had been used, allowing it to fall forward to frame an otherwise handsome face. That the face was scowling did little to detract from that fact, though the sheer look of malice blazing from the dark eyes kind of chilled the mood.

Pulling out the chair on my side, I sat down and then placed the closed folder on the desk. Folding my arms against the muscle t-shirt I was *still* wearing — the laundry service at the hotel had been terrible — I stared at the guy for a few long moments. The goon matched my move and folded his arms against his button down; he took the extra step of flexing slightly as he did so. I tried — and failed — not to roll my eyes as the not-so-subtle *Mano a Mano* move.

The guy snorted; it would have been more effective had it not sounded more like a wheeze. "So, you're the fucking boyfriend," he said as he shook his head sadly. "Pathetic."

"Fiancé," I corrected, unsurprised that he'd gone directly to a topic he thought might rattle me. I nodded at his broken nose. "And are you using 'fucking' in the literal sense? Or as a colorful adjective? Because if it's the former, I might have some questions about your grammatical skills."

He stared at me. "What the fuck are you talking about?"

I nodded. "Colorful adjective it is," I smiled. Flipping the folder open, I sorted through the papers until I found the one from the MVD that had a matching photo. "Herbert, is it?" I asked as I scanned through the demographics on the page. "That's an old name. Was your mom a fan of the former President?"

"President? Of what?"

My eyes came up from the page. "The United States, Mr. Colebrook. Or were your history studies as poor as your English curriculum?"

"I got out of high school."

"I'd love to see *that* transcript," I smiled. "Must have gotten straight-As in thuggery."

Colebrook frowned slightly but kept his own council.

"I know the officer who placed you into this room already made you aware of your rights," I continued. "Before we begin, I'd like to re-confirm you don't wish to have representation with you."

He stared at me for a few moments — long enough for me to

wonder if he was actually a poorly programmed artificial intelligence struggling to make sense of what I'd just said. "Do what?"

I sighed. "Do you want your lawyer, Mr. Colebrook?"

"I got rights."

"Yes, you do," I nodded. "Are you invoking them?"

"What?"

"Your rights," I repeated, feeling like I was stuck inside a weird version of an Abbot and Costello skit. "Are you invoking your rights?"

"Which ones?"

I looked at the guy sitting across from me and slowly began to nod. "Seriously," I sighed as I closed the folder and stood. "I'm going to step into the next interview room for a few minutes and see if your partner in crime also seems to be playing the role of a low-IQ muscle for hire; while I'm in there, my staff will be taking a deeper dive into your background." I smiled slightly as I moved to the door. "It would be best to talk to me now before I uncover your Mensa membership, Mr. Colebrook."

"I don't know what that is."

"That might be the first truthful thing you've said," I replied. "How long have you worked for Anton Cardinal?"

"I don't know who that is."

"I see." I turned and leaned against the door. "Do you work for The Cardinal Group, then? Or some sort of outside firm?"

"I'm self-employed," was the nasally answer. "Private security."

"Ah," I nodded. "An extremely popular profession in Southern California. Who are your clients?"

"I don't share names."

"Oh, come on," I smiled wider. "You must have protected *someone* famous. Impress me."

"My clients are private."

I wandered back to the desk. "Or you don't have any. How long have you worked for Anton Cardinal?"

"I've already told you—"

"Yeah, yeah," I sighed as I put my hands on the back of the chair. "And I still don't believe you."

"Then that's your problem, isn't it?"

"Not entirely," I replied. "So, if you don't actually work for The Cardinal Group, who paid you to deliver a message? I have a hard time thinking you were doing a favor for someone," I added, then paused when I saw the slight twitch on his face. "Maybe I'm being a bit too literal here. Who *asked* you to deliver a message?"

Colebrook shifted in his seat uncomfortably; it was hard not to smile at the subtle confirmation I might have scored a glancing blow. "I'm not sure I understand what you mean."

"I'm not surprised," I said. "It must have been a rather large favor you owed someone, considering what you had to do when it was called in." I reappraised Colebrook for a moment. "You *worked* — past tense — for The Cardinal Group, didn't you? Before you went private?"

The fidgeting became more pronounced. "Maybe," he answered grudgingly.

"Did you do security for Cardinal?"

"Maybe."

"I'm going to take that as a yes," I said, feeling the slight tingle that I was heading in the right direction. "And you left to, what, create your own firm?" I asked. "I'm wondering now if I'm going to find your name on the list of subcontractors Cardinal uses."

"I don't work for Cardinal—"

"I believe you," I interrupted. "I also believe you're being paid by a company that *is* working on behalf of Cardinal, so while it's *technically* true you aren't working for Cardinal, you really are." I eyed him again. "It takes capital to set up a new firm," I continued. "The paperwork you have to file for the State of California *alone* can run into the thousands. How did you pay for that?"

"I had savings."

"I'm sure," I smiled. "Am I going to find some large deposits augmenting those savings when I pull your bank account transactions?"

"You can't do that—"

"Oh yes," I nodded. "I totally can. You've been quite helpful, actually; I think I have enough probable cause now to dig around in your financials, those of your firm and the one that hired you." I leaned a bit closer. "And when I uncover the direct line between you and Anton Cardinal, your options, Mr. Colebrook, are going to shrink dramatically. Or," I smiled as evilly as I could, "put another way, the length of time you'll be inside a jail cell will increase."

"I haven't said anything!" he protested. "I'm not a rat!"

My eyebrows went up. "There's a term I've not heard in a while," I said before nodding to the door. "I'm about to leave so I can talk to your partner; you have until I close the door to—"

There was a quick knock at the door before it was pushed open, violently. Turning, my eyes narrowed when I saw the suited figure bustle into the interrogation room and move over to the seat beside Colebrook; while it wasn't anyone I had dealt with before, the leather briefcase and Madison Avenue slickness screamed *criminal defense attorney* — and also, pretty much, meant the interview was over. Narrowing my eyes further, I wondered a bit at the timing; Colebrook and his partner had been at the station since being transferred to our custody on the day Alejandro was attacked. While I wasn't sure they were tracking my suspects, someone — and I had a decent idea who — was tracking *my* movements, and had correctly guessed when the interrogation would take place. The only thing they hadn't counted on was my early arrival at the station; I saw a unique opportunity here to confirm my suspicions about who might be orchestrating everything.

"Hello," I said as I reached over to shake the hand of the new addition. "Deputy Chief Vasily Korsokovach."

The lawyer declined to take my hand. "This interview is over. You will be releasing my client immediately."

"Not likely," I observed. "He's being charged with first degree assault, and the arraignment will be happening later today. You can talk release options with the judge."

"There won't be any arraignment," the lawyer replied smugly. "I've read the complaint and there's hardly enough there for a misdemeanor let alone a felony; besides, it took place in Irvine, not Rancho Linda. You have no jurisdiction."

I cocked my head. "How do you figure?" I asked. "Did you skip over the extradition memo?"

"The... what?"

I sighed again. "I'm beginning to question the quality of your law degree, but the short version is that Irvine transferred the investigation to Rancho Linda." I paused. "It aligns with one we already had in progress."

"I see," the lawyer replied — but it seemed unlikely from his expression that he truly did. "If you don't capitulate, we'll amend our civil action to include an obstruction complaint against your department."

"Civil action?" I asked, frowning.

"We're suing the so-called victim for defamation."

"Really," I said. "And who is this 'we' you are referring to?"

"I'm not at liberty to discuss who hired me."

"Which tells me everything I need to know," I smiled as I moved back to the doorway. "I'll give you a few minutes to speak to your client in private, but then he goes back into holding until the judge is ready to see him."

"I demand that you release him!"

"Noted," I nodded as I exited the room. Chief Gilbert was coming down the hallway toward me. "That was fun," I said, rolling my eyes for emphasis.

"I could tell." Gilbert nodded at the other interview room. "He's got a lawyer, too."

"I figured." Glancing back at the room I'd just left, I folded my arms against my chest. "All things being equal, I think I've managed to confirm that I touched a nerve. A civil suit? Really?"

"Posturing?" Gilbert asked. "Or are they really going after Alex, legally?"

"Probably the former, but I'll have to assume the latter." I thought for a moment. "We're on solid ground holding them until arraignment," I continued. "And no judge is going to set bail for muscle like that. They'll be a guest of the County for a bit methinks."

Gilbert arched an eyebrow at my word choice but let it slide. "Unless he has a good lawyer."

"There's that," I nodded slowly. "That means I should anticipate a follow-up visit from our friend in there, just in case. Guess it's a good thing I agreed to your protection detail for Alex."

"Indeed, it was," Gilbert smiled thinly. "Though I wonder if I should beef it up a bit."

"You saw that guy's nose, right?" I asked. "I think we'll be fine."

"Still," Gilbert added quietly. "It might be wise to be careful for a bit."

"You know me—"

"Which is why I'm worried," Gilbert interrupted with a long-suffering sigh.

"I hear Pepto-Bismol is on sale this week at Walgreens," I replied brightly as I started walking toward the exit. "You might want to stock up."

TWENTY
RECHARGING

Somewhat flagging after the last of the caffeine had worked its way through my system, I found I had zero desire to dig through the case in my still as yet fully unpacked office; the desire for a hot shower and fresh change of clothes — not to mention the possibility of a quick nap — was too much to ignore, so I logged into the virtual in/out board for the department and marked myself as *remote* for the remainder of the day. It wouldn't stop anyone from reaching out to me, of course, but it did give me some hope I might be able to get a handle on what I was facing with a minimum of disruption.

By the time I pulled onto the 57 to head back toward Anaheim, though, I found I was smack in the middle of rush hour and all of the hell that entailed; it was clear my quick trip home was going to be anything but. Trying hard not to roll down the window and scream, I instead punched at the various presets on my satellite radio until I found the Disco station I often turned to when I was feeling out of sorts. While not anything I had grown up listening to, I'd spent enough time on the club scene over the years to appreciate how a good backbeat could make even the worst day seem palatable. I had just begun to tap my finger in time to an old ABBA tune when the radio cut out so Siri could announce an incoming call; my eyebrows went up when I saw who it was.

"Gina," I answered with a smile. "Is everyone working the early shift today in Rancho Linda?"

"No," she laughed. "Only the hard-core folks. Are you back in California?"

"Got in this morning."

"How did it go?"

"Well," I replied, "I've got another dead body on my hands, if that tells you anything."

"Shit," she breathed. "Related to your case?"

"I think so, yes. Sean Colbeth agreed to work that end of it for me so I could get back out here."

"That's convenient," Gina replied. "Why was he in Florida?"

"It's a long story," I chuckled. "Involving fracturing relationships and absent fathers. I'll have to fill you in over drinks at some point."

"I can't wait. Do you have a second? It sounds like you're driving."

"I'm attempting to get back to my condo," I replied, "without killing anyone. So yes, I can talk. What's up?"

"A few things," she replied. "First, the network is now up and running here at Headquarters; with all of the equipment finally connected, we were able to update your file with our results."

"That's excellent news!"

"It would be," she sighed. "The lighting grid on this floor blew out late yesterday afternoon; apparently, it couldn't take all of our machines running plus someone making popcorn in the break room's microwave. The Facilities team is currently trying to figure out how to undo the strangely byzantine circuitry for this building, but there's no ETA on when it might be fixed. My team is running around with headlamps and flashlights; feels a bit like we're in one of those post-apocalyptic movies where the power is never going to come back."

"One step forward, two back," I groaned. "Sorry."

"I hate to say this, but I really miss our old spot."

"So do I. You think they'll let us move back in?"

"I heard the bulldozers had already begun plowing the building over," she replied.

"Just like Cortés," I sighed. "Burning the damn boats to keep us focused on moving forward."

"Technically, he scuttled them," Gina replied. "But point well taken. Anyway, we also finally ran the prints we collected at the scene and from the victim's car."

"Anything interesting?"

"It depends," she said. "We confirmed that the site supervisor's prints were on the key safe at the construction site but had no match to another set we uncovered. That same set was present in the victim's car — on the steering wheel, the door handle and the trunk."

"Our killer?"

"Seems likely," she agreed. "I hesitate to add that we were able to get some partials from the forklift; they were pretty poor specimens, but we did manage to get a four-point match to the unknown from the safe and car."

"I can't take that to court," I mused as I swerved to avoid a minivan that had pulled blindly into my lane. "But it might still come in handy. I also find it interesting that we even *found* an unknown set of prints."

"Sort of makes the killing feel spur of the moment, doesn't it?" Gina asked.

"It does. I presume you've run those through all of the normal systems?"

"Every last one. No hit, nowhere. Which is not unusual if the person in question had no reason to be on file."

I thought about that for a moment. "We took exclusion prints from everyone at the site, right?"

"We did."

"I'm tempted to have you send a tech over to The Cardinal Group to collect more, but somehow, I suspect the current CEO is going to balk at participating. I might be able to sweet talk my favorite judge into a warrant, though, since it was their construction site."

"Good luck with that," Gina chuckled. "Let me know if the warrant comes through."

"Will do."

"One other thing," she continued. "Per our conversation earlier, I had one of the geeks pull the GPS log on the victim's phone; while the data is rather extensive – another reason I fear privacy no longer exists these days – we focused on tracing her movements in the hours leading up to her death."

"I keep intending to turn location tracking off," I said.

"Good luck if you try."

"Any surprises?"

"That's more your domain than mine," Gina laughed. "I *can* say she didn't seem to be terribly mobile during that period, though. Pretty much stayed in Rancho Linda, bouncing between the address you've listed in the file as her mother's, Vons Supermarket, the branch of First Bank of Southern California downtown and the construction site where we found the phone."

I frowned slightly. "That sort of tracks; I got the impression she hasn't reported physically to work in a while. Those locations give off a full remote worker vibe for sure."

"Well, for what it's worth, the entire thing has been uploaded to the case system; you can paw through the timings and try to make something more of the data than we did."

"Oh joy," I rolled my eyes. "More data to troll through."

"You know you love it."

"I'll never admit to that," I laughed. "Anything else?"

"Not yet, but the day is early."

"All right. Thanks, as always."

"My pleasure."

The exit for Katella appeared just as I hung up from my conversation with Gina. I sent out a solid prayer of thanks when I *finally* turned into the garage and tapped my fob on the reader; descending to the level where we had our spots, I found to my delight the bright yellow New Beetle belonging to Alex was still present. Sliding the Camaro in behind it, I grabbed my swim backpack and headed to the elevator lobby, hoping beyond hope that I might be able to steal a few minutes with my fiancé before he had to leave for work.

A sense I might be walking into something unexpected hit me hard when I went to put my key into the door of our condo; a fragrant fir Christmas wreath had appeared, fully decorated with glass ornaments bearing cheerful Disney characters in festive garb. Pushing the door open, the scent of freshly baked gingerbread immediately wafted toward me, and I paused to take a deep, appreciative breath. Growing up, our housekeeper had baked gingerbread and other goodies around the holidays, one of the few parts of my former life in Southern California I'd truly missed once I'd moved to Maine. I'd tried to make up for it by cleaning out whatever Calista's Bakery had in stock the first week of December while I'd been living in Windeport, but as good as they were, they hadn't really measured up. We'd been in Maine last Christmas, so I'd not had a chance to source anything yet in California; as I dropped my backpack in the half-bath, I thought perhaps I needn't look any further.

Following my nose like the intrepid detective I was, I found Alex in the kitchen huddled over our stand mixer and mumbling something in Spanish. My eyebrows went up when I saw he was dressed in his standard diving gear; his luscious mound of black curly hair had been pulled back by a favorite Nike kerchief in white, matching the flour stains I could see on his dark microfiber shorts. Aside from whatever was occupying his attention in the bowl of the mixer, two pots were happily bubbling on the stovetop, and a wire rack next to the sink had at least a dozen small cookies on it; the vague smell of peanut butter made me think they might be destined to be topped with a Hershey's Kiss. Most surprisingly of all, a traditional coffeemaker had materialized on the counter and appeared to have a freshly brewed pot ready to go.

Moving up behind Alex, I slowly encircled him with my arms and nibbled at his neck; the faint taste of cinnamon clung to his toffee skin, enticing me to nibble a bit more. He leaned into me, then turned so he could plant a proper kiss on my lips. "You're back sooner than I expected," he said.

"It was always an out-and-back," I replied.

I felt a frown form as I took in his face; his left eye was still a bit puffy, speaking to how swollen it had to have been a day earlier. The bruises around and below it made him look like he'd been on the wrong end of a prize fight decision; it didn't appear he'd gotten any stitches, though. I tentatively reached over and touched his cheek; the slight wincing I saw from Alex told me enough that I decided it might be best not to ask any further questions. It was harder not to comment on the matching bruises on either bicep; clearly, he'd understated just how badly he'd been manhandled. Taken in context, the manic baking began to make more sense.

"I'm glad you're home," Alex smiled.

"The gingerbread smells good," I said.

"Should be ready for testing in about ten minutes," he said after glancing at the timer on the stove.

"Happy to take one for the team," I smiled. "Where did that wreath come from?"

"The North Pole, silly," he laughed as he returned his attention to the bowl. "Along with everything else."

"There's *more*?"

"Check out the living room."

I popped back out of our kitchen and rounded the breakfast bar; the cabinets overhanging the counter had obscured just what sort of winter wonderland my fiancé had conjured up. In the brief amount of time I'd been away, the entire space had been completely transformed; a modest tree sat in the corner beside the sliding doors, fully decorated and sedately lit with LED lights of red and green. An eye-popping stack of wrapped packages had been tucked beneath the tree, carefully positioned to mimic the most romantic Christmas Card photo I'd ever seen. Garland had been strung over the slider, with more strands of LED lights woven into it; on the wall beneath our flatscreen television, two Disney-themed stockings were hanging on impressive temporary hooks. The way mine was bulging told me I was much further behind in my holiday shopping than I realized. A small advent wreath had been positioned on the breakfast bar, holding the five candles for the season; in a nod to our feline family member, the candles were fake but otherwise still quite impressive. I had to search my memory to remember the correct order for lighting them. One side table held what looked like a small crèche; the well-worn figurines bespoke its history as a family treasure. The *pièce de résistance* was sitting atop the coffee table — a complete winter village with working lights that had to have taken years to assemble.

"Holy shit," I breathed.

Alex appeared at my shoulder. "Is it okay?" he asked, his voice betraying some concern. "I was worried—"

"It's beautiful," I interrupted him. "And amazing and one hundred percent you. I love it."

"Good," he breathed a sigh of relief. "I probably should have warned you how much I'm into Christmas."

"And spoil the surprise? I think not," I laughed as I kissed him. "Though it feels a bit early."

"*Mi amor*, it's already December."

"Then I am wildly behind in my shopping. Where on earth were you storing all of this?" I asked. "Unless I was completely bewitched by your beauty at the time, I feel like you only had a few boxes when you moved in."

"Most of this is new," he said. "I did have the crèche with me; the village arrived yesterday." Alex smiled fondly. "My mother decided it needed a new home and shipped it out."

"It's incredible!"

"And has a ton of memories," Alex replied as the timer on the stove went off.

We moved back to the kitchen so he could check on the cookies. "As much as I love finding you here baking, shouldn't you be getting ready for work?"

Alex smiled. "I was in a fight, remember? I've been given a few days to recover from my injuries, such as they are."

I looked at him askance. "That must have riled your boss."

"About the only upside to this whole thing," he laughed as he pulled the tray of gingerbread from the oven, "aside from you arriving unexpectedly."

I wrapped my arms around his waist and nibbled at his neck again. "Happy to help."

"I can tell," he chuckled as he tried to work around me and move the cookies to the wire rack. Putting the baking sheet into the sink, he twisted around inside my arms. "Someone is feeling frisky."

"Can you blame me?" I asked as I pulled his face closer. "Celibacy is kind of hard for me. "

Alex dropped his eyes meaningfully to my waistline. "I can tell," he repeated.

"How long before those cookies are cool enough to test?"

"Long enough," he replied quietly before pressing his lips to mine.

We left a trail of clothing all the way to the master bedroom; I spared but a glance for the *second* Christmas tree Alex had snuck into the corner of the space before pressing him onto the comforter atop our bed. Working my way down the small groove between his pectorals, I discovered just how erotic the mixture of baking spices I was tasting with each kiss could be; reaching the edge of his happy trail, I paused long enough to look up the amazing contours of his chest to gauge how I was doing. Leaning on his elbows, he'd thrown his head back and closed his eyes, clear evidence that he was working hard to keep from going too far, too fast. Smiling wickedly, I moved further south and began to focus on other parts of his anatomy that appeared all too willing to accept my attention; the slight moan from high above me as I delicately kissed a particularly sensitive portion told me I wasn't the only one who'd been feeling frustrated.

Slipping upwards against his now damp skin, I pressed myself into him and felt a shudder beneath me; working that corner of his neck as deliciously slowly as I could, I felt his hand slowly encircle me, a leading indicator that I was not going as fast as he wanted. I returned the favor, and then was surprised when he began to grind against me with an unbridled urgency. Feeling a bit devilish — and not willing to let myself go quite yet — I gently rolled onto my back, flipping our positions and forcing Alex to adjust. Breathing hard, he pushed himself up and then straddled my thighs; his face was flushed, and sweat had begun beading along his forehead. The sly smile I saw appear gave me pause, then he reached over to his side of the bed and rustled through the drawer to come up with the small bottle of lube he kept there. Squeezing some out onto a palm, I tried not to react when he slowly — deliciously slowly — used it to coat every square inch of my cock. Tossing the bottle aside, he repositioned again so he could lower himself onto me; there was a momentary pause, and then I was suddenly inside of him, struggling to maintain my control. Alex must have seen my expression, for his sly smile widened a bit; with just a slight movement of his hips, he was able to keep my full attention but not allow me enough friction to get to release. My eyes widened when I realized I'd been outfoxed; not to be outdone, I curled upwards and pulled his face back to mine, trying — and failing — to shift him. Kissing him with a fierceness that told him I was on the verge of going fully feral, Alex returned the favor, peppering my neck with small kisses that felt electric against my slick skin.

Pushing himself back up, he shifted slightly and then began to move with an earnestness that told me the end was near. I managed to reach down and ensure that I assisted him in any way I could; within seconds, I felt the twinge that there would be no further holding back. Arching my body upwards, I fisted the comforter as waves of ecstasy washed over me; Alex shuddered nearly simultaneously, then fell onto me, completely spent. I wrapped my arms around his torso and hugged him even closer, relishing the nearness of him while basking in the afterglow of our lovemaking.

Once our breathing returned to normal, Alex opened his beautiful eyes and looked at me. "Welcome home."

I kissed him before replying. "I may have to travel more often if this is the sort of reception I'll get upon return."

"Or," he breathed as he leaned up and nibbled at my earring. "You could stay home more, and we could do this again. And... again."

"I'm — oh *shit*, Alex — working remotely today, so we could test drive that option," I said, aware that he seemed to be re-awakening my libido again. The fact I was ready so soon for a second act was interesting.

"Good," he replied as he moved down to a pectoral and then began to work over a nipple.

"I — *fuck!* — should log into my computer, though."

"Right this minute?" he asked.

"Maybe not..."

TWENTY-ONE
REMOTE WORK DAY

Somewhat fortunately, by the time I did manage to log onto my computer much later that morning, nothing significant had developed other than confirmation the case system had finally become functional. I left instructions to be called immediately if that changed, ran through the shower and then staked out a position on the couch in the living room so I could peruse the files on my MacBook. As the sheer volume of what I had under my fingertips became clear, I was rather thankful I'd opted to do it from the comfort of my condo; having fresh cookies close at hand only added to that sentiment. While I waited for the case system to load, I set the laptop on the cushion beside me so I could track down the USB stick Myrtle McKenna had given me; it was still in my swim backpack, carefully wrapped in a plastic evidence bag from the Orange County (Florida) crime scene unit. True to her word, Bernie had her tech make a copy of the stick's contents before handing it back to me for my case. Sitting back down on the couch, I crossed my legs and then went about entering the stick into *our* evidence file, then swore at myself for leaving the proper dongle in my work backpack. Getting up off the couch for a second time, I trotted into the bedroom and rifled through my cords and cables to come up with the right adapter, then folded myself back into position once again. A small plate of iced gingerbread cookies had also magically appeared on the side table, nestled into a tall mug of steaming coffee. Smiling, I took a sip of the amazing brew and only managed to snarf down two of the cookies before returning my attention to the laptop.

I already knew from having watched the Florida crime scene tech download the device that it was overflowing with more than sixty gigabytes of data; it didn't take long for it to transfer to my laptop, but uploading it to the office over the VPN felt a bit like waiting for paint to dry. I amused myself by checking into the files that Gina's team had already uploaded for me; scanning the index they had created, it seemed a rather eclectic set of information that on the face of it, didn't appear connected to anything in particular. So, I did what I always did and simply started at the very beginning and began to read through all it, one page at a time.

The first file contained genealogical information on the Cardinal family, tracing the forbears of Anton back to the *Mayflower*; it was an interesting piece of trivia, especially since the name didn't feel especially apropos for a Pilgrim. Aside from being background that could be used in any article Grandchester had planned, I had a hard time understanding why she'd pulled it together. Setting it aside, I opened a file that contained newspaper clippings from *The Orange County Register* dating back forty years; most were business articles about The Cardinal Group, including one that covered their initial formation under Konstantyn Cardinal. I smiled slightly at the obligatory half-page photo that showed the patriarch sitting behind the controls of a large bulldozer, staged to look as though he were actually doing the excavating at one of his construction sites; turning the page, I wasn't surprised to see a second, smaller photo of young Anton — all of perhaps six years old — wearing an oversized hardhat while shoveling dirt into a hole.

Looks like the internship program started early, I thought. *Poor kid.*

Returning to the main list of folders, I clicked into the next one and found another set of articles, culled from a variety of sources; some were local papers, like the *Register* or the *Times*, but the majority came from national business magazines such as *Fortune* or papers like the *Wall Street Journal*. Sorting through the images of the articles had me flashing back to an economics class I'd had to take as an undergraduate; our final project had involved pouring through mountains of data to create an economic forecast for the State of Maine, a mind numbing exercise I'd only managed to get through with the assistance of an extremely sexy wide receiver who'd had a surprising head for numbers. That he was also handy in other ways had been an amazing side benefit — one that had gotten us off track during more than a few late night "study" sessions in his private dorm room. Looking out the window of our balcony for a moment, I smiled slightly at the recollection of nearly getting caught sneaking out of his building so I could get to swim practice on time; the football team had been on lockdown in preparation for a game, so visitors (of any kind) had been forbidden. Focusing back on the laptop, I made a mental note to see if he was still coaching at that small school in upstate New York; his NFL career had run through several teams before a back injury sidelined him permanently less than six years out from graduation. I wasn't sure if that was a good run or not for someone in his position.

My eyes flicked over the various articles, scanning the text without really registering what I was seeing; much like the genealogy material I'd already gone through, it felt like Grandchester had been trying to build out a thorough background to The Cardinal Group as well. Though shaded by each publication's particular perspective, to an article they all wound up predicting a bright future for the real estate developer; those reviews became even more glowing once the firm landed in the hands of the founder's (then) young son, Anton. Several toward the end of the virtual stack even had photos of Anton in poses atop equipment that were clearly intended to mimic the ones taken of Konstantyn years earlier; the decided lack of any highlighting of further generations being prepped for the future hinted at Anton's current status as a family man, and made me think back to the snapshot I'd seen of him with Grandchester at Angels Stadium. Staring at the photo of Anton sitting behind the controls for a backhoe, I wondered a bit at why the two of them hadn't ultimately gotten together; if the diamond on Grandchester's hand had been any indication, the relationship had been pretty serious at some point.

Shifting screens for a moment, I punched up the *Orange County Register* and immediately realized I had no way to get to the back issues through their website; searching for a possible engagement announcement was going to require a visit to our library, it seemed. Returning to the case system, I stared for a long moment at that last picture of Anton; given how he looked older than the version in the Angels Stadium photo, but not as old as the guy I'd seen in person a few days earlier, it had to have been staged about the time he'd taken control of the company.

Six years or so ago is what Peg said, I thought as I backed up the reader enough to catch the date of the article. *That meshes with when this was published. A bit of PR to assure the world there were no changes coming; but when was the actual transfer? Grandchester must have that here somewhere...*

Backing out to the top-level folders again, I scanned the names of them and randomly selected another, hoping it might lead to any information the reporter had gathered about the transition. I lucked out and discovered a treasure trove of articles, though most focused on the palace intrigue that led to Anton taking over; my eyebrows went up when I discovered the father had not left the organization willingly, but in fact had been pushed out by his son. They went up further when Konstantyn unexpectedly passed away shortly after handing over the reins; the coroner ruled it had been from natural causes, but the breadth and depth of coverage over the scion's death led me to think conventional wisdom was otherwise. Shifting screens slightly, I did a quick database search through the coroner's records and found the autopsy that had been performed on Konstantyn. My eyes widened slightly when I saw who had performed it; they widened further when I saw just how brief the report was, something that was exceedingly unusual from the normally verbose person in question. Grabbing my iPhone, I found the number for the current Chief Medical Examiner and was pleasantly surprised when she picked up on the first ring.

"This is unusual," she chuckled. "To what do I owe the honor?"

"Do I have to have an excuse for calling my favorite coroner?" I asked.

"Now I *know* I'm in trouble," Peg laughed. "But two can play at this game. What can I do for my favorite boy in blue?"

"I haven't been a boy in quite some time," I replied. "Nor have I ever fit the other definition."

"I'm almost afraid to ask," Peg chuckled. "So, we'll let my joke die a horrible death right there."

"Probably for the best," I laughed. "Otherwise, I might be forced to revoke your Ally status."

"Ouch."

"Are you between things? I don't want to interrupt a postmortem."

"More or less," she answered. "I just wrapped up a ninety-year-old that met his maker while making whoopee with his neighbor at a senior living facility over in Placentia. I don't know what's going on down there, but it's the third one in the last year."

"Shit," I breathed. "I hope he died happy."

"I'm not able to determine that scientifically," Peg deadpanned. "Still, maybe you should look into it."

"The deaths?" I asked, frowning. "I think Placentia is out of my jurisdiction."

"Figures. Anyway, I'm getting a cup of coffee at the moment, so tell me what's on your mind."

"I want to ask you about a PM you did a number of years ago," I began. "It might be tangentially related to the case I'm working on now."

"Oh?" she asked. "Now I'm definitely intrigued. Let me get back to my desk so I can pull up the file. Who was it for?"

"Konstantyn Cardinal."

There was a long silence, which was more than telling. "I'm not sure I need my files for that one," she ultimately said.

"You remember it, then?"

"Oh yes," Peg replied. I heard her close a door and made the assumption she'd returned to her office. "I was the Deputy Medical Examiner at the time; it was one of my first PMs."

"I can never think of you as not being *the* Medical Examiner," I chuckled.

"My predecessor would probably agree," she replied. "She never told me directly, but I think that was one of the reasons I was hired as her assistant."

"Smart woman," I said. "I'll say as much if I ever meet her."

"She's in Barcelona now," Peg said. "Living the good life watching the bulls run and drinking sangria."

I frowned, for it was extremely unusual for Peg to not get directly to the point. "I think Hemingway made the former far more interesting than it is in real life, though I hear *real* sangria is something to behold."

"I wouldn't know."

"Look, I've got your report up on my laptop," I continued. "And it's... sparse, to say the least."

"That it is," Peg sighed.

"Did you uncover anything during the PM?"

Peg hesitated again. "I'm going to preface what I'm about to say by reminding you that I was a new hire at the time," she began. "And not entirely willing to buck my superiors."

"As well as I know you, I find that hard to believe," I said, raising my eyebrows.

Peg laughed. "It was a phase and didn't last long."

"What happened?"

"The family objected to a full autopsy due to their religious beliefs," she replied. "It came fairly late in the process, too; I had Cardinal on the table, prepped and ready to go when the deputies came in to remand the body to the funeral home." Peg sighed. "I felt like I was in one of those weird Kabuki theater situations, standing there with a scalpel in my hand while they zipped the body back into a bag."

I flipped through the file on my screen. "Ah," I nodded slowly. "I missed the form earlier; if I'm reading this right, it was the son that filed the request."

"Sounds right," Peg said. "I never saw anyone from the family."

"No one identified the body?"

"There wasn't a need," Peg replied. "Cardinal was found in his bed by his son, according to the report I saw; COD was presumed to be natural causes, but given his age and relatively good health, SOP called for an autopsy to confirm."

"Which you wound up not being able to do," I added thoughtfully.

"Exactly."

"Any whiff of foul play?"

"Aside from the sudden religious objection? Not that I know of, but you'd have to ask the investigating detective."

I shifted screens again and then swore. "That might be problematic," I added. "It was Mark Freidman."

Peg was quiet for a moment. "No kidding."

My eyes flicked to the master bedroom as I found myself suddenly awash in emotions. As much effort as I had made over the years to get past the rape, seeing Mark's name in the file triggered all sorts of memories I couldn't avoid — including having been tied, spread-eagled, to my own bed so he could slowly throttle me to death with his bare hands. He'd done plenty of other unspeakable stuff to me, too; while the physical scars had long ago healed, I knew the mental trauma would never fully recede. There were still times when poor Alex would touch me a certain way and I would immediately jump out of my skin; thankfully, it didn't happen very often any longer, but I also never knew what would set me off, either.

Swallowing, I pulled myself back into the moment. "Mark wasn't known for keeping good notes," I said. "I'm not going to get much from the file, but it does list the responding EMTs. If I'm extraordinarily lucky, they may still work for us." I went back to the short narrative in the file from Peg. "Your report more or less confirms the COD."

"It had to," she sighed. "Without running any tests, all I had was the visual observations I'd made prior to them trundling him off. The guy *looked* healthy, but beyond that, I couldn't have told you what killed him." Peg paused. "Why? Do you think otherwise?"

"I don't know," I replied honestly. "My natural inclination is to be suspicious, though, when the founder of a major corporation suddenly expires shortly after turning the business over to his son."

"I'm not sure I knew about that," Peg replied. "Though the M.E. at the time might have."

"Maybe. It's probably not relevant."

Peg paused again. "You wouldn't have me on the phone if you thought otherwise."

"True," I laughed.

"I've got to go. But if you need anything else—"

"Understood and thanks."

Setting my phone down on the couch beside me, I poked through the online directory we shared with the county for all who were employed in the public safety sector and quickly located the two names that had been attached to the incident report; both appeared to still be active with the Orange County Fire Department, though I was unable to ascertain if they happened to be on duty that day. Undeterred, I grabbed my phone and punched in the first number; it went straight to voicemail, so I left my name, number and reason I was calling before moving on to the second individual. This time I hit pay dirt: a deep voice answered after the second ring.

"Hello?"

"Yes, hi," I said, glancing at the screen of my laptop. "Is this Hank Forbes?"

"Speaking."

"I'm Deputy Chief Vasily Korsokovach, Rancho Linda Police," I continued. "Do you have a few minutes to speak? I'm working a case that might overlap slightly with a call you took a few years ago."

"I don't, actually," Forbes said. "I'm about to go back on duty; I was at lunch, which is the only reason I took your call."

"When do you get off?"

"Sunset," he replied simply.

I blinked and then re-read his entry on the active roster. "I used to work that part of the beach myself when I was in high school," I said. "Hopefully the tech is better now."

"Doubt it," Forbes laughed. "Lifeguarding is at the bottom of the pecking order."

"Why did you shift from being on an ambulance, then?"

"The hours are better," he replied. "Not to mention the view. And I can surf on my lunch hour."

"Yeah, I could get behind that myself. I've been meaning to catch a wave or two; do you mind if I swung by your stand and chatted on my way to nirvana?"

"I think I can multitask. High tide is at three, by the way."

"Noted," I said. "See you then."

Putting the phone back on the couch again, I returned to the laptop and found that the data from the USB stick had finally popped into the case system. Toggling through to the storage area associated with my session, I began to peruse the hundreds of folders that had appeared and slowly began to frown; it became clear within a few minutes that I'd been given what was known in the business as a "discovery dump," an overwhelming amount of data that was intended to be difficult to digest — and therefore capable of hiding, in plain sight, something of interest. I spent close to an hour trying to organize what I had before realizing most of my thoughts were now focused on paddling around the Pacific; bowing to the inevitable, I logged out of the case system and closed down my laptop. Assuming traffic was on my side, I had a real chance to make it to the beach just as the tide reached its zenith; getting info from the lifeguard was, of course, no less important, but honestly, I was beginning to feel as though I was running out of investigative steam.

Sliding my laptop into the backpack, I wandered into the half bath to retrieve a wetsuit and one of the Speedos I knew to be hanging over the sink from my last round of laundry; to my surprise, Alex was already in there, folding stuff from the dryer directly into a basket. His eyebrows went up when he saw me, then went up further as he watched me reach for one of the full-body black neoprene outfits; the one in question happened to be a favorite of mine, since it had contrasting panels of electric blue along each leg. Grabbing the Speedo, I started to leave when I saw the look on Alejandro's face.

"I take it there's a clue to be found down in Newport Beach," he said.

"There is, actually," I replied, suddenly self-conscious of the neoprene I was clutching.

Alex rolled his eyes. "Like you haven't used *that* line before."

I smiled slightly. "Maybe a time or two. This time it's true — I need to speak to a lifeguard who happened to have been the EMT on duty the day the founder of The Cardinal Group passed. He's on duty until sunset."

"Oh," Alex said, smiling slightly. "That changes everything, naturally."

"Naturally," I laughed. I pulled down the wetsuit he often used when we surfed together and handed it to him. "Why don't you come with me? We can call it date night and grab something for dinner at that seafood place right along the boardwalk."

Alex took the suit, but in doing so, stepped close enough to me that his chest was touching mine. His eyes danced merrily as he spoke. "I had other plans for this evening."

"Did you?" I asked.

"Yes," he said as he pressed himself into me. "They centered on a handsome hunk of a swimmer with a six pack so sharp it could cut paper."

"Do I know this swimmer?"

"I think so, yes," he breathed into my ear before nibbling at my neck.

I felt the first inklings that my afternoon was about to go off the rails. "Maybe you should demonstrate what you had planned," I whispered quietly as he worked his way toward my mouth. "So I know how much time to carve out of my schedule."

"If you insist," he said after our lips parted; in the blink of an eye, the wetsuits had been dropped to the tile at our feet, and Alex was making short work of pulling my t-shirt off.

I decided the waves could wait a little bit longer.

Twenty-Two
Surfing for Clues

In the end, Alejandro opted to remain at the condo so he could continue his Christmas baking marathon; somewhere along the line, he'd learned that Rosie loved rum cake, so he'd found a recipe online that he'd planned to make. After eyeing said recipe and determining it was more *rum* than *cake*, I figured I had a pretty good idea why Rosie might like it. Leaving him to his own devices, I quickly changed into the Speedo I'd grabbed, tossed on a t-shirt and some shorts and then hit the road; despite my rather pleasant dalliance with my fiancé, the clock on the dashboard of my Camaro indicated I'd still make it to the beach with plenty of time to spare before high tide, assuming traffic was in my favor.

Fortunately, it was; the parking lot, though, was a stark reminder I wasn't the only one trying to time my arrival for maximum surf. I was close to having to ferret out a quasi-illegal spot in one of the neighborhoods close to the beach when a small Honda backed out just ahead of me in the city parking lot; I deftly swooped in and parked the Camaro, then grabbed my iPhone so I could pay for the spot. Once that was done, I pushed open the driver's side door and stepped out into what had become a brilliantly sunny afternoon; taking a deep, appreciative breath of the salt-laden air, I lamented how little time I'd spent on the water that fall. I couldn't put my finger on any one thing that had prevented me from doing so other than the fact it had been an extremely busy period; then again, it often felt like my life was one series of emergencies that blended into each other, so perhaps that was the lamest of excuses. Surfing had long been a way for me to center myself, much as swimming often did; as I went around to the trunk to retrieve my board and wetsuit, I smiled at all of the times an epiphany in a case I'd been working had occurred while bobbing out among the waves and made a quiet promise not to forsake the Goddess of the Sea.

Wriggling my way into the skintight embrace of the neoprene was less of an adventure than normal, though I feared (karma being what it was) I would pay for that on the back end when it came time to try and shed my new second skin for the post-surfing shower. Tucking my board under an arm, I locked up the Camaro and started across the parking lot to the public access pathway to the beach; my route took me first to the long pier jutting out into the Pacific, allowing me a moment to gauge the current wave situation. As the fully parking lot had portended, business was brisk out on the water; surfers of all stripes were liberally spread out along the cascading lines of breaking waves, though not so close as to make it impossible for any one of them to suddenly stand and attempt to ride all the way to shore. There appeared as though there would be plenty of space for me a bit further up the beach, closer to the small jetty of rocks at the far end; that suited my purposes just fine, for according to the employment file I'd plucked from the Orange County system, the lifeguard I needed to speak with had been assigned to the stand just next to it.

Trundling down the steps and onto the beach proper, I smiled as my toes dug into the warmth of the sand; the number of people enjoying the late afternoon sun felt like a leading indicator than the weekend had started early for them. I passed an impromptu beach volleyball game in progress on a court that had been defined by coolers and gaudy beach towels; two college-aged guys with deep tans were tossing around a frisbee just beyond that. The inevitable sandcastle construction was also underway, too, though the toddler working on it seemed more interested in digging the moat around the lumps I presumed were supposed to be towers than actually working on the main structure. I waved at a buxom blonde perched in the second-to-last lifeguard stand as I passed by; I made a mental note to tell Alejandro later that I had further evidence Speedo's tensile strength was superior to other swimsuit brands, though in this particular case, I feared it might be on the upper bounds.

As often as I'd surfed in Newport Beach, it had been ages since I'd returned to Lifeguard Stand One. It had been my home base when I'd worked as a lifeguard myself, though I'd initially thought I'd been sent to Siberia when it had been assigned to me given its relative distance from the headquarters building on the pier. What I'd not counted on was being partnered one summer with a fellow teen asking the same questions I'd begun to contemplate surrounding my sexuality; by the time I'd returned to high school that fall, I'd finally understood who I was, and more importantly, was fully comfortable with it. My only regret was that our brief summer of love had been just that — brief; we'd parted at the end of the season, and I never saw the kid again. Every now and then I considered doing a records search just to determine what happened to my first love; I always stopped myself, though, for part of the magic of what had transpired between us lay in his mysterious disappearance afterwards.

The stand itself looked as though it hadn't changed at all. Like most lifeguard stands in Southern California, it had a wide porch facing the water, with a partially enclosed hut-like structure behind it containing the necessary rescue gear. A small patio of concrete was directly behind the stand, just beneath a lone shower head bolted to the rear of the hut; I smiled slightly to think of some of the furtive shenanigans that had occurred there between shifts, barely out of view of the beachgoers.

Forbes was standing up against the railing of the raised porch; he'd caught my approach and had shifted his position slightly so he could watch my arrival while still keeping an eye on the water. I wasn't prepared for the fine male specimen I found on display; wearing only the vibrant red board shorts that were the international uniform for lifeguards emphasized the richly deep tan he'd gained from working on the beach, a tan that strangely accentuated every muscle of his pleasantly ripped body. His six-pack abs underscored the hours spent in the gym; the carefully groomed chest spoke to an understanding of how to best display those efforts. Medium-length brown hair faded by sun exposure to almost blonde was escaping from a baseball hat on backwards; stubble of a slightly darker shade kissed a jaw so sharp, it practically took my breath away.

A smile of nearly perfect white teeth appeared when I stopped a few feet from the steps to the stand. "When you said your name was Vasily Korsokovach, I never expected it to be *you*."

I returned the smile as I drove my surfboard into the stand. "I take it my reputation precedes me."

"Hell yes," Forbes replied. "I begged my parents to stay up so I could watch your relay final in Beijing."

"Dear lord," I chuckled. "What were you, like, two?"

"Fourteen," he replied. "A lot changed for me that summer, and you had a big part in that." Forbes paused. "I never thought I'd ever have to chance to thank you for it, but damn. Here you are."

I slowly nodded. "My interviews?" I asked, thinking back to the endless hours I'd spent making the rounds as one of the first openly gay members of the US team.

"And the articles," he replied. "Discovering it was okay to be who I wanted to be, that was, like, a revelation I didn't even know I could have."

"That's why I did them," I said. "It was time for a change."

Forbes frowned. "These days, I'm not sure the country is still on board with that."

"The fight is ongoing, and I fear, always will be," I sighed. "Do you mind if I come up? I used to work this stand myself back in the day."

"Please," he said, waving at the porch.

I came up the steps to the porch and took up position beside Forbes; the late afternoon sun was incredibly warm against the dark of the wetsuit, and I could feel the first trickle of sweat along the back of my neck. "Thank you for agreeing to talk to me," I said as I unconsciously fell back into my role as lifeguard and began to scan the horizon. "I'll try not to take up too much of your time."

"It's been a fairly quiet day, so I actually appreciate the interruption," he replied.

"Quiet is good."

"And incredibly boring," he sighed. "Especially now that we are so short staffed; we used to trade off with a replacement every ninety minutes; now I'm lucky if I can get a break long enough to use the bathroom."

"Didn't you say you surfed at lunchtime?"

"They *have* to give us the lunch hour," he answered. "Legally. That's the only break I can count on."

I glanced at him. "We used to have two guards in every stand."

"It's not been that way for years now," he sighed. "They replaced that with someone roaming on a four-by-four, up and down the beach."

"That seems... unwise," I replied.

"So far, so good," he shrugged. "No one's died yet. You wanted to talk to me about the day we rolled for Konstantyn Cardinal?"

"Yes," I nodded. "Do you remember it?"

"I do," he replied.

His tone made me look at him again. "It's why you gave up being an EMT, isn't it?"

Forbes risked a quick glance at me. "Not by choice."

"What happened?"

There was a long pause. "If it were anyone other than you — or that reporter that reached out to me — I'd continue to keep my mouth shut. But I'm tired of hiding, and tired of having been silenced."

I narrowed my eyes. "This reporter — was she from the *Register*?"

He nodded. "Vivian Grandchester."

"When did she reach out?"

"About six months ago," he answered. "Said she was doing background on a feature she was writing about The Cardinal Group; she'd seen my name on the incident report the day Konstantyn died and, like you, had some questions."

"Did you give her your story?"

"Yes."

I wish I'd gotten into that den, I thought. "Walk me through what you told her."

Forbes took a deep breath. "It started off as a standard 9-1-1 call; my partner and I were the closest available unit to the estate the Cardinals own — it's just off the canyon in Rancho Linda."

"I've been up there," I said. "Million-dollar views."

"And then some," he nodded. "The housekeeper met us at the door, and we rolled our gear into this massive bedroom on the first floor; Konstantyn was in bed, face up, and his son, Anton, was sitting on the edge holding his hand."

"How'd he look?"

"The son or the father?"

"Both, I guess."

"The father was clearly dead," Forbes said matter-of-factly. "It was easy to see even from across the room; his son seemed to be in a trance of some sort and was spouting short phrases of gibberish as though the father was still alive."

"What did you do next?"

"The standard stuff," he continued. "Once we determined there was no pulse — and given the temperature of the body, realized there hadn't been one for some time — we called it and then radioed for the medical examiner."

"Why?"

He shrugged. "It wasn't clear *how* he had died," Forbes replied.

"That always triggers a postmortem, even if the ultimate answer is 'natural causes.'"

"Makes sense. Did the coroner do a liver temp when they arrived?" I asked, trying to remember if I'd seen that in the file.

"I think so, yes. I don't remember what it was, though; we were pretty much packed up and waiting to be released by the officer in charge by that point."

I frowned a bit. "So far, this sounds like a pretty ordinary call out," I said.

"We thought so too. And to be honest, once we left, I completely forgot about it."

I nodded again. "Until Grandchester reached out?"

"Exactly."

"What did Grandchester ask you about?"

"The state of the body, specifically," Forbes replied. "And the glass on the sideboard by the bed."

"Glass?" I asked, frowning. "Of what?"

"Sherry," he answered. "According to her, a source inside the family had told her it was his custom to have a glass of sherry before bedtime — had been for years. That same source informed her the glass was missing the day of Konstantyn's death."

"Was it?"

Forbes looked at me. "You know how sometimes you forget certain things, but strange details stand out to you forever?" he asked.

"I do."

He paused for a moment. "There was a stain on the sheet beside Konstantyn's face," he said quietly. "I only noticed it as I was the one who tried to find his pulse. It looked and smelled like some expensive liquor had been spilled; I've had enough experience with drunks to recognize it as such." He paused again. "I remember to this day thinking that was odd, since I'd not seen anything vaguely like a minibar in the space."

"Could it have been sherry?"

Forbes shrugged. "I don't know. Maybe? It's not the kind of thing I would drink myself."

"Interesting. Did she ask about anything else?"

"Other than confirming Anton, the son, was in the room when we arrived? Maybe a few other things — like when we arrived, how long we were there, when we left. That sort of stuff."

"And you talked to her six months ago?"

"Yes."

I thought back to what I'd seen on his employment record in the Orange County directory. "Which is when you transferred here."

"Yes," he answered, slightly more quietly.

"By choice?"

"No," he added, even quieter.

"What happened?"

He glanced at me, then returned to the ocean. "A few days after I spoke with the reporter, I found a note taped to the *inside* of my locker at the fire station," he said. "It had a letter and... photos of me and my partner. Photos that had been taken when the two of us went on a long weekend to Playa del Carmen."

"Your... ambulance partner?"

Forbes nodded. "The note said I was to recant what I told the reporter immediately or the photos would be sent to Internal Affairs." He glanced at me. "I don't know about the police side of things, but they tend to frown on fraternization on our side."

"He was your superior?"

"I was his," he replied. Forbes hesitated. "Look, I'm not terribly proud of what I did, but I was up for a promotion at the time; something like that would have derailed my career. So, I called Grandchester back and told her I was mistaken."

"She didn't believe you, though, did she?"

"No," he said. "Whoever sent me those photos found out, too, because the following Monday, I was sitting in my CO's office, being told I had two options."

"Quit or come to the beach?" I asked.

"Exactly. I figured quitting would give whoever the fuck did this to me more satisfaction, so I took the demotion." He sighed. "It isn't all that bad. The pressure's about the same, but the hours are far more consistent. And," he continued with a slight smile, "it meant I could 'officially' date George."

"I'm glad something good came out of that," I said. "Are you willing to go on the record about what you saw?"

"Fuck yes," he said. "The longer this has gone, the angrier I've become at how I handled it."

"You'll need to swing by my office, then, so we can get a proper statement."

"I'm off tomorrow, would that work?"

"Yes. I'll text you the address when I get back to my car." I reached over and shook his hand. "Thank you for coming out of the shadows."

"Did I help your case?"

"I think so, yes," I smiled.

"Good." He nodded toward the waves. "Tide's turned. Are you still going in?

"Fuck yes," I echoed as I started down the steps to my board. "See you tomorrow."

Twenty-Three
Confronting the Truth

The cold embrace of the Pacific took my breath away as it always did; coming up for air after diving into the surf, I bobbed for a moment before beginning a brisk freestyle to get beyond the current line of breakers. I dragged my surfboard behind me until I was through the worst of it, then pulled it up so I could swiftly slip onto the waxed surface. Paddling into the swells, I worked my way out to a favorite point about halfway between the pier and the breakwater, then sat up and took stock. If anything, the crowd had swelled with the change in tide, almost to the point where it was just a little uncomfortable. Frowning slightly, I let a few choice options glide beneath me while I watched the others; then, once I knew what sort of path I could carve through them, I waited for the next best candidate, threw myself up and let myself go. The rush of cruising along a cresting wave never failed to disappoint, and all too soon I found myself paddling back out to sea, invigorated and ready for more action.

While time ordinarily was rather meaningless out there among the waves, that evening I found myself unusually fixated on the sun as it slowly sank closer to the western horizon. It wasn't hard to understand *why*, for it was an unusually vivid reminder that I was getting close to the end of the case. By the time I'd ridden my third wave toward shore, I was relatively certain I had most of the pieces I needed to prove the theory that had been bubbling up in the back of my head; as I stood on the board for one last run, the sense the financials I had yet to go through might not completely confirm my suspicions was strong enough to wonder what Grandchester herself had turned up in her research. Dropping into the best wave of the night, I ducked under the crashing water and came out at the other end; diving off my board and back into the cold water, I paddled toward shore determined to finally gain access to that treasure trove, one way or the other.

Showering off the worst of the salt water from my suit, I had a few wonderful moments of torture as I twisted and groped and swore before ultimately freeing myself from the prison of the neoprene; as I trudged back to my car carrying the dripping mess under one arm, I figured the first person who produced a wetsuit that was easy to put on *and* take off would become a millionaire overnight; popping the trunk to the Camaro, I pushed my board inside and then found my hand frozen in mid-air as it reached for my towel.

I can't believe Hope didn't know what her daughter was working on, I thought. *In fact, the way she was so insistent that I* couldn't *review Vivian's files should have been a red flag for me.* Glancing in the direction of the lifeguard tower where I'd spoken with Forbes, I found myself nodding slightly. *Someone's leaning on her, too. Just like they did with Forbes. Damn.*

Yanking my towel from the trunk, I did a cursory mop-up and then threw on my shorts and t-shirt; showing up soggy and smelling like the ocean wasn't exactly professional, but as I slid behind the wheel of the Camaro, I figured expediency was now the order of the day. Punching in the address for Grandchester's home into Siri, I began considering the best approach for wrestling permission to view the files from Hope; if I were successful in my quest, delaying the deep dive into the financials would be worth it. Either way, it was shaping up to be a long night.

I backed out of my spot and then made my way through the municipal parking lot toward the exit; despite the gathering darkness, there were still a fair number of cars parked there, speaking to the vibrant nightlife the beach offered. Turning out onto the street, I could see the small seafood restaurant I'd tried to tempt Alex with was doing a brisk business; cars were stacked up at the valet stand, and the small parking lot off to the corner was completely full. It *was* Friday night, and in California, that usually meant not being able to get a table anywhere unless you'd planned ahead and made reservations. As I merged onto the freeway for my drive back to Rancho Linda, I realized I had a sudden hankering for the freshly fried baby shrimp Millie's used to serve back in Windeport; despite living along the *other* coast, I'd never found the version offered in California to quite be the same.

My dalliance at the beach meant rush hour was in its last hurrah for the evening; uncharacteristically, all five lanes headed northward were snarled enough to push the median speed to something just above a brisk walking pace. Siri was no help in suggesting an alternative to powering through, so I grimly wove between stalled out lanes while fantasizing about owning a flying car that could soar far above the mess when needed. Or a working transporter, for that matter; anything to avoid the infernal Hell of too many people on too few roads trying to get nowhere fast.

The state of Zen I'd attained from communing with Lady Pacifica managed to keep me from any major incidents of road rage, though I was incredibly thankful when the classic lines of Grandchester's home finally appeared in my headlights. Shutting down the Camaro, my eyes flicked to the structure for a moment and took in the fact that the curtains had been drawn tightly against the night; unlike the other houses along the tree-lined street, the home was completely dark, almost as though it were intentionally trying to hide in the shadows. Wondering if my impromptu visit might have caught Hope Grandchester on a night when she was out playing cards with the girls, it still struck me as odd that not even the light by the garage had been left on; it was enough of a concern that I played the cautious route and grabbed my Glock from the glovebox before clipping my badge to the waistband of my microfiber shorts.

Sliding my phone into a pocket, I locked the Camaro and then carefully walked up the driveway; the strange sense my approach was going unnoticed washed over me for a moment, and I paused to take another look at the house. Crickets from the thicket of bushes between the properties seemed unusually loud as I waited there, interspersed with the random croak of some sort of frog that must have been hiding in a water feature I'd not yet encountered. Two waste bins had been placed next to the garage door; altering my plan slightly, I walked over to them and confirmed they were both empty. Looking back at the street, I could see that no other bins were out; if it had been trash day — something I could check with the city pretty quickly — I had a strong suspicion that while Hope may have put the bins out in the morning, a concerned neighbor had pulled them back from the street at some point later in the day.

So, she's been gone for a while, I thought. *Or,* as I looked up at the dark outlines of the house, *she wants someone to* think *she's gone.*

The garage door was of the kind that didn't have windows, so there was no way to tell whether or not a car was present; sliding around to the side of the house, I found a small window for the space, but it, too, had a curtain drawn across the glass. Pulling out my iPhone, I triggered the flashlight and tried to see if there was a gap of any kind, but somewhat unusually, the thick fabric on the other side appeared to have been pinned together, avoiding any of the usual gaps that might have occurred. I didn't want to read into what I was seeing, but it was hard not to make the assumption that someone was more than a little concerned about their privacy. Turning off the flashlight function, I slipped my phone back into my pocket and started back around to the front of the house, idly noting as I did so that my soggy Speedo had soaked through the fabric of my shorts. I moved carefully up the steps to the front door and reached for the doorbell; I could hear it ring out inside the house, but when no one immediately came, I pressed it a second time, then, when even the cat I'd seen on my first visit failed to materialize, a third. Pulling the Glock from my holder, I found myself shifting into the worst-case mindset and then slowly reached out for the handle; I wasn't surprised to feel it turn easily beneath my hand, though it did little to alleviate my sense that something was wrong. Holding my gun up, I nudged the door open with my foot very, very slowly, then called out.

"Hope? Hope Grandchester? It's Deputy Chief Korsokovach. Are you here?"

Leaning forward slightly, I held my breath and listened for any indicator I'd been heard. When none came, I nudged the door further open and then tried again.

"Hope? Hope Grandchester? Are you here?"

I waited several heartbeats, then several more to allow my eyes to adjust to the semidarkness of the small foyer beyond the door. When they did, I immediately saw the form sprawled out along the rug of the hallway; keeping my gun at the ready, I slowly moved into the space, then carefully knelt beside the body. Shifting my gun to my other hand, I reached down and pressed my fingers to Hope Grandchester's neck; to my great relief, I could feel a pulse, though it wasn't as strong as I would have liked. Yanking my phone from my shorts, I snapped on the flashlight and recoiled slightly when I saw the pool of blood around her head; without moving her, I couldn't immediately see the source, but assumed the wound was on the side or back of her head. What I could see of her face spoke to having taken a brutal beating; sitting up slightly, it also appeared an arm was at the sort of unnatural angle that spoke to months of future orthopedic visits.

Damn.

Shifting my focus, I quickly dialed 9-1-1 and was immediately connected to a dispatcher. "This is Deputy Chief Korsokovach," I said without preamble. "I need an ambulance at this location immediately; I have an unconscious female, approximately sixty years old, who appears to have been physically assaulted. She's unconscious; I have a pulse, but it's not strong."

"Pinging your phone now," the operator said with the brisk efficiency of experience. "Ambulance is on the way. Do you require any other assistance?"

"I—"

The acrid smell of something burning suddenly hit my nose; it was faint but getting stronger. My eyes began to scan the space for the source and landed on a flickering orange light at the end of the hallway. Knowing there wasn't much I could do for Hope at the moment, I quickly stood and trotted down the narrow space, wrinkling my nose as the stench became more pronounced; ignoring the increasingly urgent questions coming from the dispatch operator, I stopped in front of a double pocket door through tendrils of white smoke were slipping through. Pressing the back of my hand to the door, I quickly withdrew it before sprinting back to the unconscious form of Hope Grandchester.

"Roll fire, immediately," I barked into the phone as I knelt beside Hope. "There appears to be a fire in progress at the rear of the home. I am going to try and move the victim outside."

"Roger that. Fire units are on the way; keep this line open."

"Will do," I said before temporarily sliding the phone back into my pocket.

Stuffing my gun back into the holster, I tried to ignore my impulse to dash back to the den — I was certain now that was what was currently in the process of burning to the ground — and carefully leaned over Hope; gently, I snuck my arms beneath her, then pulled her to my chest. The air had become thick, making it difficult to breath as I pushed up from the floor; my eyes began to water as I hurried toward the front door as fast as I thought I could go with my precious cargo. As I stepped out into the night air, I grimly noted none of the smoke detectors had gone off; holding Hope closer to my chest as I hurried down the steps and then across the small patch of grass for her front yard, guilt from choosing a few hours of surfing that afternoon threatened to overwhelm me. What little evidence I'd seen made me think whatever happened to Hope transpired not long before my arrival, adding to the sense that if I'd arrived just a few minutes earlier, maybe I might have interrupted whoever had done this.

Plenty of time later to beat up on myself, I thought as I picked a spot next to my Camaro and gently set Hope down. *And Lord knows I will beat up on myself.*

Pressing my fingers to her neck again, my eyes strayed to the blood staining the front of my t-shirt; under the better lighting of the street-lamp hovering over the sidewalk, it didn't take long to find the gash on the back of her head, nor to see it was deep enough to show the bony white of her skull. While the pulse was still there — barely — I intrinsically knew the odds were against Hope ever waking up. Still, that didn't prevent me from popping the trunk to my Camaro and finding two dry towels; I folded one into a vague pillow and gently put in under her head, then shook out the other to drape it over her torso. My first aid training was pretty clear, though treating for shock was probably not really necessary at that point.

Sirens in the distance slowly became louder; crouched beside Hope, I chanced a look at the house and wasn't surprised to see the orange glow growing at the rear of the structure. Smoke had appeared in silhouette, backlit by the light pollution of Rancho Linda; even to my untrained eye, it was fairly clear it was growing both thicker and darker. Whoever was responsible for the conflagration had enough of a head start that I feared the firefighters' ability to save anything short of the foundation. Reaching for her hand, I took it into mine and held it as though I could will Hope into hanging on; the coldness I felt as I squeezed it told me I wasn't going to find her pulse a third time. Shaking my head, I continued to hold her hand while literally watching my case go up in smoke.

TWENTY-FOUR
IT'S NEVER A GOOD SIGN WHEN
THE NUMBERS DON'T ADD UP

"Nothing?"

"Nothing."

I closed my eyes and rubbed at a temple. "I figured if anyone could pull something from that mess, it would be you, Gina."

"Sorry to disappoint," she said, her voice full of genuine regret. "But as you correctly intuited, the fire was set in what the house plan listed as the library; I'm still waiting on formal confirmation from the Fire Marshall, but informally she's already told me they've found the chemical signature for regular gasoline at the point of inception."

"Donna's usually not wrong about those things," I sighed, thinking of the tall, silver-haired expert I'd first met during my initial tour with Rancho Linda. "And it would explain how thoroughly destroyed everything is."

"Yeah."

I opened my eyes and looked at the photo on my MacBook; Gina had taken it from the sidewalk, looking back at where Hope Grandchester's house had once stood. Save for a small sliver of the garage's rear wall, not much was left beyond a smoking pile of rubble; it looked a bit like one of those properties you often see in an *after* photo when a wildfire races uncontrolled through a community. I'd pretty much known my chances for retrieving anything of Vivian's research had gone to zero the moment I'd seen the smoke curling out of the den; my only hope now was to piece together whatever narrative she'd been crafting from the materials I still had access to. Having spent a few days chasing the thread meant I had a pretty decent idea where she was going, though; my eyes fell to the small plastic evidence bag holding the USB stick I'd trucked back from Florida. There was no way to suppress the groan at how long the evening was shaping up to be, something that Gina heard over the open connection.

"It can't be a total loss," she said. "I mean, your victim had to have had a backup of some sort, right?"

"If she did, it's a nontraditional one," I sighed. "Your lab geeks confirmed that she didn't have much in cloud storage save for a few photos; I'm still waiting on the warrant for her email and social media accounts, but based on what I've seen so far, Grandchester seems to have been wily enough not to trust anything important to a service she didn't directly control."

"Smart, I guess."

"Especially if she were protecting a source," I replied.

"From whom?" Gina asked.

"The fucking bastards that did this," I said darkly. "I should have seen this coming, especially after they tried to take out Alex—"

"You can't blame yourself," Gina interrupted. "This isn't on you. The way I read your entry in the file, the victim would never have agreed to help your investigation."

"I could have sweet talked her, given enough time," I replied.

"Maybe. Maybe not." Gina paused. "She didn't give you any indication that she felt like she was in danger, did she?"

"No, though in retrospect I think I assumed she was protecting her daughter's legacy by keeping me from the research. Seems more than likely now Hope knew *exactly* what Vivian had."

"And was killed to keep silent?"

"Just like her daughter."

"Damn."

"Yeah," I nodded again.

"By the way," Gina continued. "One of my superstar techs managed to identify the game in that photo we recovered."

"Oh?" I replied. "How on earth did they do that?"

"We were able to blow up the scoreboard in the background and matched what was on it with the box scores on record for the team. Turns out it was the Angels - Twins matchup on Wednesday, May 30, 2001." She paused. "In what might be foreshadowing for our case, the Angels lost, 0 and 3."

"May 30?" I asked. "Must have been Memorial Day week, right?"

"Looks that way," she confirmed. "So, your victim was engaged to the now-head of The Cardinal Group more than two decades ago."

"Wild. And it also explains how young they both look in the photo."

"Exactly. I would love to know what happened between them."

"That's still on my list to discover."

"Good luck with that. One last item," Gina added. "Peg put you on the calendar for first thing in the morning; she's coming in special for you."

"I'll be there." My eyes flicked to the clock on the toolbar of my screen. "Thanks for your efforts."

"Of course. I'll update the file with our photos and notes before we punch out."

"Do we ever really punch out?" I asked with a slight smile.

"Poor choice of words," she chuckled. "Talk later."

I tossed my phone down on the cushion beside me and repositioned slightly so I could balance the MacBook on my lap a bit better. The lights were off in the condo aside from those on the Christmas tree and the strip that had been wound into the garland over the television; glancing toward the bedroom, I could see the flicker of light from around the edges of the partially closed door, the only indication that I wasn't currently alone. Alejandro had been more than a little unhappy with my tardy return home that evening, mostly because he'd spent the afternoon making a pot roast that had suffered terribly from my delay. It had been some time since he'd gotten into a snit over something so trivial; then again, my lack of texting him an updated ETA as a result of having to stick around the scene until Gina's team arrived had not helped matters, nor the funk I'd been in as a result of adding Hope Grandchester to the list of casualties associated with the case. He'd tried to extract from me what had gone wrong, though the concern on his face had shifted to one of annoyance when I'd essentially ignored him, curled into a corner of the couch and begun to review what data I still had; he'd mumbled something about catching up on a Christmas movie he'd saved to his watch list, popped some popcorn in the microwave and then decamped for the master bedroom. Glancing at the bedroom door again, I wondered if I dared risk making an appearance, or if it might be wiser to pull an all-nighter with the data so tempers could reset a bit.

No, I thought sadly, *I fucked this one up. I deserve to sit out here for a bit.*

Sighing, I returned to the laptop and the profit-and-loss statement I'd been reviewing for The Cardinal Group; I took a moment to drag next to it the official version that had been filed with the California Franchise Tax Board with their taxes for the last fiscal year, then started to compare entries. Since they were a privately held organization, getting access to their tax records had required making several phone calls, including one to press an unamused Judge Spenser for a warrant. In the end, he'd agreed with my probable cause but had made it clear I'd interrupted his night on the town — an implicit subtext that I was on the hook for something at a later date. *That* had made me roll my eyes, for the last time Spense had called in a favor, I'd been forced to be the star attraction at a charity fundraiser featuring a very cold dunk tank.

I'd begun my review with the final four years that Konstantyn had been in charge and found that each of the reports filed with the state had been identical. That in itself was extremely unusual, for the odds that the net income at *any* organization would be within a standard deviation of the prior year — or the next — were extremely long. As in win-the-massive-Powerball-jackpot long. More troubling was the fact that the State hadn't flagged Cardinal for further review; without a contact at the Feds to lean on, I had no way to know if the IRS had seen something similar, but guessed it had and also passed on any sort of audit. Not that it mattered; I was relatively certain that the statues of limitation had run out on anything from that time period, so I'd set those files aside and begun looking through the more contemporary filings. Here the information was erratically eclectic, showcasing rather starkly just how differently Anton appeared to be running Cardinal from his father. Losses began to appear the second year Anton was in charge, and then began to mount in every succeeding year; those had the net benefit of erasing any sort of tax being due to California, but again, the fact that he'd not booked *any* profit in the years since his father's death *should* have triggered some sort of review. Most companies couldn't survive bleeding red ink like that for more than a few quarters; not only had Cardinal stayed viable, but it had also expanded — at least, based on the revenues being booked.

Shifting screens again, I went back to the trove of data from the USB stick and located the list of vendors Myrtle had hidden in plain sight, then yanked out of the stack the purchase order log I'd managed to find buried beneath product catalogs and project plans. The first bottle of beer got me through separating out the orgs *funding* the efforts of The Cardinal Group from those providing goods and services to the firm; there had only been a handful in the pre-Anton days, so those were easy to catalogue, but the number had quadrupled after he took over. I spent the better part of my second bottle of beer trying to trace the various organizations through the business directories I had access to; by the start of my third, I'd managed to winnow down the shell companies to two companies, both based out of rather shady areas of Eastern Europe. Tracing the dollars would take more beer than I had in the fridge, but my gut was already telling me I was looking at some sort of elaborate money laundering scheme; what was less clear was why Anton hadn't hidden it better, for the fluctuations on the books after Anton took over were quite visibly tied to the difference between the funding he'd received and payments made to vendors.

Sitting back on the couch and rubbing my grainy contact lenses, I wondered how they'd wound up being the selected bid on the housing project, or the even scoring the demolition of the old police headquarters building; while there was physical evidence they could *do* stuff, at least on paper, they had no viable reason to exist. Cash flow was *always* negative, without fail. And yet, they continued to win contracts; sighing, it seemed likely there were other as yet undocumented payments being made to interested parties, those who could make or break a project. As the clock closed in on half past two, I tried — and failed — to understand why nothing I'd uncovered had provoked even the slightest curiosity from any agency that had oversight over Cardinal. Rancho Linda wasn't New York City, not by a long stretch; those sorts of real estate shenanigans were far less frequent in California, mostly owing to those agencies keeping such excesses in check.

Tapping at my laptop, I wondered if Vivian had put together the same pieces; if she'd actually dated Anton as the photo from Angel's Stadium suggested, maybe she'd seen something, too. Shifting screens again, I went back to that photo and stared at the young couple; whatever else had happened since, it was clear the two of them were deeply in love at the time it was taken. Or were they *still* in love? I'd scanned the transcripts from the voicemails Gina's team had uncovered, and she'd not been wrong in her characterization — there was some pretty steamy stuff in there from Anton. It made the buttoned-down version I met at his office seem like some sort of carefully crafted public persona incapable of the hot emotion clearly on display. The bi-directional texts between the two of them had filled in more of the blanks, revealing a relationship that had apparently continued long, long after the universe thought the two had split for good. The Vivian Grandchester of the text messages was diametrically different than the crusading journalist I'd known; the passion on display was, even to a gay guy, rather erotic and had me reassessing my view of the woman.

At least until the final set of messages that had flown between the two on the day she'd been killed. Moving between windows on my laptop, I pulled up the transcript of the texts and then scrolled toward the bottom; tapping at the side of the MacBook, I re-read the same section that Gina and her team had flagged, for it marked a decided change in tone between the two.

Ant: We've got to meet. This is getting out of hand.

Viv: Well beyond that. It's gone to press.

Ant: You can still pull it. Or correct it.

Viv: There's nothing to correct. Not on my end.

Ant: What is that supposed to mean?

Viv: You can't play that card any longer. But if you'd come to me sooner, maybe the outcome would have been different.

Interestingly, there was a good ten-minute space between that message from Grandchester and the response from Cardinal.

Ant: I need help. I can't get out of this without you.

Viv: Give me the details.

Ant: Not like this. Not over text. We have to meet.

Viv: Where?

Ant: You know where. Tonight.

I stared at the last message in the chain, for it was *truly* the last message; dated a few hours before Peg thought Grandchester had died, it more or less confirmed why the reporter was where we found her. The messages were tantalizingly scant on the underlying reason for Cardinal's apparent panic, but if the records I'd spent the long evening reviewing were any indication, it seemed highly likely whoever was bankrolling him would not have looked kindly upon whatever article Grandchester was preparing to publish. And that seems to have been her fatal flaw; I was certain now that Cardinal had seen through her bluff about it already going to press, giving him a pretty damn good motive for wanting to eliminate her *and* anyone else who had access to the same information she'd based her reporting upon. My gut twisted at how he had apparently shifted from lover to murdering the one he loved, but it also wasn't the first time I'd seen it; now more than ever, I had to recover what Grandchester had pulled together — and figure out how to place Cardinal at the scene.

Simple, I laughed to myself. *All in a day's work.*

Yawning, I ran my hands through my still-shorter-than-I-liked hair and reminded myself to swing past the library in the morning to confirm what I could through the archives; smiling, I mentally self-corrected to *later* that morning then closed the lid on the laptop. I was about to get up and hunt for a spare blanket in the laundry room when my iPhone started to buzz; groaning that work might be calling at that hour, my eyebrows shot up when I saw it was Sean Colbeth.

Tapping to answer, I tried to sound less tired than I felt. "You're up late."

"Your math is off," came the chuckle from the other end. "Actually, I'm just getting back from the gym; I didn't think you'd pick up, so I was planning on leaving you a voicemail about the postmortem for Myrtle McKenna."

"I'm pulling an all-nighter to go through the info we got," I explained. "Or mostly an all-nighter. I was about to call it quits."

"Find anything?"

"Yeah," I replied. "Plenty of evidence that The Cardinal Group was taking in a ton of money from overseas investors that they plowed into their development portfolio. Classic laundering that was only partially hidden in their filings."

"It wouldn't be the first time that a 'developer' took in shady money."

"Nor the last. I think my victim — the first one, that is — had figured that out, and my prime suspect eliminated her before she had a chance to reveal it to the world."

"You like that Cardinal guy for it?"

"I do," I nodded. "I don't have all of the pieces quite yet, but I'm close."

"Then heaven help him," Sean chuckled.

"I appreciate the vote of confidence. How was the PM?"

"No surprises," he said. "COD was gunshot to the head. TOD matches what we thought. About the only interesting aspect was the bullet matched rifling from an open-unsolved Bernie's been looking into. She's leaning toward this being some sort of murder for hire."

"That would fit." I felt an eyebrow arch. "Bernie? We're on a first name basis, now, are we?"

There was an uncomfortable silence. "That might be the other reason I'm calling," Sean replied. "I've spent a fair amount of time with her since you left and... I think she's hitting on me."

"Of course she is," I laughed quietly. "I could see that the moment she stepped out of her car."

The silenced stretched out again. "I... don't know what to do about it."

I started to quip something sarcastic and then caught myself when the penny dropped. "You still love Suzanne, don't you? After everything?"

"Yeah," was the ultimate response. "Yeah, I think I do."

"Huh," I said thoughtfully. "That complicates matters a bit."

"Yeah."

"Did you sleep with Bernie?"

"What? No!" Sean exclaimed. "I mean, Bernie's telegraphing she wants to go there, but I can't. I just can't."

"So what you're saying, then, is that you've not actually broken up with Suzanne," I sighed. "Contrary to everything you've told me since Thanksgiving."

There was a rueful chuckle from the other end. "I haven't seen her long enough to say much of anything, let alone actually try to end our relationship."

"It sounded to me like it had," I replied. "Ended. At least, based on what happened in New Hampshire."

"Or how we've been avoiding each other," Sean chimed in. "The whole thing's kind of a hot mess."

"That's one way to look at it," I said. "Are you going to call her?"

"Suzanne?"

"No, Bernie," I rolled my eyes. "Yes, Suzanne."

"Once I get to my dad's place," he answered. "I'll know what to say by then." He paused again. "She's still invited to the wedding, right?"

I was struck by Rosie having told me earlier to keep Sean's now not-quite-ex girlfriend on the list. "Yes."

"Maybe I don't need to call—"

"*Yes*," I emphasized, "you do. I love you to pieces my friend, but I won't have you interjecting your own drama into the one I'm sure to have at my wedding."

"Ah," he chuckled. "Fair point."

"Entirely."

"I'll call, then."

"Good," I smiled. "Now I'm going to hang up so I can get some sleep before practice."

"Okay. Talk to you after I get to Dad's? I'm heading out after I pick up some files from Bernie; I should be there tonight."

"Sounds like a plan."

I hung up on Sean and then looked over to the closed door to the master bedroom; suddenly, finding a blanket seemed like a silly idea, especially when I knew who was waiting for me just beyond it. Was he going to be angry with me still? Maybe, but as I packed up my computer and then padded across the carpet toward the room, I realized my need to simply be close to him trumped that concern. Putting my hand to the knob, I turned it as quietly as I could and then tiptoed into the darkened space; shedding my clothes, I slipped beneath the sheet on my side of the bed and nearly gasped in shock when Alex suddenly pulled me toward him. The heat from his skin immediately warmed mine; a smile formed on my face when I saw the slight glint of the low light reflecting in his eyes.

"Took you long enough," he whispered, his voice thick with sleep.

"There was a lot to go through," I replied as I reached over and pushed some curls away from his beautiful face.

"Did you find what you needed?"

"I think so."

I saw him turn to look at his phone on the nightstand. "You're not going to get much sleep," he said as he turned back toward me.

"Yeah, I know," I sighed before I felt a tentative hand at my cock. "Oh," I smiled. "I see."

"You always do," he chuckled as he pressed his lips to mine.

TWENTY-FIVE
ANOTHER AM PM

For the first time in a *long* time, swim practice was a literal drag; Alex had been true to his word and had kept me occupied right up until I had to reluctantly roll out of bed and leave for the pool. Not that I was complaining; far from it. *Any* time spent with the man who had stolen my heart was worth enduring the inevitable crash I knew would ultimately be coming, though I hadn't expected it to happen in the middle of a brutal set that had been focused on the upper body. Coming into the far wall, I misjudged the distance and completely blew my flip turn; I realized immediately what I'd done when I kicked out of the rotation, hard, and was met with only empty space behind my feet. A few dolphin kicks got me back to the surface, but I misjudged that, too, and accidentally sucked down what felt like ten gallons of chlorinated water. Spluttering like an age-group swimmer that needed water wings, I grabbed what was left of my dignity — as well as the pull buoy that had begun to float away from me — then dog-paddled to the starting block, all but conceding I was in no shape for my usual Saturday session. Fortunately, it appeared that Coach was the only person who had seen my fiasco; the slight smirk on her face as I pulled myself out of the pool was enough, though, for me to feel the heat of embarrassment on my cheeks.

I was therefore in no mood to deal with the terrible showers in the locker room and instead toweled off, then pulled on a favorite pair of shorts over my still-damp swimsuit. Shrugging into a t-shirt Alex had given me back in July that was emblazoned with a smiling Mickey Mouse in Pride colors, I grabbed my swim backpack and headed out to my waiting Camaro; since I'd cut my workout short, I was running ahead of schedule, which translated into having more than enough time to get some sugary treats for the Chief Medical Examiner. Dropping my backpack into the footwell of the passenger seat, I smiled slightly at the thought I'd might break with long-standing practice and actually partake in something myself that morning, especially if I could get the barista to quadruple the amount of expresso in it. There was no question I was running on fumes, something a sizable jolt of caffeine might be able to address, albeit temporarily.

Pulling out of my spot — and idly noting that Rosie's spot was empty that morning — I made for the exit of the lot and then crossed Rancho Linda to get back to the 57. Part of me was screaming that I'd actually driven *up* to Rancho Linda for practice only to now have to drive *down* to Santa Ana for the postmortem; glancing at the odometer in my car, I shook my head to think at how many of those miles had been logged doing that exact routing since my return to California. Traffic at that early hour was fairly reasonable, and I made good time getting to the usual Starbucks just a few blocks away from the Orange County Office of the Medical Examiner. I ordered two different holiday-themed beverages for Peg, then shifted gears for myself and instead asked for the largest drop coffee they had on offer; carrying the tray back out to my car, I paused long enough to make an impressive dent on the extremely hot coffee before heading down the street. By the time I was walking across the parking lot to the Law Enforcement entrance, the first wave of caffeine had begun to percolate through my system, giving a little lift to my step and slight reduction in the haze that seemed to have been shrouding my brain that morning.

I changed out of my workout garb and into the thin scrubs provided in the locker room, then managed to balance the beverage holder in one hand as I made my way into Peg's preferred exam room. The Medical Examiner herself was in her usual position, standing between her computer console and the stainless-steel table bearing the body of our latest victim. Her head turned in my direction at the sound of the double doors being pushed open; her intelligent eyes immediately went to the tall plastic containers I was carrying.

"Is that one... pink?" she asked as I came up beside her.

"I believe the barista told me this is 'holly berry red,'" I said as I rotated the holder toward her.

"It looks like Pepto-Bismol."

"That's what I said," I smiled, though I knew she couldn't see it beneath the mask. "I nearly got thrown out of the store."

"Never make your barista mad," Peg said as she reached for the pink beverage.

"Exactly."

I pulled my coffee from the holder and then put the remaining drink down on the sideboard; pulling my mask down slightly, I took another deep sip from the brew and tried not to swoon too much. I might not have been as quiet as I thought, though, for when I looked at Peg, I could tell from the angle of her head that perhaps an eyebrow or two had been raised.

"You never do that in here," she observed. "Who are you and what did you do with Vasily?"

I chuckled. "It was a long night," I replied as I took another wonderful sip. "Massive doses of caffeine will be the only way I'm going to get to the end of this case today."

"You realize that's not very healthy, right?"

I shrugged. "Sean's been doing it for years," I said. "It hasn't killed him yet."

"Perhaps he's not exactly the right role model for you on this," Peg said. "Promise me you'll stop if you feel heart palpitations?"

"I don't think it will get to *that* level," I laughed. "But yes, I promise."

"Good."

I nodded at the table. "I don't want to get ahead of your presentation, but I presume my victim died from blunt force trauma to the head?"

Peg nodded. "More or less," she said as she took a sip from her own drink, then put it down beside her computer so she could tap at the keyboard. "I did a little pre-work before you got here—"

Glancing meaningfully at the open Y-incision on the cadaver, I chuckled. "We have differing definitions of 'little,' Peg. The organs are already labelled and on the cart over there."

"I work fast," she replied defensively. "And I have a brunch date to get to."

"Noted."

"Anyway," she continued as she turned the monitor toward me. It was displaying an X-ray of Hope's skull, and it was hard to miss how a significant portion of it had been crushed. "Two, maybe three blows in this location resulted in massive hemorrhaging; based on the shape of the injury, I believe it was delivered by something heavy and metallic, with ridges."

I blinked. "Like brass knuckles?"

Peg swiveled her head toward me. "Yes — yes, that would fit exactly," she answered. "We have some models on file; I'll run them against the 3D scan we did of your victim's head to confirm, but the pattern fits. What made you think of that?"

"Two goons in expensive suits tried to beat up Alejandro a few days ago," I explained. "One of them had a set; they're in evidence if you want me to send them over for comparison."

"Do." Peg paused. "Is he... okay?"

"He gave better than he got," I replied. "A little banged up, but no worse for the experience."

"Thank God! Why was he—"

"I think it was supposed to be a message for me," I interrupted. "To back off the investigation, much like the message I expect whoever visited this upon Hope Grandchester was trying to impart."

"Going after your fiancé feels all sorts of personal," Peg observed.

"It is. And it won't go unaccounted for."

Peg looked at me askance. "I don't doubt it." Tapping at the screen again, it shifted to show a CAT scan of the brain; even to my untrained eye, the blotch about where the injury was seemed bad. "This created a massive stroke within minutes," Peg continued. "I don't have the exact timing yet, but I believe she was, for all practical purposes, already dead when you found her."

"Well, shit," I sighed. "That doesn't really make me feel any better."

"I know, but I also know you well enough to think you probably are beating yourself up over this." She moved back over to the exam table and picked up the right arm, then angled the hand toward me. "Defensive wounds on both hands indicate she didn't go down without a fight, but other bruising on the upper body indicates a taller, stronger individual was able to overwhelm her."

The black-and-blue marks Peg pointed to stood out starkly against the linen white color skin takes on in death. "Held from behind or in front?"

"Front, I think, based on the bruising. The killing blow came from behind, though. My read is your victim was attempting to get away, or had turned away, from her attacker."

I nodded. "And then that, as they say, was that."

"Pretty much. Otherwise, your victim is in perfect health for a woman in her age bracket. Some minor plaque in the arteries, and maybe an extra pound or two over ideal, but that's it."

"We might have trouble making a formal identification," I said. "I believe my earlier victim was her only child, and the husband died about six years ago."

"It may well be," she nodded. "I'll try to tie the two victims together via DNA but that might be the best we can do."

"Any closure is better than none."

"Speaking of," Peg said. "Did I mention this victim had defensive wounds?"

"You did." I paused. "You found something? Trace? Under the nails?"

"Yes," she nodded. "Epithelial cells from her attacker."

My eyebrows went up. "Did you match them to anyone?"

"Yes," she nodded again. "Owing to the state of Vivian Grandchester's body, it was far harder to find trace evidence, but I have some talented techs here and they managed to pull something from what was left of her hands."

That sense the final pieces were clicking together hit me, hard. "The DNA was a match."

"Yes. I also went back and examined the head injury I flagged during my initial postmortem on Vivian; I can't be completely certain, but the pattern *could* be similar to the weapon used on Hope."

"It was the same person," I said. "It has to be."

"The odds favor that, yes, but it's not conclusive," she cautioned. "You might want some harder evidence in hand to back it up."

"I think I have an angle there," I smiled. "Though it still needs a bit of research. And a willing witness."

"One sounds far easier than the other," Peg observed as she wandered back to her computer and picked up the shockingly pink drink.

"Story of my life," I said as I started toward the door. "Thanks for coming in on your day off."

"My pleasure. And Vas?"

I paused with my gloved hand on the cool steel of the door and turned back. "Yeah?"

"Be careful," she said quietly. "Given how this looks, you could be in real danger when you confront whomever you think is the perpetrator."

I smiled again. "Don't worry," I said as I pushed the swinging door open, "Alex has already reminded me just how much trouble I'll be in should I get myself killed."

Twenty-Six
Yes, People Still Do
Wedding Announcements

Returning to Rancho Linda after the postmortem did seem a bit on brand, but I had one last stop to make before I could shift into the final stages of the investigation. I was nearly certain I had everything I needed to make my case, though as the tepid water from the shower in the locker room for the morgue cascaded over me, it felt like I still had a few loose ends that I might never be able to fully tie up. The loss of Grandchester's research meant proving some of what I suspected was going to be difficult without a little help — and a healthy dose of my customary legerdemain. Scrubbing away with the terrible industrial strength body wash on offer, I decided any strategizing would need to wait until after I'd been to the research desk at the library; once I knew what I had, I might have some additional insights that would allow me to weave my final tapestry.

True to form, I'd not packed a spare set of clothes in my swim backpack, so I was reduced to tossing back on my Speedos (which were still damp from my workout) along with the shorts and t-shirt I'd worn to the pool. It wasn't ideal, but now that I had the scent of the finale in my nose, I didn't want to take the time to swing past the condo for something a bit more professional. Running a hand through my hair, I prayed it would grow out a bit faster and then grabbed my backpack from the floor to head out to my car. The brilliant blue sky I encountered as I pushed out into the day made my inner surfer whine slightly; it was the sort of weather that could induce one to grab their hunk of a significant other for a day spent canoodling beneath a beach umbrella in between sessions on the waves. By the time I reached my Camaro, I'd managed to talk myself into staying on track, but only with the silent promise that I make good on such plans at some point in the near future.

Traffic was two-to-one in favor of those heading in the direction of the surf, though, a visible reminder that I might have not chosen wisely. Still, it also meant I made exceptionally good time returning to Rancho Linda and pulled into the main parking lot outside of the library a hair past nine. I was a little surprised at how many early bird readers were already in the parking lot when I got out of my car, though as soon as I spied the young mother carrying one kid and walking hand-in-hand with another toward the ornate entrance, I suspected I knew what the main attraction might be at that hour. My theory was confirmed when I wandered inside and saw on the small whiteboard easel that children's story hour started at the bottom of the hour; having been a volunteer for such things at *The Alternative Way*, I was rather thankful the research side of the facility was on the other end of the building.

I always thought of the old fashioned Windeport Library Sean's cousin ran each time I was in the one for Rancho Linda; I'd spent many hours poring through materials there that were otherwise difficult to obtain over the internet or any other service Sean had subscribed to at the time. The Rancho Linda Library was far newer, of course, something that was reflected in its Art Deco design and Frank Lloyd Wright-esque appointments. Turning at the large circulation desk, I made my way through the stacks to the smaller Reference Desk; there, to my surprise, I found a familiar face working at the computer.

"Beverly? They have you working on weekends now?"

The striking woman looked up and smiled at me. "Hey, Vas! It's been a while."

"It has indeed," I smiled back as I leaned on the counter. "I thought being promoted meant you were able to choose your own hours."

Beverly Granell, the newly minted Head Reference Librarian, shook her head. "No, it actually means that you get to cover for everyone when *they* take the weekend off unexpectedly."

"Well, shit."

"Exactly," she laughed. "Though it's pretty quiet at this end of the library on the weekend, so I usually get to catch up on my work."

"I noticed," I replied. "Got time for a question?"

"For you, of course," she said as she eyed my work backpack slung over a shoulder.

"Do you still have back issues of all of the local newspapers?"

Beverly nodded. "We do, though since the last time you were pawing through our source material, it's been digitized. No more scanning microfilm or microfiche."

"Damn," I sighed dramatically. "That was the only reason I came."

"And here I thought it was because of how cute I am," she laughed.

I smiled slightly; as much time as I'd spent in the library — and as well-known as I'd become in the community — Beverly seemed to have a willful blind spot about my sexuality. Rather than be frustratingly annoying, I actually found it kind of endearing. "Human Resources would prefer that I not speak to that," I said.

"Yeah, I imagine they would," she sighed. "What are you looking for?"

"Wedding announcements, especially for the wealthy."

She looked thoughtful for a moment. "That's probably the only segment of the population that still puts those sorts of things in the paper. Most ordinary people just post it on their social media these days."

I raised my eyebrows. "That doesn't seem very traditional."

"Times change, Vas."

"Tell me about it."

Beverly stood from her seat and walked around the desk. "How far back to you need to go?"

Thinking back to what Gina had told me, I had a ready answer. "I think the one I am hunting for would have been printed between 1998 and 2001," I said. "But it might be wise to err a few years on either side."

"Well, lucky for you, our new software makes it pretty easy to do that. Come along to my inner sanctum and I'll show you the ropes."

I decided it would be best not to remind Beverly it wasn't my first rodeo and instead simply smiled before following her down one of the aisles between shelves of books. Contrary to my initial impression, there were adult patrons sprinkled here and there, perusing what was on offer or quietly reading the latest edition of the *Los Angeles Times* in a sunny spot beside one of the giant picture windows. While I had long thought of the library as useful resource for my day job, until that moment I'd never considered it as a place to just to hang out and chill; my tastes tended to run more in the direction of cafés like *The Alternative Way* where I could munch on freshly baked pastries while enjoying some live music. Still, having spent a fair amount of time in a library, I could completely get how appealing a place it could be for quiet contemplation.

Beverly turned and then turned again, entering a small room I was quite familiar with; several generous work surfaces hugged the walls, holding various machines that I was relatively certain anyone born after the turn of the millennium would be hard pressed to identify. We moved right past the microfilm reader and over to an extremely modern looking curved monitor currently displaying the logo for the library; Beverly reached down and tapped at the keyboard briefly, bringing up whatever application it was that had, essentially, replaced the old-fashioned process of reviewing yards and yards of film. Part of me was a bit surprised that the Rancho Linda Library had managed to forestall progress for as long as it had; the rest of me wasn't ashamed to admit I was going to miss hearing the whirring of the wheels as I sped through pages of ancient newspaper articles. Something had been lost in being reduced to tapping away at a keyboard to get what you needed.

Stepping back, Beverly gestured to the screen. "This is the master search window," she began. "Give it the date range *here*, and the keywords you want *there*, then hit the big button to get it to go. You can do deeper filters by clicking that drop down arrow over there."

"Okay," I nodded as I pulled out the chair and sat down. "And if I want to print anything I find?"

"Send them to the printer at my station," she answered. "Pages are at the usual price."

"All right," I nodded again. "Hopefully this won't take long."

"Ever the optimist," she laughed. "I'll be at my desk if you get into trouble."

"Thanks."

Beverly nodded and then withdrew, leaving me to my task; sliding my MacBook out of the backpack, I set it up on the counter and logged in. It had been literally years since I'd scribbled anything into the department-issued notebook we all carried around, though it had far more to do with the illegibility of my handwriting than the fact it seemed like an anachronism from a time long past. I stared at the screen for a moment, then punched in the date range I suspected might cover the announcement and then paused again as I tried to decide the best keyword to search for. Making the assumption that it would be bigger news about the heir to a major developer getting hitched, I added Anton Cardinal to the box, then hit the *go* button. In mere seconds, the screen filled with a list of citations, far more than I'd expected; scanning the items, I found them to be a mix of business reporting as well as more mundane social notations about Anton. I wasn't surprised to find he was a star athlete in high school (baseball), though apparently not enough of one to score a scholarship anywhere. Graduation from his MBA program at USC's Marshall School of Business was covered as though it were a royal affair, with a nearly three-quarters of a page dedicated to the event *and* a full color photo of a very young Anton in robes. I wasn't all that surprised to see that the reporter who had written the article was, in fact, Vivian Grandchester; her trademark clipped phrasing and direct-to-point style was one that had been deployed against me nearly two decades later.

Wondering if that was the first time she'd covered Anton, I side-tracked myself for a moment and did a cross reference between her as the reporter and Anton as the subject; that shrunk the citations by nearly half, which in itself was extremely interesting. Starting from the oldest, I scanned through them and found that Grandchester's first article about Cardinal was shortly after she started at the *Register*; it was a fluff piece about some sort of strip mall being designed by the firm, and Anton — who, if the dates were right, would have been in the first year of his MBA at the time — had been the one leading her through the community elements of the plan. I smiled to think of the flowery phrasing Anton had used to describe what had wound up being a pedestrian retail outlet on the outskirts of Rancho Linda; since returning to work for the department, I was relatively certain the main tenant had changed at least four times, a telling sign about the viability of the location.

It wasn't clear to me how long Grandchester had been assigned to the business beat for the paper, but it was long enough that I could watch Anton's path as it first veered away from doing anything with his father's company to suddenly taking over everything. Only then did the tone of the articles shift ever so slightly; it wasn't that they had been overwhelmingly *glowing* about the capitalist-in-training, but once Anton was in charge, they shifted ever so slightly into something more acerbic. Bylines with Grandchester's name on them then began to thin out about a decade ago, though every once in a while, an article would pop up revealing some rather unsavory business practice at The Cardinal Group, one that would be hastily stopped (or better hidden) according to later follow-up reporting. I would need to do a cross-reference against Grandchester's entire body of work, but it certainly hinted at her rise as an investigative journalist. Scrolling to the end of the results, I noted the most recent exposé written about The Cardinal

Group had been just a few months earlier; Grandchester appeared to have been extremely interested in how Anton had been financing their latest efforts — including the housing project by the reservoir — and found that same connection I'd seen in the financials to those rather sketchy overseas investors. From the way the story had been written, uncovering the money trail had involved digging through multiple shell companies that had been little more than a series of post office boxes in various large cities forwarding to each other. My eyebrows went up when I saw that two of the companies seemed to have been on the list of organizations sanctioned by the Feds, making me wonder again why no one had flagged the organization earlier; another firm represented the interest of a sovereign wealth fund based in the Middle East, something that felt like it would have required far more vetting than ultimately appeared to have happened..

Sitting back in my chair, I rubbed at my chin thoughtfully and was startled again at the stubble beneath my fingertips; it was an itchy reminder that I'd had rather erotic plans for the weekend that had yet to transpire. Grabbing my iPhone from where it was resting beside my MacBook, I turned on the selfie camera and took a good look at myself; save for a brief flirtation when I'd first arrived in California, I wasn't one for facial hair of any kind and frowned at having let myself go that long without cleaning up. Twisting my head, I sighed deeply at what had become of my hair; having it shaved off at the hospital meant I was seeing my natural hair color for the first time in forever, and the experience was less than thrilling. Giovanni — the hairdresser Alex and I shared — had assured me I was *maybe* a month away from being able to do something — *anything* — with it. Putting my phone back down on the counter, I grumbled to myself a bit about how the universe was working against me at the moment before returning to the task that actually mattered.

Backing up slightly, I reset the date range and then went through the archives a second time hunting for the wedding announcement I was certain would be there. I knew the small postings in the paper were an anachronism from another time, but as I read through what turned out to be a substantial list of them, I smiled at the thought that at the end of the day, humans tended to be creatures of tradition no matter how small they might be. Reviewing the photos felt a bit like rewinding the clock, too; hairstyles I'd not seen in decades reminded me of the bouffant my mother used to wear when she entertained at the family mansion in Newport Beach, and the massive aviator glasses everyone seemed to be rocking further proof that my fixation on contact lenses was well placed. Shoulder pads became rounded then disappeared; clean-shaven men shifted to carefully manicured stubble, then flowing beards. Unsurprisingly each couple had that glow about them or at least were *trying* to put out there the image that they'd found true love at last. I wasn't all that shocked that the preponderance of the postings were, of course, for hetero couples; the effect of California legalizing same-sex marriages kicked in on the back third of the entries, finally showcasing the diversity of what love could *actually* be. My eyes lingered on one entry toward the end of the list; two guys, maybe in their mid-twenties, were holding hands and looking into each other's eyes like the rest of the world didn't exist. It was the most truthful photo I'd seen yet, lifting my heart in ways I found hard to quantify — maybe, perhaps, because I felt the same way each time I got lost in those beguiling dark brown eyes of my fiancé.

Frowning slightly, I realized I'd not come across anything for Grandchester and rewound the list to the top so I could start over. When I didn't find anything on my second review, I sat back in my chair for a moment and pondered the possibility that I was wrong about their relationship; all I had was anecdotal evidence they'd been a couple, with nothing but a single photo from a random ballgame and steamy sexts to possibly back it up. Turning to my laptop, I sifted through the case system until I was able to pull up the photo in question, then zoomed in again on the ring Grandchester was wearing; given the size of the diamond, it was *extremely* unlikely the ring wasn't of the engagement variety, but then again, the wealthy tended to play by a different set of rules than the rest of us. There was a chance, however small, it was a weirdly expensive gift, but as I stared at the ring, I felt myself shaking my head. Zooming back out again, I took in the stolen moment the photo had captured and the unvarnished emotions on display; shaking my head again, I felt even *more* certain something was there.

That, I thought to myself, *is nearly as truthful as shot as that gay couple. Those two are in love.* Looking at the list of wedding announcements, I frowned. *Where the fuck is your entry, then?*

There are times when I marvel at how my brain makes connections; as I stared accusingly at the library computer, it happened again when the conversation I had with Rosie at the diner suddenly popped into my head.

I'd forgotten about that. A bit of a scandal at the time now that I think about it.

I managed to prevent myself from slapping the palm of my hand to my forehead and instead went back to work on the database. In moments, I'd pulled up everything posted into the *Around Town* sections from any of the papers published in Orange County; while purporting to be a local eye on events in the various communities that made up the O.C., in truth it was usually thinly veiled and scantily sourced gossip. Four entries in, I hit pay dirt with an article published nearly twenty years earlier.

HUNKY HEIR TO FORTUNE DATING ONE OF US - (Rancho Linda) - Jaws dropped around Southern California yesterday when dreamboat Anton Cardinal was spotted dining with up-and-coming journalist Vivian Grandchester. Cardinal, 26, has apparently taken time out from prepping to take over from his father in order to woo the vixen who is apparently just a year older. Considering the depth and breadth of eligible maidens in the O.C., it remains to be seen if this match is a solid one or just a momentary fixation.

I frowned slightly at the terrible prose, not to mention the use of the word *maiden*; I was relatively certain no woman had ever wanted to be called that, even when it was in fashion during the late Middle Ages. *Vixen* also seemed to portend the sort of coverage the couple was slated to receive, something I quickly confirmed with succeeding entries in the database; one of the final missives seemed especially venomous, making me think the family might have had a hand in getting it published.

IS SHE AFTER HIS MONEY? - (Rancho Linda) - A friend of the family has confided worries that the playboy son and heir to the Cardinal fortune might be blind to what is actually going on, especially since it seems clear his purported fiancé is actually a social climber that will jettison him once she has access to his trust fund.

As was normal with such tabloid fare, the "reporting" relied more on innuendo and background whispers than any sort of direct quotes from primary sources. Rolling back through the entries, I tried to discover where the tone of the coverage shifted from fawning to scathing; it wasn't hard to see that the dates roughly aligned with the first hard-hitting article Grandchester published about The Cardinal Group, hinting that the family was less than thrilled with the spotlight she'd placed on them. Since she had apparently continued churning out hard-hitting investigative pieces about the firm, the smear campaign on the gossip pages had not affected her in the least, though I did wonder how quickly her relationship with Anton had dissolved after the first one had been published. I didn't feel like I knew Grandchester well enough to gauge whether she would have been the kind of journalist to use her relationship with Anton to gather material for an investigation; it did seem likely, though, whatever access she might have enjoyed would have evaporated once she'd gone public with her reporting.

So, the relationship went south — which feels like a fair assumption — but that doesn't prevent her from continuing her work, I mused and then found myself struck by a thought. *I wonder if I'm reading this backwards — what if that first article came out* as a result *of Grandchester being cast aside?*

Splitting the screen, I lined up all of the articles the reporter had written beside the gossip articles; knowing that it wasn't entirely an appropriate correlation, I wasn't all that surprised to find that first in-depth piece on The Cardinal Group was published *after* the gossip tide had turned against her. Sitting back in my chair again, I ran my hands over my scalp as I tried to poke holes in my theory. Had she done her work in retaliation? Was that why she'd been so fixated on The Cardinal Group over the years? I needed more information than the newspaper articles were ever going to provide, but my gut was telling me I was on to something — especially since it pointed to a possible motive for her death.

She uncovered something, something big enough that Anton or his cronies couldn't erase with some vitriol in the Local section of the paper, I thought. *I know how thorough Vivian can be, so it's not a stretch to also assume her reporting would have been backed up by solid research. Research,* I sighed, *that went up smoke. Damn. If only I'd been a few hours earlier, or she'd had the presence of mind to keep a copy—*

I sat bolt upright in my chair.

Shit. Of course she had a copy! And I bet I know where it might be, too.

Shifting back to my laptop, I went through the list of items we'd recovered from both the crime scene and Grandchester's car. I found what I was looking for on the fourth page and smiled rather grimly for having overlooked what it might have represented. Grabbing my iPhone, I speed-dialed Judge Spenser's private number and impatiently waited for the call to go through.

"Vas?" was the puzzled response when my friend picked up. "What an unexpected delight on this marvelous weekend morning. Please tell me you've finally decided to join me for jazz brunch."

"I need a favor," I said without preamble.

"Mother of God," Spense sighed. "If it were anyone else, I'd hang up now."

"I've just solved my case but need a search warrant in order to prove it."

There was a pause. "Is this in regard to that dead journalist?"

"It is."

"I told your office earlier this week that it's a much higher bar—"

"Spense," I interrupted. "She's dead and could give a flying fuck now about any possible Fourth Amendment violations. I'm also reasonably certain her mother was killed last night as payment for keeping her daughter's secrets from me — not to mention all of her research went up in smoke when the house they shared burned to the ground."

"Wait, what are you talking about—?"

"They even came after Alex," I continued, playing my last trump card. "This is my last, best shot at closing the case."

The pause was longer this time and felt more thoughtful. "You have probable cause?"

"I do." I waited a beat. "I know I'm right, Spense. I just need a little leeway to get there."

"You don't ask for much, do you?" he sighed. "Walk me through what you have…"

Twenty-Seven
In The Vault

First Bank of Southern California was housed in a beautiful Art Deco building in the heart of downtown Rancho Linda. I'd never been inside the structure despite it just being a few blocks from our original headquarters building; not being a fan of commercial banks in general, I'd kept my accounts with the small credit union I'd used when I'd been working in Windeport and, given how much I could do online, had no desire to shift anything to one based in California. I knew my parents had private customer privileges with one of the large New York-based banks; I'd always assumed it was some sort of status symbol to be fêted by a personal banker, though I also wondered just how many digits had to be on your balance in order to get such a high level of customer service. Me? I was completely happy snapping a copy of a check with my iPhone and calling it a day. It was the little things, truly.

It had taken all of my charm and then some to get Judge Spense to issue my search warrant; he'd been more than a little skeptical of my reasoning and extremely wary with respect to the thin circumstantial evidence I'd provided him. Still, I'd yet to lead him astray when making such requests; while there was always a chance this could be that fateful first time, I felt confident I was right. Pulling into the parking lot close to three that afternoon, I glanced at the paper folded in half on the passenger seat beside me and for a moment felt that confidence falter.

No, I thought as I turned off the Camaro and grabbed the warrant, *I'm right.*

Locking the car, I dashed across the pavement to the front door and pulled it open only to find a well-dressed guy standing there wearing a surprised expression and holding a set of keys. "Sorry," I smiled as I tried to sneak past him. "I didn't see you there."

"We're closed," the guy said as he stepped back and then blocked my path to the counter.

"Really?" I asked. "That seems early."

"It's Saturday," he replied.

"It is," I nodded. "Is the manager around?"

"I'm the manager," he said. "And we're still closed."

"Vasily Korsokovach," I smiled as I flashed him my badge and then held out the warrant. "Deputy Chief, Rancho Linda Police Department. I have a warrant to access a safe deposit box tied to one of your clients"

The guy frowned as he took the warrant from my outstretched hand. As his eyes flicked over the text, I finally saw the slim metal name badge clipped to his lapel. "You do indeed," Harold Weaver sighed. "And of all days, too. My kid has to be at a pool party this afternoon and I'm already late to pick him up from the ex."

"I do apologize," I smiled slightly, "and will try to make this as quick as I can."

Harold looked at me. "Actually, screw it. She owes me one — I didn't want to go anyway, and she can deal with the precious cherub. You can wait in my office; I need a moment to lock up and get the tellers started cashing out for the day."

"Thank you," I said, wondering slightly if I was seeing why Weaver had an ex.

The office was nicely appointed with the standard plastic Ficus in one corner and generic framed landscape oil painting on the other; about the only unique item was a handsome globe that appeared to be made entirely of wood. Each continent had been meticulously scribed into the surface of the sphere, with key details like capitals or landmarks. I was tempted to spin the globe much but decided against it; instead, I perused a glossy brochure on possible investment planning options sponsored by First Bank. Thankfully, Weaver rescued me before I got too far into it.

"All right," he said as he breezed into the office and sat down at the large wooden desk. Tapping at the keyboard, he looked at the warrant. "Vivian Grandchester…" he murmured as he scanned the screen. "Yes, she does have a box with us." He looked up at me. "I presume you don't have her key?"

"I do, actually."

I pulled the small evidence bag from the pocket of my shorts and held it up to him; while I'd been waiting for the warrant to work its way through the system, I'd made a mad dash to our new headquarters building to retrieve the key from the evidence locker. How I'd overlooked the unique cut of the key the first time was beyond me, but to be fair, I wasn't sure how many people still used such things as safety deposit boxes anymore. I'd only managed to recognize what it was after realizing the GPS data from Grandchester's phone hinted at where she might have stashed her work; it was, perhaps, another sign that I was working on too little sleep and way too much caffeine.

Weaver looked at the bag. "I'm almost afraid to ask what has happened to Ms. Grandchester."

"Probably wise not to," I nodded.

He looked at me for a long moment. "The safe is this way," he ultimately said as he stood up.

I followed him across the ornate lobby that felt as though it had come straight out of a Walt Disney movie, then waited as he pulled out his ring of keys to unlock a golden gate that barred access to the massive safe. Unlocking it, he swung the gate open and then stepped inside; I was right behind him, my impatience at wanting to finally get to the end of the case on full display. Weaver paused to read the small numbers inset on each box before finding the right one; inserting another key from his ring, he twisted it and then pulled the container backwards, smoothly removing it from the wall. Holding it carefully, he turned and nodded toward the door to the safe.

"There's a viewing room just outside," he said as he moved in that direction.

"Sounds good."

We exited the safe and immediately turned into a small space just off to the left; Weaver went directly to a table in the center of the room and placed the box down on top, then snapped on a small ornate task lamp that was sitting beside it. "I'm going to check on how the tellers are doing with their cash out," he said as he stepped backwards. "I can check back with you afterwards."

"Thanks."

I waited for Weaver to nod and then bow out of the small room before I dug a pair of latex gloves from my backpack; snapping them on, I grabbed my iPhone and took a few photos of the exterior of the box before I opened the evidence bag to retrieve the key. It turned easily in the lock on top of the small rectangular box, and once engaged, served as a sort of handle to flip the lid open. Tempted as I was to play dramatic music to mark the occasion, I opted instead for the muted hum of the air conditioning as my soundtrack as I peered inside the small box. Snapping a few more photos, I set my iPhone down on the counter and then began to remove what was inside; the first thing was a small box in brown leather, which I placed directly beneath the small task lamp. Taking another photo, I then carefully cracked it open to reveal the extravagant diamond ring I'd first seen in the photo from Angels Stadium. Leaning closer, I marveled at the cut of the diamond; even in the poor light of the room, it sparkled a blue white that spoke to just how expensive it was. Gently closing it, I unzipped another pocket of my backpack and produced a few more evidence bags; sliding the ring inside, I signed and dated the bag and then set it aside.

Next out was a small, zippered pouch; nestled inside were four USB sticks labelled as being one terabyte in size. Each had a small notation on them, which might not have made sense to anyone who hadn't already been trying to piece together the work that Grandchester had been doing; one was marked *Finances*, while another had the tag *Foreign Investors*. The third said, simply, *Anton*; the last one, though smudged, clearly read *Supply Chain and Finale*, confirming perhaps my hunch about the nature of the journalist's plan for publishing her articles. Those went into separate evidence bags, which I sealed and added to my pile; I'd have to wait to review their contents until Gina's team had cleared them.

A small laptop was next; turning it over in my gloved hands, my eyebrows went up when I saw the inventory label from The Cardinal Group. Popping open the lid, I was able to confirm the battery was quite dead; I had to hunt through my backpack for a bigger evidence bag for the device. As I slid it inside, I prayed that whatever Grandchester had needed from it would still be accessible to my tech nerds.

Beneath that was a leather-bound notebook; pulling it from the box, I discovered it was actually an old-fashioned accounting ledger of the sort I'd only ever seen in period movies. Thinking I knew what I was looking at, I gently opened the cover and found a meticulous record of entries going back nearly twenty years; it was no mere historical record, though, for the final pages listed dates as late as the prior August. Running my gloved finger over the line items, I slowly began to nod; having just gone through the official tax filings of The Cardinal Group, it was clear I was looking at the *real* books for the organization, and they painted (unsurprisingly) a wildly different fiscal view than what the State of California had been led to believe. I was going to need time to digest the information, but the series of sticky notes that had been added to various pages told me Grandchester had already done most of the legwork; I nodded again in grudging admiration at how she had doggedly matched up entries and tied them to specific entities doing business with Cardinal; some matched the shady names I'd already uncovered myself, but others were not familiar. Not that it mattered, for the pattern was pretty clear: Cardinal's true business model had been taking in overseas investments and washing them enough that they were squeaky clean at the other end, no matter the project. That anything was being built at all felt like something of a miracle, though it did begin to explain why our new headquarters had felt so shoddily constructed.

Lowest cost bidder my ass, I thought.

Closing the ledger, I slipped it into another evidence bag and then returned to the box. At the very bottom, sealed in plastic, were two tickets; holding them up to the light, I smiled slightly to see they were for the Angels - Twins matchup on Wednesday, May 30, 2001. The seats were good, too, though I could also see that prices had increased quite a bit in the decades since. Turning the package over, my eyebrows went up when I found a small handwritten note behind them; my heart broke ever so slightly as I read it.

05/30/2001

The happiest day of my life

It wasn't much of a stretch to assume Cardinal had proposed to Grandchester that day; the fact she had kept the tickets as a memento of the occasion seemed especially poignant, given how they were hidden among the evidence she was likely using to take down her one-time fiancé's organization. Humans could be a complicated mess of contradictions at times, something I was uncomfortably aware of. Opening one final evidence bag, I slid the tickets into it with care, then took another long look at it before sealing the flap and signing the exterior. Looking the pile of items I'd pulled from the box, I felt once more that I'd never truly known Vivian; we'd had our differences, to be sure, but now I wondered how we might have gotten on had I been able to get past what she had done to me. People could hold the strangest grudges, and I was certainly no exception; in that case, the loss was all mine.

I'd just finished putting all of the bags into my backpack when Weaver reappeared. "Do you need any more time?" he asked with just enough of a tone to indicate he wasn't entirely willing to grant any.

Zipping up my backpack, I shook my head. "I'm done," I said, answering more than just the question he was asking.

Twenty-Eight
Showdown

There was a significant part of me that knew I'd never get a confession out of Anton Cardinal, especially if I tried to drag him down to the department for an interview. Still, that was the fastest way to ensure I could get his ass behind bars with a minimum amount of fuss, so once I was back behind the wheel of my Camaro, I immediately began to plot how to get him there. The direct approach seemed like my best option, so I dug through my wallet for the business card Cardinal had given me and then dialed the wireless number showing just below his title. Somewhat surprisingly, the man himself answered on the first ring.

"Anton Cardinal."

"Hi," I said cheerfully. "This is Vasily Korsokovach. We met earlier this week?"

There was a pause. "You're that police officer, aren't you?"

"Yes," I replied. "Look, I just wanted to let you know that my team is headed back to the construction site where we found our victim; we have new information that the murderer may have left something incriminating behind, so we've got to go back through the scene again."

"Seriously?" he said, his voice tinged with anger. "I lost a full day of work the last time you were there."

"Which is why we're going tonight," I said. "It shouldn't take long. And, to be perfectly honest, it's just me heading back. My Chief isn't willing to pay the overtime to roll the entire crime scene unit. But I should be in and out — I'm pretty sure I'm about to close this case."

"Really?"

"Yes," I said, trying to sound as certain as possible. "So long as I find what I'm looking for. Thankfully, our victim left me a trail of clues."

"Did she?" Cardinal said, making his first mistake.

"Oh yes," I smiled to myself. "A very *clear* trail. I just wanted to let you know what was going on if anyone called you. I assume someone will be on site tonight?"

"No," he replied. "We don't staff after hours."

"Oh, right," I said as though this were the first time I were hearing that. "Well, any chance you could get someone to let me in?"

There was a long pause. "Yeah, I can make a call."

"Great!" I replied enthusiastically. "It won't take long, I don't think."

"And it's just going to be you?"

"Just little ol' me," I answered, then iced the proverbial cake. "I can't stay long, either. I've got all of the victim's records with me and need to get them logged into evidence. It's going to be a long night."

"Sounds like it. I'll make sure the site it unlocked for you."

"I appreciate that."

"Good luck."

"Thanks."

I hung up and then immediately dialed Alex. "Hey," I said when he picked up. "I'm about to do something stupid and need your help."

"That doesn't sound promising," he replied. "Do I want to know the details?"

"It depends on how angry you want to be with me."

"Fuck," he breathed. "What are you getting into?"

"I'm about to take down the guy who ordered the hit on you."

There was a pause. "I'm in. What do you need?"

I blinked. "I thought you'd tell me to call my boss."

"Would you if I did?"

"No," I replied honestly. "Because he's gonna be even angrier than you."

"That's what I thought."

"Are you at the condo?"

"No, actually," he answered. "I snagged my favorite suit in the hot tub tonight after practice and since you appeared to be working late, I decided to get a replacement; the sporting goods store at the Rancho Linda Mall is the only one in Orange County that carries the colors I like in my size. I'm literally standing in the parking lot outside the mall."

I frowned. "I thought you were going to take it easy while you healed."

"I am," he replied. "I didn't do any handstand dives."

"We are quite the pair, aren't we?"

"That we are."

"Hang tight, then," I said as I started up the Camaro. "I'll be right over."

"Will do."

I hung up and immediately pulled out of my parking spot, then set a new land speed record getting to the mall. It wasn't hard to locate my fiancé — he was the only hunky diver with luxuriously thick black curls casually standing on the sidewalk in front of the main entrance. Pulling to the curb, I rolled down the passenger window so he could lean inside. "This feels a bit illicit," he smiled.

"More so after I give you this," I replied as I handed him my work backpack. "This has everything from the case I'm working on. Go straight to Rosie's mansion and lock yourself in, then wait for me to get there."

Alex's eyes widened. "Why does this suddenly feel more dangerous?"

"Because it is," I answered. "If you don't hear from me by midnight, call Chief Gilbert. Tell him I told you I was heading to the construction site where we found the victim to confirm a theory."

"Vas, I take back what I said earlier: this is nuts. I don't care if you're going to settle a score—"

"I'm already committed," I interrupted. "My suspect knows I'm heading over there. I need to turn up, or this is all for nothing."

"Fuck," he breathed.

I leaned over and kissed him. "If this goes right, we'll do that later."

"It better," he frowned. "Or there will be Hell to pay."

"Don't I know it."

"I really don't like this."

"Me, either," I replied. "See you soon."

I pulled away from Alex before he had a chance to talk me out of my scheme and zipped across the parking lot; glancing in the rearview mirror, I could tell even from a distance that he was extremely unhappy with me. I worried a bit that he might act rashly as a result, but there was no time to deal with that particular issue; pulling out of the mall parking lot, I shifted lanes and then turned my attention toward what was about to transpire. Traffic flowed reasonably freely for a late Saturday afternoon; since we were on the cusp of winter — meteorologically speaking — the sun was low enough on the horizon the hills surrounding Rancho Linda had begun to cast long shadows across everything. The irony that it was nearly a perfect setup for a horror movie wasn't lost on me, especially given the rather gruesome death that had already taken place at the construction site. While I had no intention of adding another body to the count, I was quite aware just how unpredictable suspects could be once they were cornered. Maybe it was how Alex had been looking at me as I'd handed him my backpack, or perhaps I'd finally figured out the lesson of what had happened to Sean back in August; whatever the reason, while I waited for a break in traffic to turn onto the access road for the construction site, I speed dialed my boss. There wasn't any way he could stop me at that point, but at least he might be quick to respond to what could turn out to be an epic disaster.

Gilbert picked up on the first ring. "I don't suppose ordering you to turn around would do any good," he said without preamble.

I sighed. "Alex called you, didn't he?"

"Fuck yes," he replied. I thought I could hear a siren in the background. "Why that man puts up with your shit is beyond me. I'm on the far side of the city; two other cars are en route but we're at least ten minutes out."

"I don't need—"

"Like *hell* you don't. Watch your ass and don't fucking do anything stupid until we get there."

There was no point in responding as my phone decided to do the triple beep indicating the line had been dropped; turning onto the access road, I wasn't sure how I felt about Alex turning me in. On some level, I'd kind of expected it; no, as my Camaro rumbled up the dirt road, my heart finally acknowledged that I'd essentially *banked* on him doing exactly what he'd done — while adding the warning that if I ever revealed I'd more or less manipulated him into it, he'd kill me himself.

I wasn't all that surprised to find the gate to the fence wide open, nor the dark Mercedes sitting in the very empty de facto parking lot just beyond. There were lights on in the small portable construction office, and as I pulled the Camaro in beside the Mercedes, I thought I spied something flickering on the ground level of the first building. Shutting off my car, I grabbed my gun from the safe in the glovebox, then shrugged into the shoulder holster that I detested; clipping my badge to the waistband of my microfiber shorts, I snagged the industrial strength flashlight from the glovebox and then exited the Camaro. Aside from the soft hiss of traffic cruising by far below the site, it was deathly quiet; the shadows of the early evening had plunged the site into early twilight, causing the songbirds to call it a day — along with just about every other critter in what passed for the woods in Southern California.

Gravel crunched under my sneakers as I carefully made my way toward the construction office; procedure dictated that I call out my presence, but I intrinsically knew there wasn't anybody inside waiting for me — a suspicion confirmed when I found the door wide open, and the space inside thoroughly tossed. My eyes widened slightly at the carnage, for I'd only said what I'd said to try and draw out Anton Cardinal; the fact that he truly *thought* something tying him to the murder was still present at the scene was an unexpected bonus, one I could turn to my favor. Backing out of the office, I made my way across the lot to the first building; as I passed the storage yard, it was hard to miss that the gate for the heavy equipment was also unlocked and open, a mute warning that my suspect might be planning an encore later. The concrete of the recently poured sidewalk in front of the first building masked my approach slightly, but discretion seemed the better part of valor at that point; pulling my Glock from the holster, I checked to make sure the clip was full, then held it at the ready as I moved up the walkway to the framed-in lobby for the structure. It was dark enough by that point that I snapped on my flashlight and washed it over the space as I entered; not being a construction expert, it was hard to know how much progress had been made since my last visit, though I thought the electrical wires that seemed to be hanging everywhere was new.

Despite the framing, I felt quite exposed standing there at the entrance; pausing for a moment, I tried to discern if I were alone and then decided to split the difference. "Anton!" I called out. "It's over."

There was movement at the far end of the hallway, and my attention shifted for a split second — long enough that I nearly missed the figure that dropped out of the ceiling above me. Something hard hit my hand, twice, and sent the flashlight clattering across the concrete; I instinctively brought the gun up and rammed it into the chin of whomever it was standing beside me. The distinctive crack of bone fracturing was nearly as satisfying as seeing them sag to the floor, dazed, but I took no time to appreciate my work; diving sideways, I slipped behind a partially completed plywood wall just as a gun went off in the distance. Wood splintered about where I'd been standing, showering me with small toothpick-sized pieces that stung like a thousand wasps across my exposed skin. Rolling into a crouch, I kept low and moved as quickly as I could through the apartment I was apparently in, then dove across a side hallway to get behind a massive stack of drywall. The gun went off again, allowing me to gauge how close I was to the shooter; the fact that they were still raking over the lobby told me they'd not seen me take off — or they were mistaking the poor soul who'd tried to take me out for me.

Glancing upward, I was acutely aware I'd not attempted to clear the space above me; thankfully, no one else appeared to be waiting in the eaves, but I'd not entirely anticipated Cardinal bringing his own form of backup, either. Given the time from when I'd originally called him, I presumed he'd brought only what the Mercedes could carry — meaning at best, there might be four adults, including Cardinal, somewhere on the property. More blasts from the gun attracted my attention, and I managed to catch the slight flash of the muzzle in the distance; I waited another moment for my eyes to adjust more fully to the semidarkness of the interior, then quickly worked my way toward that end of the building. Boxes of construction supplies were in the final apartment, and in an inspired moment, I shoved my gun into the holster long enough to quietly climb onto them; timing it as perfectly as I could, I leapt up to grab an overhead beam, then did one of the most difficult pull-ups I'd ever attempted. Hooking a leg onto the partially finished floor above, I rolled onto the plywood and took a half second to breathe before yanking my Glock back out of its prison. The scent of freshly cut wood filled my nose as I quietly crawled across the under flooring; reaching the edge of the building, I shifted directions slightly and then found a spot where I could look down into the hallway below.

Anton Cardinal was just beneath me; as before, he was dressed impeccably in a tailored suit, though this time the impression was less that of a New York businessman than a really bad villain from some *James Bond* movie. He was holding a commercial version of my Glock in his hands in double-fisted style that meant his only experience with one had been on a shooting range with a poor instructor. It was also an indicator of why he'd likely missed me completely; I decided it might be best to leave that portion of the story out, though, when I ultimately told Alex about it. I held my breath for another moment and was rewarded when a second figure came into view, also holding a Glock.

"Is he dead?" I heard Cardinal ask.

"No," the other figure replied. They had an accent that I couldn't quite place. "But Vlad is. There's blood, though, so I think you might have gotten him. He can't be far."

I blinked, and then quietly did a once-over; as far as I could tell, I'd not been shot. Then again, it wouldn't be the first time a burst of adrenaline had masked an injury.

"We need to find him," Cardinal was saying. "It's the only way to shut down this whole investigation."

"One you could have stopped a long time ago."

My ears perked up, and I quickly grabbed my iPhone; triggering the recording function, I prayed to whatever deities worked with cops that the microphone was sensitive enough to pick up what was going on below me.

"There were too many people in the loop," Cardinal replied. "Too many people that would have to have been paid. You know that as well as I do. We don't have the money for that scale of payoffs. Not now. Not after everything."

"You only needed to pay off *one* person," the other man said tartly. "If you had acted when we insisted." The way the guy pronounced the letter *w* made me think of my mother's infamous Ukrainian accent.

"She wouldn't take the money; Viv operated from a different playbook. Her ethics would never have allowed it."

"Her *ethics* are what got her killed."

Cardinal snorted. "We could've learned a thing or two from her, you know? Erasing her didn't prevent the world from imploding around us any more than killing my dad resolved our financial issues. If anything, the situation has gotten far worse."

"Your father knew what he was getting into, just as much as you did when you accepted our offer."

"I never wanted to run the company," Cardinal replied. "I had a life—"

"You had *nothing*," the other man interrupted. "And you never did. We own you."

There was a stony silence. "What's one more death, then?" he asked.

Oh shit—

The gun went off once, and I heard a body drop to the ground; I'd managed to open my mouth to announce my presence when it went off a second time. Swearing, I swung around the beam I'd been balanced upon and shimmed down a support column to the hallway, dropping the final feet to the concrete in my hurry to get to the latest carnage. Three steps and I was beside the crumpled form of Anton Cardinal, his eyes staring upward sightlessly as blood began to spread from beneath his head. In the semidarkness of the hallway, I could just make out where the bullet had entered his right temple, though thankfully I was unable to see the sodden mess that was what was left of the back of his head. The gun was still clasped in his hand, and even from my distance, smelled hot from having recently been fired. Standing, I moved over to the other body and found a middle-aged man also in a business suit sporting a bullet hole in the forehead; he'd fallen onto his back and was no longer a concern to the rest of us mortals. His Glock was a few feet away, dropped, presumably, when he'd been felled by the unexpected assassination.

Turning off the audio recording for my phone, I snapped a few photos to document the scene and then moved to lean against the partially completed hallway wall to wait for my boss to arrive. Oddly, even though I knew this represented the end of the case, it felt like the hollowest of victories; while there was a certain justice to how my killer had been rung up for his crimes, I far preferred watching the book get thrown at them by a jurist incensed with someone taking the life of another. Glancing at the structure around me, I wondered if the project would ever get completed — especially once whatever was left of The Cardinal Group was finally held to account. For in that moment, I knew I would do whatever it would take to get Vivian Grandchester's article published; despite our differences, it was clear we shared an affinity for righting wrongs whenever possible.

It felt like a fitting epitaph.

EPILOGUE

The rest of December sped by in a blur, and before I knew it, I was waking up beside Alejandro late on Christmas morning. He'd insisted on opening our presents at the stroke of midnight, something I'd not been all that upset about doing; the surprises that had been waiting beneath the tree had been well worth it, as had the rounds of passionate lovemaking we'd engaged in afterwards. Somewhere around the wee hours of the morning, Morpheus had finally demanded his due and I'd drifted off to a blissful, peaceful sleep full of dreams of the two of us walking hand-in-hand up Main Street, U.S.A. for our dining reservation at Club 33. The restoration of my membership to the elite club — and my fiancé's hand in it — had been an amazing surprise, accentuated by the handwritten note from my mother that had nearly sent me to tears. Seeing Alejandro's expression when he'd opened my gift, though, had been worth all of the surreptitious phone calls to his mother back in Tucson, as well as tracking down a former high school friend working for Disney Feature Animation capable of producing the exquisite art I was looking for. The family tree I'd been able to piece together based on his conversations with me — and the blanks his mother had filled in later — had been something to behold, especially given how important his heritage was to him. Still, I felt a bit like I had shirked my Christmas responsibilities, for the tickets to Comic Con he had scored — along with the amazing Aquaman costume — had gone above and beyond. That had led me to begin plotting for something super special during our wedding in January, though to pull *that* off was going to require the assistance of a certain multimillionaire author I knew had connections everywhere.

Shifting Chat slightly from his spot between our pillows, I snuggled in closer to Alex and rejoiced silently in the nearness of him. The scent of our lovemaking was still heavy in the air and led to certain stirrings that I was relatively certain my soulmate would be unable to miss. When he subtly pressed himself into me, I knew it was the green light I'd been looking for; throwing a leg over his thigh, I slowly began to guide myself into him while simultaneously nibbling at his neck. Chat decided he'd seen enough and quickly leapt from the bed; I reached over Alex's warm body and began to work him over, relishing in the soft moans that began to escape his lips as I carefully moved him ever closer to release. It didn't take long for our skin to become moist with the exertion; soon, I felt his body begin to tremble as he tried to hold back the inevitable. For my part, I took that as a sign to slow down; the anguished cry from Alex made me smile slightly, for we both knew there wasn't anything quite so nice as delayed gratification.

So, naturally, that was when my iPhone decided to go off.

Ignoring the stream of curses emanating from my fiancé, I leaned back as far as I could without actually withdrawing from him and searched for the offending device; my hand finally hit on the cold metal of the case and I dragged it to my face, then groaned when I saw who was calling. Leaning back into Alex, I gently kissed his damp shoulder before whispering into his ear.

"It's my boss."

"Of *fucking* course it is," he said huskily. "Can you just let it go to voicemail? It's fucking Christmas."

"He'll just call back," I replied. "Or send in the troops to find out why I didn't answer."

"*Fuck*," he swore with a vengeance. "He has a sixth sense—"

"That's why he's the boss," I laughed, "now hush while I try to get him off the phone."

Alex grumbled something under his breath about nixing the Chief from the Christmas Card list next year as I tapped the answer button. "Merry Christmas, Vas," came the cheerful voice of my boss. "Sorry to interrupt your festivities, but I've got a bit of a dilemma."

"More fallout from the Grandchester case?" I asked.

"No," he quickly answered. "Despite how highly irregular it was for a Deputy Chief of Police to co-author a long form investigative piece for a local newspaper, both Internal Affairs and the City Council can't find anything in our policies barring it from happening."

"I was pretty thorough in looking through the regs, Chief," I reminded him. "That almost took longer than stitching together the article Grandchester had written."

"I know," he replied. "And, off the record, our Public Affairs Officer thinks it was a stroke of brilliance. Now the *Register* owes us one."

"I can't wait to call in that favor," I smiled. Alex chose to grind himself into me at that moment, and it took everything I had not to groan into the phone. Taking a deep breath, I tried to sound like I wasn't making love to my fiancé as I continued. "I don't suppose we can say the same about the Feds?"

"Hell no," Gilbert said. "Despite handing them everything on a silver platter, none of the alphabet agencies will even admit to our help in shutting down a significant international money laundering scheme here in Southern California."

"Well, I'm happy to let them take the credit if that keeps them off our back the next time something big comes along."

"Fat chance," he chuckled. "Are you working out? I don't mean to interrupt."

"Just finishing up," I replied, which was mostly true. "What is your dilemma?"

"I know you've got some time off next month for your wedding and honeymoon," he began.

"Oh shit," I said. "Do *not* tell me something's come up—"

"No, no, nothing quite like that," Gilbert said hastily.

I thought about that for a moment. "Then what *is* it like?"

The long pause made me more uncomfortable. "I've been asked to temporarily loan you to the Orange County Sheriff's Office," he said. "They've got a case that has them stumped, and for whatever reason, asked for you by name."

"Orange County?" I asked, perplexed. "They want *me*? For a case?"

"Yeah," he replied. "I know your friend Sean is usually the one that consults, but since you're going to be out there—"

The penny finally dropped. "Orange County, *Florida*?"

"Yes."

"Let me guess: the request came from Bernadette Carver?"

"Yes," Gilbert answered. "As I said, you appear to have made quite an impression when you were out there."

"Sean worked with her more than I did, honestly," I replied. "She probably should ask for him."

"Already did," Gilbert said. "She wants *both* of you." He chuckled. "I guess your respective reputations preceded you, so to speak."

"We haven't worked a case together in some time," I hedged. "And I'm getting married! I don't have time to work a case—"

"They're flying you out there first class, so long as you can leave tomorrow. I'm looking at the tickets now."

I glanced at Alex. "I had plans for New Year's, Chief—" I started before cutting myself off. "Tickets? *Plural*?"

"Alex can go with you," he continued. "Isn't he off until the wedding anyway?"

"Campus is closed through New Year's, and then he was taking vacation for our trip, yes," I replied.

"Good. Then pack your bags and enjoy some extended time away from California. I think you've earned it."

"By working someone else's thorny case?" I laughed mirthlessly. "Not my idea of a reward, Chief."

"Knowing you, you'll solve it quickly and then have the rest of the time to yourself."

"I appreciate your faith in me," I replied.

"Will you do it?"

I sighed. "It goes against my better judgement, but yes. Send me the tickets."

"Already in your email."

I sighed again. "I need to surprise you more."

"I'm okay if you don't," he chuckled. "Have a nice trip."

I hung up and dejectedly tossed my phone to the nightstand; to say my libido had cooled was an understatement, though I tried to make a good showing to ensure that Alex finally got the release he'd been patiently waiting for. It wasn't lost on him that I'd not climaxed with him, though; as gently as he could, he pulled off me and then turned to face me. His beautiful eyes searched mine for a moment, and then he leaned his forehead into me.

"All that matters," he said quietly and with a fondness that I wasn't currently feeling like I deserved, "is that we are going to be together. Whether that's here at home or in Orlando, it doesn't matter." He pulled away from me. "Being *with* you does."

"Are you sure?" I asked, my heart overflowing with love for this man.

"More than anything," he smiled.

ACKNOWLEDGMENTS

I've long been an avid news consumer. For as long as I can remember, the daily paper has been delivered to whatever house I've lived in, and more than one wonderful Sunday has been spent pouring through the bonus sections that are only printed once a week. Even with the shift to having more of this content online, there's still something faintly magical to me about seeing the news in print — almost as if documenting the changes in our daily lives in that way will hold them in place, however briefly. Those that work in news — be it on the local level or the far more widely known national organizations — are to me a very special breed, one dedicated to getting the facts right and the story of our time accurate to the final letter. Recent events have made me think that fewer of these hardcore for-the-record folks exist than in years past; still, the ones that do maintain a level of excellence that others can only strive to reach.

The idea for this novel came out of a chance conversation with a now-former colleague about local news outlets; I'd been toying with the idea of a journalist who finds out more than they bargained for but needed a better understanding of just how news gets gathered in a very practical sense. As it happens, my colleague lived through the strange times that were the pandemic years and had a front row seat to people who decided they didn't like what they were seeing on the television. While that wasn't the exact angle I was working on for my *particular* story, it did give me an appreciation for the vocation — and the quiet danger that is constantly lurking from those who willingly choose to ignore the protections the Constitution provides to the Press. When one of us is silenced, all of us are; it's an important lesson that feels far more prescient than I would have ever expected in 2025.

I'd like to extend my appreciation to **Alexis** for pulling back the curtain on what goes into making a daily newscast. Her help and thoughtful guidance proved invaluable for crafting the environment my fictional journalist existed within; I wish her all the best in her new career and, frankly, miss our hallway conversations.

And, of course, I could not have done this without my own beautiful soulmate, **Paula**. She is well aware of the struggle that went into writing *Silenced* and the strange decision I made to attempt to write two books at the same time; her quiet support and calm insistence that I could do it helped me over a number of humps, reminding me yet again that I am truly blessed to have her by my side.

—C

May 25, 2025

ABOUT THE AUTHOR

Born and raised in Maine, Chris has spent nearly three decades as an IT nerd, writing just about everything other than a novel in the process. That changed in early 2019 when he was advised to find a way to wind down from his day job; sifting through his options, he recalled a childhood ambition to become a writer and quickly found himself weaving an entirely new world from the comfort of his laptop. *Silenced* is his ninth book in the *Vasily Korsokovach Investigates* series.

Despite his love for the Northeast, the author escaped the cold for Arizona, where he currently resides with his beautiful wife and a Staffordshire Terrier rescue who insists on being walked as frequently as possible.

For all of the latest information, including hints about upcoming books and an exclusive reader newsletter, please visit the author's website at https://chrisjansmann.com

instagram.com/chrisjansmann

facebook.com/christopherjansmann

amazon.com/author/chrisjansmann

bookbub.com/authors/christopher-h-jansmann

goodreads.com/chrisjansmann

mastodon.coffee/@chrisjansmann